Dragonlords
Andrakis Book Three

30th Anniversary Edition

Tony Shillitoe

First published in 1993 as Dragonlords by Pan Macmillan.
Re-published in 2006 as Dragonlord War by Altair Australia.
Republished in 2024 as Dragonlords on Amazon.

Cover art by Kirsi Salonen
http://www.kirsisalonen.com

ISBN: 978-0-6458658-4-4

For Meg, Leah, Jaimee and Kim –
the true sources of magic in my world.

THE KINGDOM OF THANA

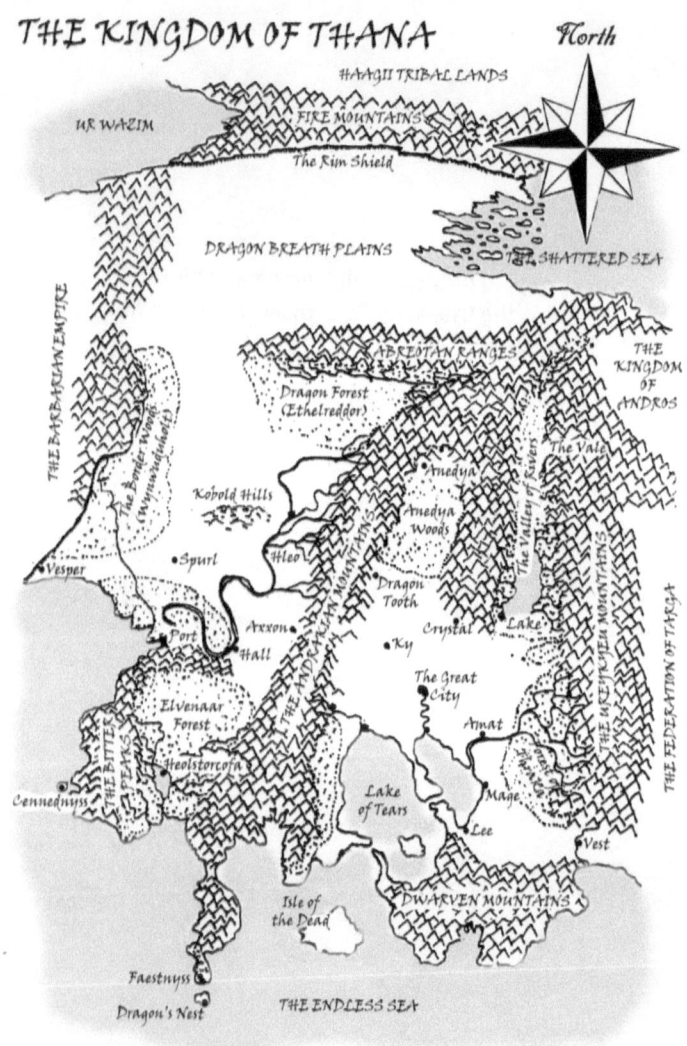

RANU KA SHEHAALA

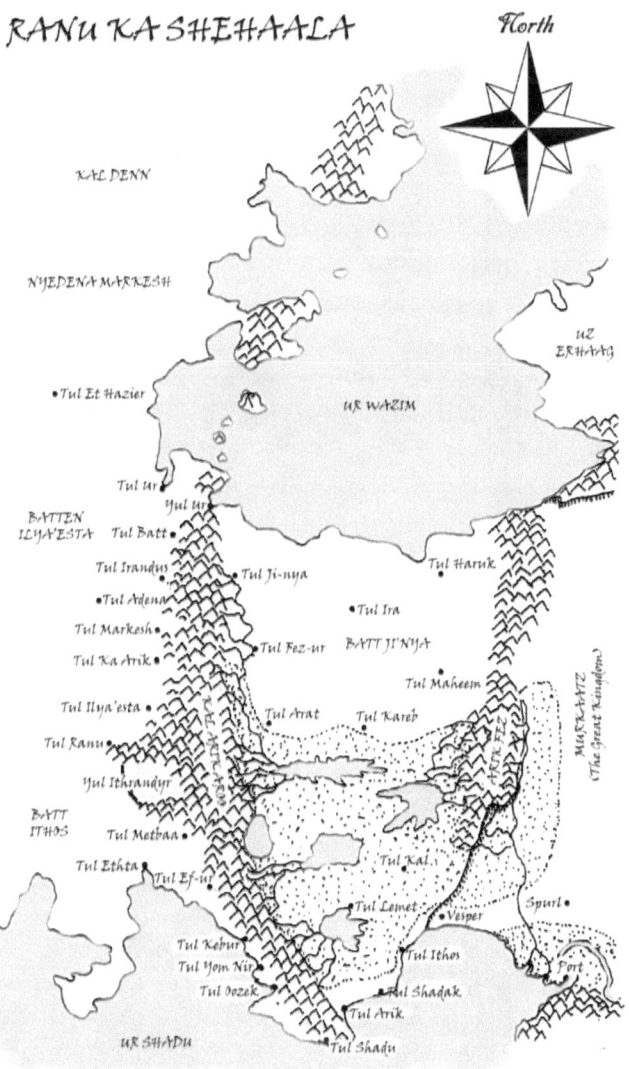

North

KAL DENN

NYEDENA MARKESH

UZ ERHAAG

• Tul Et Hazier

UR WAZIM

Tul Ur

Yul Ur

BATTEN
ILYA'ESTA   Tul Batt

Tul Harúk •

Tul Irandus

• Tul Ji-nya

• Tul Adena

• Tul Ira

BATT JI'NYA

Tul Markesh •

Tul Ka Arik •

• Tul Fez-ur

Tul Maheen •

Tul Ilya'esta •

Tul Arat

Tul Kareb

Tul Ranu •

Yul Ithrandyr

BATT
ITHOS   Tul Metbaa

Tul Ethta •

Tul Ef-ur •

Tul Kal •

Tul Lemet •   Vesper •   Spurl •

Tul Kebur

Tul Yom Nir •

Tul Ithos •

Tul Oozek •

Tul Shadak •

Tul Arik •

UR SHADU

Tul Shadu •

Port

MUSKAATZ
(The Great Kingdom)

v

—

"Philosophers talk of journeys and cycles, prophets promise outcomes and returns – but I warn you: be wary of them. They are liars. For what does it mean to say that we have reached the end, or that we have returned to where we started? It means nothing. We can never return to where we started. If there were ends to our journeys, we would all cease to move, once we got there. If it was possible to return to exactly the place from where we left, then why would we ever bother to leave in the first place? We leave because we know that leaving will bring change. Change is all that we can ever be sure of. Even the place toward which we journey will never be the place we reach, just as the place we leave behind can never be the place to which we return. There is always change – no matter how infinitesimal. Always."

Translated from the Ranu text, *Ashka Ilya'esta Irandu*, a philosophical inquiry by Farsiz Areem.

One

'There,' Tim whispered.

Sasha followed the direction of his hand. The darkness refused to yield, so she sensed rather than saw movement beside the low wooden bungalow. Two silhouettes briefly appeared and disappeared in the night shadows. Tim tapped her shoulder, and they slid noiselessly behind their buildings, parallel to their quarry.

Something was amiss. The Haagii army encircled the Great City. Only the Eyes and Ears remained on duty to warn of Haagii incursions after dark, and no members of The Hand or the Guild were stirring. Terence sent a message to Tim, through the Maze, from his watch at the outer edge, warning strangers were creeping into the city. Tim and Sasha guessed where they might be, and lay in wait. Their guess was good.

The intruders weren't Haagii. They moved with the practiced silence and fluidity of highly trained assassins. Tim thought he lost them, four times, but patience, and intuitive guessing each time, brought him back on their trail. They disappeared into the darkness whenever Kingdom soldiers passed, and avoided open doorways and lighted windows, resorting to scaling walls and roofs wherever the street was lit. Tim was certain they were heading for the castle road, and the castle itself. If they were assassins, there would be no point confronting them, because they would fight to the death, or commit suicide, rather than be taken, but he was curious to know who they were, where they came from, what their purpose was, and who they worked for – if he could take one alive.

Sasha tugged his arm. Three voices echoed along the street that branched from the castle road into the Great City, and soldiers came into view, obscured by the darkness. Without a light, because of the siege laws, they moved slowly, talking to break down the darkness.

At the point where Tim knew the hunted were pressed against a building wall, a soldier toppled forward. His companions went to catch him, and they also slumped to the ground. The night remained silent and motionless, as if holding its breath, until two figures emerged to drag the bodies of the hapless soldiers out of sight. Tim squinted and watched the two figures pull on the dead soldiers' garments and buckle on their weapons, his Aelendyell night vision letting him see his quarry as clear as if it was daylight. He nudged Sasha. They lifted their tiny assassin crossbows and fired. Both victims leaped sideways as the darts struck home.

Tim and Sasha sprinted across the street. Tim deliberately aimed to wound his target, but the stranger had already wrenched the dart out of his shoulder and was struggling to his feet by the time Tim reached him. Tim swung a sharp kick at the man's head, but the victim rolled with the blow and came up, short sword glinting in his hand. Tim flicked a dagger from his belt and jumped back as the sword-wielder lunged. His opponent made two more swings, sweeps Tim dodged easily, despite the wielder's unusual speed, but the sword suddenly kept coming, the throw catching Tim across the side of the neck as he evaded its point. Two daggers appeared in the stranger's hands, and the man was on him, forcing him to the ground. Tim tried to roll his attacker off, but couldn't, and every move to force the antagonist off-balance was counteracted. He was a professional, a good one, and his strength surprised Tim. As he slowly forced his dagger points closer to Tim's vulnerable windpipe, Tim tried to lever his right knee under the man's chest, but his attacker resisted and pressed down harder. Tim summoned every ounce of strength remaining, to halt the dagger points. Already one was touching his skin. This is a stupid way to die, he thought. The dagger point began to cut.

Then his attacker sighed and tension in the man's body relaxed. Tim heaved him over his head, with an upward thrust from his knee, and as the man's body thumped against the side of the building and slid to the ground Tim leaped to his feet to finish him off, but Sasha grabbed his wrist, and twisted her bloodied dagger directly before Tim's eyes. 'Relax,' she said, grinning. 'He's had enough. You owe me one, Tim Gaelus.'

The red banner weaved through the sea of Haagii warriors encircling the Great City. Standing on the hastily erected wooden tower in the west corner of the castle, Andra watched the banner's steady progress, and wondered how many Dark Warriors served the Dragonlord, and why they chose to do so. A soft breeze stirred a lock of his black hair, teasing his cheek, and as he swept the lock aside he ran his fingers along his long locks to the silver circlet that clasped it in a tight ponytail. How long since I first wore the Guardian ponytail? A bare two years? he pondered.

His world had changed beyond imagining. Sent unwillingly from his home in The Vale, as a raw, naive youth to serve in Great King Thana's army, he witnessed bloody battles, slept with a woman, felt love stirring in the Aelendyell forests, watched friends die in agony, faced death a hundred times, and slain a dragon. Slain a dragon – he reached across his left shoulder, his fingers touching the gilded hilt of Abreotan's sword. So much had changed – from Guardian to King. He was the Inheritor, according to the ancient legends and the prophecies, because he carried the sword.

The flapping red banner halted near the foremost Haagii ranks. From his tower, atop the castle wall on the edge of the plateau cliff, Andra couldn't discern details, but the Dark Warriors were dismounting among a thick knot of figures.

Haagii encircled the entire Great City. In every direction, across the vast plains of Ky, the hordes of the Dragonlord spread like a plague, defying any scourge to remove them. By day, the besieged in the Great City stared at warriors beyond number ranged against them, and knew they faced inevitable defeat. By, night the plains were a sea of campfires, flickering brazenly, as far as light could carry.

There was no escape for the defenders. The Kingdom had been reduced to the survivors trapped in the confines of the Great City and the castle.

Andra's gaze shifted to the distant purple smudge in the west that defined the Andrakian Mountains, and he focussed on the dark blue cloud hanging ominously above the peaks. Elvenaar Forest was burning. The Haagii were incinerating the Aelendyell stronghold. It seemed even their ancient magic, the powers they inherited from their Elvenaar ancestors, couldn't halt the blood-crazed march of the Dragonlord's armies. Had Wudufaesten collapsed too?

He recalled the friends he made in the far western forest – Terath, Mirith, Freyar – the Aelendyell people who carried him from the dust of Dragon Breath plains and gave back the breath of life. Time and circumstance separated them. The prophecy made him King, but the Dragonlord's invasion brought war and death to the Aelendyell forests. Had the Elder's magic held against the Dragonlord's minions?

He lowered his eyes to survey the army drawn up outside the old city's perimeter. Most of the Dragonlord's army were Haagii, tribal warriors, from a thousand different clans, who'd made an indefinable bargain with Mareg Dru'artha Sutnavanistra to wage war against the Kingdom. And others were numbered in their ranks, strangers like the Dark Warriors, and the bowmen, and still others who lived in regions north of Uz Erhaag. The Dragonlord drew upon unpredictable and unknown reserves to bolster his multitudinous forces in the war.

Some change or plan was afoot in the enemy's ranks. The Haagii made frequent skirmishes against the Great City's poorly constructed perimeter defences, without seriously attempting to scale the low walls, as if content to play cat-and-mouse, like they did for weeks at Central Gate. At any time, they could overwhelm the remaining defences, and pour into the city. Andra knew High Lord Surdrok's warriors were ready to retreat to the safety of the castle on the plateau. The holding of the Great City's walls was a military game, nothing more. But the action below suggested to

Andra the Haagii leaders were preparing something else. In time, he would learn what it was, because intelligence reports would be brought directly to him, now that he was King.

He pondered his last thought. Great King Andra. No, just King Andra. He already let it be known he would not accept the title 'Great', which implied something he was not. Two days ago, he was Andra, a Guardian of The Vale, a warrior chosen by destiny to bear the sword of Abreotan to the Great City. Now, everyone bowed before him, in awe, because he bore the sword – because he slew a dragon on the stone bridge at Cennednyss – because he was a prophecy incarnate – because they believed he would defeat the Dragonlord and save the Kingdom. If only he knew how.

Andra drew the sword from his back scabbard and searched its shining blade, examining the intricate and ancient runes etched there by Elvenaar sorcerers. It was a magical blade, a weapon forged by the Dwarven, and blessed by the Elvenaar, to aid Aian Abreotan fight and defeat the Dragonlord host in the ancient Dragon Wars, a thousand years ago. There was no weight in the weapon, and whenever Andra held it, his fingers and arms tingled with power as it melded into his being, became an extension of his arm, and transformed him into something beyond mortal warrior; into something he could not yet comprehend. He wished the dragon dead at Cennednyss, focussing his fear and hate into the sword, and it generated a pulse of energy that ripped through the dragon's armoured scales and boiled its heart: killing the beast, and nearly killing Andra. The energy came from within him, draining his strength, and the shock rendered him unconscious. He turned the sword in his palm. Who was master? He held a potent weapon, yet he did not know how to control it. How could he learn its secrets?

He felt pressure on his leg. Artega, the war dog, looked up with inquiring eyes, black tail wagging expectantly. The temporary wooden steps to the tower platform creaked under the weight of someone approaching, and Claarn's giant form ascended. The warrior's red locks flamed about his head like an angry forest fire, but the giant man's battle-worn face grinned beneath his bushy red beard.

'Good watchdog, that one,' said Claarn in greeting. 'No one can sneak up with him guarding you.' Andra smiled and patted the dog's muzzle. 'Still puzzled by good fortune?' Claarn asked, and he laughed as he drew up to his full height, a full head taller than Andra.

Andra glanced back at his sword and smiled sheepishly as he lowered the point. 'Still puzzled by what I don't understand,' he replied.

'You're King,' said Claarn, with a deferential, but mocking bow. 'That's easy for we of lesser rank to understand,' and added, after a pause, 'Your Highness.'

Andra returned the sword to its scabbard and frowned. 'You know there's no need for that. Being King doesn't change anything.'

The giant warrior guffawed loudly, and said, 'Tell that to your subjects. You can't ignore what is.'

'I mean nothing's changed between us,' Andra argued, endeavouring to force the seriousness of the matter onto the grinning warrior. 'You're a friend, and friends don't bow to each other.'

Claarn chuckled at Andra's answer. 'If you're to be King, my friend, you'd best get used to lots of people bowing to you. As for me, I swore allegiance to the Great King, and since you're now the Great King I swear allegiance to you. You're stuck with me.'

A smile crept across Andra's lips at Claarn's exaggerated protestation of loyalty. 'As it is,' he said, reviving the Guardian acceptance of matters. Claarn clapped the reluctant King on the shoulder, petted Artega's head, and turned his attention to the movement in the Haagii lines far below.

From the gate tower, the Royal Chancellor observed the two friends talking on the temporary wooden scaffold. Like Andra, he'd climbed to a vantage point to see what was brewing in the Haagii lines that morning, but his interest was quickly drawn to the presence of the new, uncrowned King on the western tower.

The new King was an enigma. His arrival on horseback at night, in the Great City, the fiery amber beacon of Abreotan's sword held aloft, as his party charged through the Haagii army, was already woven into a new legend among the people. A Ahmud Ki could do nothing but let events take their course, until the euphoria of the initial days evaporated, but he was vexed that his careful planning had gone quite wrong, and events escaped his direct control, with the death of Liam at Cennednyss and the arrival of Andra in his place.

He was philosophical about the current outcome. The prophetic telling of Abreotan's successor was accurate, because Andra bore the mark of the moon on his cheek, albeit a crescent-shaped scar, and he retrieved Abreotan's sword from a glyph constructed to keep pillagers at bay. A Ahmud Ki made a mistake in creating an artificial saviour out of Liam, that's all. If his minions, like Peret, were more observant, there would have been no error. Instead, he would have taken earlier control of Andra, instead of Liam, and the issue would have been without doubt his to decide and direct. The punishment for rash action would be patience, for the interim, but eventually he'd work a way to bring the new King under his influence. Then he would be full master of the Kingdom again, as was his rightful destiny.

Claarn's arrival on the tower beside Andra amused A Ahmud Ki. The new King's naive trust in his friends would prove a useful weakness to exploit. Andra lacked the necessary political wariness that might interfere with his plans, and he seemed keen to gather his friends around him, suggesting he felt vulnerable and unsure in his new capacity. As with Liam, this one provided levers to manipulate his psyche. A Ahmud Ki would foster his confidence and make him reliant on the Royal Chancellor's advice and powers, so Andra would come to see A Ahmud Ki as another friend in his new court. The dead King, Thana, foolishly blundered blindly into the same trap, by appointing A Ahmud Ki as Royal Advisor, and finally as Chancellor, before he engineered Thana's assassination with Aelendyell arrows fired by hired assassins. There was no necessity to kill this new King, not with a prophecy to fulfil, because he was an essential tool in A Ahmud Ki's climb to ultimate power as successor to the Dragonlords, and A Ahmud Ki had to control him accordingly.

There was also the sword. Andra slew a dragon at Cennednyss, a feat that struck even A Ahmud Ki as astounding. Peret witnessed raw magical energy erupt from the sword to pierce the dragon's chest, and said that only the new King seemed able to generate magic from the weapon. A Ahmud Ki's logic told him the sword was the source. The warrior, Andra, displayed no magical abilities of any magnitude.

Yet there remained nagging incongruities in the legend surrounding Thana's successor. Peret described Andra at the battle of The Rim Shield as an unstoppable warrior, who wielded, with inhuman ability, what turned out to be nothing more than a finely crafted sword. Andra was left for dead in the grey dust of Dragon Breath Plains, only to reappear in the Great City, alive and robust. People in the castle, overawed by the growing stories of how he cheated death before the Dragonlord's host, and walked alive out of the scourge of Dragon Breath Plains long after others died, spoke of him as the one who died and was reborn. In the Bitter Peaks, he faced one of Mareg's sorcerers, slew him, and survived a spell attack, again cheating death, before returning to Cennednyss to claim Abreotan's sword. And he single-handedly killed the most fearful beast in the Dragonlord's menagerie, walking unscathed through dragon flames, before slaying the creature with a mighty surge of power. There were too many unaccounted factors, too many unexplained happenings to make A Ahmud Ki comfortable that Andra didn't possess personal magical ability. He would have to be cautious.

The watcher was being watched. Dark eyes followed the Chancellor's silver-cloaked form, as A Ahmud Ki descended the gate tower to disappear in the castle. Drycraefter Waeron Ardath stroked his flowing white beard. The Chancellor was ambitious, and no doubt he was plotting new schemes with the arrival of the new King.

Ardath turned his gaze toward the wooden tower, where the new King and his warrior companion were observing the Haagii. He saw the outline of the sword on the King's back – Abreotan's sword. The Dragonlord's days were numbered. The ancient prophecy, stemming from the dying ages of Abreotan's reign, after the Dragon Wars, was coming to completion, and the Dragonlord's nemesis waited in the wings, with his sword of fire, to return peace to the world's stage.

Ardath saw two more figures climb the tower's wooden steps to join the King, and recognised High Lord Surdrok's stocky build and black armour, but the other, a woman warrior with raven hair, was unknown to him. The group briefly conversed, before all four descended. He knew their intended destination because he was going to join them. The King's Table was assembling for the first time since the new King's arrival. Thana's unfortunate and untimely assassination left the Chancellor at the head of the assembly of Lords.

Not that many decisions were needed. The Kingdom's armies had withdrawn from Central Gate before the massed onslaught of the Dragonlord's forces, and retreated into the Great City, where rough defences were built to shore up the half-completed outer wall that people hastily and inadequately constructed under Thana's orders. The King's Table was powerless to order anything, except withdrawal or suicide. The Dragonlord offered no other options.

Ardath understood A Ahmud Ki. The Chancellor's name came from the western Ranu language, and literally translated into 'the seeker of power'. All too apt, Ardath decided, because the Chancellor is power hungry. Ardath preferred to avoid the political games that possessed the other Lords of the King's Table, the constant jockeying and bartering for status that consumed their waking time and unsettled their sleep. He preferred to observe and record, which was his official capacity in court. Drycraefters were the Kingdom's historians.

In his life, he'd watched lords bicker, scheme, and fight for favours, gain and lose status, live and die in the game of politics, but of them all A Ahmud Ki was becoming the most ruthless and efficient. He'd engineered political assassinations and a legend to promote his reputation. His only flaw was his choice in Liam as the prophesied saviour.

Although he kept out of the political arena, Ardath gained satisfaction from observing its competitors, especially when they stumbled or fell, and A Ahmud Ki certainly stumbled with the advent of Andra. In the interim, the bearer of Abreotan's sword was immune to A Ahmud Ki's clutching greed, but Ardath knew that time would be brief. A Ahmud Ki was driven by his warped perception of history, by a passion Ardath vaguely understood, but could not yet detail or describe, and the only thing standing between the new King and the Chancellor was the sword. It was the key. The legends and the prophecies pointed directly to it. Whoever controlled it, controlled the Kingdom's destiny, indeed the destiny of every being within the Kingdom, and possibly beyond its boundaries.

That was Ardath's dilemma. The world he understood was changing faster than he could record, and three figures were emerging at the hub, their existence and their destinies influencing the destinies of everything else. The Dragonlord's hate and power seemed immeasurable. If he triumphed, there was no future beyond eternal agony, perpetual warring, or death for everyone.

A thousand years had passed, since Aian Abreotan wielded his magical sword to consign the Dragonlords and their creatures to death, or imprisonment. Before that time, they reigned supreme, carving out the world's boundaries between their lust for power and total domination, playing their games of war and treachery against each other, and devastating everything in their paths. Abreotan ended that era and brought peace – until A Ahmud Ki's meddling released Mareg Dru'artha Sutnavanistra. Enraged but free, Mareg fled north, into the realm of Uz Erhaag, where he gathered an army of millions beneath his brutal control, an army which he unleashed on the Kingdom, and other lands, to return to absolute rule, and plunge the world back into the chaotic hell that existed before Abreotan.

But the prophecies said he could not triumph. King Andra was his nemesis, the wielder of Abreotan's mighty weapon, a spirit of truth and freedom. The prophecies promised he would slay the Dragonlord. With the new King, there was hope.

And then there was A Ahmud Ki, who complicated the potential of the future with his insatiable lust for dominance. What was he seeking, beyond himself? Or was there to be nothing beyond himself? Was he an aspiring Dragonlord, a fledgling abomination thrown up by an accident of circumstance?

For the first time, Ardath felt the need to take sides. Written deep inside the Ancient Lore, among the oldest records, in a coded language only the successive Drycraefters had learned, and taught to their descendants, was information vital to the new King. Without it, the prophecy could fail. Ardath feared A Ahmud Ki's intentions toward King Andra. He was certain, without proof, that Thana's assassination was the work of the power-mad Chancellor, not angry, vengeful Aelendyell as was commonly promoted and believed. A Ahmud Ki was too keenly interested in the sword and the new King, for Ardath's liking, which meant someone had to become the new King's mentor and protector. Ardath, too, had a part to play in the prophecy's outcome.

Two

The assembled Lords awaited Andra's entrance. A Ahmud Ki offered Andra Thana's griffin crown to wear into the meeting of the King's Table, but he refused the symbolic gesture, saying he wasn't yet formally the King. As he turned from the disgruntled Chancellor, he glanced at Claarn, who nodded approval, before he led Andra into the meeting room of the King's Table.

The Lords stood and bowed respectfully as Andra entered, until he reached the golden chair at the head of the long oak table. Andra noted the black cushioning and symbol of the dark green griffin worked into the fabric: Thana's heraldry.

'The Great King is before you, Lords of the former Kingdom of Thana!' A Ahmud Ki announced, as he followed Andra into the chamber. 'Be seated.'

The Chancellor's announcement startled Andra from his reverie. Bemused, he turned to the attendant Lords. Faces: most of them strangers. He knew Surdrok, the High Lord of the Great King's Armies who replaced Mara, under whom Andra served. Mara died at The Rim Shield, along with ten thousand warriors and Andra's closest friends from The Vale – Alain and Stephen – slaughtered by the Haagii who now sat on the plains of Ky.

'When Your Majesty is ready?'

Andra's eyes met the Chancellor's grey eyes.

'Your Majesty?' Claarn interrupted, pulling out the King's golden chair for Andra to sit. Andra accepted the giant's offer.

Surdrok coughed, and stood. 'With Your Highness' permission, I'll be brief,' he began, but a wave of disapproval erupted, over which the Chancellor's controlled, commanding voice rose.

'If the Lords would remember why we are here,' he

asserted, and he glared at Surdrok. 'Your manners are terrible, as always.'

Surdrok gave the Chancellor a fierce look, but could not sustain the fire in his eyes, under the Chancellor's direct gaze, and looked away. Disgruntled, chastened, he resumed his seat.

Lord Haephus stood, his orange and red priestly robes flowing elegantly. 'With permission, Your Majesty?' he politely asked. Andra could only nod, feeling decidedly uncomfortable in his new role. 'As Lords of the Kingdom,' Haephus began, 'and on their behalf, I wish to pledge our support and allegiance to the new King, Great King Andra the First, Bearer of Abreotan's sword, The Inheritor, and Dragon Slayer. By all that is praised by Our Blessed Goddess Teka, I welcome you to your station.' As he spoke, Haephus advanced, carrying a heavy silver sceptre, carved remarkably like an elongated dragon's head and neck.

Simultaneously, the silver-robed Chancellor lifted a platinum chain, preparing to place it over Andra's head.

Andra flinched at the sight of the neck chain, Liam's ghostly features coming to mind as he remembered the heavy platinum yoke he'd worn, and the neck chains he glimpsed on assassins in the Maze. He glanced along the rectangular table, and saw the white-robed, white-haired figure at the far end subtly shaking his head, as if warning him not to accept the chain.

'As your attendant servants, we assemble to anoint you, O Most Noble of Successors, Lord over all the Kingdom,' Haephus continued, reciting the ceremonial litany usually reserved for great occasions of state when the whole population assembled to witness the coronation of a new King. Current circumstances demanded a circumspect and immediate ceremony. 'And with these blessed symbols of your mighty station, King of Kings, we -'

'Wait!' Andra cried and jumped to his feet. His unexpected interruption flabbergasted Haephus, who stumbled sideways, fumbled, and dropped the Royal sceptre. Claarn reached for his sword, seeing Andra's awareness of danger.

'What is the problem?' A Ahmud Ki asked, lowering the chain to ease the weight on his arms, as he scrutinised the warrior who was to be King. Perhaps his nagging fear this new King had inconceivable magical power was justified. How else could he suspect the chain, except that he sensed something about it? Or had someone told him? A Ahmud Ki shot a glance at Ardath, at the far end of the table, but the Drycraefter masked his feelings.

'I'm sorry, but no ceremonial,' Andra announced. 'There isn't time. When the Dragonlord is defeated, then I will accept the ceremonies appropriate for a King.'

Haephus was petulant. 'I wish I understood. The King must have Teka's blessing to be King,' he said, looking annoyed.

'Then bless him afterwards,' scowled Surdrok, misinterpreting the purpose of the new King's interruption as a sign of dislike for frivolous ceremony. 'There's a siege taking place. The Haagii aren't interested in Royal time-wasting, priest. I pledge my allegiance to Great King Andra without question.'

Surdrok's blunt statement started a wave of echoed pledges from the other Lords, and they stood and bowed formally.

'As it is,' said Andra, who bowed in return. He sat, and the others followed suit, including the Chancellor, who moved to his chair at the left hand of the King. 'I will be honest with you,' Andra began quietly. 'I have not chosen to be King. I don't even know what a King has to do.'

'Judging by the last one, not a lot,' growled Claarn in the background. All eyes turned to the giant, some glaring, like Haephus, and some grinning, like the young Lord Gerran whose face seemed designed for mirth more than serious matters of state.

'You might start by curbing the manners of your bodyguard,' suggested Surdrok, but his jibe was good-natured, since Surdrok had placed Claarn second-in-command at the defence of Central Gate and held a healthy respect for the giant warrior's fighting prowess. Claarn responded with a deliberately clumsy bow toward the High Lord.

Andra waited until the by-play ceased, before he continued. 'In the interim, High Lord Surdrok commands the castle's defence. He answers to no one, but me. Under him, I appoint Claarn and Marella. We all know our survival depends on the strength of the castle, and the courage and ingenuity of our defenders. So must it be.' Andra paused to watch the reaction of the Lords to his decisions. No one appeared fussed. Surdrok looked pleased. 'As for matters pertaining to each of your individual duties, I'll speak alone to you, and you can teach me what a King needs to know,' he concluded, but added, 'And the title Great King is not to be used. I am simply Andra.'

A Ahmud Ki leaned over the wooden bench that curved to meet the tower wall, and contemplated the platinum chain. The magical light sphere made the links glow, as if they emanated the magic worked into the chain. Once he knew Andra had supplanted his protégé in winning Abreotan's sword at Cennednyss, he expended important energy modifying the chain to suit his purpose. The embedded control spell was more powerful and far subtler than that used to manipulate Andra's Guardian friend. If he was to ultimately rule the Kingdom, in the intervening period he needed a King who acted naturally, intelligently, even when his decisions and actions were dictated by A Ahmud Ki's mind. His practical research into the range of Ithosen, Targan, and Aelendyell mind spells, and subsequent synthesis of them into his own unique magic, enabled him to accomplish his aim in the chain. All he had to do was to get it around the neck of his victim – and he failed.

He crossed to the amber crystal sphere, mounted on a marble pedestal, near the opposite space in the room, held his right hand above it, and concentrated, until a face appeared within: Peret, the Apprentice who accompanied the expedition to retrieve Abreotan's sword from the ruins of Cennednyss.

'Yes, Master Ki?' Peret asked.

'I want Lord Ardath watched closely. I want a daily report of his every movement,' A Ahmud Ki instructed.

'Yes, Master Ki, it shall be done,' Peret replied, and averted his face.

A Ahmud Ki lowered his hand to end the communication. He had no reason to suspect Ardath's involvement in this new King's refusal of the chain at the King's Table. The Drycraefter always remained aloof from political intrigues. In fact, he freely supplied A Ahmud Ki with details concerning the sword's existence and the words of the prophecy. He neither hindered, nor schemed. Waeron Ardath was hardly a foe, but A Ahmud Ki was teased by a niggling doubt, despite his logical conclusions. Ardath never had anything to lose before. He could afford to stay aloof from his colleagues' political manoeuvrings because he had no desire for power. He inherited his Drycraefter role, and he did not want to be King.

However, there were changes taking place, important changes affecting Ardath's future as much as anyone's in the Kingdom. The new King was the key to a prophetic future, but his naive nature, and lack of self-interest, made him vulnerable to political misfortune. Might Ardath feel sorry for him? Would he be prepared to risk his safety to prevent anyone tampering with the prophecy, recorded through the centuries in his Drycraefter Ancient Lore?

Ardath was a real threat to A Ahmud Ki for three reasons. First, he practised magic. He could thwart A Ahmud Ki's mind spells with ease. That irked the Chancellor, who wanted no one to be able to match his prowess in magic.

Secondly, he held the Ancient Lore – the records of the Kingdom and its events from the time of King Abreotan – a thousand years of history and observations in one work, that was only marginally repeated in a thousand other volumes, in the Great King's Royal Library. The Drycraefter shared his work with no one, and A Ahmud Ki wanted access to it.

Lastly, Ardath never revealed what he truly held. A Ahmud Ki was being provoked by his own precept: that true power lies in never fully revealing to your enemy the extent of your powers. Ardath was an unknown quantity, a user of magic, a bearer of knowledge who gave little away about the full extent of his abilities, and that made the Drycraefter truly dangerous.

Three soldiers on night watch, at the eastern sector of the road leading to Amat, stared anxiously at the fires, burning bright and warm, amid the Haagii ranks. Silhouettes passed across the fiery backdrop, and sometimes the shadows paused to enjoy the heat.

'By Teka, Clem, I'd give an arm to be standing beside a fire tonight, away from this cold,' one soldier muttered, as he shivered at the icy touch of the spring air.

'And you'd lose a sight more than your arm if you were invited out there,' Clem growled. 'Just be thankful you're alive to see them bastards keeping warm.'

'I just wish they'd come,' said the third. 'I'd sooner die fighting than waiting.'

'Hush your words, Marron,' the first hissed. 'Don't go bringing bad luck on -' His sentence never ended. He sighed, deeply, and slumped against the wall. Before his companions could react, they also dropped silently to the ground, small metal shafts embedded in the base of their skulls.

Four shadows slipped over the Great City's outer ring wall, paused, and melted into the night among the nearest buildings. Beneath the street, along which the figures loped silently, Milly began running, carrying another warning to Tim Gaelus, and the members of The Hand, deep inside the Maze.

Three

The Great City was burning. Fires erupted, sending tongues of yellow flame leaping into the night. Golden red and orange sparks spiralled across the purple sky, and shadows danced on the plateau cliffs.

From the gate tower parapet, Andra saw the lines of blazing torches, carried by eager Haagii, spreading through the city's streets, pouring toward the King's Way junction, where it branched to become Castle Road. The city's outer ring defences had collapsed under the first major assault, and barely ahead of the tide of fire Kingdom troops and city folk were racing for the castle's safety. Although Andra knew this moment was inevitable, throughout the eight days since arriving with Abreotan's sword, a pang of fear gripped his stomach and pumped through his veins. Step by inexorable step, the Haagii were breaking down the Kingdom's resistance, pushing toward the annihilation of everyone who stood in their path. Yet, from previous encounters, he knew the Haagii were only warriors like him, forced to serve a Lord for a cause they did not embrace. No, he reminded himself, they aren't like me at all. He was the master in the Great City now, and his Great City was burning.

Surdrok's strident command bellowed across the battlements, 'Open the gates!'

Iron chains rattled, as the massive wooden and iron doors swung apart, and a fully armed Haardrishii company rode out to descend the road toward the converging rivers of torches at the base of the plateau. Soldiers spread out along the castle parapets, heavy crossbows loaded, and manned the ballista mounted above the gate. Shouts and orders echoed, as the castle defenders prepared to repel their enemy.

Andra descended the stairs and strode into the bustle of warriors gathering weaponry in the square behind the great gates. He saw Marella buckling on her breastplate, and crossed to her, grabbing a buckle to help. 'Where's Claarn?' he yelled, close to her ear.

She pointed to the gate. 'Gone down to help the rear guard!' Andra didn't recall seeing him ride out with the Haardrishii, but darkness could disguise anyone in the confusion and haste. 'Thanks,' Marella said, as Andra tightened the last buckle. She flicked back her dark hair, and headed for the small entry gate, beside the main gateway. A knot of warriors hurried after her.

'Wait for me!' Andra called, and headed in the same direction, but as he reached the small gateway a restraining hand caught his arm. He turned to face the shorter, stocky figure of Surdrok.

'Pardon, Your Majesty, but where are you going?' the High Lord asked.

'To help,' Andra replied, startled by Surdrok's unsolicited attention.

'You can't do that.'

'Why not?'

Surdrok looked as if he failed to comprehend Andra's question, and replied, 'Because you're the King,' with an undertone that highlighted his explanation obvious and irrefutable.

Andra didn't understand the implication. 'I am a warrior,' he stated calmly. 'I was a Guardian before I was a King.'

Surdrok held Andra's arm firmly, staring into the Guardian's eyes, as if seeking an elusive answer, while around them warriors and soldiers hurriedly prepared for the impending conflict. He released Andra's wrist, bowed stiffly in his Haardrishii armour, and moved out of Andra's path through the exit door, saying peremptorily 'I beg your pardon, Your Highness. I am a fool.'

Andra unhitched Abreotan's sword from his back scabbard and stepped through the doorway.

Alone, Surdrok was aware of a small group watching him. He glared and barked, 'What are you idiots gawking at?' and the group dissipated, like petals in the wind, fearful of the

21

High Lord's wrath. Surdrok checked with Devi Karl that the defences were organised, according to his plans, and he also quietly slipped out of the front gate, and headed down the darkened castle road, toward the battleground.

Milly frantically waved at four soldiers staggering through the smoke-filled street, but they didn't see her in the cottage doorway, and stumbled past, so she yelled at their receding backs.

One soldier turned, and shouted, 'Run kid! The devils are loose in the city!' before they disappeared into the pall of smoke and flare of building fires.

Milly ducked inside the cottage, as a pack of Haagii warriors charged along the street brandishing torches and weapons. An object thudded against the thatch roof and she knew it would burst into flames. With practised agility, she opened a trapdoor, and dropped into the Maze.

'Any more up there?' Patti asked, as Milly landed.

'The last ones ignored me,' she replied, 'but the Hagmen have set fire to this building too.'

'Never mind, young lass,' the stout madam said, grinning, as she ruffled Milly's short brown hair. 'We're probably in enough trouble, bringing the others down here against Orrin's wishes.'

'But we had to save them,' Milly insisted.

'Of course we did,' said Patti, 'and we have.'

'Then damn Orrin,' the girl cursed, and spat.

Her outburst brought a broad smile to Patti's podgy cheeks. 'Here now, young lady, you be mindin' your language. I won't have Andra learnin' you've taken to swearing since he come back. You know Royalty now,' the fat woman chided.

'But when can I see him?' Milly asked.

'Soon enough, lass, soon enough.'

Patti and Milly walked quickly along the low, dim tunnel, until a space opened to their right, where eight people waited: four soldiers, three women, and a child. They turned

22

their faces to Patti, as she waddled in. 'Anyone else?' one haggard woman asked, a plaintive appeal in her sullen dark eyes.

'That's everyone,' said Patti. 'There's only the filth up there now, burning everything.' The haggard woman lowered her head and wept silently, and her companions put their arms around her shoulders to comfort her. 'There's little time to tarry,' Patti explained. 'The girl will lead you to a place where everyone else who's got underground is gathering. You'd best go as fast as your legs'll carry you. There's a lot going on up there, and down here.'

As Patti spoke, Milly saw three Guild members slide past, carrying the hand-held crossbows that were normally the property of The Hand assassins. They were going to kill Haagii. She wished she could go with them, instead of leading the people they dragged to safety. She wanted to see Haagii die. They killed her father. She would never forgive or forget that fact.

'Come on, Milly lass,' Patti urged, nudging her to attention. 'There's no time to daydream down here. Get on with it.'

Milly led the party along a twisting route, that rose and fell and twisted and turned, through the heart of the Maze. Before the Haagii came, outsiders who blundered into the Maze, the territory of the Great City's Thief Guild, had their throats slit. It was a forbidden world. Even in the first days of the siege, Guild Master Orrin said the Shadow's Voice expressly forbade the presence of city people within the Maze, but humanitarian voices, led by Patti and Tim Gaelus and Sasha, protested the instruction, and a common agreement spread, between members of The Hand, sanctioned by Death's First Hand, that the Shadow's Voice's order would be contravened when the Haagii assaulted the city. By offering shelter to the refugees escaping the Haagii, they were acting against the Guild's head authority.

Milly agreed wholeheartedly that saving people was much more sensible than letting them perish just to keep a few tunnels secret. The meeting place in the Maze for the

23

refugees was the Deep Cave, because it was the largest space for assembling people in the thieves' underground network. By the time Milly brought her group there, close to two hundred people were gathered.

Her friend Aaron waved and trotted to meet her, as she entered, but Milly's attention was attracted to Jen, who was tending to an injured soldier, near a large rock at the cave's centre. 'This is exciting stuff!' Aaron grinned.

Milly spotted two small daggers tucked in his belt. 'Where did you get those?' she asked.

'Picked them up.'

'Who from?' she persisted.

'Who knows? Want one?' He drew a dagger and handed it to her.

She held it up to the guttering light, flickering from a multitude of torches around the cave walls, and noted how the blade was pitted and chipped. Though it was poorly kept, she didn't have her own weapon, and she felt the need to have one. 'Thanks,' she said. 'I'll sharpen it later.'

'I'd like to sharpen mine on a Haagii throat,' said Aaron, with a twisted smile. 'I'm going to be an assassin when I'm old enough to be accepted.'

Milly stared at the boy. 'I'm going to live in the castle as a princess,' she said quietly, and smiled at the fluttering shadows made by the crowd of people on the Deep Cave walls.

The clanging melee reached Andra's ears, as he pushed through the mob scrambling up castle road to escape the Haagii. Kingdom warriors remained in the Great City, after the Haagii encirclement, but men, women, and children, from the poorer quarters on the western side of Dragon River, were running to save their lives. Some clutched bags full of personal possessions, hastily grabbed when the Haagii charged into the city's heart, but most ran empty-handed, hearts full of fear. Ahead, a wall of torchlight, and a dark line of riders blocked his path. The King's elite Haardrishii, black armour glistening, held the foes at bay. Haagii reached at the horsemen, trying to pull them down, but Haardrishii swords glinted in the flickering light as they slashed mercilessly at the attackers. A shadow relief of the battle adorned the cliff wall, the shadows elongated and twisted into heroic scale, warriors and horses locked in combat. A knot of warriors battled the enemy, ahead of the Haardrishii.

Andra searched for Claarn and Marella in the maddening throng, until, above the din of conflict, he heard a rallying bellow that could only come from the giant of Tressel Deep. He reached over his shoulder for Abreotan's sword and willed the blade to flame. A white aura grew rapidly into an amber glow, and the blade erupted into a tongue of fire. The tingle of magic thrilled through his arm.

'Then it is true!' whispered a deep voice to Andra's left. Surdrok replaced his astonishment with his usual grim expression, as he looked up at the prophesied King, and said, 'I am with you, my Lord,' with humble obedience, and together they pushed between the jostling horses, into the fight.

Andra swept aside every Haagii who opposed him, but most retreated from the warrior wielding the fiery sword, pushing their companions aside in their frenzy to escape the phenomenon. He heard Claarn's roar of greeting, and Marella moved to his right. Surdrok swung and thrust with cool precision, his assassin training honed to perfection, despite his restrictive Haardrishii armour. The Haagii lost impetus, as their numbers fell at the hands of the four barring their progress, until they collapsed behind their torch wall, leaving a gap between the two factions.

Claarn laughed, as he wiped the sweat and blood from his shaggy brow. 'We are too much for them. They've lost their will to fight.'

'Hardly,' grumbled Surdrok. 'Open your eyes, giant.'

Claarn saw the Haagii torch-wall part to allow a group of armoured warriors through, their long blond locks flowing from beneath their helmets, wicked spikes curved from the shoulders and sides and elbows of their black plate, their long swords gleaming.

'Dark Warriors,' said Marella quietly, 'at least fifteen.' A number of Haardrishii dismounted behind Andra's small party and joined them, while the warriors, who were helping Claarn and Marella hold the road, withdrew.

'A stand-off,' Claarn growled.

'I doubt it will be for very long, judging by their behaviour,' said Marella.

Behind the Dark Warriors, the Haagii began beating on their shields, softly at first, but the clamour grew, spreading through their ranks, down the short section of Castle Road. Surdrok gave an instruction to a warrior, who melted through the ranks beyond the horse line. The drumming rose to a crescendo, a fierce battle cry at its peak, at which moment the Dark Warriors advanced.

From the outset, Andra felt the Dark Warriors were pressing toward him with fanatical determination, and the first to confront him almost leaped onto the blade of Abreotan's sword. As he toppled aside, his face contorted from the searing flame and razor-sharp blade, a second, and a third, each resolutely inspired to kill or die, attacked Andra. He'd never fought warriors so unconcerned with death.

Though the Dark Warriors fought with exceptional skill and ferocity, their single-minded purpose to attack Andra gave Claarn, Marella, and Surdrok an edge. Not that Claarn needed assistance. Having nearly died at the hands of Dark Warriors in the Bitter Peaks on the quest for Abreotan's sword, his sword arm was lit with a different fire than the magic in Andra's weapon: a lust for vengeance burned, and the flame-haired giant wrought his vengeance with brutal delight as he felled two foes.

The conflict was bloody, but short. As Andra's flaming sword sliced through the shield and breastplate of the last Dark Warrior, the victim sprawling onto the corpses piled on the road, the Haagii battle cries dissipated, and an eerie silence settled.

Andra stared at the Haagii. Thrown into relief by the guttering torches, they looked the monsters the Dragonlord needed to command to wantonly kill the people of the Kingdom without mercy, but he could see a clear expression on their faces: disbelief at the slaughter of fifteen of their feared Dark Warriors by Andra and his companions.

'They are lost,' said Claarn. 'They are no match for Andra. Or us,' he added, with a contemptuous smile.

'At cost,' Surdrok replied. He had a long cut across the back of his sword hand. Marella's shoulder bled from a gaping wound. Six Haardrishii were dead. 'We couldn't hold another attack like that. We have to retire.'

Claarn started to protest, his thirst for appeasement on the battleground unsated, but Andra turned, and said, 'High Lord Surdrok's right. We can't hold back an army here, especially one this large. The city's lost. The castle's our best hope.'

Claarn lowered his sword, and grinned, saying, 'The King speaks. I hear and obey.' Andra smiled at the giant's acquiescent sarcasm. Claarn was too good a friend to lose in hasty battle.

The withdrawal began. The Haagii front ranks dogged the defenders', never closing but never widening the gap, as they edged up Castle Road toward the gates. Halfway up, the front line Haagii started shouting and brandishing their spears.

'Watch them,' Claarn growled. 'Their courage is returning.'

As if in answer to his warning, a spear dropped out of the darkness into the flank of a Haardrishii horse. The wounded creature whinnied with pain, and its rider dismounted to calm his horse. More spears fell among the retreating defenders.

'Quicker!' Surdrok shouted. 'Get the horses to safety!'

As the Haardrishii wheeled their horses, and rode up the road, a blood-curdling shout rose, and the front Haagii ranks charged. Andra and Claarn met them in the centre of the road, flailing their swords, wreaking death.

'We'll hold them!' Claarn shouted at a group of warriors who ran to join the defence. 'Everyone else to the castle!'

The brightness of the flames on Abreotan's sword intensified, as Andra appeared to double his speed and ferocity, while the hard-pressed Kingdom warriors fought courageously to stop the Haagii charge. Claarn hewed and hacked, determined none of the enemy reach the castle gates before him.

Again, the Haagii dropped back. Again, the steady retreat renewed. The Kingdom warriors carried and dragged their wounded companions, hampered by their weight and pain. Marella called, 'The horses are safe! Hurry!'

Thirty paces from the gates, Surdrok ordered the defenders to run. Andra gestured for the stragglers to obey, while Claarn and he continued to walk steadily backwards, anticipating the stalking Haagii to make a final desperate attempt to bring down the two Kingdom warriors who had punished them.

Twenty paces from the castle gates, the Haagii charged. Andra and Claarn braced for the last twenty paces of fighting retreat. The flames of Andra's sword burned brilliant white, lighting the road like daylight. As the Haagii came within sword's length, dozens toppled backwards, hit by a deadly shower of arrows. The surviving handful crashed into Claarn, and Andra, to be cut down before they could understand what was unfolding. A second burst of arrows cut a swathe across the Haagii ranks, giving Claarn and Andra space and time to sprint into the castle. Within the castle compound, Andra looked up at the line of blond Longbowmen, on the parapets, going about their trade with deadly efficiency.

Four

Tim scrambled through the gap in the rock fall to join Sasha, where her torchlight revealed another section of the tunnel from the Deep Cave, blocked by a massive metal door. 'It's locked,' Sasha said.

'And probably barred,' Tim declared, as he ran his fingers over the pitted and dented surface. 'Others have tried to force it.' He looked up at the ceiling, and turned to his left, assessing the space. 'My guess is it leads under the castle, probably right into it.'

'That would account for the door,' said Sasha. 'The Great King wouldn't appreciate our people popping up in his castle grounds.'

'Hasn't stopped anyone before,' said Tim, with a sly grin. 'Look for levers, panels, anything that could hide a mechanism for opening from this side,' he continued, adopting a professional manner. They meticulously searched the walls and floor, checking every crack, every imperfection, but found nothing significant. 'Grim pickings,' Tim muttered, and grunted with frustration as he sat on his haunches.

'I'll get Holly,' said Sasha. 'If there's something to be found, she'll know where to look better than us.'

Tim nodded. 'Do that. I'll wait. Who knows, I might think of something we've missed.'

'I doubt it.' Sasha retorted, shaking her head. 'You lack feminine ingenuity.'

'So how come you can't find anything?' Tim mocked, but Sasha ignored him, and climbed through the rock fall to fetch Holly.

At the end of the long, sloping tunnel into the Deep Cave, arguing voices made her hurry. A woman and a man faced each other at the cave's centre, beside a large rock, surrounded by onlookers riveted to the scene, and Sasha recognised the pair. Guild Master Orrin, dagger drawn, platinum neck chain glinting in the torch light, was glaring at a defiant figure wearing an assassin's black garb, dark hair flowing loosely over her shoulders: Death's First Hand. The confrontation she and Tim had feared was taking place. Sasha pushed through the crowd.

'You'll pay for this insolence, Kara!' Orrin snarled viciously, biting on his words. 'The Shadow's Voice has no mercy for those who disobey him.'

'The Shadow's Voice is a fiction of your power-hungry ego, Orrin. Don't expect me to cringe before your ghost. Everyone in the Guild knows your game now.' Sasha recognised her technique. Death's First Hand spoke slowly, deliberately, goading Orrin into making the first move. Kara wanted to fight.

Orrin turned his dagger menacingly. 'Don't try to force my hand, Kara. I know the game as well as you. Better in fact. That's why I'm Master of the Guild.'

'For how much longer?' Kara challenged. 'Now everyone knows there is no Shadow's Voice? You're getting old. What are you? Forty-five? Fifty? That's old for a thief.'

'I'm more than a match for a man half my age,' Orrin growled with growing anger. 'Or any woman,' he added pointedly. 'Now get these vermin out of the Deep Cave!' he ordered, with a sweeping gesture at the survivors of the Haagii attack.

'First, you must shift me,' said Kara.

Sasha felt the tension reach climax. Orrin had an irritating stalemate, a poor result for the Master of the Guild, especially before an audience of Guild and non-Guild people. If he backed down, he was signing his death warrant, by demonstrating weakness in failing to discipline an insurgent Guild member, and no Guild Master would be accepted after a glaring show of cowardice. He had to make the first move. Kara, Death's First Hand, had successfully called his bluff.

Orrin glanced nervously at the watching circle of strangers, and Guild people. Choice of action was taken from him. The Shadow's Voice specifically instructed him to deny access to the Deep Cave to any thief, upon pain of death. Now Kara had brought city refugees into the forbidden place, in open defiance of his ruling. 'Damn you, Kara!' he whispered sharply, and thrust viciously with his dagger.

The fight was poorly matched and brief. Kara took the force of Orrin's attack backwards, into a roll, throwing the Guild Master onto his back. She rolled with the motion, and came up, thrusting her knee into his diaphragm, forcing the air from his lungs. He reacted instinctively, but she wrenched on his arm and elbow, making him stab himself deep under the ribs. Orrin groaned with pain and shock, and bucked, throwing the woman off his chest. Freed, he pulled the dagger from his chest, and straightened awkwardly; but the damage was done. Sasha saw the crimson bloodstain spreading across Orrin's jerkin. He swayed, eyes glinting like glass beads, and Sasha recognised the touch of death with her clinical assassin experience. He lurched backward and crashed like a heavy sack to the ground.

'We had a crisis before,' said Lord Kerry emphatically. 'Now we have a disaster!'

The King's Table was animated, and Andra quietly observed the bickering Lords. Tempers were frayed after the night's retreat into the safety of the castle, and by morning the extent of the devastation was visible from every part of the castle's parapets. Smoke drifted into the morning sky, from the ashes and ruins of what had been the Great City. Most buildings were gutted piles of charcoal, and the few stone buildings were dark hulks in a sea of black and grey ash. Haagii squads moved through the desolation, like carrion-eaters, picking at the remains, stoking the fires to finish the destruction of the human city. Nothing was spared.

'How many do you estimate are on the grounds?' Waeron Ardath asked of the boyish Gerran.

Gerran glanced self-consciously around the gathering, before answering the Drycraefter. 'There are at least six thousand soldiers Lord Ardath, but that is an estimate.' He caught Lord Surdrok's eye for confirmation of his figure, but Surdrok chose only to return the young Lord's stare, until Gerran broke uncomfortably away. 'Of the people who escaped the city last night, and in the past two weeks, my people estimate some eight thousand men, women and children.'

'Fourteen thousand!' screamed Kerry, jumping to his feet. 'Fourteen thousand people crammed in the confines of the castle? We'll starve in a week! There's not enough water!'

'Will you sit down?' asked Haephus, in a bored tone.

'How can I sit down?' Kerry questioned, full of incredulity, his emotion taking hold. 'We don't have to wait for the Dragonlord to kill us. We'll kill ourselves, locked up inside this fancy prison! We'll starve, or die of disease, or thirst!'

'Kerry has a point,' the rotund Lord Eustice chimed in, becoming more agitated as Kerry drew his picture of impending doom. 'There are too many people.'

'Exactly!' said Kerry, delighted to receive support. 'Too many people.' He thumped his fist against the oak wood table to emphasise his point. 'Too many people!'

'And what do you propose we do?' asked Ardath.

The question spun Kerry to face the Drycraefter. The Lord of Internal and Foreign affairs paused, and a manic glint filled his eyes. 'Get rid of them!'

'Get rid of who?'

'The city people – anyone who isn't able-bodied with a weapon. The women. The children. The old folk.'

'Now you really are crazy!' Haephus exclaimed, glaring indignantly at Kerry across the table's expanse. 'By Teka, the Profound Goddess of our Great City, I would not allow this to happen.'

'There is no more Great City, Haephus!' Kerry retorted. 'Your profound goddess is as dead as the ashes in the streets.'

Haephus' hands disappeared beneath his orange and red robe and re-emerged, clasping a short, thin bladed sword. 'I will not tolerate blasphemy against the Temple of Teka!' the priest hissed, and he pointed his weapon at Lord Kerry, who visibly whitened with fear as he hastily stumbled back from the menacing sword aimed at his throat. Time paused, in a tableau of brooding violence, and Andra noted the fears of two Lords who were meant to be his vassals.

'Sit. Both of you!' the Chancellor commanded, fingertips touching his chest, his eyes fixed on the point of conflict at the King's Table. Haephus looked self-consciously at his drawn sword, before he sheathed it, and sat. Lord Kerry edged nervously back into his chair. 'Hardly appropriate behaviour at the King's Table,' A Ahmud Ki observed, 'especially with the Dragonlord's army on our doorstep.' The Chancellor bowed his head politely to Andra. 'If I may, Your Majesty?' Andra nodded, allowing A Ahmud Ki the right to stand and take control of matters. 'Fools panic,' the Chancellor said, reinforcing his discipline of Haephus and Kerry. 'What we need are simple facts. Then we can look at all the possibilities.' He fixed Kerry with a glare, and added, 'The positive possibilities.' Everyone nodded in agreement.

Andra remained the observer, not a participant, and saw that he was the King in status only. The real ruler, the controller, was the Chancellor, who held the Lords in his palm, as he asked how many people were in the castle grounds, how much food was stored away, how many rooms were available to shelter people, how many wells dropped into the plateau water supply. His intelligence, his charismatic presence, outshone everyone. Even Surdrok was obediently involved in the gathering and sharing of facts, led by A Ahmud Ki. Andra was learning that, if he was to be a successful, efficient King, he needed A Ahmud Ki's support. That was obvious at the King's Table. His natural distrust for the Chancellor had to be overcome, because he was too valuable to be cast aside.

Tim's jaw dropped in astonishment at Sasha's news. 'She did what?'

'It's true,' confirmed Holly, who stood beside Sasha, before the metal door. 'Everyone in the Deep Cave witnessed it. Death's First Hand killed Orrin, in a fair fight.'

Tim ran his hand through his fair hair and leaned against the door before he looked at Sasha and Holly. 'You realise what this means?'

'Of course we do,' said Sasha. 'Death's First Hand is successor to the Guild Master. That's Guild Law.'

'If she wants to be,' Holly reminded them. 'She can choose not to take the position, but name her replacement.'

'Who would she name?' asked Tim. 'She's the only real contender.' Sasha and Holly couldn't immediately think of an alternative candidate for Guild Master. Orrin had been Guild Master for a long time. 'And what does the Shadow's Voice think of all this?' he asked.

'You believe in that?' Sasha responded, arching her left eyebrow.

Tim shook his head. 'A ploy by Orrin to keep us on our toes.'

'That's exactly what Death's First Hand accused him of,' said Holly.

'We'd best get used to calling her Guild Master Kara,' Sasha said, as she inspected the door again. 'There will need to be a successor from The Hand to the role of Death's First Hand now.'

Both Sasha and Holly looked at Tim. He shrugged. 'Any one of us is eligible, Sasha,' he replied, and turned the conversation from the subject. 'But first, we must find our way past this door. If it leads into the castle, as we suspect it does, then we can move the rest of the people to safety, and we can let Andra know the danger he's in.'

Holly ran her fingers across the cold metal surface and cast a glance along the walls of the tunnel, back to the rockslide. 'Have you dug away any of that?' she asked, indicating the collapsed tunnel.

'No,' said Sasha, looking at Tim. He shook his head.

'Then let's start there,' Holly decided.

A Ahmud Ki's revelation left everyone at the table with their jaws slack in astonishment, and awkward moments passed before Surdrok broke the silence. 'You're telling us that, under this castle, there's another castle carved in the plateau?'

A Ahmud Ki turned his serenely satisfied gaze on the speaker. 'Yes.'

'Tunnels? And rooms?'

'Whole galleries,' A Ahmud Ki replied, with a generous sweep of his arms to emphasise the expansiveness.

'How in Teka's name do you know this?' Haephus threw Surdrok a cautionary glare at the profane mention of the goddess' name, which Surdrok ignored.

'The Great King's Royal Library is full of information, if only you'd read,' A Ahmud Ki said, sarcastically. 'I'm not the only one in the room who knew this little secret.' He directed his comment at Waeron Ardath.

'You knew about it?' queried Lord Eustice. Waeron Ardath nodded. 'Then why in Teka's name didn't you tell us, you old fool?'

'I won't put up with any more profanity at this table,' Haephus cut in, peeved at Eustice's outburst.

'Shut up, priest!' Kerry growled.

'You don't tell me anything!' Haephus retorted, and the two locked eyes.

'I won't warn either of you again,' the Chancellor cautioned. Haephus rocked in his chair.

Everyone turned to Waeron Ardath, and A Ahmud Ki watched with amusement as the Drycraefter realised he, not the Chancellor, was the centre of interest about the plateau's secrets. He coughed.

'Tell us what you know,' Surdrok ordered.

Ardath looked at Surdrok, as if he was contemplating saying nothing, but he relaxed, and stroked his flowing white beard. 'It is recorded,' he began, 'in the 'Ancient Lore', that King Abreotan and his followers drove one army of the Dragonlords onto the Great Plains, forcing the Dragonlord,

Andrakis Va'ristrin Nyavardenet, to seek refuge in his fortress. Andrakis' fortress was carved from a large plateau that jutted abruptly from the Great Plains. After many months of siege, during which time King Abreotan left to deal with another of the Dragonlords, he returned, penetrated the fortress, and defeated Andrakis, sealing him forever, in a tomb, deep in the heart of the plateau rock.

In celebration of his victory, King Abreotan ordered a castle built, atop the plateau, to become one of his seats of power. After the Dragon Wars, Abreotan made the castle his home, and the people came to live in the city, at the foot of the plateau, along the Dragon River, which springs from the plateau's heart. You sit in that castle. Below you, locked inside the rock, is another castle, one once owned by the Dragonlord, Andrakis Va'ristrin Nyavardenet.'

Ardath's revelation held the Lords speechless. Andra was awed at the prospect a vast complex, one that had been the refuge of a mighty Dragonlord, sat beneath his feet.

'So how do we get into this fortress?' asked Surdrok, his mind filled with myriad possibilities such a site would provide for defence.

'You don't,' Ardath replied.

Surdrok's face darkened. 'What do you mean, Drycraefter? There's a fortress at our feet. How do we get into it?' the High Lord asked, with a hint of anger on his tongue.

Ardath shook his head slowly. 'King Abreotan ordered the fortress, and all its entrances, sealed after his death.'

'What?' Haephus exclaimed.

'Why?' Surdrok demanded.

'Because,' Ardath explained, tiredly, 'he wanted no one to ever interfere with the Dragonlord's tomb, or use anything that bore his imprint.'

'That's absurd!' Lord Eustice complained. 'It's a perfect place for safe refuge.'

'You mean there's no entrance to this fortress at all?' Surdrok asked, his frustration on the boil. He would not be denied access to the military tool he needed, to keep the

Haagii and the Dragonlord's forces at bay.

'None,' replied Ardath, with a gentle sigh. 'That's why I never told you about it.'

Surdrok smashed his fist against the table. 'By Teka, I'll find a damned way into this fortress of Andrakis if it kills me!' he snarled and stood to leave.

The Chancellor's steady voice stopped him. 'There is a way into the fortress, Surdrok. Sit down.' The Chancellor held out his left hand, indicating Surdrok should resume his seat. Surdrok looked at the other Lords, who were also waiting for him to take his chair, because they were eager to hear what the Chancellor was about to reveal. He sat.

A Ahmud Ki motioned to a figure in the doorway to approach the table. The Apprentice, Damon, bowed low, quickly crossed the room to his master's side, and held out two books, and a scroll. As A Ahmud Ki accepted Damon's offering, the Apprentice dropped to the floor and abased himself. Andra heard the Chancellor whisper a dismissal, after which Damon rose to his feet, keeping his eyes averted, and hurried from the room. A Ahmud Ki opened the first book to a map. 'This,' he said with authority, as everyone stared at the ancient sketch, 'is Andrakis.'

Five

Andra waited, until the three serving youths turned back the gold-inlaid cover on his bed, and adjourned from his chamber, before he locked his door. He pulled the heavy green satin curtains shut and surveyed the chamber's details. Great King Thana spared little on his comfort – silk and satin, the finest crafted woods, gold and silver. The bed was larger than any bed Andra had seen and could easily accommodate four or five sleeping adults. Six oak wood posts supported a silken canopy. Gilt chairs were dotted around the chamber, and a broad chest of drawers, bedecked by an equally broad mirror, sat beside the entrance door, the back of which was covered with beaten silver, and inlaid with rubies and emeralds. Animal hide rugs covered the marble floor. Near the window, sculpted from the marble floor, a miniature bathing pool, deep and long enough for two people, was empty of water, but he intuitively knew the servants would fill it, should he desire that luxury.

The symbols of Thana's reign – dark green and the rampant griffin – were worked into everything. The malformed beast, cross between a lion and an eagle, fascinated Andra, and he wondered if such a weird creature really existed? After all, he disbelieved the tales about dragons when he heard the stories and legends shared around campfires, until the black beasts swooped on the Great Armies at The Rim Shield, belching gouts of flame. He'd seen too much to disbelieve the possibility of anything happening. If someone told him, when he walked out of The Vale, he would become the king, he would have laughed at the absurd notion, yet he was standing in the King's chamber because he was the King, Thana's successor, the inheritor of Abreotan's legacy. How much more could happen?

He turned to the tapestries hanging on every available

wall space. Some depicted tranquil scenes of tan fawns, and small multi-coloured animals, gambolling in beautiful green forests. Two very large tapestries depicted battles between the Dragonlords and Aian Abreotan.

He moved closer, to study the detail of Abreotan, the kingly warrior. In both pictures, Abreotan was depicted as larger than anyone else, the muscles in his arms and legs and shoulders bulging ludicrously while he dealt out death to his enemies.

In one tapestry, Abreotan's great sword of flame was sweeping through the necks of two massive black dragons, sending the creatures' ugly heads rolling to the earth, and Abreotan hung in the air like the beasts he was slaying, as if he could fly. Questions whirled through Andra's mind: Was Abreotan a master of magic? Did the sword have the power to lift him off the earth, at will?

The second tapestry showed Abreotan in conflict with a Dragonlord who sat astride a fire-breathing dragon. The dragon's fire was aimed at Abreotan, but the flames spread around him without appearing to touch him. Andra recalled his confrontation with Mareg's black dragon on the stone bridge at Cennednyss. The sword shielded him from the creature's fiery belch, and he slew it with a pulse of raw magical energy. In the tapestry, Abreotan's sword was glowing with bright amber light and a single beam was shooting toward the Dragonlord, whose face was contorted in a strange mixture of hatred and terror. Around the central trio, bodies were strewn across a vast bloodied battlefield that stretched into darkness at the furthest visible point. The tapestry weaver highlighted intricate detail on the armour and weaponry, and equipment of other figures in the scenes, even on the corpses littering the battlefield.

Andra noticed significant features of Abreotan's portrayal. The warrior King not only wielded the legendary sword, he wore a suit of golden chain mail and plate armour with a golden helmet. He carried no other weapons, or encumbrances. Andra's eyes widened as two tiny, but significant, details sunk into his consciousness: the scar, and the ponytail. They were there – obscured, but there. A crescent scar marred the legendary hero's right cheek. Andra's fingertips rose to his own left cheek and traced the moon-shaped scar he bore. Perhaps it was a flaw in the tapestry. But when he looked closer, he knew the scar was real. The revelation stunned him.

He turned, unwilling to stare any longer at the tapestries. He felt exposed, insecure, unsure. Who was he really? Had fate created amazing coincidences, or was there no Andra, just Abreotan reborn to face the Dragonlord? No. The latter idea was absurd. If he was merely reincarnated in another body and time, why couldn't he remember how to generate the power of his sword? He was Andra, not Abreotan. He was Andra.

As he wrestled with the dilemma, he looked at the sword leaning against the large mahogany desk, near the bed. He picked it up, drawing it from the makeshift scabbard he hadn't replaced since returning to the Great City. The sword's weightlessness puzzled him. It was bulky to the eye, with a long thick handgrip embedded with amber studs, a dragon carved in the pommel with amber eyes, and a broad blade, moulded with jagged points. A sword designed like it should be unwieldy, impractical. He savoured the familiar tingle spreading up his arms as he grasped the hilt and swept the blade before his eyes to gaze at the runes etched into it. They had to be the keys to the sword's magic. If he could understand their meaning, he might be able to unlock the power within, and harness it. As it was, he could only call upon the weapon to light and flame. And, once only, he unleashed an awesome burst of magical energy to slay the dragon at Cennednyss; but that was a clumsy, passionate reaction, not mastery.

Someone knocked, so he leaned the weapon against the chair. He opened the door and was surprised to find the Royal Drycraefter. 'May I come in, Your Majesty?' Lord Ardath asked.

Andra studied the Drycraefter, as he entered. With his halo of white hair and long beard, the man was another fascinating member of Thana's leadership team. He seemed to keep to himself, except at the King's Table, where it was obvious he played the role of an observant watchdog. Andra sensed antagonism between Ardath and A Ahmud Ki. Ardath was an historian, a recorder of facts and events, but because Andra knew little more than that about the Lord, the visit might be a good opportunity to learn more.

Ardath's eyes rested on the sword. He moved to it, and began to reach out, but he turned to Andra, and asked, 'May I, Your Majesty?'

'No,' Andra warned. 'No one else can touch the sword. There's a powerful spell woven into its fabric preventing anyone, except me, from using it.' Ardath's eyebrows lifted inquisitively, as Andra explained. 'I don't understand it, except that a bracelet I wear –' He paused to rub his wrist, feeling the invisible Elvenaar band he received from Hyacinth and the Treekeepers in Ethelreddor forest. 'You can't see it, but it protects me from the sword.'

'I understand, Your Majesty,' Ardath graciously replied, and tilted his head toward Andra out of genuine respect. 'If I may inspect the runes on the blade?'

Andra saw no harm in letting the Drycraefter look at the runes. Something about Ardath's whole manner and presence said he could be trusted. 'Go ahead,' Andra said. As Ardath kneeled before the blade and studied the runes, he seemed to completely forget Andra's presence, and when he stood again from the weapon's resting place Andra saw a distant look on the Drycraefter's face, as if he was wandering through a forest of thought. 'What is it you see, Lord Ardath?' Andra asked carefully, trying not to rudely disturb the Drycraefter.

Ardath blinked. 'I had hoped the prophecy in the 'Ancient Lore' would come to be in my day, but I never really believed it would. You bear the heaviest load of all men, Your Highness.' Andra waited for Ardath to explain his statement, but the Drycraefter crossed the room, and sat on a chair, near the centre, and he indicated Andra should draw up a chair beside him. 'I apologise for what may seem as an

41

abrupt interruption, Your Highness,' Ardath began, as Andra sat, 'but I believe you must understand the nature of the legacy you have inherited. You are in great danger, my Lord, from within and without the castle, and there are secrets I must share with you so the prophecy can be fulfilled in its entirety.'

The mention of internal threat set Andra on his guard. 'Who threatens me within the castle?'

Ardath shook his head and glanced about the room. 'It would not be prudent of me to reveal my fears yet, Your Highness, in case I am mistaken in my judgments, but I will warn you to watch carefully those closest to you at the King's Table.'

The Chancellor, thought Andra. Who else could Ardath be referring to? His initial reservations about the Chancellor were well founded. Liam had too close a connection with A Ahmud Ki, and died because of it. Peret and the Apprentices, and their sinister actions, were directly linked to the Chancellor. Ardath had no reason to apologise. He was only voicing what Andra suspected. 'What secrets can you teach me about the sword?' Andra asked, leaning forward eagerly.

Ardath went to answer, when astonishment filled his features. Andra heard a click behind him, where Ardath's eyes were fixed, and instinctively rolled off his chair. He heard Ardath gasp, but he dared not take his eyes from two figures pressed against the curtaining, before the large window that overlooked the castle courtyard. Wrapped in assassin black, faces covered, except for eyes that stared straight at Andra, they held spent miniature crossbows, the kind he'd learned to use in the Maze.

The assassins dropped their crossbows, drew curved, serrated daggers, and advanced on Andra, stalking him swiftly across the chamber. He retreated, but the assassins had cut his path to the sword, circling to make their attack. Ardath's body was slumped against the chair on which Andra had been sitting. He could cry out – there were palace guards in the hallway – but, sensing his intention, an assassin leaped. The young Guardian barely avoided the man's dagger as he dodged and caught the assassin's arm, swinging him against the heavy chest of drawers. As he released the first man, the second lunged. Andra dived onto the bed, and as the assassin chased him, he pulled on the silk curtaining, which came swirling down over the assassin, briefly entangling him. 'Guards!' Andra yelled. Incited by his call, the first assassin flipped his dagger and threw it. Andra ducked, but the weapon grazed his shoulder, before thudding into the wall panel. Instantly, the assassin had a second dagger in his hand. His companion disentangled himself from the bed curtain, and they closed in.

Andra wanted the sword. If only he had the sword. As he refocused on the assassins, preparing to fight, his right hand tingled with the sword's presence, and his attackers' eyes widened with disbelief. He held it. The sword came to him. He had no time to consider the miracle. Advantage lost, the assassins attacked with maniacal determination, but Andra swung the twice. The chamber door burst open, and six Royal Guards charged in, astonished to see their king standing over the twitching corpses of two assassins and the Royal Drycraefter.

They excavated the collapsed tunnel section and shored the weakened ceiling and walls with strong beams brought from the store in the Maze. Holly's search of the exposed portion of wall revealed no clue to how the metal door would open. 'It's locked by a magical device,' she said, shaking her head, as she sat dejectedly against a fresh beam.

'Hardly,' argued Tim. 'More likely it's sealed this side and can only be opened from the other side.'

'Makes sense,' Sasha agreed, dropping to sit with Holly. 'The Great King wouldn't really want thieves in his basement.'

'Maybe,' Holly muttered.

'Don't be such a sourpuss,' chided Sasha, with a playful push on Holly's arm. 'You did your best to find a secret lever. You can't do much if there isn't one, can you?' Holly shrugged. 'Can you?' Sasha persisted with another nudge, forcing a smile from Holly.

'We've got to find a way through,' said Tim, as he studied the door again. 'We can't get our information to Andra any other way, except by sneaking through the Haagii camped in the city ruins and on Castle Road.'

'That's far too risky, even for you, Tim Gaelus,' said Sasha.

'But if Andra doesn't know about these special assassins, he can hardly protect himself from them,' Tim argued. 'If I have to get past the Haagii, I will.' He levelled his eyes at Sasha to emphasise his determination.

'Then let's hope you won't have any reason to prove your point,' Sasha said quietly.

'What about digging through the wall?' Holly suggested.

'No,' said Tim. 'I bet the metal door is set into a stone foundation, and that might take days to break through.'

'Not with Shaddite help,' Sasha cut in.

'There aren't any Shaddites here,' said Tim, and he sighed. 'The few who lived in the outskirts of the Great City left for the Dwarven Mountains months ago, when the war threatened the Kingdom. The only others are up in the castle, as soldiers.'

'Do you have to be so negative?' Sasha asked.

'No. Just practical.'

Approaching torches interrupted their discussion. Tim looked up and saw Milly and Aaron. They were on an errand. He admired Milly. She had learned the way of the Guild very quickly. She had enormous natural talent, superb reflexes for a child of her age, and she was intelligent. He'd already decided to ask her to be his apprentice when she turned fifteen, but he wouldn't tell her until she came of age, as was the Guild custom. His choosing was also dependent on Andra's interests in the child. After all, Andra rescued the girl from the marauding Haagii on the western plains, and brought her to the Great City, and, as King, he had a great deal to offer her, much more than an assassin of The Hand could promise.

Milly walked straight to Tim, held up her torch, and announced, 'Guild Master, er Mistress, Kara says she wants to see you immediately.'

'Do you know why?' Tim asked.

'She didn't tell me or Aaron anything, but I guess it's about being Death's First Hand,' Milly replied, with a grin.

He shot a glance at Sasha and Holly, who were grinning too. 'I think it will be something else, Milly,' he said, and ruffled the girl's hair.

'Is that a bet?' she asked slyly.

'Don't bet with her,' Aaron burst out. 'She never bets on nothing that she don't already know is a sure thing. Believe me.'

'Shut up, Aaron!' Milly snapped. 'You just don't understand the odds.'

'Do too, Milly smarty-pants,' Aaron grumbled, and turned his back.

'Take it easy, you two,' laughed Tim. He slipped an arm over Milly's shoulder and lowered to her height. 'I'll bet you a gold coin it's about something different.'

'Done,' Milly said, confidently.

Tim straightened, and turned to Sasha. 'I think we're wasting our time here. We need to think of another way up to the castle.'

Sasha looked at Holly and shook her head. 'We'll stay a while longer,' she replied. 'While you find out what Kara has in store for you, we'll give more thought to a way around this obstacle.'

'Not more women's intuition,' Tim grinned wickedly.

'You're pretty smart,' Sasha said, with a warm smile, and added, as he turned to go, 'for a male.'

The women watched Tim, Milly and Aaron recede, until they disappeared around a slight bend in the descending tunnel, before returning their attention to the door. 'No levers. No panels. No locks. No magic,' said Holly.

'A stone wall foundation and support surrounding it,' added Sasha. 'How do we get through?'

Sasha's question went unanswered. Holly stared at the

door, open-mouthed, astonished by the vision, and Sasha turned to see A Ahmud Ki passing through the centre of the metal door, as if it was an illusion.

Six

'How many slain?'

'Eight, including the two who made it into your chamber,' Claarn replied to Andra.

'But it cost us,' Surdrok broke in. 'I lost twelve guards on the castle walls where the vermin came over.'

'What do we know about them?' Andra asked, looking to the others in the room. He'd called a special meeting, to determine how to combat the unprecedented attacks by assassins, sent from the Haagii army, but the only Lord present was High Lord Surdrok. The Chancellor was summoned, but he hadn't come, a fact Andra noted. Ardath was lying near death, in his chambers, from crossbow wounds intended for Andra. The others present were Tim Gaelus, Kara, the new Guild Mistress, and Claarn, as Surdrok's second-in-command: people whose input and judgment Andra most valued on the matter to hand.

'They're highly trained,' said Tim. 'I was hard pressed in single combat with one of them. They're strong, and very agile.'

'They're hell-bent on death,' said Surdrok. 'They're not satisfied, until they kill or are killed.'

'You're clearly their target,' Tim stated.

'The Hand stopped twelve before the Haagii burned the city,' Kara informed them. 'They work in pairs.'

Tim nodded. 'There's something else,' he added. 'Have you seen their eyes, when they're alive?' Claarn and Surdrok shook their heads. 'There's no sparkle, no life – just hatred and death.'

'That's their job,' Surdrok said bluntly.

'No.' Tim persisted. 'I've never yet met an assassin who doesn't have a trace of fear, or excitement, or some emotion in their eyes. But these ones have nothing living. They're not afraid to die.'

'They're already dead,' murmured Andra.

Tim and the others turned to him. 'Exactly!' said Tim. 'They're already dead. Death's got nothing to frighten them with.'

'But they walk and fight,' argued Claarn. 'They die like anyone else.'

'Do they?' Tim asked. 'Then why aren't they afraid, even when they're trapped with no escape?' Silence settled on the meeting.

'We need to capture one,' Surdrok suggested. 'If we can get one to talk, we might learn what we're up against.'

'Good luck,' Tim said sardonically, 'but I don't like your chances.'

'Got a better idea?' Surdrok snarled, his annoyance with Tim's presence clear to everyone.

'No,' Tim replied, as he sat back in the chair normally occupied by Lord Eustice. 'Not yet.'

A Ahmud Ki sat patiently, while Damon methodically plaited his silver locks. The Chancellor was annoyed and frustrated. There were more complications than he anticipated. The new King was still out of his control, and Abreotan's sword remained a threatening mystery. Now, Haagii-employed assassins had seriously wounded the Drycraefter, Ardath, in the King's chamber, but A Ahmud Ki wanted to know why Ardath was visiting the King so late at night. There was Orrin's death, through which he lost his influential control of the Thieves' Guild as the Shadow's Voice, and the woman, Kara, usurped Orrin's title. Worse, the thieves and city people were freely moving through the Deep Cave, his only point of access to Andrakis' tomb, and the potential power waiting for him to tap. He considered Kara would not be a problem. As the Shadow's Voice, he would bring her into line. He smiled at a notion that she was already wearing Orrin's chain as her badge of office – the platinum chain containing the controlling spell he used to make Orrin obedient. He would have to be more circumspect in his visits to the Deep Cave, with people coming and going during the siege. His preparations were nearly complete to attempt entry to the Dragonlord's tomb. Timing was crucial.

And then there was Ardath. What exactly does the Drycraefter know? Why is he showing so much interest in the King? he pondered. Obvious: the prophecy.

He accepted he made an error fabricating his version of the prophecy in Liam, especially since he learned Ardath knew the truth of the original prophetic words. That's why Ardath kept the volumes of the 'Ancient Lore' from him – a tactical move that gave Ardath power over the him, and it irked him that anyone could so easily threaten him. It is time the Drycraefter shared his secrets, A Ahmud Ki mused, so he could gather all the knowledge he needed to know about the Kingdom, Abreotan, and the sword.

'Enough,' A Ahmud Ki said, as he stood. Damon dropped to the floor, face averted, and waited until his master passed through the floor before he began tidying the chamber.

A Ahmud Ki walked through the gardens and entered the palace section of the castle. The Apprentice at the entrance prostrated himself, until A Ahmud Ki turned the first right corner and disappeared, before he resumed his post.

A flight of steps led to the room in which Ardath lay. Two Royal Guards outside the door bowed politely as A Ahmud Ki walked between them. He had been to the Drycraefter's personal chamber before, and saw the collection of miscellaneous junk that cluttered Ardath's room, but the room he lay in at present was tidy and darkened, except for a single candle burning by the bed.

A young, dark-haired woman looked up, as A Ahmud Ki approached. 'Leave us,' he ordered quietly. She nodded obediently and withdrew. A Ahmud Ki took her place on the stool and stared at the Drycraefter in his deathbed.

Ardath's white hair flared like a mane across his linen pillow, whiter than the clean bed sheets, and his snowy beard was neatly combed. His eyes were shut, and a peaceful expression filled his face. A bloodied bandage covered the old man's chest, soaking up the rust-coloured discharge from his wounds. A Ahmud Ki studied the old man's wrinkled lines and cracks. The Drycraefter's breathing was shallow and erratic.

'Dying time,' A Ahmud Ki whispered, 'and no successor, Ardath: very clumsy. Who will keep your records now?'

As if responding to A Ahmud Ki's question, the old man's eyes flickered open, and he rolled his head to look at the Chancellor. 'I - thought it might - be you,' he rasped, struggling to push the air out of his punctured lung.

'Disappointed?' A Ahmud Ki asked.

'No,' Ardath replied with a weak smile. 'Pleased.'

His cryptic response made A Ahmud Ki curious. 'Why pleased?' he asked, but Ardath simply smiled and closed his eyes. A Ahmud Ki watched the Drycraefter drift into the realm of sleep, and wondered why Ardath was pleased to see him? What did Ardath know that he did not?

A Ahmud Ki sat back and generated a mind spell to probe Ardath's thoughts. Asleep, and ill, the Drycraefter's strong powers of resistance would be down, making A Ahmud Ki's entry easy. He had longed to break through Ardath's defences, to discover what he hid in his memory and subconscious, and the layers peeled away as he descended through the sea of latent pain washing Ardath's conscious thought. Deeper, he probed the core of the Drycraefter's self, searching for memories attributed to the King, the sword, the Abreotan legend, the prophecy. He moved his concentration to its peak, searching – until a presence moved near his own. He shifted focus.

You persist where you are not invited, Ardath projected.

You deny what you dare not, A Ahmud Ki replied. There's no point resisting me any longer. You are dying.

But I am not dead yet.

Don't be a fool. I have more power at my fingertips than you can even comprehend. Tell me what you know about the sword.

If I refuse? Ardath felt laughter ripple through his mind, not his own, but a deep, sinister, threatening laugh.

Then I take what I need to know anyway.

Ardath was tired, very tired. Resisting the Chancellor was draining the precious strength he clung to. Do you believe in dreams?

The thought caught A Ahmud Ki off guard. No.

Pity. I had one that might have interested you.

Tell me.

It would take too long.

Tell me, A Ahmud Ki insisted.

Ardath's sleeping body released a heavy sigh, that nearly broke A Ahmud Ki's spell, but his thoughts flooded into A Ahmud Ki's mind. A warrior stood on a hill, overlooking a bloodied field of battle, where two armies swirled in a chaotic river of limbs, locked in conflict, no one winning, no one losing. Two Dragonlords also faced each other, across the valley. The warrior lifted his sword, and it flamed with fire so bright the sun hid its face in shame behind a sea of dark clouds. The Dragonlords ... turned their faces away then ... disappeared. Left alone above the turbulent war, the ... warrior brought his shining sword ... down ... against a rock, shattering its blade.

And?

I ... don't know. The dream ... ended ...

You're a fool. Keep your senseless dreams. I want the truth about the prophecy. I want to know all of it. Tell me the secret of the sword. Ardath? Ardath? Ardath damn you! I've got to know!

Around A Ahmud Ki's probing spell light faded, pulling in darkness that threatened to suffocate his consciousness. Recognising the danger, he broke contact with Ardath's mind, and the calm candlelight of Ardath's resting chamber swung into vision, throwing soft shadows across Ardath's peaceful face. The old man's empty eyes stared at the ceiling, defying A Ahmud Ki, in death, to take what he would not allow to be taken.

Lord Rheims at last had something to do. Thana's former Chancellor and Personal Valet scurried about the

Drycraefter's chamber, arranging his burial and personal effects, delighted to oversee a very responsible duty of state, because, since the new King's arrival, he'd been shunned, ordered by his successor, A Ahmud Ki, to keep out of sight, lest he become an unnecessary nuisance and lose the post of Personal Valet. Rheims wrung his bony hands, worried he might find himself demoted below the servants of whom he took charge in the palace. The Chancellor was too efficient and too callous to be ignored, so Rheims remained in the background. But now the new King asked him to make arrangements for Ardath's burial.

There was protocol to consider, even in war; even given the unfortunate circumstances of the castle being under severe siege. Rheims was impressed with the young King's decision to inter the Royal Drycraefter in the newly opened section of the fortress discovered in the plateau. He seemed to possess an innate understanding of the correct way in which things ought to be done, meaning he was going to be a pleasure to serve, after the obnoxious Thana.

Rheims directed two older women to prepare Ardath's corpse, while he busily flitted from room to room, in Ardath's chambers, cleaning and sorting through the weird and varied assortment of items the Drycraefter collected in his lifetime. There were strange instruments, and odd phials of liquid, and a multitude of ingredients defying Rheims' description or identification.

He loaded six pageboys with heavy chronicles, most covered in dust, and directed them to carry their burdens to the black tower in the Royal Gardens, where A Ahmud Ki's servant, Damon, was waiting to receive them. Rheims didn't question the Chancellor's instruction to deliver Ardath's library to him, because he assumed the King sanctioned the order, and he also knew, from experience, that A Ahmud Ki was a law unto himself. He doubted he would have changed.

In the long, but entertaining, process of cleaning Ardath's chambers, Rheims discovered a freshly written parchment on the Drycraefter's desk addressed to 'King Andra The Inheritor'. Tempted as he was to open the document, and read it, because it was likely to be the dead Drycraefter's last piece of writing and might contain instructions as to the fate of his belongings, Rheims knew better than to tamper with anything he was not instructed to meddle with, especially if it was addressed to the King. He rolled the parchment and sent a girl, with it, directly to find the King.

Satisfied, the King's Personal Valet set to finishing his task, casting a watchful eye on the owl perched above Ardath's desk. The creature's huge, yellow, prying eyes unsettled Rheims.

Andra shuffled impatiently in the antechamber, leading from the King's Table to the inner rooms, where a waiting game was under way. Tim had set a trap to capture an assassin, using Sasha as a decoy in Andra's bed, and planting members of The Hand in the chamber. As much as Andra insisted on being part of the trap, Tim and Claarn refused to allow his participation, on the pretext he was in too great a danger. He'd been tempted to assert his authority as King, but he knew neither Claarn nor Tim would be intimidated.

They had no guarantee the assassins would come. Three nights had passed without another incursion, and much was happening, elsewhere, in the castle. The Chancellor revealed the existence of a fortress in the plateau, linked to the Maze, and soldiers and other people, including the Guild, were surveying and mapping the hundreds of rooms and corridors under the castle, making it ready for habitation. Lord Ardath was dead. Whatever secrets he wanted to share with Andra, the night the assassins struck the secrets died with him. The next meeting of the King's Table would be crucial. So much had to be decided.

He started at the sound of a soft voice. Milly was talking in her sleep. Overjoyed to see him again, after so many weeks apart, she prattled on about his kingship, and how she was going to grow up to be a princess in his court, and how Patti and Jen and the Guild whores were going to be her handmaidens: so much that everyone started laughing happily at the visions Milly evoked of Patti's cumbersome squat body, squeezed into a fine evening gown, standing petitely in the throne room, waiting for a lover to sweep her off her feet. The raucous tomfoolery that followed bewildered Milly, and she was upset to think others were making fun of her dream, until Patti took her aside and explained the full reason why everyone was laughing. Milly still didn't think Patti would look funny in fine clothes. Her observation touched the old madam's heart, and she hugged the child warmly to her ample bosom.

Andra gazed fondly at the sleeping child, curled on a bed in the corner of the antechamber, and smiled. It was good to be reunited with her. She had grown, even in the short weeks since he'd found her – a dirty, beaten captive of Haagii mercenaries. Since the link with the Maze was opened, she virtually lived in the Haardrishii stables, patting and cooing to the horses, brushing their coats, until they shone. She loved horses. Andra recalled her natural empathy with the pair they borrowed from the Sisters of Veras, the horses being slaughtered by the Haagii outside Bear's home. When all this warring is over, he decided, I will give her the finest horse in Thana's stables.

He felt pressure against his leg. and he looked down to find Artega's black snout seeking attention. 'We don't get enough time to play, do we?' he said to the dog, and Artega's tail wagged slowly. 'I hope they look after you in the barracks.'

Shouts broke his reverie. He crossed to the door, leading into the chamber where the King normally slept, but, as he reached it, Sasha flung it open, nearly hitting him in her enthusiasm, and grinned as she announced, 'We've got one!' Behind her, soldiers pinned a writhing black-robed figure to the floor. Artega growled and his fur bristled.

Seven

Andra held the parchment and studied the unsteady elongated handwriting. The girl who brought it to him explained that Lord Rheims found the document on the Drycraefter's desk. Curiosity aroused, he carefully unfurled the parchment and read.

"I must be brief, though there is much I must write. Time moves in anticipation of what I do.

You are the inheritor of Abreotan's power, being the bearer of his sword. What you will, so the sword will do. It is powerful, perhaps the most potent magic ever forged into a single item. And only you can unlock that source. Believe in yourself and the sword. There is one thing the runes will reveal. The sword amplifies spells. The orb on the Chancellor's tower has the same ability. They are both legacies of the Genesis Stone. I warned that you carry a great burden. The runes on the sword, I'm certain, will confirm my fear.

Magic has been dying, since Abreotan imprisoned the Dragonlords. The magic of our lifetime is a mere shadow of what once was, even the legendary magic of the Aelendyell, except I suspect one among us gathers more about him. When the sword is destroyed, the last potent magic of the ancient world will perish with it. I don't know why or how. The 'Ancient Lore' does not explain it. Only you will find that answer.

One final thing I must write. Beware the greed of those who claim to be your friends."

Andra perused the document again, studying Ardath's observations. He closed the parchment and sat on the gilt chair in the King's Table chamber. Artega slumped against the chair, and Andra's hand slipped down to rub the black dog's ears. He stared at the Dragon War tapestries, the familiar motifs of battle with Abreotan reigning supreme.

The sword featured prominently: was even worked into the border designs. Ardath must have started the letter before deciding to visit Andra, but his untimely death prevented him telling Andra about the sword's powers. Only I can tap into its magical source, he recollected. What I will the sword to do, it will do. He remembered the sword answering his summons when the assassins had him cornered. All he had to do was concentrate on it being in his hand.

He rose, stepped over the sprawled dog, crossed to the far end of the table, extracted the sword from its scabbard and placed it on the table. He walked to the other end, stood beside the gilt chair, and concentrated. Come to me, he thought. Come. The sword vanished from its scabbard and reappeared in his hand, its blade gleaming, magic thrilling through his arm. Andra smiled. He concentrated a second time, willing the sword to return to the scabbard. The presence melted from his grip, and the sword filled out the ragged scabbard, as if it had never left it. He was the sword, the sword was him. So it was. Its secrets were unlocking.

Lord Gerran bent over his tally sheet and counted again. At best, there was enough food for everyone, for two weeks, including using the livestock corralled in the castle grounds. After that, they would have to kill the horses, and that would provide meat for four more days, without grain or vegetables. When the horsemeat was gone, the garrison would start the slow process of starving. At least water wasn't a problem. The subterranean supply, feeding Dragon River, provided the fortress with an endless source through wells within the plateau. Gerran dismissed his assistants, who brought him the stock-take figures he needed to give the King an accurate estimate of the food situation and headed for the meeting at the King's Table.

'We've tried all the methods at our disposal, Andra,' said Tim, 'but he refuses to talk. He's able to turn off all pain when we interrogate him. He retreats into himself. It's an old assassin's trick, but somehow this one has it perfected beyond the normal.'

'He needs a warrior's persuasive touch,' Claarn snarled, leaning over the bound figure, flexing his biceps and cracking his knuckles.

'If he won't talk for me, you great ox, he certainly won't find you much of a threat,' Tim retorted, grinning cheekily, but he stepped back as Claarn fixed him with a scowl. 'Sometimes you're more of a threat as a friend than an enemy,' he added, and a broad smile creased the giant's cheeks.

'It doesn't leave us much to take to the King's Table,' Andra said, disappointed. 'How can we fight what we don't understand?'

'Perhaps I can help,' A Ahmud Ki said, as he entered the chamber. His presence automatically made Andra wary, remembering Ardath's belated warning.

'How can you help?' Claarn asked, sizing up the Chancellor's tall, slim build. Like Andra, he didn't trust A Ahmud Ki. The Chancellor took Cedwyn's sword from him, to give to Liam, to enhance the hoax that Liam was the saviour, come to free the Kingdom from the Dragonlord's threat. Claarn hated magic, and the Chancellor exuded an arrogance he associated with excessive and destructive ambition.

A Ahmud Ki studied the face of the man tied to the chair. 'There are methods not always physical. If you give me a little time with him, I will have answers to any question you desire to ask.'

The Chancellor's cold, emotionless voice made Andra less comfortable, and he looked at Tim, as he considered A Ahmud Ki's offer. 'I'd prefer to remain while you do whatever you have in mind,' said Tim. 'Since I arranged the prisoner's capture, I have no intention of lending him, unconditionally, to anyone else.'

A Ahmud Ki threw Tim a harsh stare, a stare Tim returned without flinching, refusing to be intimidated. 'If that is the King's wish,' A Ahmud Ki said slowly.

Andra saw Tim's determination, and a nudge from Claarn emphasised the situation. 'That's my wish,' he replied.

A Ahmud Ki hesitated, dissatisfied with the response, but he shrugged and smoothed back his silver hair. 'So be it,' he said quietly. He focussed on the prisoner.

Andra watched the assassin, as the Chancellor worked his magic. Initially, the stubborn resistance, the vicious hatred of a being filled with bloodlust, stared defiantly at A Ahmud Ki, until a subtle change appeared. The captive's eyes slowly widened, and his breathing rate increased. He fought the power infiltrating his mind, but he was losing the battle, losing his composure, his stolid features melting from hatred into abject fear. Sweat beaded on his brow and spread across his face. He began shaking, and, in the final moments, the dull light permeating his dead eyes brightened noticeably, as the full horror of what was happening revealed itself inside his consciousness. He struggled against his bonds and screamed for mercy, but as Claarn grabbed the Chancellor's arm to intervene the prisoner's body went into paroxysm, jerking so violently he tipped the chair and crashed against the stone floor, breaking A Ahmud Ki's concentration and ending the spell. The three observers were staring, white-faced, at the Chancellor, who smiled at his success.

'Death squads: that's a translation from their tongue. They call themselves Sharvan. They're carefully chosen from the northern province of Yarrigha, in Uz Erhaag. The province people pride themselves in developing outstanding assassin talents in the chosen boys sent to the Yarrigha School of Death by their villages. There's considerable status held by the Sharvan graduates and their families.'

The Lords, and Andra's chosen companions, listened carefully to A Ahmud Ki's dissertation gleaned from the captured assassin's mind, and the Chancellor basked in the audience's appreciation of his knowledge.

'I take it,' Surdrok interrupted, 'they've chosen to join

forces with the Dragonlord.'

A Ahmud Ki smiled. 'There's no choice. The Dragonlord is supreme master of all Uz Erhaag. They obey because it is his will.'

'Then the Dragonlord is sending the assassins, these Sharvan Death Squads, to kill Andra,' said Kara.

'No,' replied the Chancellor. 'Not exactly. They're only following the orders of a general, or head of the army, surrounding us. I couldn't find any link to the Dragonlord in the captive's memories. The man involved is Koor, or The Snake. I assume he's in charge of the Dragonlord's forces. He's sending the Sharvan Death Squads to kill Andra.'

'Was there any memory link to the Dragonlord?' Haephus asked.

'Only a deep-seated fear – our captive's never seen him,' A Ahmud Ki explained.

Surdrok pushed back against his chair and grunted in disgust. 'So, there's nothing magical about our desperate friends after all,' he said angrily. 'They're just highly trained assassins.' A Ahmud Ki laughed at the High Lord's naive assumption. 'What's so amusing?' Surdrok demanded.

'The Sharvan are more than highly trained assassins, Surdrok. They're dead souls. They have no fear of death. This Koor uses a strong form of hypnotism on them, takes over their rational minds with a powerful influence spell. You could do with soldiers like that. Imagine an army with the capacity to march into battle, completely committed, and totally unafraid.'

'What if this Koor uses his power over that whole army besieging us?' Kerry piped in nervously. 'They'd march right over us.'

'He doesn't have that great a power, Kerry, or we'd already be worm's meat,' A Ahmud Ki responded, 'but he's a nuisance, so long as the Death Squads are sent against us.'

'Then we best find a way to get rid of him,' suggested Claarn.

'How?' asked Haephus. 'You can't exactly walk right into the middle of the Haagii camp and kill him, can you?'

'It's been done before,' Tim remarked, and grinned, but his laconic comment brought an irritated glance from the High Priest.

'The only alternative,' A Ahmud Ki said slowly, gauging his listeners' reactions, 'is to make the King totally secure from their attacks.'

'How is that possible?' Surdrok asked.

'They will never penetrate my tower.'

Andra threw the cup of water angrily against the wall, and watched it shatter. 'How can you suggest I run and hide like a coward?' he said turning to Claarn, Tim and Marella. 'Even worse, you expect me to cower inside that Chancellor's black lair. I'd rather take my chances with the Death Squads. At least I know what they intend to do.'

'I don't like the idea any more than you do,' agreed Tim, 'but it's the only logical thing to do. We can't afford to take unnecessary risks.'

'That's why I don't want anything to do with that black tower. You know how I feel, Claarn?' Andra argued, appealing to the giant warrior for support.

'I don't like magic, and that Chancellor carries too much of it to be trusted,' said Claarn. 'I would not go into the tower.'

'You'd rather see your friend dead at the hands of the Sharvan?' asked Marella, her dark eyes serious.

'I would die first, before I would let any of these killers get near Andra,' Claarn resolutely replied.

'I've fought these assassins,' said Tim grimly. 'That might be the outcome, if Andra remains exposed to their attacks.'

'But why the tower? Isn't there more chance of hiding me in the Maze, or in the fortress?' asked Andra.

'That was my first thought,' answered Tim. 'But I assessed what I could do if I was a Sharvan assassin. Even as I am, unenhanced by magical influence, I could slip in and out of the Maze undetected, dressed as an assassin. Who would dare question me in my own territory?'

'I don't trust the Chancellor,' Andra replied flatly. 'Even Lord Ardath warned me to be wary. Everything points to him being more concerned with his own power than with the defeat of the Haagii.'

'Ardath warned you?' Claarn asked, curious to hear what the dead Drycraefter had said against the Chancellor.

Andra slipped the scabbard from his shoulder and withdrew the sword. A piece of crumpled parchment tumbled from inside the scabbard, to the floor. Andra retrieved it, and handed it to Tim. 'Read it.' Tim read and passed the letter to Claarn and Marella. 'You see?' Andra asked.

'That warning could be about any one of us,' said Tim, 'but I see your point. I don't trust him either.'

'What's this Ardath trying to say about the sword?' Claarn asked. 'He says the powers are unlimited, dependent only on your will.'

'Watch,' instructed Andra. He crossed the room and concentrated on the sword lying on the floor. It flashed into his hand. Tim, Marella and Claarn were astonished.

'How?' Claarn muttered quietly.

'And again,' said Andra. The sword vanished.

'Now, where is it?' Tim asked, his innate curiosity overcoming his astonishment.

'I've still got it,' Andra replied. He crossed to a low stool near the door and made a slashing motion with his apparently empty fist. The stool fell apart, sliced by the invisible blade.

'By Teka, that's amazing!' Claarn gasped.

'I'm glad to see it's more than just a fancy torch,' said Tim.

'If you've got that weapon, you hardly need fear staying in the Chancellor's tower,' argued Marella, as she examined the neat edge to the cut the sword made through the stool. 'I'd say the Chancellor has more to concern him about you.'

'I'm learning,' said Andra, as the sword reappeared in his hand. 'I just need some imagination to work out what I can do.'

'Don't look to Claarn for magical inspiration,' teased Marella, and she pulled a face at her giant companion. 'He lacks imagination for anything.' Her jibe made the four companions laugh, and their revelry brought Milly searching to see what caused their merriment.

Guild Mistress Kara was astounded by the enormity of the complex they were exploring inside the heart of the plateau. Since Sasha and Holly encountered the Chancellor at the metal door, several days before, not long after her brief encounter with Orrin that left her the role of Guild Master, her Guild was searching and mapping the interior of the fortress the Chancellor called Andrakis. The map revealed enough accommodation to comfortably house most of the Great City's population. If they could overcome the food shortage, they could hole up in the fortress forever against the Haagii. There were only two known entrances: via the Deep Cave, or through the castle's secret corridors that connected at the entry point behind the King's Royal Library. Both entrances could be barricaded by huge metal doors, denying anyone access to the plateau's heart. The corridors followed random patterns, making travel through the complex confusing, at first, and a vast number of cul-de-sacs, and alcoves in the walls, provided enormous potential for defence, even if a force penetrated the doors. The information she was gathering, about the fortress' defensive strengths, pleased the surly High Lord Surdrok, though he avoided smiling in her presence.

One significant feature kept recurring in the mapping, and it puzzled Kara. At the heart of the plateau, from the uppermost chambers to those they traced to the depth of the Maze, was a rock-filled section blocking access through the centre of the plateau at all levels. As the mapping picture took shape, it was apparent the rock-falls contributed to the blockage of a central shaft, eighty to a hundred paces wide. The enormity of the fill defied Kara's comprehension. She reasoned it was the dumping ground for all the rock and earth excavated in the creation of the fortress, but something kept annoying her logical conclusion, suggesting there was a vastly different purpose behind the filling of so large a shaft in the plateau. She made a mental note to pass her feelings on to the King's Table when the mapping was completed.

Eight

Surdrok climbed the rickety wooden ladder to the top of the temporary lookout, constructed against the castle's eastern wall, and stood beside Claarn's tall, muscular frame. The early morning golden rays, rising above the distant Ureykyeu mountain range, washed the stone castle walls in soft yellow, and he could feel the sun's heat building on his face. The giant warrior turned to Surdrok and nodded in the direction he wanted the High Lord to look.

The entire eastern section of the besieging Haagii army was in dusty turmoil. Troops were dismantling their crude shelters, loading the pack animals, assembling in ragged lines, and preparing to march in the wake of others streaming eastward, across the plains of Ky, toward the Ureykyeu. Predominantly Haagii warriors formed the contingent on the move, but Surdrok also noted two cavalry troops of Dark Warriors, nearly out of vision across the plain. Surdrok stared at the chaotic withdrawal, assessing the number of enemy involved in the movement, while trying to determine their purpose. He also watched troops from the southern and northern sectors of the Haagii army steadily move to reseal the encirclement of the plateau. 'When did this start?' he asked Claarn, without taking his eyes from the scene.

'Not very long ago,' the giant replied. 'I sent for you when I saw it for myself.'

'How many are leaving?'

Claarn shook his head. 'I am not a man for numbers, Lord Surdrok. It is a large army that leaves, but a much larger one that stays.'

Surdrok looked up at Claarn. The tall warrior's red shaggy head looking like it was surrounded by a mass of writhing flames in the glow of the rising sun. He peered over the castle grounds below, watching people going about the few morning chores. 'I'd say at least fifteen to twenty thousand are heading east,' Surdrok mused, 'about a quarter of the army. By their direction, east south-east, the towns around the Lake of Tears are doomed.'

The pair remained, silently observing the withdrawal, until shouting from the northeast tower drew their attention. Three Kingdom soldiers were waving their arms, and pointing at the sky to the northeast, above the Andrakian Mountains. Surdrok focussed on three black dots flying rapidly east, southeast. 'Dragons.' Claarn muttered and spat.

Surdrok watched the beasts move like arrows, and spoke steadily, half to Claarn, half to himself, as he saw them disappearing over the tips of the Ureykyeu. 'The Haagii take their war to Targa. The black beasts go to herald the Dragonlord's approach.'

'The Dragonlord is tired of waiting here and gaining nothing,' Claarn replied.

'No,' said Surdrok calmly. 'He already considers this siege won. He wants fresher victories.'

Tim slid into the trapdoor, brushing ash from his hands, as he loped along the underground corridor. The pack on his back was cumbersome, but necessary for the night's work, he reminded himself. A large heat shape, and a smaller one, lurked in an alcove ahead. He greeted the assassin and his errand boy. 'What Haagii movement above here, Gus?' he quietly asked.

'A little,' the adult, replied. 'The trapdoor here's buried under a lot of charred wood from Redrin's old stables, so we can't lift it, and the Haagii can't find it.'

'West?'

'Along Pattern Street?' asked Gus. Tim nodded. 'We think they're searching for basements or cellars. Rafferty told me she heard a lot of scratching in the cellar of Havner's cottage, and thought they found the trapdoor there, but there's been no Haagii inside yet.'

'Good,' said Tim. He clapped Gus on his bony shoulder, ruffled the lad's hair, and headed further south, through the Maze. He inquired after the state of affairs at each checkpoint The Hand and Guild had established to report on Haagii movement in the city ruins and warn of breaches of the Maze.

He reached the southernmost section, and the last checkpoint, which was watched by Alisha and Emery, thieves with reputations as speedy runners in the days before the war descended on the Kingdom. They were also lovers, so Tim prudently coughed, as he approached their checkpoint, in case he found them in a less than compromising position. His cough was met with laughter, and a torch flickered into life. 'Very noble, Tim Gaelus,' scorned Alisha, as he entered the circle of light. 'What might you think we'd be doing?' she asked coquettishly, tipping her head to the left to let her ash-blond, straight hair fall to her shoulder.

Tim didn't have a great deal to do with Alisha, under normal circumstances, but the few times he'd seen her, he decided she was a very attractive lady, lithe in proportion and tall, and he understood why Emery was enamoured by her. 'On guard, of course,' he answered, and grinned.

'Of course,' she said, smiling in return, her eyes searching quickly over him, a gesture that made him feel mildly uncomfortable.

'Where's Emery?' he asked, glancing over Alisha's shoulder to catch sight of her companion.

'He's keeping an eye out at the trapdoor under Reish's old seed store,' she replied.

'Any more news about our friend?' Tim asked. Alisha nodded, and indicated he should sit. He unhitched his burden as he lowered to the floor.

She reached into a cloth sack at her feet, and withdrew a flat loaf of crusty oaten bread, which she broke, passing one piece to Tim. He went to refuse, but she pushed it into his hand. 'The friend you ask about doesn't move from his pavilion, although a lot of people go in and out during the day, and women are taken there at night.'

'Women?' Tim started, surprised at Alisha's revelation.

She nodded to confirm her statement. 'Captives. They're taken, bound and gagged, to the pavilion in the evening, and dragged out quite a bit later. Sometimes one, sometimes there are two or three.' Alisha explained. 'I wouldn't like to be one of them.'

'Kingdom women?'

'In all probability,' she answered. 'From the towns and villages they've already destroyed.'

'Where are they being kept?'

'We don't really know. Haagii guards bring and take them from some place to the west of this area.'

Tim chewed the last of the bread offering, contemplating Alisha's new, complicating information, and swigged a mouthful of water from Alisha's water sack to wash the crumbs from his mouth and throat. Then he asked her to take him to Emery.

Emery was crouched in the shelter of a collapsed stone wall, an artificial cave in the ruins. Tim followed Alisha out of the trapdoor, fortunately missed by collapsing debris when the Haagii destroyed the city, and settled beside Emery. A wordless greeting passed between them, and Emery nudged Tim, pointing to a spot of light in the darkened nightscape.

Tim watched the light, determining it emerged from a partially open tent flap. His Aelendyell vision let him see details in the darkness hidden from the humans. Three Haagii guards stood beside the entrance, and a dozen more Haagii squatted by a fire to the left, about four paces from the pavilion. Eight more figures stood beside a second fire, slightly obscured behind the pavilion. They weren't Haagii. Their build and carriage were human, and two of them shouldered bows. The firelight revealed a maroon colouration to their clothing. Campfires dotted the darkness, their light spilling over each other in many places, illuminating the shadowy figures sitting around, and moving between, them. Sneaking through the Haagii encampment would be virtually impossible, even for an elite assassin, Tim decided. He tapped Emery on the shoulder to follow him, and dropped noiselessly through the trapdoor into the Maze.

'If the target is who I hope it is,' said Tim, as he began to unpack his baggage, 'then a few of the current problems we face might disappear.'

'If not?' asked Alisha, watching with interest as the assassin went about the business of disguising himself with brown and tan Haagii garments he pulled from his pack.

'Then I start again,' he said, with a nonchalant shrug.

'Everything we've observed from here confirms what you've asked us to look for,' said Emery. 'I've seen three pairs of these assassins come and go from the pavilion, and the man within dresses like a practitioner of magical arts.'

'Then he must be Koor,' said Tim. He adjusted the ill-fitting Haagii leather breastplate straps, before he picked up the pitted short sword he collected from his hapless victim earlier in the night. 'If not, at least someone who's potentially a nuisance won't be afterwards.' He grinned, and as he headed for the trapdoor exit, he nodded to his two companions, saying, 'Wish me the luck of Teka.'

The stench of the dead Haagii from whom he took the disguise was nauseating. Though he wasn't always a regularly bather, Tim doubted the Haagii ever washed the sweat and grime from their bodies, and he ruefully wondered how many lice he would inherit from his dead benefactor.

He emerged from the ruins, cautiously checking if anyone observed him in the darkness and, when he was certain no one had, he stepped away from the building and walked casually toward the light emanating from the pavilion, skirting campfires to avoid attracting undue attention. There were more Haagii around the pavilion than he estimated, and there was greater activity than he anticipated. Warriors were busily sharpening swords and axes beside their fires, some noisily shared meals, and mock fights were underway.

Nearing the pavilion, he became aware of three Dark Warriors riding between the campfires. Their path intersected his, so he paused to give them right of passage, bowing his head as he imagined a lowly Haagii would if confronted by a superior. As he concentrated on the dark fetlocks of the passing horses, to avoid chancing an upward glance out of curiosity, the blow to the side of his head came as a shock. He crumpled left, slightly stunned by the unexpected impact, and allowed himself to sprawl clumsily, without the natural skill of an assassin who would roll with the force and return to his feet. Out of the spinning darkness, he heard a low, spiteful voice growl 'Kastraana!' and someone chuckled. He waited for a second attack, ready to react to protect himself, but heard only the soft hooves of the horses plodding away. Voices cursed in an incomprehensible tongue, and a heavy boot sank into his ribs, nearly winding him. Tim rolled from his attacker, pretending to be in greater pain than he was, but in doing so he cleverly avoided a second vicious kick. He pretended to stagger to his feet, and saw a heavy arm swinging toward his head, but this time he rolled with the impact, deadening its effect, as he fell in a smartly executed awkward fashion away from his attackers. His fall was followed by another string of vehement Haagii curses, and someone spat on him. He struggled to all fours and scampered out of the firelight to the relative safety of the darkness, pursued by a wall of abuse and raucous laughter.

He checked if the rumpus attracted interest from the pavilion. It hadn't. The guards were ignoring the incident, apparently familiar with similar incidents. He assessed his injuries. The blow to his head from the Dark Warrior ached, but he could bear that. The kick to his ribs from the annoyed Haagii whose campfire he unsettled hurt far more. He had difficulty breathing, without sharp pain shooting through his left side into his shoulder. The rest were trivial scratches and bruises. He squatted on his haunches, in the dark patch between fires, and observed the pavilion. It had one entrance, as near as he could tell, and guards all round. Approaching it, under the circumstances, was suicidal. He needed a distraction, an event to draw the guards away.

He circled the pavilion, until he was opposite the

bowmen he spotted earlier. Several were relaxing, gazing into the yellow-red flames of the fire. Three were asleep, under a hide shelter supported by upright swords stuck into the ground. He edged toward the shelter, watchful, and retrieved an unguarded bow and a quiver. Then he slipped silently into the night.

His keen eyes searched for the Haagii party who bashed him for interrupting their night by attracting the wrath of the Dark Warriors, and, spying them, he nocked an arrow in the stolen bow, taking careful aim. A Haagii jerked backwards and fell into the fire, with a flurry of sparks, before his startled companions. Tim moved quickly, in case the thrum of his bowstring attracted a curious warrior, and repeated his attack, sending a second Haagii reeling forward, an arrow shaft lodged squarely between his shoulder blades.

Confusion ensued, as the Haagii scrambled for their weapons and stared fearfully into the surrounding campsite. Then one warrior broke the arrow shaft from his dead fellow's back and held it aloft, as others crowded around. A bellow of rage erupted, and the Haagii mob, brandishing torches and swords, headed angrily toward the rear of the pavilion, where the maroon-garbed bowmen were watching their approach with bemused disinterest. Harsh words were exchanged, the arrow shaft thrown to the ground in rage, and the confrontation disintegrated into a brawl that rapidly escalated into a bloody fight, attracting everyone within the vicinity, as onlookers or participants.

Tim shifted again, to avoid being caught in the chaotic rush to the scene. Even the pavilion guards left their posts to watch, though not to intervene. The diversion was wonderfully effective. Tim ran to the pavilion entrance, ascertained he wasn't being observed, and slid inside.

The Dark Warrior was as surprised to see a Haagii in the pavilion, as Tim was to see the Dark Warrior, but the disguise gave Tim the advantage because the Dark Warrior casually moved to discipline the intruding Haagii with the back of his mailed gauntlet. He didn't expect his victim to slip deftly under his swinging arm and stab him in the exposed armpit joint with an assassin's stiletto. Mortally wounded, the Dark Warrior staggered back, as Tim pushed him away, horror written deep in his bright blue eyes. He looked as if he wanted to speak, lifting his hands shakily before him, before he tottered sideways and collapsed, his long blond hair flowing over the cruel shoulder spikes of his black armour. Tim sidestepped the body and pulled back the thick woollen curtain dividing the little entranceway from the main chamber inside the pavilion.

The chamber was lit by three hanging lanterns whose pale light cast a soft creamy glow over everything, but he was drawn to two figures in black, kneeling on the floor. Directly ahead of them, a third stood in a blue robe, holding a rainbow-hued serpentine staff, in both hands, above their lowered heads. The entire chamber was bedecked with rainbow silken curtains, and an incense burner smoked in the far right corner beside the oval bed, its sickly sweet fragrance filling the chamber.

Tim's sweeping eyes were arrested by three women near the bed, bound naked to upright tent support poles, their frightened eyes fixed on the ceremony. He let the curtain slide into place and listened for sounds outside the pavilion suggesting someone was approaching, but he heard only shouting and cheering from the melee behind the pavilion where the Haagii and bowmen were settling imagined scores. Satisfied there was no external danger, he pulled his assassin's dart crossbow from beneath his Haagii garments and loaded a dart. Then he edged his favourite dagger into the top of his boot, feeling its smooth bone handle between his fingers. With a deep breath, he threw back the curtain.

The target had shifted. The two Sharvan were standing, facing each other, and the sorcerer in blue was behind one of the bound women, caressing her breasts with his staff. The shot was too difficult. He'd lost the initiative.

The Sharvan reacted, drawing their daggers and leaping toward him. He fired his lethal dart at the nearest Sharvan, and dived sideways into the chamber, avoiding the upward thrust of the second attacker. As he rolled to his feet, he flicked his dagger from his boot and threw it. His target was too quick, and his dagger ripped harmlessly through a strip of hanging silk. The Sharvan leapt at him, so he dived underneath. The Sharvan crashed awkwardly into a pile of small chests, and the brief respite gave Tim a chance to see what the sorcerer was doing. He had moved from the woman to watch the fight from a position near the pavilion's rear, partly obscured by the decorative materials.

The Sharvan was on his feet again, and circling, changing his method of attack now he knew his opponent was not a warrior. Tim circled as well, but tried to avoid being steered into a position where his back would be exposed to the sorcerer, while he extracted his stiletto from his belt. The Haagii armour was confining and uncomfortable, and he knew he couldn't wear the Sharvan down in the unwieldy costume. The fight had to be brief. He had to take a chance.

The Sharvan edged closer, driving him back a step, guiding him in front of the sorcerer. Tim concentrated on the Sharvan's dark eyes. They were his best hope. The Sharvan's stare was solid, deep – until Tim saw the slightest flicker of an eyelid, the barest break of contact. He dropped to his knees, spun, and threw his stiletto with all his strength. The narrow knife sliced through a partition of yellow silk and pierced the blue-robed sorcerer's chest. Simultaneously, the Sharvan groaned, and a heavy body dropped to the floor, but Tim dared not turn to see what had happened. Instead, he ran to the wounded sorcerer, pulled the deadly stiletto from his chest, and cut the man's throat.

When he stood, he looked across at the second Sharvan. The serpentine staff, thrown by the sorcerer at Tim, had impaled the assassin. He retrieved his ivory-handled dagger and dart from his first victim, and cut the three women loose from their bonds, warning them to keep quiet. While they grabbed garments, he listened at the front of the pavilion. The fighting had died down. Voices were arguing, different voices, authoritative voices. He was running out of time.

Tim beckoned to the women to hurry, ducked back inside the inner chamber, unhitched a lantern from an upright pole, and threw it against the bed. As burning oil spilled over the skin covers, setting them alight, he led the freed captives out of the pavilion into the darkness, moving quickly, preferring to risk discovery at a run than at a walk. Two watchful Haagii called after them, but Tim used his dart crossbow to silence their protests. The party dodged two patrols, more intent on running toward the blazing pavilion than searching for escaping prisoners, and they scrambled into the stone ruins, where Alisha and Emery awaited Tim's return.

Nine

Tim's news was greeted with relief in the castle. If Koor was dead, then it wasn't necessary for Andra to seek security in the Chancellor's black tower. Surdrok was happy to learn there would be no more attacks from the Sharvan, because he lost many good defenders keeping them out of the castle. Still, he ordered the castle watch to maintain vigilance, because there was no proof the man Tim slew was Koor. Only time would provide that answer.

Sasha chastised Tim for taking a grave risk without consulting anyone, reminding him that Kara had made him Death's First Hand in the Guild, and as such he had greater responsibilities to consider before making foolhardy excursions into the enemy's camp. He laughed, and replied he could only lead The Hand assassins by example.

The Haagii reaction to Tim's single-handed raid was swift. The following morning, reports channelled through the Maze showed the Haagii were intensifying their efforts to uncover entrances, and from the castle walls the Kingdom soldiers witnessed hundreds of Haagii tearing the few remaining blackened city buildings apart in their frustrated effort to break into the underground system. Sensing imminent danger, and without seeking Surdrok's permission, Claarn and Marella organised a company of warriors, and the two hundred strong force descended into the Deep Cave, where Guild Mistress Kara was marshalling her defence of the Maze. 'Your help's greatly appreciated,' she told Claarn, as his warriors assembled in the torch-lit cavern.

'Where do we go?' the giant asked, eager to fight.

Kara was distracted from answering by a small boy, who ran up to the Guild Mistress, and whispered in her ear. She ruffled his hair, and sent him out of the Deep Cave, toward the plateau fortress' upper levels. 'You've come just in time,' she said, returning her attention to Claarn. 'The Haagii are forcing their way into the Maze, near the southeast quarter. We'll need fifty warriors there to hold them.'

'Consider it done,' Claarn replied. He told Marella what Kara required, so she organised a squad, and Kara appointed a thief as her guide.

'Take care,' Kara warned, as Marella was about to lead her squad after the guide. 'We've trapped a lot of the Maze. Touch nothing other than what Dafid tells you is safe.' Marella nodded understanding, smiled at Claarn, and left.

'Now what?' asked Claarn.

'More of your warriors will be useful here, as a last stand,' Kara explained, 'but we need support along the tunnels leading from the city centre. I'll assign thieves to lead groups of twenty or thirty.'

Claarn straightened and grinned beneath his thick red beard. 'This is more like warrior's work,' he said, chuckling.

Marella pressed her back against the cold earthen surface of the tunnel wall, feeling grains of dirt grate against her mail shirt. She held her sword blade to her chest, while, behind her, eight warriors waited, swords ready. The approaching torchlight moved with the uncertainty of intruders in unfamiliar and dangerous territory.

The Haagii were suffering horrific losses in the Maze. Marella's warriors were defending a section that was formerly a holding cellar, beneath a small pothouse the Haagii found by sheer accident when one fell through charred floorboards. Three doors led from the cellar into the Maze, and only one entrance led into it from outside, so each Haagii warrior who entered could be attacked from three sides by the defenders. A second entry was found thirty paces from the cellar, and the Haagii who scrambled in ran foul of myriad trapping devices the Guild members laid. But a small party was spotted moving further east, through the Maze, having dug out another of the hundreds of entrances and exits through which the Guild operated, before the devastation of the Great City, and Marella and a select band crossed to intercept them.

As the Haagii torchbearer turned the corner, his leathery face and heavy jowls under lit by the flames, he was caught unaware, and fell backwards into his party, howling with terror, as Marella thrust through his leather cuirass and the Kingdom warriors attacked.

Surdrok watched the last heavy wooden catapult being pulled into position, in the castle's lower courtyard. Men and women, detailed for the duty, carried rocks excavated from inside the fortress, and piled them beside the ten war machines. The crews cranked the great wooden arms, reinforced with metal bracers, down to load their first shot. He considered the use of the catapults, at so great a range from the castle, highly inefficient. Even having the machines in the castle was absurd. The Haagii brought their war machines, only to find they were useless against the castle because of the height of the plateau above the plain. Storming the castle was impossible, except via Castle Road, which only allowed, at best, ten warriors abreast, and the road was exposed, from bottom to top, to firepower from the castle's defenders. That's why the Haagii had made no attempt to attack in the week since overrunning the city. But, he decided, a handful of boulders dropping from the castle's height, into the Great City ruins, might frustrate the Haagii rooting in the ashen waste for trapdoors, and one or two boulders might find a mark.

Two Haardrishii Devis, directing the degree of aim and strain on the catapults, looked to the High Lord for the final order. Surdrok raised his arm. 'Release!' he yelled, as he dropped his arm. The ropes and flexible arms of the catapults twanged in unison as they launched their loads into the morning, and ten boulders tumbled in graceful arcs, through the blue sky, until they thudded into the ruins far below. Plumes of ash exploded where they hit, and two sent shattered building fragments spiralling into the air. Haagii warriors scattered like ants from the targeted sites, an effect that pleased Surdrok. He turned to watch the crews loading their second round, and allowed himself a faint smile of satisfaction.

The thump above them precipitated a shower of earth and dust, and they dived against the wall. 'What in Teka was that?' Claarn growled.

The thief beside him shook her head. 'I've no idea,' she replied, looking warily at the tunnel ceiling. 'Maybe the Haagii have other plans for breaking in.'

'I think we need to move around the corner,' Claarn advised, gathering his sense of purpose. He signalled to the accompanying warriors and led his group into a larger room running off the tunnel. As they filed in, they heard another heavy thump, followed by others, softer, further off. 'Catapults,' Claarn mumbled, recognising the cause of the overhead noise. 'Surdrok's trying out the castle toys.' His sarcastic observation raised a quiet chuckle from those nearest. 'Where now?' he asked the woman guiding his band. She turned to point to a door on the far side of the room, but as she did it burst open, and Haagii warriors charged in, wielding swords and axes wildly. With a throaty roar, Claarn met their attack head on.

The news was bad. Each time another runner sprinted into the Deep Cave, Kara learned how much further the Haagii had penetrated the Maze, how many more entrances had been discovered in the city ruins. Some pockets of resistance were strong, like Marella's group, who were holding the Haagii back admirably, having lost no ground, but other sections were being pushed back by sheer weight of numbers, and some had collapsed, surrounded and cut off, and overwhelmed by too many of the enemy. Communication with Claarn's band had ceased altogether. A young girl sent to find out what was happening there barely escaped a large pack of Haagii forging toward the Deep Cave. She lost them by taking a circuitous, confusing route through the middle tunnels, a strategy that gave Kara time to dispatch more runners to warn other defenders access to the Deep Cave might be soon cut off, if the Haagii coming from the southwest were large in number and not stopped.

'Are you sure?' Tim asked, gently holding Aaron's shoulder. 'The big warrior with the flaming mane?'

'Yes Tim,' Aaron nodded. 'Mistress Kara sent Brenda to bring news about his group, but she was chased back by Haagii. She said they were all caught or dead.'

Tim threw a quick glance at Andra, as he sheathed his dagger, and said, 'I'll go.'

'Wait,' the young Guardian King said. 'I'm coming.'

Tim shook his head, as he went to follow Aaron. 'Too risky, Andra,' he argued.

'I'm coming as well, Tim Gaelus,' Andra declared. 'And not even you will stop me.' He gazed up the fifteen silver steps of the proscenium at the griffin throne he was studying before Aaron's arrival, fixing his eyes on Abreotan's sword, which he left leaning against the side of the throne. The sword materialised in his hand, sparkling with blue light, and he strode toward Tim and the exit from the Throne Room toward the Royal Library.

The Chancellor stood near the opening to the fortress tunnels in the Royal Library, watching Tim, Andra and the young boy approach. He stroked his trimmed black beard and waited for the three to draw alongside, before speaking directly to Andra. 'What's the emergency, my Lord?'

'The Haagii have broken into the Maze, and they have Claarn,' Andra said.

'You take the sword against them? Isn't that careless?' A Ahmud Ki asked, employing a diplomatic tone.

Andra stared at the Chancellor. 'Claarn is a friend. I owe him my life,' he stated firmly, and he followed Tim's receding back into the tunnel between the castle walls.

A Ahmud Ki smiled as the King and his companions descended. Noble - very noble, he thought. The new King has significant weaknesses - his friends, and his sense of justice. Both can be exploited. The opportunity to get him alone in his tower was thwarted by the assassin, Tim Gaelus, who would eventually pay for interfering, especially as there was a touch of Aelendyell about the thief, which added doubly to A Ahmud Ki's intense dislike of him. Tim Gaelus must be eliminated, he decided.

'Withdraw!' Marella shouted, above the clash of swords. Reluctantly, her courageous squad began a perilous and hectic retreat along the twisting paths of the Maze, following Dafid, who seemed able to make perfect sense out of a chaotic tangle of corridors and rooms. Time and again, Haagii cut their escape, or charged into the midst of their group, threatening to split them, but Marella rallied her fellow warriors and they pressed on, leaving a trail of Haagii dead. Not without loss, though. The Haagii encounters took their toll, whittling down the number in the retreating band, until barely twenty made the final dash into the Deep Cave, where a solid phalanx cut down the Haagii foolhardy enough to charge into the entrance.

From other quarters, thieves leapt to safety, many sorely wounded in their flight from marauding Haagii, but very few appeared after Marella's hard-pressed band. The Maze had fallen to the enemy, and only the Deep Cave remained to defend. After that, Kara expected to withdraw to the metal door into the fortress. She felt regret at losing the home ground of her Guild to the Haagii, but she knew the Haagii paid a terrible price for their victory at the hands of her thieves and Claarn's warriors, and they would pay even more to gain access to the Deep Cave.

Three boys emerged at a run from the Royal Library entrance to the fortress and A Ahmud Ki ordered them to halt. 'What's the news?' he asked, feigning polite interest.

A mousy-haired scrap of a lad, replied, 'The Haagii are almost in the Deep Cave proper.'

The information flabbergasted A Ahmud Ki. He nervously flexed his fingers. 'Who are you seeking?' he asked.

'We have to tell High Lord Surdrok what's happening,' the boy explained. His companions were edging toward the large Royal Library entranceway.

'Then do it,' the Chancellor ordered, with a flick of his wrist, sending the three scuttling from the library, eager to escape the tall, silver haired man's threatening presence.

A Ahmud Ki stared at the entrance to the fortress. If the Deep Cave fell into Haagii hands, his plan to enter the Dragonlord's tomb was jeopardised. He could not allow that, under any circumstance. He'd waited too long to learn the secrets from Ardath's books and refine his spells. He could wait no longer. The Haagii had to be stopped. He headed for the corridor.

'You can't risk it!' Marella shouted. 'There're Haagii everywhere in that place!'

'We can't leave Claarn in there!' Andra yelled back.

Tim pushed beside him. 'Kara won't tell me anything,' he said, shaking his head, 'but Brenda says Claarn's party were last headed toward the tunnels and rooms beneath the Inn of Dragons territory.'

'Then let's go,' said Andra, with a determined expression.

The pair pushed through the phalanx of warriors at the Deep Cave's entrance, ignoring Marella and Kara's emphatic cries to return, and headed into the near tunnel. Haagii, astounded to see two enemy warriors among them, attacked eagerly, but Andra parried their sword thrusts with uncanny ease, and ruthlessly cut five opponents down in rapid succession. Tim downed two others. Then Andra willed his sword to flame, and lunged recklessly, sending the Haagii scrambling for safety from the fiery sword.

'This way!' Tim yelled, tugging at Andra's arm, and they

darted down the steps of a narrow tunnel leading from the main one.

The Maze was too complicated for the Haagii to infiltrate in its entirety. The Hand assassins, keen to move silently and undetected, even among their own kind, built narrow, low passages through large portions of the general underground system, many beneath the level of the Maze corridors. Tim led Andra through secret inner passages, avoiding the corridors overrun by the Haagii, but constant bending made the young warrior King's legs ache, and he reminded himself of his need to regain the fitness he had as a soldier under Trainer Murdok. Three times, they fought past Haagii who stumbled upon The Hand's lower highway, until they emerged through a disguised door in a room Andra thought he recognised: the lodgings he shared when he returned to the Great City with Milly.

Shouts, and smashing, rose from an adjoining room. Tim crept to the door and listened. More Haagii. He turned to warn Andra, but the King's foot heaved the door open, and he strode into the room with Abreotan's sword aloft.

'Shut your eyes, Tim!' he yelled, and closed his own.

The shocked Haagii backed away from the mad figure, but recovered their courage when they realised only one human entered and started to advance, laughing at the pathetic enemy. An explosion of light from the sword's blade sent them reeling, clutching their seared eyes and screaming in agony.

When Andra ended the surge of energy, he motioned to Tim to join him. The assassin blinked, his eyes adjusting to the sword's softer magical light, and crossed the room, staring in astonishment at the blinded Haagii, curled up or groping in their permanent darkness. 'I'm glad you warned me,' he whispered, as he resumed the lead in the corridor beyond.

'There's fighting ahead,' Andra said, as they paused to listen at the next corner. The clash and ring of metal echoed along the tunnel, mixed with cries of pain and anguish. Dead Haagii were strewn to the t-junction, and random bodies of fallen Kingdom warriors. A sudden, loud and familiar bellow rang out. 'Claarn!' yelled Andra.

'Who else?' quipped Tim, as he followed his friend along the tunnel.

Claarn's tiny remnant was hard-pressed against a wall, in a room Andra guessed was a large meeting and eating hall. He recognised the basic layout, but there were many places alike in the Maze, part of the design to confuse intruders. A barricade of broken chairs and tables separated the Kingdom warriors from a blood-lusting pack of Haagii who were prodding and poking with swords and spears, mocking the surviving defenders. At the centre of the Kingdom warriors, stood Claarn in defiant defence, hair and beard matted with blood, arms and armour stained red, and his sword blade dripping, and in the low-ceilinged room, surrounded by the broad, stocky enemy, the giant of Tressel Deep looked larger than any mortal human could possibly be.

Andra saw the battle-strained grimace of his friend, as he beat off another probing Haagii spear, and wondered how long the giant man had held out against impossible odds, or could continue to hold out. He remembered the strength, the courage, and the fury of the warrior at The Rim Shield, in the face of the overwhelming numbers of the Dragonlord's army. Claarn would become a legend by his deeds. If he, Andra, was to be King after this siege of the castle, he'd see that Claarn received the hero status he deserved. Shouting Claarn's name, Andra brandished the flaming weapon of Aian Abreotan, and plunged into the Haagii, Tim beside him.

A Ahmud Ki stood silently at the foot of the natural staircase leading up to the crystal lake, formed from the subterranean springs that gave birth to Dragon River, and observed the Kingdom warriors fending off sporadic Haagii attacks against their shield wall. The Haagii were more persistent and more numerous by the minute. A full-scale attempt to push into the Deep Cave was certainly due.

He considered his options, cursing the young King for

foolishly charging into the Maze with Abreotan's sword. If he died, perhaps the prophecy was nothing more than an elaborate coincidence. He conceded that scenario was highly unlikely, because the text of Ardath's 'Ancient Lore' clearly explained the certainty of the prophecy reaching fruition.

The sword held magic. Others witnessed it. Peret was a reliable servant, and he saw it slay a dragon. To lose it on such a trivial errand, trying to rescue the idiotic giant who waded in against innumerable odds, was proof of the immense weakness A Ahmud Ki recognised in the new King; but what a waste! He could help the warriors hold the Haagii at bay, in the hope the King would return, or he could seal the entrance immediately with a glyph. The latter meant giving up the sword and the prophecy.

The Haagii attacked the defenders again, furiously, and the phalanx wavered under the renewed pressure, as Kingdom warriors fell. Behind the three lines, Marella and Surdrok moved back and forth, exhorting the defenders to hold their ground. For a moment, the front line seemed about to capitulate, and A Ahmud Ki steadied himself, preparing to cast a fire spell to discourage the Haagii, but the defenders rallied, and the Haagii eased back to regroup for a renewed assault.

It seemed a pity to lose the sword and the new King. He wanted to learn the sword's powers. The texts he gathered from Ardath's library revealed very little, only that the wielder would grow to understand its magic, an explanation A Ahmud Ki found most unsatisfactory. He also read cryptic suggestions its powers were limited only by the wielder's powers. Did that mean it was more powerful in the hands of a Dragonlord than a mere warrior? Would his powers be projected and enhanced by the sword? Could he wield it? He cursed the inexperienced King for leaping into the dragon's mouth of the Haagii army with the sword. Even Thana hadn't been that stupid.

Noise erupted in the Haagii quarter again. Warriors at the mouth of the Deep Cave jostled and pushed, but they were turning away from the shield wall, facing into the depths of the Maze. A Ahmud Ki was fascinated. What were the Haagii trying to do? Then he saw their flickering, unsteady torchlight consumed by a brighter intensity approaching out of the left tunnel, as the sword of Abreotan flashed into view, slashing and hewing through the Haagii like a reaper's scythe through dried grass. Andra pushed forward, drawing Tim, Claarn, and half a dozen Kingdom warriors in his wake, as if nothing could prevent his passage. Inspired by the vision, the warriors in the Deep Cave pressed at the Haagii's backs, cheering the arrival of their new King, who defied the Haagii army and returned unscathed with those presumed lost.

As Andra's band moved to safety, and the Kingdom warriors reformed their phalanx to hold back the awestruck and infuriated Haagii, A Ahmud Ki strode from his observation point to stand directly behind them. He ignored the fuss being made over the new King's heroic return and Abreotan's sword, concentrating fully on the Deep Cave's mouth, the brief space separating the warring factions. Only an Elvenaar glyph would suffice.

The deep currents of his years of study in four cultures stirred, and arcane words dropped silently from his lips, as he lifted his hands toward the entranceway, palms pressed up and out, thumb tips touching, letting the energy within transfer to the air on which he focussed, willing it to form into a shield of power no Haagii could penetrate. Barely a thumb span ahead of the closest Kingdom warrior in the phalanx, the air crackled and warped, causing the startled defenders to retreat from the sudden alteration in the air's fabric. The nearest Haagii leader, misinterpreting their movement, rallied his companions with a war cry and charged into the vague shimmer of the closing glyph. A dozen unsuspecting warriors struck the magical wall and were enveloped in an aura of crackling, burning energy. They writhed and screamed in agony, for several violent moments, until the glyph threw their charred and twisted bodies backwards against their terror-filled fellows, who halted in shock before the new menace barring their way.

A Ahmud Ki remained intent on finishing his work, until he was certain his glyph was locked. Then he relaxed his mind and arms, and turned to the astonished crowd of defenders who witnessed his exhibition of magic for the first time, knowing now that no one would question his right to respect or power in the Kingdom – not even the inheritor of Abreotan's sword – because he, alone, had closed the last easy access to the fortress of Andrakis.

"When the dark days drew upon us, those seeking courage looked to the young and the old. While the adults complained bitterly during the siege, the old slipped away with silent resignation, and the young bore suffering with patience and hope. The old and the young taught the rest of us how to face death."

an excerpt from Markim's diary, written during the siege of Andrakis, Year One of the reign of King Andrakis I

Ten

Below the castle, as the long hot days of summer dragged into weeks, the Haagii sweltered listlessly through the heat on the plains of Ky, a black mass of inertia. The siege reached stalemate with the sealing of the Deep Cave, and they could only wait for the defenders to starve or surrender. So, they waited.

Food in the fortress ran out, nine days after the battle in the Maze. The last crumbs were set aside for the children, and once the food was gone the entire population settled down to the quiet act of starving. Fortunately, there was no shortage of water, but at best they could survive three weeks at the outside. Lord Haephus and his yellow-robed priests moved among the people every day, offering the blessing of their goddess Teka, and giving encouragement to those whose fears were surfacing in the lean, hungry time.

King Andra was impressed with the priests' work, especially with Lord Haephus, whom he first viewed with disdain as another power-hungry parasite of Thana's court. Haephus had ambition, but Andra saw it was touched with humanity, and his respect for the High Priest grew daily.

On the other hand, Lords Kerry and Eustice played chess in the Throne Room, and complained bitterly about the lack of food, constantly railing at Lord Rheims to find something edible in the palace, a request Rheims could only refuse because there was no food. Andra was tempted to throw them out, but he decided to leave them to themselves, recognising their selfishness would infect the morale of people who came into contact with them, if they were forced to mix with the others. Survival depended on as many people as possible maintaining a high morale.

Surdrok, Claarn, and Marella organised the Devis and Haardrishii to continue daily training of the warriors, and willing volunteers who escaped the sacking and burning of the Great City, to keep their minds from the lack of food. Claarn and Surdrok bullied and cajoled the soldiers to greater efforts, but Marella was subtle in her approach, working with individuals to demonstrate finer, more ruthless techniques of a war-hardened warrior. If the worst came, they would all have to fight their way out of the fortress, the only dilemma being there was no place to run.

In the same fashion, Tim settled into his new rank as Death's First Hand, taking aside volunteers to learn assassin arts, and directing Sasha and others in instructing boys and girls with weapons. Milly and Aaron were first to ask to be involved. He argued for a long time, with Guild Mistress Kara, for permission to alter the rules about assassin secrecy, emphasizing the necessity for openness to survive the siege, and she finally capitulated, allowing him to carry out the training sessions in his own manner, something she knew he'd do, with or without her express permission.

The surprise to everyone was Lord Gerran. No sooner had Tim asked for volunteers than Lord Gerran asked to be included. His boyish countenance and initial clumsiness were the source of much amusement, but soon Tim was recounting to Andra the amazing learning and change taking place in Gerran.

'He's missed his vocation in life,' Tim said with a grin, one morning. 'For all his gangly manner, he throws a dagger with unerring accuracy, and he has an uncanny knack with setting traps.'

Gerran seemed to grow in stature as the siege lengthened and the hunger increased. Like Haephus, the deteriorating circumstances revealed his finer qualities that the pomp and finery of Thana's decadent court subsumed in the past.

The mystery in the fortress remained the Chancellor. Three days after he sealed the entrance to the Deep Cave to hold the Haagii back, he retreated inside his tower and remained there. The praise and wonder that surrounded the tale of his spell casting in the Deep Cave faded soon after his withdrawal, and it wasn't long before Andra overheard the old criticisms of the Chancellor re-emerging. 'He cannot be trusted,' Kerry warned looking up from his chessboard.

'Probably has his own food supply stored inside that infernal black tower to keep him and those damned bald Apprentices going for years,' Eustice chimed in.

Andra ignored their comments, but he was plagued daily with thoughts about A Ahmud Ki's purpose in remaining aloof and untouchable in his tower, locked away with his Apprentices, who'd withdrawn with their master. He'd witnessed the Chancellor's power and recognised its might in the glyph. An entire council of Aelendyell Elders worked to conjure its equivalent in Wudufaesten to hold back the Haagii, but A Ahmud Ki created his glyph alone, with consummate ease, in the Deep Cave, displaying formidable magic. He was as much a key to their escape from the Dragonlord's clutches as the sword, so Andra wondered why he remained distant, and threatening?

A Ahmud Ki lifted the amber pyramidal crystal from his white marble bench and carried it reverently to the centre of the circular tower room. He descended through two floors, to the lowest room, where his Apprentices waited, foreheads pressed against the cool floor. He ignored their presence, keeping them obediently in their places, as he positioned the crystal at the centre of their circle, and pulled three scrolls from his black robe. 'Kefha,' he called.

At the mention of his name, an Apprentice raised his bald head, but kept his eyes averted from his master's gaze.

'Stand, and come here,' A Ahmud Ki instructed.

The obedient Apprentice rose silently to his feet and moved to A Ahmud Ki's side. His heart raced. The Master had chosen him above others, which was a great and unexpected honour, but he focussed on controlling his emotions. A good Apprentice has control, he repeated in his mind.

That is precisely true, Kefha. Control.

The intrusion of the Master's voice inside his mind startled the Apprentice, but he concentrated and relaxed.

Look into the crystal, Kefha.

Kefha's eyes moved to the pyramid. He could see his reflection in its polished amber facets. Its clarity was perfect. It was beautiful. He felt something like a hand tugging at his thoughts, and recoiled from the sensation, but metaphysical fingers reached for his mind, grasping at his consciousness, pulling forcefully at him. Kefha was seized by horror, horror that his mind was being ripped from his body by a force he couldn't comprehend. He felt a rush, as if he was being wrenched physically through the air and a great coldness enveloped him. An instant later, he was staring up at a hideously distorted face peering at him from beyond an amber barrier.

A Ahmud Ki lifted the pyramid and studied the formless shadow darkening its interior: Kefha's mental entity. He marvelled at the way the shadow slowly took form, mirroring the Apprentice's bewildered facial features, even though the Apprentice's lifeless body was sprawled on the chamber floor. The spells worked perfectly. All that remained was to perfect the method for extracting the victim's knowledge from the pyramid, but he already knew how to overcome that minor detail. With satisfaction, he smiled at the terror-stricken visage trapped inside the crystal.

The guard at the entry to the fortress tunnels was certain he heard someone approaching, but when he looked there was no one in the library. Later, he was stupefied to find himself waking at a table, face down in an open book, because he couldn't read. He couldn't remember sitting or selecting a text from the shelves. No one had touched him. He hadn't been drinking wine – regrettably, not much remained in the castle. The pieces didn't fit. Perhaps my hunger is playing cruel tricks, he decided.

Tim received word the Chancellor and his Apprentices were in the fortress, but when he sent a thief to check the report A Ahmud Ki and his followers were nowhere to be found. Several witnesses recalled hearing footsteps, but seeing no one, which made Tim wonder if there was a connection between the incidents, but he didn't pursue the matter, suspecting little harm in the presence of the Lord Chancellor in the fortress.

The garrison guarding the Deep Cave was puzzled by a weird phenomenon that same evening. Late in the night, most warriors were sleeping, leaving ten on watch at the glyph. By coincidence, one warrior, due to take his turn, later told his Devi he dreamed he woke to see the Chancellor, surrounded by sixteen servants whose raised hands suspended the Deep Cave's massive central boulder high above their heads. The warrior's comrades, who were meant to be on watch with him, were all asleep. He thought that odd. Then the Chancellor's eyes turned in his direction, and his dream ended. No one could confirm his story. The huge boulder in the centre of the cavern was fixed firmly in place, but the second watch somehow missed waking the third watch at the right time. They all lost part of their night, but no one could explain how, or why.

The Sharvan moved silently up the castle wall and drifted into the night shadows, waiting patiently for the guards to pass, before they eased over the parapet and dropped noiselessly into the Royal Gardens. They crept stealthily toward the tower, until they pressed against its cold, smooth base, their black garments blending perfectly with the tower's wall.

Against the tapestry of stars in the summer night sky, their target loomed like a black smudge blotting out the natural light. Its seamless, perfect surface posed a major obstacle. They had entered the castle secretly on two previous nights to climb the tower, only to be thwarted by its polished ebony face that offered no purchase, even to the most skilled Sharvan. This time, however, their master provided a resin to apply to their hands and feet, which would enhance their abilities to cling to the tower's surface.

They spread the sticky substance liberally on their gloves

and foot wadding, and made their first experimental attempt to scale the wall. The resin stuck, almost too efficiently, forcing the Sharvan to pull hard against the surface, to release their feet or hands, and move upward.

The climb was long and arduous, even for Sharvan, and the resin added to their difficulties, but they knew, without it, their task would be impossible. As they climbed, they were constantly aware of tingling in their hands and feet, as if the surface was alive with energy.

When they reached the curved summit, both assassins were exhausted, so they paused to gather their breath, bathed in the soft purple glow of the Orb of Radiance that A Ahmud Ki mounted there to keep the dragons at bay. Driven by the will of the master who sent them, they approached the Orb, one carrying a small opal sphere. The sphere-bearer lifted it above his head as instructed and repeated the words his master taught him. 'Veribis Aknaa Mareg Dru'artha. Veribis Etnae Sutnavanistra.'

The opal sphere radiated an intense red light that penetrated the Orb's steady glow, setting in motion a chain reaction, a swirling kaleidoscope of colours that increased in intensity and speed. Overcome with fear, the Sharvan backed away from the wildly erratic light emanating from the Orb of Radiance, but as they reached the edge of the tower the Orb exploded in a massive red ball of fire, engulfing the luckless Sharvan and hurling them into the dark gardens below.

The fiery explosion atop A Ahmud Ki's tower brought everyone rushing into the Royal Gardens. Guards woke Surdrok, who immediately sent word to Andra. The cause was a mystery. Had the Chancellor been experimenting with a lethal spell? Had the Orb been affected? The familiar purple glow was gone. No one had an answer, and A Ahmud Ki was nowhere to be found. Worse, because his tower was impenetrable, if he was inside and safe, no one would be the wiser.

'But he surely would have emerged upon hearing the explosion at the top of his tower?' people argued.

'Unless he instigated it,' others whispered.

A Ahmud Ki did not emerge. Neither did his Apprentices. The mystery surrounding the explosion deepened. Surdrok set five Haardrishii on guard at the tower's base, after a mandatory search in the dark for clues, with express orders to send for him the moment anyone tried to enter or leave the tower.

In the morning, the extent of the explosion's damage became apparent to the soldiers on the watchtowers adjacent the Chancellor's tower. The Orb of Radiance was gone. Though the tower summit appeared intact, the magical sphere the Chancellor stole from the sacred Aelendyell tomb in Heolstorcofa no longer existed. Word of the dire consequences facing the castle spread rapidly through the defenders' ranks, and fear of dragons drove many deeper into the fortress. Later in the morning, searchers in the Royal Gardens discovered the scorched corpses of the Sharvan who perished.

Surdrok began to piece together the previous night's scenario, but still couldn't account for the absence of the Chancellor or his Apprentices. Had the Sharvan successfully penetrated the tower? How had they reached the Orb? Surdrok had been an assassin. He knew the tower walls were too slippery to scale by normal means. Then the first of the cryptic experiences of the guards inside the fortress reached the High Lord's ears to add to his confusion. Had the Chancellor left his tower before the Sharvan entered? Where was he going? The more he uncovered of the night's events, the less he understood. Perhaps hunger was playing havoc with his logic. The last thing he needed, in the middle of a debilitating siege, was more problems.

Eleven

The light sphere illuminated the face of the collapse, as A Ahmud Ki patiently supervised his Apprentices, who were excavating rubble from the corridor. The blockage was familiar. When he escaped the wrath of Mareg Dru'artha Sutnavanistra from the Inner Sanctum beneath the city of Targa by leaping into a teleport mirror, he emerged in a huge cavern, deep in the plateau, under Great King Thana's castle. His upward escape brought him to this collapse where he used a shaping spell to dig through in the form of an ant. This time he intended to walk through. The blockage was longer than he remembered, and the manual task exhausted his sixteen Apprentices, but when they cleared the way the party descended a flight of steps, uncovered in the digging process, to reach a level corridor.

Several paces along, the corridor was blocked by a massive metal door, secured with bolts and bars and chains. Inscribed in the door's face was an order, in an ancient Kingdom script A Ahmud Ki learned from texts in the Great King's Royal Library, warning that beyond the door '...Lay Death Itself: Go No Further!' countermanded by His Highness King Aian Abreotan. A Ahmud Ki knew the door was a full arm span thick because he passed through it previously. It denied access to the Apprentices because only he could cast a passing spell, but he anticipated it and instructed Peret and Damon to implement the second part of his plan. The Apprentices withdrew segments of ebony rod from beneath their grey robes and began constructing two halves of a portal frame.

While they worked, A Ahmud Ki took two completed rods he secured inside his robes, concentrated, and used a passing spell to walk through the metal door into the corridor beyond. There, he engineered the receiving portal, and within moments the Apprentices saw their master return.

He inspected their frame without comment, extended his arms and uttered the Targan word. 'Haeraeni.' Sparks crackled between the pair of rods, spreading into a crystal blue haze that shimmered in the portal frame. 'One at a time,' A Ahmud Ki instructed, and pointed to Damon to lead the Apprentices through the portal.

The corridor opened into an antechamber, but again the way was blocked by a rock-fall. A Ahmud Ki hadn't been further, except down through the antechamber, but instinct told him to seek beyond the rock fall, so he set the Apprentices to work again to dig through the debris, under Peret's guidance, and motioned to Damon to follow him into the antechamber.

The pair descended a spiralling stone stairwell, the fascinated servant Damon obediently following A Ahmud Ki, filled with awe and curiosity at the wonder of the tunnels his master discovered in the rock. He would never have dreamed such a place could exist, nor that he should ever set eyes on it, but his master was leading him into the world's heart, and he was pleased to serve so great a master.

The stairwell opened into an immense cavern, the size defying his comprehension. The gentle light generated by his master's sphere touched the wall behind them and the floor for a good fifty paces, while the rest of the cavern remained invisible.

As if hearing Damon's thoughts, A Ahmud Ki ran his nimble fingers around the light sphere and launched it into the air. It rose, its light intensifying fivefold, until the whole cavern was bathed in bright white light.

Damon was astonished. The cavern floor was smooth, as if it had been polished, and it was filled with colours, ranging from black through deep reds to light tans and yellows. The walls, like the floor, were smooth, lit by the same parade of colours, curving toward the central dome of the ceiling. Only the ceiling was marred. Some fifty to eighty paces of it degenerated into rough, featureless rock, completely alien to the beauty and texture of the rest of the chamber. Damon studied the aberration, ignoring his master, and saw it was yet another rock-fill, blocking what would once have been a vast chute or shaft leading out of the chamber.

A Ahmud Ki saw the rapture on his servant's face and decided to leave Damon to his thoughts. Though he stood in this chamber before, he never dared illuminate it as clearly as the hovering sphere lit it now, because he arrived through the portal from Targa in a state of shock, worried he'd stumbled into another portion of Mareg's lair and afraid his light would attract the Dragonlord's attention. He walked away from the gawking Apprentice to a point nearer the centre of the cavern, where he found the fragments of green crystal that once formed a portal mirror connecting with Mareg's Targan tomb. He picked up a shard, examining it for residual magic, but it was lifeless.

He thought of the sorceress, Seralinna, the woman he grew to love in Targa. She taught him her magic, believed in him, was with him when he triumphed over Lady Tarnyss, died when his lust for power inadvertently released the Dragonlord, and as much as he tried to deny the truth he knew he killed her with his willfulness. He felt the rising pain in his heart and closed his fist on the shard, burying its sharp point in his palm.

He became aware of a figure at his feet and looked down to find Damon prostrated before him. He opened his hand, saw the blood pooling in the creases of his palm, and threw the shard across the vast emptiness, listening, until he heard it strike the floor. Pain heightens the senses, he reminded himself from his Ithosen training under Karrilyon. He turned his attention to Damon. 'You wish to speak?'

Damon looked up immediately. 'If Master Ki doesn't mind, may I explore the cavern?'

A Ahmud Ki nodded. 'Explore That's why I brought you down here. I want to know every intimate detail of this place, especially any exits, other than the stairs we descended by.'

'Yes, Master Ki.' Damon answered enthusiastically. 'It will be my pleasure.'

The excavation of the corridor seemed interminable and, weakened by a lack of food, the Apprentices steadily tired of their labours, despite fearful respect of their master.

A Ahmud Ki hid his frustration from the Apprentices. He relied on them to break through the rubble to open the hidden chambers of the Dragonlord's tomb he was certain lay beyond the rock fall, because even his power was limited in such a task. He would expend too much personal energy removing the rubble with spells, and there was the possibility the excavation would only lead to another empty chamber. He allowed them to rest more frequently, salvaging the reservoirs of energy dwindling from their hungry bodies as the time drew on. Water was a risk, until Damon's exploration of the cavern yielded a major supply trickling from the wall into a very deep pool, more water than they would ever need.

Damon discovered other features, including a shell fragment far too large to carry to A Ahmud Ki. When the Chancellor descended to look at his find, he was methodical in his examination of the speckled red fragment. He searched the area near where Damon found the specimen and noted a well-worn hollow in the cavern's floor. The shaft, the water pool, the hollow, and the eggshell fitted into the picture A Ahmud Ki imagined. The cavern was a dragon's den, a stable for the Dragonlord's fearsome beasts; an observation he kept to himself.

A Ahmud Ki re-organised the Apprentices to work in rotating shifts of four. The non-working fours slept and rested, conserving their strength for when their turn came to continue digging. They rotated through three shifts, before the last blockage was removed, but what they found disheartened them. The corridor, much as A Ahmud Ki feared, ended at the gigantic boulders filling the central shaft. There was no chance they could ever make headway through the shaft fill because the boulders were too large to move, and too tightly packed. Their tunnelling had been futile – until Peret discovered the narrow gap between the corridor's end and the first massive boulder.

When Peret drew A Ahmud Ki's attention to it, the Chancellor ordered him to squeeze through the gap, and he cast another light sphere for the Apprentice. The gap was a tight fit, and Peret squeezed through a long tunnel formed by the shaft wall and boulders pressed against it, above and below him. If the gap reached a dead end, he was going to have difficulty edging out backwards. At least the light sphere is a comfort, he decided, as he nudged it ahead.

The tunnel emerged in a small space where he could kneel comfortably, trapped between wall and rock. A second, larger gap led on, following the curve of the shaft. He realised the tunnel was the remains of a gallery, or ledge, that circled the perimeter of the vertical shaft. The boulder fill destroyed most of the ledge, but enough remained to keep the boulders from sealing the shaft against its walls, thus creating the tunnels. He called back to his waiting master that he was continuing and scrambled into the wider gap.

Peret's discovery of another chamber, and a second metal door inscribed with an unknown ancient language, thrilled A Ahmud Ki to the core, though he was careful to hide his rush of excitement from the Apprentices. Crawling through the twisting tunnels formed by the boulders, was an infinitesimal burden for the reward he anticipated waiting beyond the door. He'd been kept from the promise too long. Finally, after so much waiting and manoeuvring, he was nearing the taproot of power trapped within the tomb of Andrakis, and his inheritance of the Fifth Ki.

When he emerged in the chamber where Peret led him, he focussed on the metal door. It was worked with complicated designs, based on dragon motifs, and like the previous door they encountered it was heavily chained and barred to seal it permanently. In its centre, at eye level for A Ahmud Ki, were a series of embossed, jagged letters in a language he could recognise from his years of study and experience. He read them silently: 'Andrakis Va'ristrin Nyavardenet: Turn Traveller From The Face Of Death!' He found what he sought. Without a word to Peret, or the other Apprentices crawling through the gap into the chamber, A Ahmud Ki cast his spell and passed through the metal door.

He stood, staring at the figure bathed in soft green light, for a long time. The Dragonlord stood to attention, in a golden suit of plate armour, a massive golden battle-axe dangling at his left side. His fine head was bare, exposing his braided silver locks that hung to his armoured shoulders, framing his delicately sculptured face, the high cheekbones and oval eyes marking the link with the ancient Elvenaar culture. As he had with Mareg, when he studied the Dragonlord's visage before attempting to drain his magical force in Targa, A Ahmud Ki felt as if he was staring into a mirror, seeing his face sketched in the Dragonlord's features. The solitary difference between the slumbering Dragonlord's face, and A Ahmud Ki's, was the latter's dark, closely cropped beard: the legacy of his bastard birth right, as the son of a human father and Aelendyell mother. He self-consciously rubbed his bristles as he studied the Dragonlord trapped in the magic of Abreotan's thousand-year-old justice. Andrakis' eyes were closed, but A Ahmud Ki sensed the life force sleeping beneath Abreotan's spell, and knew there was power, the immense power of the Fifth Ki, lurking beneath the spell's restraint, a power he wanted to harness to master all five Ki of magic. He was the new inheritor, the new Lord of Magic. That was his destiny, and in Andrakis' tomb he would fulfil his destiny.

A Ahmud Ki withdrew a crystal pyramid from his silver robe and approached the Dragonlord's prison of green light. A pace from the light's perimeter, he placed the pyramid on the floor, one facet facing the Dragonlord, stepped back and studied Andrakis again, for a long time, before deciding to search the chamber.

The chamber was hexagonal, the walls clad with fine leaves of beaten gold, each individually shaped leaf wrought and fitted perfectly with its neighbours to produce an even cover. The Dragonlord occupied the wall opposite the entry door. To his left and right were second and third doors, identifiable from the wall by the presence of door handles carved in the shape of dragon claws. The rest of the chamber was bare.

Curiosity got the better of A Ahmud Ki. The doors were locked when he tried them, but he was determined to learn where they led. He passed through the right door, into darkness so complete his Aelendyell vision gave no clues as to the nature or size of the chamber. When he created a light sphere, he discovered he stood at the head of steps.

He descended, and at the foot of the steps a corridor opened, lined by a dozen doors. Many doors were battered, and the corridor was strewn with skeletons of warriors, killed in an ancient battle. Most skeletons wore chain armour, after the style of the Kingdom soldiers, a style that had changed little from the time of the Dragon Wars. Others had remnants of golden plate mail, like that worn by Andrakis, though there were few of them. The fighting had been ruthless and bloody, judging by the rents in the armour and the smashed weapons and scattered bones. The doors opened into barracks, bedrooms, eating spaces, and what must have been servant quarters. They'd been pillaged, stripped of everything.

Beyond the left door from the golden chamber, A Ahmud Ki found an alcove with flights of steps leading up to the left and right, and a flight leading down directly ahead. He chose the down steps.

The stairway led into a large chamber, but like the other areas it had been stripped clean of all furnishings, so A Ahmud Ki couldn't determine its original function. The only remaining feature was a bubbling water fountain, in the shape of a playful baby dragon spouting water from its mouth into a hollow in its rotund stomach, a sculpture A Ahmud Ki considered utterly distasteful. No doors led from the chamber, so he returned to the alcove and ascended the right stairs.

Three skeletons lay on the floor of the first chamber at

the top of the stairs, and he discovered four more in the next, but apart from the skeletons nothing remained. Disappointed, though hardly surprised, he descended and climbed the last set of steps leading left. They culminated in a landing before a door that had not been forced. Neither was it locked, he discovered. He turned the dragon claw handle and pushed it open.

The chamber within was as bare as the others, but his gaze fixed on a green shimmer emanating from an archway in the wall to his right. He stepped into the room and found a glyph. Beyond its magical haze, he saw something even more wonderful, more than he expected to see in the Dragonlord's tomb. The long room was intact, its shelves and tables undamaged by those who brought about Andrakis' downfall, and lining the shelves were books and assorted items. Whether the glyph was created by Andrakis in a vain effort to prevent Abreotan destroying his power and his knowledge, or whether Abreotan had sealed the room with a glyph to keep his warriors from pillaging the greatest treasures a Dragonlord could gather, was immaterial at that moment to A Ahmud Ki. What he had, almost within reach, were the physical secrets of a Dragonlord's power, and if he could possess them his destiny would be complete.

Filled with utter exhilaration at his discovery, A Ahmud Ki broke into spontaneous laughter for the first time in years, and laughed until his ecstasy reverberated through the Dragonlord's corridors.

Twelve

Breaking down a glyph was a long, wearisome task, and A Ahmud Ki lost all awareness of time as he laboured, casting spells to test the composition of the glyph's magic, learning its secrets, and unlocking the wards binding it. He artfully probed its static energy, gently touched the magical wall with psychic fingers, until he found a clue, a weakness, and then he eased aside the binding spell at that point, before resting to replenish his strength.

Powerful glyphs were complex amalgams of spells, and often the most potent were constructed cooperatively between users of magic who wove and moulded their individual fire and making and passing spells into an energy formula only they understood. Glyphs cast by individual spell-casters were only as powerful as the caster's art, and few could aspire to the magnificence of the glyph A Ahmud Ki now worked to unravel. It was a glyph he expected of a Dragonlord. Abreotan could not have constructed so elaborate a formula, he decided, which was why the glyph still protected the library and store in the room beyond. It was Dragonlord Andrakis' last creation — and it was beautifully crafted.

He lost count of the spell locks he slowly identified and released, as he moved from level to level in the glyph. As he progressed, the shimmer of the magical barrier faded, little by little, until only a shadow of its glory remained in the doorway. Then it was gone. He'd unlocked the ancient barrier.

A Ahmud Ki stared through a veil of elation and exhaustion at the unprotected archway, his feet unwilling to take the first triumphant steps toward the Dragonlord's secrets. He forced himself to walk and entered the chamber that had remained sealed for a thousand years. Books and jars, and small chests, were scattered everywhere. Scrolls cluttered a dozen shelves. The heart and soul of Andrakis was exposed, and A Ahmud Ki was happy: but he was fatigued beyond all measure from the labour of dispelling the glyph, and he ached from head to toe with weariness. His legs felt soft and weak. Overcome, A Ahmud Ki slumped to the chamber's floor, letting the darkness of sleep close over his mind.

Reading and sleeping dulled the sharp tooth of hunger gnawing at his stomach, but time was unimportant. He moved from the chamber only when he had no choice but to drink from the absurd baby dragon fountain, or fulfil bodily functions away from where he studied. The treasure of texts was feeding his real appetite – his appetite for knowledge and magical power – and he read with insatiable voracity. He rapidly assimilated the difficult and ancient Dragonlord language, until it was as familiar as the other tongues circumstance and necessity forced him to learn during his years of travel and study, and, as he read, his understanding of the Five Ki blossomed.

The First Ki was innate magic inherited by arcane beings, like the Aelendyell from whom A Ahmud Ki gained half his birth right. He begrudgingly owed the base of his power to the people he scorned as a bastard child: half-human, half-Aelendyell. Between the races that had descended from the ancient Elvenaar and Dwarven, individual magical properties differed, but the underlying essence of the First Ki remained immutable. The passing through generations of the amber rings and bracelets and necklaces symbolised the tradition of the First Ki.

The Second Ki was contained in the studies of the Elvenaar sorceresses, whose works were detailed in the Aelendyell Book of Lore, the text A Ahmud Ki stole from his village Chanter when A Ahmud Ki was still Terin, the unwanted illegitimate. The Second Ki was magic exclusive to the Elvenaar, although, as he read, A Ahmud Ki learned it was all one to the Dragonlords. It was the magic of the natural world, of trees, and animals, and the four elements of earth, fire, air, and water.

The Third Ki was the province of the gods and goddesses, the holy magic of the Ithosen, and perhaps even of the priests of Teka; magic based on faith. He travelled the path to the Third Ki under Karrilyon's guidance, and the Ranu god Berak N'eth became his powerful, if somewhat silent, mentor. The Third Ki was a philosophy of how magical powers develop and exist rather than pure magic, but without its training regimen A Ahmud Ki knew he could never achieve the power he wanted.

The Fourth Ki was magic of the self. The Targan sorceresses learned Specialties from their mothers, spell forms they developed and embellished in all possible variations, but it was a form of magic limited to the potential of the user and her, or his in rare cases, ability to learn how to project magic from within.

The Fifth Ki was the knowledge and skill of combining the other four Ki into a single, unlimited form.

A Ahmud Ki sat back, closed the huge volume he was reading, and shook his head with ironic disbelief. The Fifth Ki: he already held it. He'd been searching for a power he already possessed. Experimentations with different spells, his cloning of magic to form new, stronger variations of spells taken from individual Ki, were manifestations of his true power, his ability to draw together the Four Ki to create the Fifth. That ability separated the Dragonlords from all other ancient races, and from their descendants – the ability to master and alter all forms of magic to create their own laws, their own powers, their own greatness.

He laid the book on the floor and stood to stretch his back and shoulders. There was no longer a secret hidden from him. He was the secret. Somehow, by a weird twist of destiny, he was born to inherit the legacy of the Dragonlords. He, A Ahmud Ki, was a Dragonlord. The uncanny likenesses between his features and those of Mareg and Andrakis, a similarity marking them as brothers of one family, products of a single race, weren't coincidental. As he always believed, he was destined to be the most powerful being of time. He knew the truth in its entirety. He could be denied no longer.

The first great black beast swept in from the north on the third morning after the destruction of the Orb of Radiance, gliding with ugly grace over the castle, its passing shadow casting a cold chill through the defenders who witnessed its arrival. The dragon turned in a wide arc to the west and descended to land at the far edge of the Haagii army. 'The vultures come,' Claarn growled and spat, as he turned to stride along the parapet, taking the news to Andra.

Surdrok ordered his Devis to assemble crews for the castle's giant ballistae. Kara's thieves found eight machines stored deep in the fortress, each almost three times the size of the weapons mounted on the castle walls and towers, and the bolts with them were as thick as a strong man's arm, designed, they all assumed, to be used against dragons a thousand years earlier during Abreotan's reign. Mounting the giant ballistae on the castle walls was impossible because of the space required, so all eight were dismantled and hauled to the roof of the palace building, and fixed there, but the work of fully reassembling the ballistae had yet to be completed. Surdrok set soldiers to the task.

Andra summoned the sword and walked with Claarn toward the western tower. How many dragons will the Dragonlord send? Andra wondered. He hadn't perfected control of the sword's powers to feel confident facing another dragon. The incident at Cennednyss was a fluke, and a near fatal one. Yet, if the dragon attacked, he knew he had little choice but to face it. That was his destiny now. From the tower, he could see the dragon's black form hulking over the enemy who cowered from its presence. As he watched, the dragon lifted its left wing and began preening, like a bird.

'Farrer says the creature had a rider,' said Claarn, his eyes fixed on the dragon. 'He saw someone dismount after it landed.'

'Remember The Rim Shield?' Andra quietly asked.

'I never forget it,' said Claarn.

'I saw a rider then, on the back of the dragon that Derik O'Dale tried to slay.' Andra's thoughts fled to that moment, when lightning exposed the winged monster poised above his Longbowman friend. In that moment, he believed the heroic stand of Derik and the thousands on The Rim Shield would turn the tide of battle against the innumerable Haagii, like heroes always managed to do in the fireside legends, but the one tremendous burst of dragon fire that engulfed that futile heroic vision obliterated the last images of legend from his naive warrior's mind forever, along with his friend, and all near him.

Despite Surdrok's orders to keep the news of the dragon's arrival silent, it spread to the fortress' general population, and men, women and children flocked to the castle walls, drawn by an innate fascination to see the embodiment of their fears. Many Kingdom warriors had seen, first-hand, the destruction a dragon could wreak, but the people of the Great City only heard stories brought to them, before A Ahmud Ki raised the Orb atop his tower. At so great a distance, the dragon, though dwarfing living creatures near it, seemed small, innocuous, and some of the ill-informed made foolish bravado of its presence – but most people saw the terror the Dragonlord's beast could bring to their castle, and, caught between hunger and the new threat, they began to despair of hope.

Andrakis' golden armour gleamed in the yellow light. Though he knew there was no point risking dismantling the green glyph imprisoning the Dragonlord, he desired the exquisite armour and the impressive axe Andrakis possessed. Perhaps later, he told himself, and turned his attention to the crystal pyramid.

With confidence bordering on arrogance, he recited the entrapment spells he perfected in the isolation of his tower. The crystal's amber hue intensified. He thought he heard an indefinable movement, and looked up – into the open, glaring, red eyes of the Dragonlord. Andrakis stared at A Ahmud Ki from beyond Abreotan's imprisoning glyph with such ferocity he almost lost his concentration, but he steadied, and met the Dragonlord's gaze, while he continued his litany, watching Andrakis' face for movement. Only the burning red eyes stared, full of hatred. Then, as A Ahmud Ki completed the final sentence of his incantation, the Dragonlord's eyes enlarged, as if witnessing an invisible event of terrifying proportion, but the brief expression of abject horror vanished, and the Dragonlord's eyes closed again in eternal sleep.

Amber mist swirled in the pyramid at A Ahmud Ki's feet. He lifted it and watched the mist slowly take an ethereal shape, mirroring Andrakis' features. The Dragonlord's initial expression of terror changed to sneering contempt, a change that brought a smile to A Ahmud Ki's lips. He concentrated on projecting his thoughts at the mental energy trapped inside the crystal. Surprised? The response was harsh, insulting, a mental thrust designed to injure A Ahmud Ki's mind. Don't waste your precious energy, Andrakis, A Ahmud Ki explained. The crystal protects me from primitive attempts at injury.

The eyes in the pyramid glared with angry frustration. Who are you? Andrakis demanded.

Your master and your inheritor.

A Ahmud Ki's reply inflamed the Dragonlord's anger. I am Andrakis Va'ristrin Nyavardenet, the Golden Dragonlord! I have no master, only slaves! Who dares presume otherwise?

I am A Ahmud Ki. I am your master. You are my slave. There is nothing else for you but eternal oblivion, A Ahmud Ki calmly informed his captive. Aian Abreotan sent you there, and I keep you there, if I wish.

I am Andrakis! the mind inside the crystal insisted. For Dragonlords there is no death!

But you are already dead, replied A Ahmud Ki. Inside my crystal, you are nothing more than the sum collection of your thoughts and memories. The body you had is gone, and there is no body for you to go to. You are nothing but a shadow of what was a Dragonlord, a memory, preserved history. What was once Andrakis' is now A Ahmud Ki's. I am your successor. I am the new Dragonlord. A Ahmud Ki felt the impact of his revelation seep into Andrakis' consciousness, and, sensing the welling passion, quickly closed his mind to the horrible, silent scream of anguish that rose from the tortured entity imprisoned inside the crystal's amber mist.

Hunger made him feel light, transparent. In Yul Ithrandyr, he heard stories of Ithosen monks who deliberately starved, twice a year, to gain visions of their god or goddess. Now he understood why a state of excessive hunger appealed to them. When he concentrated, he imagined the awesome presence of his Ranu god, Berak N'eth, God of Power, moving through the chamber, and he prayed quietly to the omnipotent being that chose to sustain him. Time was transient. Being was reality. He existed, regardless of Time.

Andrakis was being stubborn. Despite his wretched imprisonment, the Dragonlord's arrogance sustained his will to defy A Ahmud Ki for as long and as stoutly as he could, and he fought despair to block A Ahmud Ki's mental probes. But A Ahmud Ki relaxed each time Andrakis set up a new stumbling block and adjusted his assault to probe from a different angle. With every change, A Ahmud Ki could sense Andrakis' resistance weakening, like a chess opponent, who knew the game would ultimately be lost, but was determined to lose it only after a protracted and honourable battle. A Ahmud Ki wanted it no other way. If he was to master Andrakis, as inevitably he would, it was to be absolute mastery, the kind only achieved over an opponent who uses every move to avoid defeat.

Between the rounds with Andrakis, when A Ahmud Ki sat cross-legged on the floor before the pyramid to battle the Dragonlord's psyche, he immersed his mind in books in the Dragonlord's library, learning everything about the Dragonlord's studies, about his conquests and few failures, about the empire he amassed, before Abreotan disenfranchised all Dragonlords. A Ahmud Ki read to learn the extent of his inheritance so that, when the time came, he knew what he could rightfully claim.

During one such reading session, A Ahmud Ki chanced on the amazing secret of Dragon Tooth, the structure that jutted like a massive dragon's tooth out of the plains of Ky, north of the Great City. Sealed deep in its catacombs was an army, the Dragonlord's army, an army Andrakis was unable to mobilise against Abreotan's warriors during the Dragon Wars, an army of golden warriors, waiting to be animated to fight for their Dragonlord.

The disappearance of the Chancellor and his Apprentices niggled at Surdrok, even more than the presence of the dragons. A second dragon appeared, two days after the first, circling high above the plateau stronghold in the late summer afternoon, before descending to roost near the first beast. Like the Haagii army, the dragons seemed content to wait, mimicking the vultures to which Claarn compared them. The Chancellor, though, had been gone six days.

Surdrok was sure he wasn't in his tower, certainly not since the destruction of his precious Orb. There were those, like Kerry and Eustice, and even Haephus, who believed A Ahmud Ki had deserted, used his magic to escape the rat-hole they were trapped in. Kerry went so far as to suggest A Ahmud Ki had joined the Haagii. Surdrok, like Andra and Claarn, held no truth in their allegations. A Ahmud Ki valued the magical power of the Orb he'd stolen from the Aelendyell, and was very unlikely to let its destruction pass without retribution. In fact, all the reported evidence from the last night the Chancellor was seen, the night the Sharvan assassins destroyed the Orb, proved the Deep Cave held the answer to A Ahmud Ki's whereabouts.

Surdrok searched the cave, especially near the central boulder, hoping to find answers to the riddle that plagued him. When he gave up, frustrated, he posted two guards to watch the boulder, independent of the garrison guarding the glyph, in case the dream one warrior recounted to his Devi was more fact than fantasy. So, of everyone in the castle, Surdrok was least surprised when a soldier burst into the Throne Room, late in the afternoon of the sixth day, to report to King Andra he'd witnessed the Royal Chancellor emerge from the centre of the great boulder in the Deep Cave, and that the Chancellor wanted an urgent interview with the King.

Thirteen

A Ahmud Ki was waiting in the library. The first thing Andra observed was that the Chancellor appeared taller and thinner. Six days of starvation significantly altered his features. 'I come as you requested,' Andra said, in greeting.

A Ahmud Ki bowed his head. 'I'd like you to accept an invitation to my tower, Your Highness,' he said. 'I've learned something that concerns us both, and it will have a major impact on our destinies, and the fate of everyone in Andrakis.'

Andra suppressed his astonishment at the Chancellor's invitation, although his instinctive distrust of A Ahmud Ki rose. 'What discovery?'

'Here is not the right place to explain,' A Ahmud Ki replied. 'And you need not be so concerned. I have no hidden agenda.'

Unprepared for the Chancellor's candid confession, Andra paused, before continuing. 'You could at least tell me where you've been these past days.'

'I will,' A Ahmud Ki said, and smiled, 'if you accept my invitation.'

The Orb was destroyed. When he heard the news, A Ahmud Ki headed for his tower and entered, ascending cautiously through each level, in case intruders or traps awaited him, stopping to place the pyramid on its pedestal on the top floor, before rising through the roof. He found nothing: not even ash. The Orb had disintegrated, leaving not even a fragment for A Ahmud Ki to reform with a restoration spell.

From the height of his tower, he could see the panorama of the plains of Ky and the vast Haagii army. He searched for the dragons he guessed would have arrived with the Orb's destruction, and saw the pair of beasts gliding on warm eddies, several thousand paces south of the castle. He watched them soar in the blue sky, as he pondered his alternatives.

The siege's outcome hinged on whether he could convince Andra to portal to Dragon's Tooth. How much could he safely tell the King? The less the better: true power, he reminded himself, is in never letting your enemy know as much as you know. That way you maintain an advantage.

He laughed silently, thinking of the trapped Dragonlord in his crystal prison. Even so mighty a being succumbed to him, and was yielding all he knew, piece by piece, through his resistance, thereby forgetting the quintessential principle of power. Andrakis was a fading Dragonlord, a relic of the old time. A Ahmud Ki was the new age. The crucial difference between the two generations was intellect.

Andra would be allowed to take companions. The King's weakness was his friends. If he could make the new King feel secure, he would go. The extra companions reduced risk-taking within Dragon Tooth, because Andrakis no doubt had long-established unpleasant surprises for unwelcome visitors inside the rugged tower.

The dragons were flying west, toward the Andrakian Mountains. He wondered why. Perhaps they're roosting there, he thought. One day soon, he would command dragons, and usurp Mareg's pretensions to rule the many lands of the world, ruling in his place as the one and true Dragonlord of the new age. Then he would soar in the skies, mounted on his own winged creature, and all people would abase themselves to him.

He wondered how Damon and Peret were fairing, along with the other fourteen Apprentices he abandoned in the Dragonlord's lair. Circumstances required urgency. He had little time to waste, to ferry the Apprentices up the shaft under the Deep Cave's central boulder, so he ascended alone, telling them to remain until his return. They didn't dare question his instruction. He imagined them practising the skills he made them labour over in the darkness below the plateau, skills of patience and concentration, trying to master the insignificant, limited spells they practised daily, hoping to produce magic from their futile efforts. Having established his authority and position in the Kingdom, he no longer needed petty servants to bolster his status, and with Andrakis' power and wealth at his fingertips soon everyone in the Kingdom would be his servant to command, which made the Apprentices essentially expendable. Perhaps he would leave them to guard Andrakis' tomb permanently.

He looked one last time at the space where the Orb of Radiance had existed, shrugged, and descended into the Spell chamber to continue his mental chess with Andrakis.

'He wants me to meet with him in the tower,' said Andra, turning to stare out the turret window.

'Again?' gasped Tim. 'Doesn't he take hints?'

'He's a determined man,' said Sasha, leaning against a small round wooden table in the chamber. 'He has a lot to gain from Andra's cooperation.'

'Like what?' asked Andra, turning to her.

'Status. Prestige. Power,' she replied. 'All the precious things Lords pursue with religious fervour.'

'He's already got those things,' said Andra.

'And he wants more,' she responded. 'He's like Orrin was in the Guild. The more power he got, the more he wanted.'

'Killed him,' noted Tim, with a wry smile.

'It always does,' said Sasha, flicking back her hair. 'People who want more than what they've got are one thing, but those who keep chasing more, instead of enjoying what they've got, end up getting hurt, or killed by their greed.'

'You're becoming a pretty philosopher,' said Tim to Sasha, with a faint touch of mockery, before crossing to Andra's side. 'You refused,' the assassin stated, assuming Andra's distrust for A Ahmud Ki had driven his sense.

Andra looked at Tim with a serious expression. 'No.'

'Oh!' grumbled Tim, slapping his thighs to emphasise his exasperation. 'You mean I risked having my throat cut to kill Koor, so you didn't have to seek refuge in that infernal

Chancellor's tower, just to have you walk in on his invitation a week or two later?'

'There's more to it.'

'Oh? What?'

'He said it has something to do with his and my destiny. And yours. Everyone's.'

'No doubt it has,' Tim agreed, but shaking his head in disbelief. 'His especially, I bet.'

'Anything the Chancellor does seems to have a bearing on our destinies,' said Sasha.

'I know,' said Andra. 'But this time -'

'You know what I've learned about him, since being cooped up in this Andrakis fortress?' asked Tim, turning to Andra, cutting through his reply. Andra shook his head. 'I'll tell you. First, I learned from Gerran that he appeared out of nowhere, apparently as a Targan emissary. He seemed to go out of his way to establish himself in the good books with Great King Thana. In fact, he promised Thana he'd keep the Dragonlord out of the Kingdom. Gerran said everyone suspected he was behind the assassination of High Lord Nisus. Remember me talking to you about that incident?'

Andra nodded. He remembered Tim's anger and concern The Hand was implicated in the murder of a top official of Thana's court.

'Then those useless fools you keep in the Throne Room, Eustice and Kerry, keep spreading their malicious gossip in conversations I overhear. Seems the good Chancellor was involved in the release of this Dragonlord whose army is marching against us. Now I don't believe much of what they say, but Gerran tells me that's common knowledge among the Lords. He's responsible for this whole tragic mess.'

Andra listened silently to Tim's unfolding rumours. His instinct for avoiding the Chancellor was being strongly vindicated.

'And there's more,' Tim continued. 'He's gone out of his way to turn the Kingdom away from the Aelendyell, at every opportunity, making accusations about their loyalty to the King. He stole the Orb of Radiance from Heolstorcofa, murdered Aelendyell there, and called for their outlawing when the Great King was assassinated on the evidence of three arrows any competent assassin could have fired. Can you see what I'm getting at?' he pleaded.

'I understand.' Andra said, although he was lost in thoughts about the Chancellor's trustworthiness.

'You never told me any of this, Tim Gaelus,' said Sasha.

'I've only just fitted a lot of the pieces together,' he replied. 'I knew about the Aelendyell, but his involvement with the assassinations only started to come together when I spent time talking to Gerran. The connection with Nisus, and the fact he became Lord of the Royal Assassins after that murder was blamed on The Hand, started me thinking about all those hits Orrin ordered for the Shadow's Voice. It all fits together.'

'You seriously mean The Shadow's Voice -' Sasha began.

'Is A Ahmud Ki,' Andra finished.

'Exactly,' confirmed Tim.

'It doesn't change the situation,' said Andra, moving back to the window. 'I've agreed to meet him in his tower this evening. And I'm taking two friends.'

'Who?' Tim asked.

'You.' Andra turned to the assassin. 'If you're willing.'

Tim caught Andra's steady gaze with a grim expression and broke into his usual affable grin. 'Try going without me,' he said. 'Who's the other lucky visitor?'

'Marella.'

'What about me?' Sasha asked, but her question went unanswered when a burst of intense heat exploded through the turret window, flattening all three companions.

As Andra scrambled to his feet, he heard cries and orders yelled from outside their chamber.

'The damned dragons!' cried Tim. 'Come on! There are people to get to shelter!' Tim and Sasha dashed down the turret steps.

Andra looked at the steps leading to the turret parapet and glanced down at the receding backs of his friends. Somewhere distant, in the castle grounds, he heard more shouts and screams, and above the din the dragon cry he dreaded since The Rim Shield nightmare. He concentrated on the sword in his back scabbard and it appeared in his right hand. His path was chosen, but he could only walk it if he was willing to discover his destiny. It was The Way. The Guardian Master taught him to flow with the current when it moved too powerfully to resist, and so it had been since the day he walked out of his home in The Vale as an offering to the Great King's Armies.

He ascended the steps with grim determination, as he considered how pertinent The Vale's teachings had become so far from his home. His nostrils recoiled from the stench of seared flesh, as he emerged on the parapet, and his eyes rested on its source: two Kingdom soldiers unfortunate to be on duty when the dragon made its first pass. Holding down a desire to vomit, Andra turned to survey the chaos.

Fire and smoke spread over the southwest quarter of the castle, and a portion of the palace roof was aflame. Two giant ballistae had been there, but they, and their crews, if any had been on duty, were gone. The remaining six machines were being cranked into position as quickly as the men and women operating them could work. Surdrok bellowed orders to a squad of Haardrishii in the castle foreyard, and on the eastern wall Claarn was organizing a contingent of the Longbowmen. Their efforts would be token and futile, Andra decided, with memories of Derik at The Rim Shield and the Aelendyell at Wudufaesten, because dragon hide was impervious to ordinary shafts. He had to warn Claarn to take the Longbowmen to safety.

A sudden screech overhead drew his attention to the dragon, as it swept by, black wings outstretched, its shadow flitting across the buildings. Andra studied the creature's long slender neck, carrying its ugly diamond head, the hulking great back legs, with scythe-like claws tucked neatly under its charcoal belly, and its stiletto tail. He saw, in the beast, a beauty he could admire, but it was a cruel and deadly beauty. The dragon was a creature of awesome magnificence that could only ever instill terror in people's hearts. He glimpsed a shadowy figure, thin wraith-like, in black robes and helmet, clinging to webbing that served as reins and saddle. The vision was as brief as the instant when lightning on The Rim Shield revealed a similar rider on the dragon hovering above Derik O'Dale.

Banking high to the north, the dragon wheeled toward the castle, scooping massive pockets of air with its wings to gain momentum, and began an attacking run.

Devi Hannan, directing the ballistae, raced back and forth, urging the crews to aim true. The dragon came on at terrifying speed. Overawed by the oncoming image of their wildest nightmares, two ballistae crews scattered, running fearfully from the black wings of death bearing down on them, despite Devi Hannan's exhortations. The dragon's brutal jaws opened, as the remaining four ballistae crews fired their bolts, and a gout of crackling flame enveloped two ballistae.

The beast swept over, and crossed the southern castle wall, but it faltered, losing height as it turned in an arc over the outer edges of the Haagii encampment, and Andra wondered if a ballista bolt pierced the creature's scales. He kept close watch, as the dragon glided out into the plains, and lost sight of it when it descended behind a hill. He waited, but the dragon didn't rise again. Was it hurt? Abreotan kept the ballistae in the fortress of Andrakis, so they must have been powerful enough to satisfy him.

But when he returned his attention to the palace roof he was appalled by what he saw. The dragon's last pass ignited the remaining roof, and through the nearer flames he saw the metal skeletons of two ballistae. The roof they were mounted on collapsed into the upper storey of the building. In one pass, they lost their best external defence against the dragons.

He searched the flames for bodies, though he doubted the people operating the ballistae had any chance of survival. Below, Haardrishii warriors led their horses from the stables into open space to ensure the horses weren't in danger from the spreading conflagration. People emerged, carrying buckets of water to douse the smaller fires, but the palace was an inferno beyond saving. The Throne Room, the King's Table, the King's Chambers, the Royal Library – the entire building was burning out of control. The library entrance to the underground fortress was undoubtedly under threat from the fires. Kara or Tim would've ordered the large metal doors closed to keep out the smoke. Those people above ground would be isolated, until the fires diminished, unless they used the difficult shaft entry under the Haardrishii stables.

Andra turned toward the distant hill that hid the dragon from his sight, and savoured the tingle from Abreotan's sword as he meditated on how he could use the sword against the next dragon attack. He was the sword. What he willed it to do, it would do.

Tim Gaelus herded the last soldiers down the tunnel, five members of the Royal Guard, who were in the Throne Room when the ceiling collapsed in a stream of dragon fire.

Sasha and three others heaved the gigantic metal door closed, blocking off the growing heat and billowing smoke pouring from the burning Royal Library, and sealed the easy entrance from the castle grounds into the fortress. The only other way in was by rope-drop, down a treacherous chute from the Haardrishii stables. 'I'll listen here awhile, in case anyone else escapes through the fire,' said Sasha, as she dismissed her three helpers.

'No one else will come,' said Tim, as he approached. 'That fire's too fierce. The whole palace is burning.' Even as he finished speaking, the pair heard a muffled rumble beyond the metal door, and something solid thudded against it. 'The palace walls,' Tim said, concern lining his brow. 'The heat's making them collapse.'

'What will happen to the others above?' Sasha asked.

Tim's thoughts immediately flashed to Andra. 'They'll have to survive, best they can, until the fires are out.'

Fourteen

The beating drums washed across the black sea of Haagii warriors, steadily rising to a crescendo, before dying out to recommence the rhythmic cycle. Dark Warriors rode through the ocean of enemy, in squads of fifteen to twenty horsemen, bearing long lances bedecked with red pennants, their passage drawing them together at the foot of Castle Road. A gigantic war machine, a battle-ram on wheels, was being hauled along the King's Way by a team of Haagii, and around the base of the plateau, every three to four hundred paces, figures in green assembled, bows across their backs, and lengths of heavy rope wrapped around their arms. The enemy were preparing a full-scale assault.

Andra watched the vast army's preparations, evaluating their modes of attack, studying the groups from his vantage point atop the gate tower. The Dark Warriors rode up the winding Castle Road at a steady gait, keeping several paces ahead of the hundred or so Haagii hauling and pushing the massive ram, and behind them a wall of Haagii warriors marched to the rhythm of their war drums.

On The Rim Shield, the Haagii came at a silent run, like a tide sweeping down from the mountains, a flood of death to drown the Kingdom's soldiers, an attack that was eerie, and frightening. This was different. The Haagii were coming toward the castle's gates with sheer arrogance, as if they knew victory would be theirs. Longbowmen moved to the castle walls, and trained their weapons on the advancing troop, waiting for them to come into range.

Claarn stepped up beside Andra. 'They come to their deaths,' the giant grinned with bitter pleasure.

'They come,' said Andra.

At their leader's order, the first volley of shafts flashed from the longbows and crashed into the leading Dark Warriors. Riders and horses collapsed, as if struck by a mighty hand, but their companions did not falter, except to avoid tripping on the fallen as they continued to ride forward. 'They are either fools, or the bravest warriors this Dragonlord has,' said Claarn with a respectful shake of his head. A second wave of arrows cut through the Dark Warriors, reducing the troop to half its number, but still they came at a controlled walk, as if the rain of deadly shafts meant nothing.

'Jump!' Andra screamed to the giant, and he grabbed Claarn's mailed back to pull the warrior with him.

Claarn toppled down the steps of the gate tower, as a rush of flame exploded along the parapet, and the silhouette of a dragon whistled past. Before the pair could scramble to their feet, a second roar of fire engulfed the space above them, driving them further down the steps. 'By all that is ungodly, those beasts are the foulest!' Claarn roared.

'That's why the Dark Warriors came on,' said Andra to Claarn as they descended to ground level. 'They kept our attention from the creatures long enough to surprise us.'

They stumbled out of the tower, into the courtyard before the great gates, where Andra grabbed two Haardrishii who were waiting to help defend the gate and told them to order everyone off the walls. Then he searched for Surdrok, whom he was certain would be organizing the gate's defence and found him at the front. 'Keep everyone under the shelter of the tower stone!' he yelled to the High Lord. 'It's the only protection we have against the dragons.'

Surdrok looked askance at the young King, but he nodded politely. He'd already realised that much. Without arrow and oil fire from the gate tower, the enemy would take a very short time to batter through the old iron gates. Holding the castle was next to impossible.

'I'm going to find Marella!' Andra yelled to Claarn, as he turned from Surdrok.

'Then I'll come with you,' the giant replied.

They waited, until a second dragon made its fiery pass over the tower, before they sprinted to the entrance of the gutted palace, dodging from wall to wall to avoid attracting the dragons' attention. 'She was defending the western flank, last I saw her,' Claarn revealed as they ran, and they cut across the barracks square reserved for the Haardrishii, to the western wall.

When they reached the relative safety of a burnt-out stone building against the wall, Andra glanced back at the smoking gate tower and southern wall where the Longbowmen had stood. No one remained. How many survived and made it back down, he wondered? He heard the first thud of the enemies' ram against the gates. How long can we defend?

Andra followed Claarn up a flight of steps, onto the lower parapet of the western wall, and emerged in a broil of battling figures. Green-clad warriors, bows harnessed to their backs, were harassing separated Kingdom soldiers. Claarn plunged into the fray and hacked at the enemy who inexplicably scaled the plateau cliff. Andra turned right, dodged a vicious sword thrust, and dropped his attacker over the parapet edge with a solid punch from the heel of his left hand to the warrior's chin. Flourishing Abreotan's sword above his head in an arc, he joined the melee, and in a matter of moments Claarn and Andra turned the tide against the attackers. Rallied by the giant's and the King's efforts, the defenders drove the remaining enemy over the castle walls to their deaths: just in time.

Spotting the dragon turning from the south and sweeping toward the western wall, Andra yelled a warning, and watched his warriors scramble or leap to safety. But he remained. The dragon came at frightening speed, jaws gaping open, but Andra held the sword before his body and concentrated, as a jet of fire spewed from the creature's mouth and enveloped him. An instant later, the flames were gone, the dragon past, and Andra turned, unharmed, to watch the ebony creature swing to the east, across the northern perimeter of the castle grounds, dipping as its wings flashed past A Ahmud Ki's black tower.

'Come down!' Claarn cried from below, a horrified expression marking the giant's broad brow.

Andra checked for the second beast, saw it stoop to attack the eastern section of the castle, and looked down at Claarn. 'Get as many people as you can into the shaft under the Haardrishii stables!' he yelled. 'Only the few who aren't afraid of death can remain! This battle's lost! Our hope lies in the fortress!' The giant hesitated, bowed obediently, and ran to do his King's bidding.

Andra's attention was drawn to another dragon hovering directly above the Chancellor's tower, its huge wings struggling to suspend it in the air. The beast drew in its breath and exhaled a sustained burst of fierce white-hot flame directly on the ebony wall of the tower. Unable to maintain its awkward position, having lashed the wall with flame, the dragon dropped into the Royal Gardens in an ungainly manner, and out of Andra's vision, but from where he stood he could see the tower suffered no apparent damage. The magic holding A Ahmud Ki's creation together was powerful.

He searched for the dragon that attacked him and saw it sweeping toward him. Balancing the sword in both hands, he climbed onto the crenellations. This time the creature's rear legs were extending as it swept in, its huge talons glinting in the bright summer sunlight like gigantic razor-sharp scimitars.

At the precise moment the dragon's right leg lashed at him, Andra leaped from the wall toward the parapet, eyes closed, and swung his sword with all his strength at the dragon's foot. The impact, amazingly less than he expected, sent him sprawling to the parapet edge, and only a quick push of his elbow prevented him plunging to the solid earth, ten spans below. He thought he heard a twisted scream of brute pain, and something thudded into the stone tower several paces beyond him.

When he steadied his balance, and looked up, he saw the dragon's taloned foot lying against the tower, shocked nerves impulsively twitching, dark blood boiling from its severed arteries. He jumped to his feet, and scanned the sky and horizon for the creature, but it was gone. He glanced at his smoking blade and was aware of an incandescent glow shimmering along its length. The power of Abreotan's sword pulsed through his arm.

The pounding of the ram at the tower gates increased in ferocity, and he heard a rumble, like distant thunder, and a roar of brutish triumph erupted from the invisible Haagii massed outside the castle gates. The gates were giving. As he turned to descend the stone steps from the parapet, he saw Claarn and Marella waiting at the bottom. 'Why are you still here?' he asked, when he reached them.

'I've done as you ordered, Your Highness,' Claarn said. 'As many as we could find have taken refuge in the fortress, but the process of lowering people down the shaft is slow.'

'There isn't enough time for us to go,' Marella added with a disarming smile, despite the smeared ash and blood on her face.

'Has Surdrok and his men gone down?' Andra asked, as they ran toward the front gate.

Claarn laughed. 'He's as stubborn as we are. He would hate to miss a good fight.'

Andra was angry his friends hadn't escaped. Within the fortress of Andrakis, the Haagii and the dragons couldn't get them. Besides, he'd thought of a contingency plan to be the last to drop down the shaft, using the sword's power to protect him from the fall. Now there were complications.

Surdrok and fifty Haardrishii waited in phalanx defence at the main gate, and behind them, pitifully few Longbowmen, those who escaped a fiery death on the gate tower, were lined up on overturned benches, their extra height giving them a close, safe shot over the Haardrishii. Six warriors stood behind them, swords in hand. The ram pounded furiously, and the gate metal buckled more severely with each blow. Large gaps appeared between the supports and gates proper. Then, with a screeching groan, the left gate was smashed from its hinges, and it lurched drunkenly in and slammed against the gate wall.

A flood of Haagii charged through the breach and crashed against the Haardrishii shield wall. At first, the

Haardrishii held their ground, and the Longbowmen's accuracy stalled the flow through the breach, but the numbers of enemy multiplied too rapidly, until the orderly phalanx began to disintegrate. Like a bursting dam, the defence collapsed, and broke into disordered, desperate melee.

The greater the number of Haagii pressing against Andra, the more fluid and lethal his movement became, as he let the controlled rhythm of his Guardian training rise to join with the unerring power flowing from the sword, and the combined forces transformed the young warrior into a complete weapon, cutting and hewing through the enemy, as if they were unable to touch him, or escape his will. The battle boiled around him like a distant dream, action that moved slowly, a scene he seemed able to touch and yet not be affected by. How many Haagii fell in his circle of power he couldn't estimate, but while they poured past him and around him, they seemed increasingly more reluctant to approach or confront him, until he stood in his circle of protection, sword in hand, without an opponent, only enemy warriors staring and backing away, or leaping past to get at more mortal foes.

The pitifully few defenders were losing rapidly, despite Andra's dominance. The green-clothed archers emerged from the east and western areas of the castle to encircle the defenders, and the way to the stables was cut by a horde of Haagii streaming through a new breach in the near wall.

Surdrok called the twenty surviving Haardrishii and handful of warriors to a fighting withdrawal, between the walls of the burnt-out palace, and the defenders forced a path through the green archers, until they were pinned against a corner of the high wall surrounding the Royal Gardens. The Haagii fought hand-to hand in the confined space, the restricted area bringing the enemy almost to a one-on-one confrontation that heavily favoured the defenders' prowess.

'We're too much for them,' Claarn bellowed and laughed, as the Haagii retreated several steps, warily eyeing the warriors, terrified of their leader with the glowing sword.

'Where do we go now?' Marella asked, glancing at the closed access. 'Look!' Her outcry forced all the defenders to look ahead. The Haagii were moving aside for the green archers to form three precise rows. Ten paces away, they unhitched their bows, and drew their shafts. 'This is getting decidedly uncomfortable,' Marella hissed between her teeth.

'Fight with us, you cur dogs!' Claarn roared. Marella and Andra had to grab the giant's great arms to restrain him from charging in headlong fury at the enemy, and his passionate outburst brought jeering from the Haagii, who cat-called and taunted their trapped enemy to initiate a suicidal charge. 'Let me fight and die like a warrior!' Claarn demanded, glaring at Andra, and pulling his great arm free. 'I refuse to be a bull's-eye for mongrel archers!'

'No,' said Andra. 'You won't be. There's another way.' He turned the sword toward the wall and drew a large circle. As he completed the circle, a hole appeared in the stone. 'Get through,' he instructed, and turned to face the enemy archers. He lifted the sword at full arm's length, and it emitted white rays that hit the arrow shafts and burned them before a single shaft was released. The archers dropped their weapons in shock. Panic-stricken Haagii pushed against the tide surging behind them, terrified the sword's sorcery might be turned on them.

In the chaos, Claarn and Marella shepherded the surviving defenders through the hole, and Claarn called to Andra to follow. With a backward glance, Andra checked the enemy were unwilling to attack, before he slipped through the hole to join his companions in the Royal Gardens. After he passed through, he reached back with the sword's tip to touch the hole, closing it again.

Surdrok and his Haardrishii were terrified in the presence of the great black beast on its haunches before the Chancellor's ebony tower, and they crouched in the cover of garden undergrowth, gaping at the dragon, until Andra tapped Surdrok on the shoulder to indicate he was intending to circle to the creature's left. Claarn went to follow Andra, but the Guardian King silently indicated he wanted no companions before he disappeared into the undergrowth. Disgruntled, Claarn beckoned for Marella and two warriors to follow him, and they crept to the right, bending low.

Andra stopped eighteen paces from the rear of the dragon and saw the creature's black scales shift along its narrow spine as it breathed. He also saw a shadow detach from the tower wall and scurry toward the edge of the garden, where Surdrok and his Haardrishii were secreted. The figure seemed intent on the dragon's preparation to spray its caustic flames against the tower facade, but it spun to stare at the foliage and screeched in alarm. The dragon's massive head turned, and its brute jaws opened, revealing white dagger-like teeth. The Haardrishii were paralyzed by fear, but High Lord Surdrok defiantly heaved a spear at the beast in a futile heroic gesture.

Andra cried a challenge, as he leapt from cover to draw the creature's attention from the Haardrishii, but his voice was drowned by a searing rush of fire roaring through the foliage, turning the multitude shades of green to smoking black, twisted shadows of branches bedecked with gold and yellow flame leaves. For one fantastic moment, Surdrok was rigid in the charred chaos, as if the dragon's flame left him unharmed, until the corpse, encased in its terrible suit of melted black metal, toppled into the smoking embers.

Andra screamed at the dragon, and ignited Abreotan's sword with his rage, the flames crackling white against the tapestry of the smoke-smeared sky. Hearing the challenge, the dragon's head snaked around, until its fierce red eyes fixed its antagonist. Reptilian hate burning through the black slits in its pupils, it spat a short burst of fire, but the flames rushed past the human ineffectually, and ignited the foliage beyond. Andra laughed. He flexed his arms, a surge of magical energy poured through them, and he grew in stature: taller, broader, expanding to meet the dragon on equal terms.

Seeking the initiative, the dragon lunged, jaws wide,

teeth glinting viciously, but Andra met its attack with a sweep of Abreotan's sword, the flat of the blade smacking against the creature's head, sending it reeling against the side of A Ahmud Ki's tower, and when he swung the sword back he sliced neatly through the dragon's chest scales, releasing a fountain of steaming maroon blood gushing across the gravel path. The dragon screeched in agonised torment, before spouting another ball of flame, and raised its wings to take flight, but Andra jumped forward and swung the sword in an arc that cut through the beast's left wing. Incapacitated, writhing with pain, the dragon collapsed onto its left side, wreaths of flame bursting from its jaws in a last impotent attempt to ward off its attacker. Andra stepped up to the creature and brought Abreotan's sword down across the dragon's exposed neck, severing its head in a single blow. Like a fantastically grotesque chicken, the dragon's body kicked and jerked involuntarily, its huge and powerful rear legs running in air to escape what had already struck. The beast's great body shuddered and was still.

Claarn and the survivors emerged from the cover of the remaining gardens and stared in disbelief at Andra as the young King shrank to normal proportion, and their eyes moved from him to the lifeless dragon and back again, as they struggled to comprehend what they had witnessed.

Only Andra spied the shadow slipping through the foliage toward the ruined archway of the devastated palace, and he turned the sword toward the fleeing dragon rider, but the being moved too quickly, disappearing through the arch, as a dozen Haagii entered the gardens.

'Our troubles worsen,' Claarn muttered, and brandished his sword, ready to fight again. The remaining warriors, barely eight counting Marella and him, formed a semi-circle, backs against the dark tower, as the Haagii poured through the archway. 'Somewhere inside this infernal thing that cursed Chancellor's probably watching all this and laughing,' Claarn growled.

Andra studied the seamless curve of the ebony wall, oblivious to the fearful silence settling on his enemy as they set their eyes on the butchered dragon. He gripped the sword between both hands and wished for a door to appear in the wall. As he concentrated, a shimmer on the wall became a widening ripple, and the surge of energy through the sword intensified. He sensed magical resistance to his wish operating against the sword, but the rippling effect ceased, and the wall opened. 'In!' he shouted. His astonished companions, and the surviving Kingdom defenders, scrambled to safety inside the Chancellor's black tower.

Fifteen

A Ahmud Ki was deeply engaged in a séance with Andrakis Va'ristrin Nyavardenet when the first burst of dragon fire washed against his tower. Though the flames didn't harm the structure, a fraction of intense heat penetrated the Spell chamber, making him uncomfortable about the attack.

The Dragonlord sensed his disturbed concentration. Afraid? he taunted and laughed.

A Ahmud Ki returned his attention to the crystal pyramid, annoyed to reveal the faintest fault to his prisoner. Fear is something I forgot long ago, Andrakis. Don't presume an unexpected side-thought is weakness. Where you remain, don't presume anything.

Mareg will crush you, the Dragonlord's bitter mind replied. You're nothing but a moment in time. Dragonlords are immortal.

Immortality means nothing to anything trapped within a crystal prison, you poor limited fool. Mortality surrounds you. When I finally tire of your company, I will smash the crystal and you with it. I may be a moment in time now, but soon I will be time. And you will be nothing but dissipated cloud, scattered across the universe. He felt Andrakis trying to close him out, and another gentle flow of heat reminded him a dragon was testing his tower's strength. He concentrated, burning into Andrakis' trapped psyche, until he could feel the Dragonlord scream from the agony of his invasion. That's so true, Andrakis. You will yield everything, until there's nothing more to give. The only immortality you have to cling to is your knowledge in my mind. Stop resisting what you cannot resist. Give. I am your master. You cannot refuse me. I am A Ahmud Ki.

He closed the communication and approached a mirror to study his appearance. The face in the mirror was changing. Where there had been a beard was clean skin, but he hadn't shaved. Starved of food, the cheeks were hollow, the features gaunt. The Aelendyell eyes were strikingly more prominent, and the eyes burned with a faint reddish flame that tainted their natural grey. In the amber light, he imagined they burned red, like the eyes of Andrakis; the eyes of a Dragonlord.

He had no recollection of passing time. Outside, before he began the long and exhausting struggle with Andrakis, dragons and men were locked in another battle, and he sensed they were there still, but he knew little of what transpired – or for how long. He remembered a dragon used its flame against his tower to no great effect. That was all.

He descended through the floor to the Study chamber, and called a light sphere into being, but as the sphere brightened he felt a ripple in the fabric of the tower's spell, a surge of energy threatening to unbalance the harmonies holding his construction together. He responded immediately, focussing on the wall, working to repel the unseen magic, and for a moment he forced the intruding source to retreat, but it surged again, determined and more powerful, and he was overwhelmed, caught off-guard by an opponent with greater arcane strength than he anticipated. Before he could recompose his energy to drive the alien magic out of the fabric of the tower, he heard voices echoing a storey below, in the Visitor's chamber. Someone had broken into his impregnable home.

Sensitive to the potential danger of intruders who could command so powerful a source of magic, A Ahmud Ki conjured a spell to test their minds. The first contact he made was with a mind that recoiled at his probing touch, and he thought he recognised the astonished reaction of Claarn, the giant warrior from Tressel Deep.

Astonished to discover the intruders weren't foes, but castle defenders, A Ahmud Ki moved to the stairs and descended without the aid of spells, until he saw Claarn at the base of the stairway, along with the female warrior, Marella, a handful of dishevelled soldiers, and the Guardian King. His eyes rested on the incandescent sword. The magic that disarmed him came from it – or the King. Which one? 'I'm glad you saw fit to accept my invitation, Your Majesty,' A Ahmud Ki said, with a polite smile, as he reached the bottom of the stairs, gathering his composure. 'But normally I expect visitors to announce themselves. You've caught me unprepared.'

'You're an idiot!' Claarn growled vehemently, glaring down at the Chancellor. 'Half the Haagii army stands on your doorstep!'

A Ahmud Ki pretended to ignore the warrior's outburst, as he moved to Andra, bowing his head faintly when he reached him. 'The castle has fallen?'

'Damn well it has!' Claarn interrupted from behind. 'And where were you, Lord of the Royal Assassins? Hiding?'

Claarn's vicious barb stuck. A Ahmud Ki turned to face the giant, anger welling in his face, and for a moment Claarn swore he saw the pupils of the Chancellor's eyes turn bright red, and form slits, like a cat, but the mysterious vision disappeared as A Ahmud Ki relaxed, and said, 'There are matters your limited mind would fail to comprehend, warrior, matters of great import.'

Claarn responded to the antagonistic jibe by squaring up to A Ahmud Ki, his great threatening bulk looming like a vast storm above A Ahmud Ki's silvered head. 'Then you might be so kind as to explain these 'great' matters to one so limited,' he prompted, his cutting sarcasm evident to everyone in the chamber.

A Ahmud Ki flexed his fingers. One other man dared to taunt him in this manner – Boeris, Tarnyss' spy in Jasmin's castle – when he was learning magic in Targa, and he regretted not repaying that arrogant fool for his manner. This giant of a man facing him needed a lesson. But the King was watching. If he disciplined the rude friend, he would lose the King's trust, and he was already working too hard to gain that. Later, then: the fool giant was sure to provide another opportunity. He was too easy to arouse to anger and rash action. Later, then. With an exaggerated nod of his head, A Ahmud Ki indicated the stairs. 'If you will all follow me up to the Visiting and Study Room, I will explain. But we must hurry.'

Claarn led the party up the stairs into the next chamber. Though the tower was black on its exterior, the interior walls resembled polished white marble, better for reflecting light. The room they were leaving was austerely furnished, a low table and tapestry cushions the only accoutrements, but the space at the top of the stairs was a library, with books and scrolls stored in curved shelving around the wall, and a low reading table at the centre with four stools. Light emanated from a floating sphere near the room's ceiling, and the magical globe made Claarn uneasy. He wondered whether they made a grave error, running from certain death at the hands of the Haagii into the Chancellor's tower, where nothing was certain.

A Ahmud Ki followed the weary warriors up the stairs, a step behind Andra, studying the King who held Abreotan's sword in his hand as he ascended. He knew it was a source of powerful magic, most likely the most potent object created in the Kingdom, but he was puzzled as to how the King could manipulate its magic. To do that, he had to have some powers. When the group assembled at the table, at A Ahmud Ki's instruction, he threw Andra a glance that told Andra he was reluctant to explain everything in the presence of the others, but circumstances prevented an alternative.

Andra looked at Claarn and Marella, and decided he would have it no other way, even if the circumstances were different. He was only disappointed Tim wasn't present, because he'd come to highly-value Tim's judgment, skills, and friendship.

A Ahmud Ki cleared his throat, as he stretched out a small parchment, a map of the plains of Ky, though a very old one because the Great City did not appear. The fortress plateau was marked by ancient symbols, and Andra recognised a pictorial representation of a landmark to the northwest, the feature he noticed when he descended from the Andrakian Mountains with Milly – Dragon Tooth the carter called it. 'This map is part of my explanation,' said A Ahmud Ki. 'There are things I do not know, as yet, but I have learned our salvation lies in the catacombs of this place.' He pointed directly at Dragon Tooth. 'Somewhere in here there is an army.' He lifted his head, after his revelation, to study the astonished faces – except for Claarn, who seemed unimpressed.

'An army,' Claarn mocked, disbelief ringing in his voice.

'Yes,' A Ahmud Ki replied, 'a sleeping army of five thousand warriors, waiting for their master to call them to arms.'

'And who might their master be?' the giant persisted.

A Ahmud Ki indicated Andra. 'How can this be?' Andra asked, trying to make sense of the revelation.

A Ahmud Ki moved from the table to a set of shelves, talking as he walked. 'Each Dragonlord had his own army, before the Dragon Wars.'

'Each?' asked Marella. 'You mean there was more than one?'

'There were,' answered A Ahmud Ki, 'but Abreotan condemned each of them to magical prisons, as he defeated them. I've already informed the King that one Dragonlord is sealed beneath the fortress. But don't be concerned. Unlike Mareg, Andrakis will not rise again.'

'How can you be so sure?' Claarn asked warily.

A Ahmud Ki fixed him with a stern look, and said, 'I am sure.' For once Claarn didn't doubt the Chancellor's word, but he sensed something sinister lurked behind his tone.

'So how does this involve us?' Andra asked.

A Ahmud Ki returned to the table. 'You must go to Dragon's Tooth and call Andrakis' army to life. Your sword possesses the power to do that.'

'And you?' Andra added.

'You need me to guide you there. I will construct a portal.'

'How do you know these things?'

A Ahmud Ki allowed a conspiratorial smile to dance on his lips. 'Some things are best not shared,' he said cryptically, 'not in this place.' His explanation completed, the Chancellor

135

ascended through the Study Room ceiling, much to his guests' disbelief, with a promise to return with necessary artefacts for constructing a portal to take them directly to Dragon's Tooth.

Claarn expressed his unease as the Chancellor disappeared. 'I trust him less than I trust Haagii. At least I know they want to slit my throat. He's unpredictable.'

'We're not in any circumstance to do otherwise,' Marella wisely pointed out. 'Besides, we have the protection of Abreotan's sword.'

At the reminder of the sword's power, they turned to find Andra engrossed in a separate matter: learning the names of the surviving warriors who entered the tower with them. He bid them not to bow in his presence as he addressed each one.

'I am Will, Your Highness,' a broad-shouldered youth said, with courtly politeness despite his obvious rustic heritage. 'And this is Ben, but he doesn't speak much.' The dark-haired, dark-eyed warrior beside Will nodded and grinned a toothless cavern of a grin.

The other four introduced themselves, in turn. Andra recognised the features of a man who called himself Dirk, a soldier he saw on several occasions, on duty, on the walls, since the siege began. Dirk was tall, and thin, in many ways an easy target for the enemy, but he was surprisingly agile, and efficient with a spear.

One female, besides Marella, had escaped with their party: a surly warrior named Tara. With cropped blond hair, and a muscular physique, Andra thought she easily matched Marella's strength, though Tara was shorter, and stockier than the woman from Tressel Deep. Her mood was verging on violent, even when she constrained herself respectfully before the King. Andra made a special note to be wary of her volatile nature.

Second to last in the group was a rat-faced individual, who said he was called Rekka. His slight, short stature didn't especially suit Andra's image of a warrior, causing him to consider Rekka was more likely a renegade thief who inadvertently found himself caught in the last stand at the gates because he was too slow to escape to the fortress refuge.

The last warrior wore a helmet he hadn't removed, even inside the Chancellor's tower, and he seemed gangly in build, awkward. When Andra spoke to him, he nodded, and shifted nervously when Andra pressed him for his name. There was something familiar about his mannerisms, Andra thought, and he ordered him to remove his helmet and reveal his identity. Reluctantly, the warrior obeyed his King's direct command. Helmet in hand, Lord Gerran sheepishly bowed.

'What are you doing here?' Andra asked with genuine disbelief. 'I thought you were keeping the assassins company in the fortress.'

'Pardon, Your Majesty, but I was curious to find out what a soldier did as well. The new skills Tim Gaelus imparted to me, they, well, make me feel, braver. I wanted to see what was happening in the castle,' the young Lord quietly replied, looking less comfortable than ever with his disguise exposed.

'You certainly found out what was happening,' grumbled Claarn from behind Andra's shoulder, and added, 'The last thing we need is a soppy Lord to nurture.'

Gerran's face flushed at Claarn's comment. 'I have not been a burden. I fought beside you at the gate and at the garden wall.'

'I can vouch for that,' laughed Marella, pushing Claarn's massive shoulder with her open hand. 'He's not a slouch with a sword, even if his face suggests innocence.'

Andra cast a cursory glance over the party. 'You all understand what might be happening here?' he asked. They nodded in unison, except for Tara, who remained impassive, and Rekka, who seemed more interested in what he could tamper with in the Study room. 'I have no idea where the Chancellor will take us. You heard what he had to say.'

'Not much,' noted Marella.

'Not enough,' Claarn added.

'If there is an army beneath Dragon Tooth, then we must go,' said Andra. 'There's little else left to do.'

At that moment, they became aware of the Chancellor's presence in the chamber. A Ahmud Ki held two ebony rods. 'I normally leave this in my upper chambers,' he explained, as he began to position the rods on the floor in an upright position, a pace apart, 'but you can't ascend there. So, I'll reconstruct a portal here.'

Andra watched the Chancellor step back from the rods and pass his hand across the plane between, uttering the word 'Haeraeni,' in the process. A blue haze formed between the poles. A Ahmud Ki concentrated, hands pressed palm to palm before the portal, and Andra thought he discerned a subtle change in the glow. Then it turned red.

'I've improved the spell,' A Ahmud Ki said, in a matter-of-fact tone, as if congratulating himself. 'The portal has connected with one in Dragon's Tooth, enabling us to pass.'

'How did you know there would be a similar device at that place?' Claarn asked, suspicious of the Chancellor's confident understanding of matters.

'As I told you before, there's the power of magic, and there are warriors. You only know what you are.'

Claarn didn't fully comprehend the Chancellor's cryptic allusion, but he understood its intent. At sword's length, he'd dearly love to make the Chancellor dance a different tune.

'There's no time to waste,' the Chancellor said to Andra, and with that he stepped into the red haze and vanished. Andra looked to Marella and Claarn, nodded, unhitched his sword, and followed A Ahmud Ki into the portal.

'I have a bad feeling about all this,' Claarn growled, as Andra disappeared into the shimmering red light.

Marella smiled, retorting, 'You always have a bad feeling about something, you big lummox,' and she prodded her reluctant friend toward the portal. Claarn drew his sword, spat to his left, and stepped into the red glow.

Sixteen

Andra was aware of a shaft of sunlight angling into the small chamber via a narrow window slit, two arm spans above the floor, and it shone on a crystal on the opposite wall, creating a spectrum of colours. As his eyes adjusted to the gloom, he sensed others moving behind him. Turning, he saw Tara and Rekka emerging from a dim red oval mirror, and Claarn, Marella and Gerran stood to his left. A glowing orb appeared on his right, cupped in A Ahmud Ki's palms, before he commanded it to float a half arm span above his head. The light revealed a new dimension to the chamber, because the walls, ceiling, and floor were crystalline, carved and polished from the heart of the place.

'This place is an entire opal,' Rekka blurted, and he began chipping at the wall with his short dagger.

Andra saw flecks of blue, purple, green and orange fire through the black surfaces and marvelled at the chamber's beauty.

'Leave that,' A Ahmud Ki ordered.

Rekka considered ignoring the instruction, in the face of fabulous wealth awaiting the picking, but thought better when he imagined he saw red fire in the pupils of the Chancellor's eyes. He sheathed his dagger and moved toward the exit.

'Where are we?' Marella asked.

'At a guess, somewhere inside the Dragon Tooth pinnacle,' A Ahmud Ki replied. 'Look for passageways.'

Rekka found one exit, which led down a set of ebony stairs. Then Gerran noticed a flaw in the opal opposite the exit in the chamber, and closer inspection revealed a neatly concealed panel.

'Check it,' A Ahmud Ki ordered.

Claarn used the point of his sword and pushed the panel cautiously. As it swung open, a musty odour escaped, with an inexplicably chill breath that ceased an instant later, though lingered long enough to make the giant shiver.

'You having another bad feeling?' Marella asked.

'There's something evil beyond that panel,' Claarn snorted.

'We're hardly likely to see what's in the room without looking, are we?' A Ahmud Ki said sarcastically. Claarn glanced at Marella, stooped and entered the dark space. 'Well?' A Ahmud Ki called impatiently. 'What can you see?'

'Nothing without light,' Claarn snapped.

Before A Ahmud Ki could cast a second light sphere, a stifled groan came from the chamber, and Claarn roared with a mixture of shock and pain.

Andra heard something shatter, and a heavy thud against the floor, and pushed between A Ahmud Ki and Marella to enter the darkness. He urged his sword to shine and white light cascaded through the small chamber. Claarn was pressed against the far end, his sword drawn, eyes wide, his bearded visage white with fear. Blood trickled down the side of his burly neck. Andra glimpsed a shadowy creature retreating from the light, its humanoid form blurred, even in the sword's radiance, and it reminded him of the creature he saw escape from the Royal Gardens after he killed the dragon. He edged toward it, cornering it beside Claarn.

The giant, recovering his composure once he could see what manner of creature attacked him in the darkness, stepped back, staring at the alien being. It held a short, black dagger in its claw-like grip, and shining eyes gawked greedily, though it seemed terrified of the light. 'What is that thing?' he hissed.

Andra shook his dark ponytail. 'I don't know.'

'Do you feel the coldness coming from it?'

'Yes.'

With nowhere to run, the creature crouched, ready to pounce, as Andra closed in. Squealing, it leapt, opening a mouth filled with serrated teeth, filed to points. Andra dodged one step and sliced through its midriff. The creature howled with a tortured cry that sent a shiver down the spines of the whole party, and fell, severed in half. Dead, it seemed to become more substantial, and Andra imagined he could see the separated torso and limbs of a human warrior in its blurred silhouette.

'One of Andrakis' special pets,' A Ahmud Ki noted, as he entered the chamber. 'We're certain to find more.'

'What is that thing?' Claarn asked, temporarily forgetting his animosity toward the Chancellor.

'A dracabeorn,' A Ahmud Ki nonchalantly replied, studying the dismembered shape lying on the opaline floor. 'A dragon warrior. Dragonlords had special minions, like the King has his Royal Guards, except these servants know only to serve. They have nothing in them but the spirit the Dragonlord breathes into their souls.'

'You mean they're dead?' asked Marella, as she moved in to see if Claarn's wound needed tending.

'You might say that. Then again, they live for as long as the magic sustaining their synthesis from living to living-dead isn't tampered with,' A Ahmud Ki explained. He cast a quick glance at Andra's glowing weapon. 'But you tampered effectively with it.'

'Why was that thing in here?' Andra asked, returning the sword to his back scabbard.

'There are many possibilities,' mused the Chancellor, 'but my guess is there's something in this chamber he was meant to guard at all costs. Dracabeorn have no fear of death, and usually exist to prevent access to an important item or place. Get the others in here, and we'll search for other hidden panels.'

The party searched the narrow confines of the chamber thoroughly, but found nothing. 'Seems this thing didn't have a job to do,' Claarn grumbled.

'I'm not convinced,' A Ahmud Ki replied. 'There is another way.' He turned to the others. 'Everyone else leave the chamber.'

'Why?' asked Andra.

'With respect, Your Majesty, but do as I instruct,' A Ahmud Ki politely responded. 'I want no interference with the magic I must conjure.' Andra looked at Claarn and Marella, nodded, and the three followed the others out of the small room. 'Close the door panel,' A Ahmud Ki added.

Satisfied he was alone, A Ahmud Ki intensified the brightness of his light sphere, and quickly ran through a litany of words, learned from the Targan sorceresses, to conjure a spell to disclose any object or opening disguised by magical means.

As he completed his arcane work, two changes occurred in the chamber. A tiny opal gem in the crystalline wall began to glow with a feeble blue light, and, on a hitherto invisible shelf, two arm spans from the floor, a staff appeared. A Ahmud Ki regarded both objects bemusedly, before he crossed to the gem. Aware there might be a trap to catch the unwary, he vigilantly pried the gem from its place, revealing a tiny recess carved into the crystal. Seated there was a stubby, gold cylindrical rod, with notches and ribs dotted along its surface. He was certain it was a key to an unseen door. He worked a second brief spell and drew the key from its hiding place. As the key moved, a sharp needle flashed in and out at the opening to the storage hole, precisely where an unwary hand would've reached. A Ahmud Ki smiled grimly, as the key floated to his hand on his spell.

He turned his attention to the staff, atop the shelf. He reached up, touched the nearest end guardedly, and, believing it safe, he pulled the staff down.

From crown to toe, the staff was inscribed with ancient runes, the written lore of the Dragonlords. The knowledge he extracted from Andrakis' entrapped mind enabled him to decipher the writing. Its function was primarily as a weapon, capable of bursting into flame without harming the wielder, but it also had charismatic influence exuding from it. Clearly the Dragonlord used the staff to bolster his image before his minions, but essentially it was a toy, an invention Andrakis created at a whim for his amusement, since he already possessed more power than the pathetic staff could ever duplicate. Nevertheless, A Ahmud Ki decided to keep it. It would serve as a visible emblem of his status. He glanced one more time, around the room, before he cancelled his spells, including the light sphere, and stepped out of the door.

Andra studied A Ahmud Ki, as he emerged from the adjoining chamber. He saw the new staff the Chancellor carried, but he was conscious of the physical changes he already noticed in the Chancellor, since stepping into the tower. The Chancellor's features were finer, more handsome, acutely Aelendyell, and yet different. There was majesty in his features. His beard was gone, though that alone was of little consequence, because he could've shaved. Perhaps that was creating an illusion, Andra considered. No. A Ahmud Ki had changed, enough to be called change, and the subtle alterations puzzled Andra.

'So, what did you find?' Claarn demanded, as soon as A Ahmud Ki straightened.

'This,' he answered, referring to the staff.

Claarn looked at the staff suspiciously. 'What does it do?'

'You'll discover in good time,' A Ahmud Ki retorted sarcastically, and started for the exit leading downstairs.

'Where are you going?' the giant asked, annoyed the Chancellor should treat him with so little respect.

'The army's in the catacombs, that means down,' A Ahmud Ki explained, and with a flourish of his silver and black robes he disappeared into the stairwell, the second light sphere following him.

'Damn him,' Claarn muttered, turning to follow.

'So long as he doesn't damn us,' Marella noted quietly, beside her giant friend.

A Ahmud Ki only led for a short distance, after which he indicated Claarn and Marella should lead. The stairway was narrow and steep, and the steps difficult to see because they were black, smooth and shiny, like the walls and ceiling. The opal interior disappeared, replaced by obsidian. They descended at least fifty paces, by Andra's estimate, before Marella found a landing. 'There's a door to the left,' she indicated, 'and the stairs continue down.'

'Go down,' A Ahmud Ki ordered.

One by one, they passed the door, except Rekka, who

slipped silently aside, until the last one, Gerran, followed the rest downstairs. He checked the door, found it locked, but recognised the mechanism, withdrew his lock picks from his pocket, and began fiddling. The light from the party's sphere rapidly waned, but he replaced it with the yellow glow of a small taper he carried, and continued attempting to pick the metal lock. He had no interest in fabled armies, but, if he guessed right, this weird place was certain to house wealth. A locked door wasn't worth ignoring.

Marella and Claarn alighted on a second landing a further ten paces down, and a third a similar distance after that, both with adjoining doors that A Ahmud Ki instructed should be left alone. The obsidian stairway continued to wind ever downward into the bowels of the pinnacle, but a few steps beyond the third landing a strangled cry echoed through the rock and the stairwell from above. 'What was that?' Will gasped, wrenching his sword from its scabbard.

Andra eased Abreotan's sword from his back, and heard Tara scowl with disgust, 'That bloody idiot Rekka! He's not here.' Andra quickly checked those present and confirmed her observation. He started up the stairs.

'Don't waste your time,' A Ahmud Ki impatiently growled, and turned to continue down, but Andra ignored the Chancellor's dismissive statement, and the others watched the Guardian King, sword shining, circle up and away from them.

'I'm going with him,' Gerran said, and followed Andra. Claarn pushed past A Ahmud Ki with a scowl, and Marella climbed in the giant warrior's wake. Realising he couldn't stop their leaving, A Ahmud Ki shrugged and leaned against the wall to await their return. He knew they'd return, and soon. One thing was certain. Rekka wouldn't return. Andrakis' traps would have seen to that.

Andra reached the top landing and found the door ajar. He edged toward it, and, sword ready, he peered anxiously into the chamber. Initially, it seemed bare, lacking windows or other exits, but then he saw Rekka's body slumped across an open chest, against the left wall. Blood pooled on the floor beneath the victim. Gerran, Claarn, and Marella joined Andra, staring into the chamber. 'Dead?' asked Gerran.

'I think so,' said Andra.

'What killed him?'

'A trap,' said Marella.

'What kind?' Gerran persisted.

'Go and find out,' Claarn muttered, annoyed by the young Lord's constant questioning.

Before Claarn or anyone could stop him, Lord Gerran walked into the chamber, crouched, and crept across to Rekka's corpse, where he gingerly inspected the body and the chest. He edged back to the others. 'Darts,' he informed them. 'Four. My guess is they came from the chest. Three are embedded in his neck, and one caught him in the eye. The chest's empty.'

'You're damned lucky you're alive to tell us that,' Claarn said, anger crackling in his voice. 'If the trap was set to come from the floor or walls, you'd be a dead pretty Lord instead of a live one.'

Andra continued to stare into the chamber, studying its barren walls, and began to appreciate why A Ahmud Ki led them past. Whoever built this fortress was determined no one would rob its spoils without dear cost. For all his suspicion, Andra held increasing respect for the Chancellor's astute advice and leadership.

A Ahmud Ki was still leaning silently against the wall when Andra and his companions returned. He indicated no interest in what they discovered, and he didn't ask what had become of Rekka, but Andra felt as if A Ahmud Ki knew the answers. The Chancellor checked they were assembled and turned to continue the descent.

The stairwell wound deeper into the rock, twisting back on itself several times, with nothing to break the obsidian's black monotony, until they emerged in a large chamber where A Ahmud Ki's light sphere reflected a deep green glow of jade from the ceiling and the walls.

The floor remained black, like the stairwell. Despite its rugged carving, and its hard crystal facets, the interior of

Dragon's Tooth had a shining beauty that appealed to Andra in a manner not unlike the Aelendyell forests, though the two places were poles apart. The forest lived, breathed, and was soft and forgiving. Dragon's Tooth was cold, hard, and dead.

Apart from the entrance through which they descended, the party discovered three other exits from the jade chamber. One led deeper into the earth, one ascended a set of jade steps and turned out of view, and the third was a narrow, low passageway carved through the jade. 'My guess is this one leads outside,' said Marella, peering along the third tunnel.

'There are no openings at this level outside of Dragon's Tooth,' said Will quietly.

'How do you know that?' she asked.

Will cast a quick glance at Ben, before looking back at the dark-eyed Marella. 'Ben and I've been here, before the war.'

'Looking for treasure,' said Dirk.

Andra noticed it was the first time the tall soldier warrior spoke since stepping through the portal. He was reserved, though nothing like the silent, brooding Tara.

'The army is down,' A Ahmud Ki said firmly.

'I want to look in there,' said Lord Gerran, pointing to the steps leading up.

'Rekka got curious too,' Claarn warned.

'No. Let the boy look,' A Ahmud Ki replied.

Alarmed by A Ahmud Ki's unexpected concession, Andra and Claarn were too slow to prevent Gerran scrambling up the steps and disappearing to the right. 'If he comes to any harm,' Claarn growled, glaring at the Chancellor, but A Ahmud Ki ignored the thinly veiled threat, and waited as the giant and the King pursued Gerran.

Five paces after the bend in the stairway, they found Gerran on a landing, surrounded by a dull red glow emanating from a source immediately ahead of him. He was staring into a chamber of diamond, lit by a soft white light exuding from the crystals forming the ceiling. 'What magic is this?' Claarn breathed between his teeth.

At the chamber's centre was a statue of a diamond warrior, and at his feet, seated, staring from lifeless eyes back at the three stunned faces were six dracabeorn, like guard dogs. Beyond the statue, at the rear of the chamber, Andra's eyes fixed on a suit of golden plate battle-armour. The metal gleamed in the soft diamond light. A helmet lay at the foot of the armour, full visor closed, bright red plumes seeming to radiate light in the chamber. 'You see the armour?' Claarn whispered.

'Yes,' Andra replied, gazing in awe.

'It is as fine a suit as I have seen,' Claarn added. 'Worthy of a King.'

Andra let Claarn's words seep through – worthy of a King. Gerran took a cautious step forward, toward the red shimmer, but Andra's hand halted him. 'Glyph,' he warned.

'Very observant.' A Ahmud Ki's deep voice broke the trio's reverie. The rest of the party followed Marella and A Ahmud Ki to see what they discovered. 'It appears you've found part of Andrakis' treasure,' the Chancellor explained. 'If I guess correctly, what you see, in there, is his battle-suit. Any warrior wearing that armour would be virtually invincible because of the magic wrought in its design.' A Ahmud Ki turned to Andra. 'Perhaps it's destiny you should discover it. You are the Inheritor. With Abreotan's sword and Andrakis' armour, who could resist you? Not even Mareg himself.'

Andra stared at the armour again, saw the crafted lines and the jagged points erupting from the shoulders and elbows, saw the power and the oppression. 'It's too well guarded,' he said.

'If you don't take risks, you gain nothing worth risking for,' A Ahmud Ki replied, resorting to an Ithosen maxim Karrilyon taught him during his years of training.

'What of the glyph?' Andra asked.

'A minor matter,' said the Chancellor, and he began breaking down the spells binding the glyph's energy.

Andra turned Abreotan's sword in his hand. The others drew their swords. 'There's no point coming with me,' Andra said to Claarn and Marella. 'The dracabeorn are magical. Your weapons aren't likely to affect them.'

'One way to find out,' Claarn answered.

Andra considered ordering them to retire, but at that moment the red glow of the glyph disappeared and the waiting dracabeorn rose to their feet, hissing through jagged teeth. Andra pushed ahead of his companions, determined to protect them from the Dragonlord's minions, and the sweeping Abreotan's sword cut down two shadowy creatures in the first blow, but the remaining dracabeorn spread to separate foes, and a melee erupted. Andra turned, slew a third dracabeorn attacking Gerran, and a fourth confronting Tara, but a cry of pain to his left drew him toward Will. He beheaded the black figure grappling with the warrior, but not before Will received a mortal wound. Claarn and Marella were embroiled with the final dracabeorn, being driven toward the watchful A Ahmud Ki because their swords had little effect on the creature, despite their dealing it blows that would have killed mortal warriors a dozen times. Andra turned from the gasping Will and moved to assist them, but A Ahmud Ki wove a pattern with his fingers, and the dracabeorn stiffened, its eyes locked on the Chancellor. Seeing his chance, Claarn smote the shadowy being a massive blow with his great sword through its skull, and the dracabeorn staggered, nearly fell, but straightened, still staring directly at A Ahmud Ki. Exasperated, Claarn heaved his sword high to strike again, and Andra swung Abreotan's sword ready to destroy the dracabeorn.

'Leave it!' A Ahmud Ki ordered.

Suspended by his cry, the two weapons hung menacingly above the shadowed form as their wielders looked to A Ahmud Ki for explanation.

'This being is no longer a threat to us,' A Ahmud Ki said, concentrating intently on the dracabeorn.

'How is this possible?' Claarn asked, determined to slay the manifestation of evil standing under his naked blade.

A Ahmud Ki smiled. 'This one no longer serves Andrakis,' he said, approval purring through his voice. 'His soul is mine.'

Andra lowered his sword, staring at the black creature standing rigid before A Ahmud Ki. Claarn spat to show his disgust, and turned to speak to Marella. Ben's low moan confirmed his friend, Will, was dead. Two already, thought Andra, turning to gaze at the body of the warrior he was too slow to save. How many will pay the price for finding this army?

A Ahmud Ki watched the Guardian King's face for emotion and read his pity. Tempted as he was to peer into the Guardian's mind, he restrained himself, knowing timing for that act would be crucial. First, he wanted to get the King into Andrakis' armour, and build his self-confidence as rightful heir to the Kingdom – under A Ahmud Ki's guidance.

Seventeen

The first to die was Lord Rheims. Thana's ex-Chancellor, relegated to Royal Valet, the stick-thin old man narrowly escaped the dragon attacks on the palace, but his weakened constitution couldn't repel his gnawing hunger, which reduced him to a fragile figure of skin and bone. Two days after the great metal door was sealed, a serving girl found the old man dead in his sleep.

Later that day, two elderly soldiers who shared their scant food during the siege with children, also died, and slow starvation began to claim its share of survivors with the certainty that accompanies death. The old and the children were suffering most. Malnourished little bodies began to display distended stomachs and hollow, dark eyes. Mothers wept for the hunger of their children. Warriors despaired of hope. High Lord Haephus' priests strove to uplift flagging spirits, but their own energies diminished as the days dragged, and the fall of the palace spread greater lethargy through the population trapped in the fortress catacombs.

The disappearance of King Andra, the Chancellor, High Lord Surdrok, most of the Haardrishii, the Longbowmen, and Lords Kerry, Eustice, and Gerran, all presumably dead or taken by the Haagii, destroyed the meagre hope of many defenders, and the fortress halls sank swiftly into sorrow, and resignation. People started singing soft death-songs beside their small smoky fires, and their melancholy melodies haunted the long corridors and deep chambers of the hold that witnessed the defeat of a Dragonlord a thousand years beforehand.

Some, in the blind numbness of hunger, fancied themselves as prophets, and whispered, to those willing to listen, that the wheel had turned full cycle, and they were paying the price for the victories of Aian Abreotan with the restoration of the Dragonlord to that which was rightfully his. Others pointed to history, saying the fortress was cursed to be a tomb.

There were exceptions, especially among the children, who seemed reluctant to let go of the vitality life breathed into them, and foremost was the orphaned thief girl everyone knew as Milly, the child once favoured by King Andra. She emerged as a leader of the children, organizing games for the smaller ones, teaching her peers skills she rapidly acquired from Patti, Tim, Sasha, Jen and others, and she was eager to learn new skills as the days slipped by. She was constantly talking to adults, especially older folk, bringing them witty cheer, and carrying water to those whose lethargy combined with physical weakness to immobilise them. Milly's broad smile and positive humour, under trying circumstances, was a beacon to everyone, and some began calling her the Girl of Light, saying she was blessed by Teka, the goddess who seemed to have abandoned the rest of them to the Dragonlord's hordes.

Milly was oblivious to the aura created in her footsteps. When Tim mentioned it, thanking her for trying to bolster the defenders' spirits, Milly laughed, and said it was fun, a lot better than sitting and moping the days away.

Without the old King's Table quorum, Lord Haephus being the surviving member, the fortress leadership fell on new shoulders, a hastily convened interim committee, consisting of Haephus, Guild Mistress Kara, Tim Gaelus, and Patti. Tim and Patti were content to let Haephus and Kara make the decisions, but, unexpectedly, Haephus insisted on their participation in the committee because, as he pointed out, most able-bodied defenders were Guild members, and they would more readily respond to orders from a committee of their own people. So, the three Guild members and the Priest of Teka took on the responsibility with calm and cooperative resolve.

The Haagii tried beating down the metal door when they eventually uncovered it in the palace ruins, and when that failed they resorted to heat, trying to melt it, or weaken it. These attempts also failed.

'There's little point them trying to break in,' Sasha argued, as she sat beside Tim before a fireless hearth. 'They only have to wait until we starve.'

Tim slid a gentle arm across her shoulder, a touch of affection he restrained in the past, but the changed circumstances made his feelings for his assassin friend strengthen beyond comradeship.

Sasha accepted his caress, and eased deeper into his arms. 'You know,' she said softly, listening to the regular rhythm of his heartbeat, 'I nearly believed the prophecy was true.'

Tim squeezed her arm. 'It's true,' he reassured her. 'You've seen the power of Abreotan's sword with your own eyes.'

'But where is Andra?' she asked, her concern rising. 'He couldn't be still alive and free up there. Not after three days.'

Tim gently lifted Sasha's head to gaze at her. The flickering torch masked her beauty in shadow, but he saw the torch gleam in the languid pools of her eyes and drank from their essence. 'Believe me,' he said softly, 'he's alive. I never doubt that for a moment. He's come to fulfil a prophecy so ancient it can't be anything but true. He will defeat the Dragonlord, and rule for a long and prosperous time.'

'How can you be so certain?' Sasha gasped.

Tim bent to kiss her lips, and whispered, 'I just know.'

The Haagii discovered the source of Dragon River inside the plateau. Milly brought Tim the news. 'Aggett and his crew found them creeping into the Deep Cave from the lake cave. They swam underwater, through the plateau cleft,' she explained rapidly, as Tim followed her down the winding passageways.

Aggett had five Haagii corpses lined up for Tim's inspection by the time Death's First Hand arrived. 'Caught 'em sneakin' down yonder steps,' he said. Tim glanced at his shaggy headed compatriot, noted that, human face apart, the burly thief-come-warrior could easily pass for a Haagii in dim light.

'Then we can expect some more,' said Kara, who joined the small group perusing the bodies.

'Not if these don't return,' said Tim. 'My guess is they've been sent in to see if there's an easy way into the fortress.'

'We've kept 'em out of sight of yon entrance,' Aggett explained, indicating the cavern arch that A Ahmud Ki sealed with a glyph to prevent the Haagii invading via The Maze.

'Good,' said Tim. 'Then they won't know if this lot made it inside or not. So long as we let them think that, they won't try sending others in that way.'

'I've got six good men on watch of the lake,' Aggett added.

Tim clapped the thief on the shoulder. 'You're developing quite a knack for this, aren't you?'

Aggett grinned broadly, proud of his efforts and pleased to receive a public compliment from Death's First Hand. Before the siege, such an acknowledgement would have considerably raised his status among his fellows, marking him as a candidate for the title of Master Thief. He wondered if that chance would ever return. Perhaps.

The yellow-robed priest bowed to Tim, a courtesy Tim never encountered, and said in an urgent voice, 'Lord Haephus requests you come at once.'

Tim signalled to Sasha to follow him, and the pair trailed the priest as they hurried toward the upper levels. The Haagii incursion through the river into the lake had already disrupted the morning's routine, and whatever trouble was brewing, so late in the day, certainly rounded out the time. Though there were tiny light and airshafts extending out through the plateau cliffs, day and night in the fortress blended into wakefulness and sleep, and sleep was a luxury Tim learned to take whenever an opportunity presented.

At the head of one corridor that branched toward the upper metal door, they encountered a large crowd of people blocking their way. Over their heads, Tim could see the distant hood and robes of Lord Haephus, who was determined to hold the crowd back. 'What's all this?' Tim asked a man.

The man didn't look at him, as he responded. 'We're sick of starving. We want to go out and fight.'

'The Haagii will slaughter you,' Tim argued.

'Better to die with a sword in hand, like a warrior, than to die like a rabbit in a burrow.' As he answered, the man turned, and immediately recognised Tim as one of the leaders. A hint of fear appeared in his face. 'I didn't know it was you I was speaking to,' the man hastily apologised.

'You can say what you like,' said Tim with a faint shrug. 'In a way, I feel exactly as you do.' Despite Tim's friendly response, the man shrank into the crowd to avoid further conversation.

'There's another way around,' said the guiding priest, realising they would not be able to force past the crowd in the corridor, but Tim was already heading along the alternative passage. When he reached Haephus, a heated argument was in process, and tempers were becoming violent.

Two men at the front of the crowded corridor were threatening Haephus with weapons. 'Out of the way, priest!' one yelled. 'Teka hasn't saved us. She won't save you either!'

'I won't open the door for you,' Haephus said, as calmly as he could.

'Then I'll open it!' growled the second man, waving his pike. 'And if I have to, I'll open your guts too!'

Tim pushed past the half dozen priests, and three thieves, who formed the barricade to the crowd's progress, to stand between Haephus and his antagonists. 'Put away your weapons!' he ordered.

'Get out of the way, Tim Gaelus!' a voice shouted from the crowd.

'Move or I'll gut you first,' the pike bearer threatened.

Tim measured his opponents. Neither looked dangerous, just heated and desperate. Hunger ruined men's senses. He glanced over their heads, making out familiar faces of Guild members in the torchlight. 'I advise you to put away the weapons,' he repeated, returning his attention to the two at the front. 'This isn't the way to resolve the problem.'

'Stop your talking, thief!' the pike bearer spat. 'We're not waiting any longer to starve here. My wife's sick. My little kid's died already. I'm not waiting to watch my other kid and wife die here.'

Tim recognised the bearded pike bearer, father of a newborn who died because his mother couldn't sustain feeding him. Grief and hunger drove him. Of the two men, the pike bearer would be the more dangerous, the less predictable. He made one more plea. 'The Haagii will butcher all of you, if you leave. If you wait, King Andra will save us.'

'The King is dead!' several voices shouted.

'You know that better than us all,' the pike bearer's companion added.

'Get out of our way or join your bloody King!' the pike bearer screamed, and he thrust the curved point of his weapon squarely at Tim's chest.

Tim easily avoided the man's wild attack, kicked up, and disarmed him in a movement that sent him reeling into the men gathered behind him. 'There's no point continuing this,' he said in a cool, even voice. The pike bearer spat, and reached for his pike on the floor, but Tim held it fast with his foot and warned, 'Don't be a fool, my friend.' Enraged beyond common sense, the man lunged at the assassin, only to meet a solid knee that sent him staggering backwards again with a bloodied nose. Tim made an open-handed gesture to the others, especially the Guildsmen behind the pike bearer. 'Save him further humiliation. Take him, and meet with us in the Deep Cave tomorrow morning. I'll send word for everyone to attend. This decision affects everyone in the fortress.' The crowd acquiesced. Arms restrained the pike bearer, and they withdrew, muttering and talking as the corridor emptied.

'That was most uncomfortable,' Haephus said, as Tim

turned around.

The assassin grinned. 'You're a much braver man than I figured,' he said casually.

Haephus bowed his head very slightly, accepting Tim's comment with good grace, but he was unsure as to whether it really was a compliment.

Someone was shaking him forcefully. Milly's voice broke through the thick vale of sleep. 'Wake up, Tim! Tim! Wake up!' she cried. He opened his eyes to find the girl bent over him with a candle. 'Come on, Tim! The fortress! It's flooding!'

He lifted his right hand from Sasha's breast, and sat up as Milly pulled frantically on his left arm. 'Alright, I hear you, Milly,' he said wearily. How long had he slept? He never slept so long, or so soundly. Was it the hunger? Or the lovemaking?

'Tim!' Milly squealed with frustration.

'I'm coming! Just let me dress.' He threw off the light cover and gathered his clothes.

Milly unashamedly watched him dress, studying the assassin's masculine body out of girlish curiosity. Despite the thin edge starvation was giving his frame, he had the lithe beauty of a cat.

Tim ignored her, his mind filled with urgency. The fortress was flooding? Absurd. How? Pulling on his boots, he cast a wistful glance over Sasha, who slept despite Milly's shrill insistence, before following the girl at a run through the corridors.

By the time he reached the Deep Cave, water was lapping along the floor, an armspan deep, pouring down the stairway that led up to the lake cavern where the springs bubbled Dragon River into life. Figures stood gawking in the sloping corridor. 'When did this start?' he asked a woman who was on duty in the Deep Cave.

'A while back,' she replied.

Gauging the water's depth, Tim quickly estimated the Deep Cave would be submerged within a short time, and the water would gradually rise through the lower chambers of the plateau because there were no outlets until halfway up. 'Wait here,' he told Milly, and plunged hip deep into the rising water, heading for the stairway to the lake cavern. He had little difficulty reaching the steps, climbing, and he disappeared. A short while after, he reappeared. He crossed the Deep Cave, wading around the central boulder.

Kara and Haephus, and a host of others, came to the sloping tunnel to see what was happening. 'I told you!' a man yelled from the crowd. 'I told you all! Now we won't starve, we'll drown like rats! This place is cursed!' Tim recognised the pikeman he subdued earlier.

'Well?' Kara asked.

'The Haagii have blocked the river's exit from the plateau. They've sealed its path, and it has nowhere to go but back into here.'

'The Chancellor's glyph holds it in as well,' Haephus noted, looking at the glimmering entrance to the Maze. Haagii shadows moved beyond the eerie wall of rising water.

'We'll all drown!' the deranged pikeman screamed again.

Annoyed by the man's panicky persistence, Tim turned to the gathering in the corridor. 'We won't drown. There are vents halfway up the plateau that prevent the waters rising higher. But we'll lose the lower chambers in the flooding.'

'We don't have to.' Sasha's statement surprised Tim. She pushed through the crowd to stand beside him. 'There's one chance,' she said, 'but I'll need as many strong hearts and arms as I can get.'

'What are you going to do?' Tim asked, wondering what scheme his lover had in mind.

'We'll shift the central boulder.' she replied. 'You told me yourself you believe there's a shaft under it.'

The rising water was shoulder height for most of the volunteers who half-swam, half-waded to the centre of the Deep Cave. Sasha counted fifty-two heads. She knew the boulder was incredibly heavy, and that it had resisted attempts to shift it before, but she also knew heavy things were made lighter in water. She hoped her assumption proved accurate. 'This needs everyone's cooperation,' she explained, as they formed a circle around the point where the boulder dipped beneath the surface. 'When I count to three, we all take hold and lift. Understand?' The sodden volunteers nodded. 'Good,' she said. 'Now get a deep breath. One, two, three!'

Four attempts at shifting the boulder proved futile. Despite Sasha's efforts to coordinate the lifting, once underwater the organization lost impetus. Twice she was certain they were about to budge the boulder, but nothing happened.

'It's no use!' one man sputtered, struggling to stay above water because of his short stature, and he floundered in the direction of the corridor to join the waiting crowd who watched what many considered to be folly.

'One last try!' Sasha yelled. 'Just one more.'

On the count of three, they submerged, and wriggled fingers under the boulder. Tim strained with all his remaining strength, feeling the pain of so much hunger, so much weight, stretching his resources to the limit as he held his breath. The boulder lost its grip on the earth and rose. Simultaneously, Tim felt a force suck at his leg with incredible strength, and realised the water was plunging into whatever vortex they created beneath the raised boulder. Fighting panic, he released his grip and pushed against the boulder, pulling his leg free as the pressure subsided, and lifting his head out of the swirling water.

Other heads bobbed into view. Sasha emerged, spluttering and coughing. 'Get away from here!' she yelled, and she disappeared again.

As the others swam and struggled away from the whirlpool, Tim scrambled across the appearing summit of rock toward the point where Sasha vanished, and reached into the circling waters. A frantic moment passed as he probed the water, feeling for his lover. Then hair tangled around his searching fingers. He pulled, but couldn't free her. Determined not to lose her, he braced against the rock and pulled harder. Sasha's hands shot from the water to grip his wrist like a vice, but to his horror, as the rapidly receding water level revealed the tangled mess of hair he held, the pale hands relaxed and slipped softly into the water. No! he cried passionately, in the silent void of his heart. No Sasha! Hold on! Hold on!

Eighteen

The moment Andra stooped to pick up the golden helmet from the floor of the chamber, a rasping screech drew his eyes to the diamond statue Gerran was studying. The young Lord leapt away, staring in disbelief, and gasped, 'It's alive!' Even as Gerran voiced his shock, the diamond warrior lowered his crystal sword, and turned on his low base to gaze through bright crystal eyes at Andra.

'By Teka, this place is accursed beyond all measure,' Claarn whispered, picking up his weapon, and Marella eased to Andra's right to retrieve her sword. A Ahmud Ki remained unmoved, though fascinated by the unexpected turn of events, as the crystal warrior stepped off the base. 'What's caused this to happen?' Claarn asked, as he shifted to the crystal warrior's right, where Ben crouched in awe beside Will's body.

'I suspect,' suggested A Ahmud Ki, carefully considering the magic, 'that he is supposed to guard the armour against intruders.'

'I thought you knew what the Dragonlord had organised for intruders in here,' Gerran complained from behind the statue. A Ahmud Ki made no effort to respond. He was too intent on studying the magical being advancing on Andra.

Andra shifted left and the crystal warrior turned to follow. It was pursuing him: no one else. He was the first to touch the armour, so the diamond warrior wanted to punish him. He lifted Abreotan's sword from the wall and prepared to defend himself.

Claarn struck first, but his great sword clanged harmlessly against the warrior's diamond surface, and to everyone's dismay the statue didn't acknowledge Claarn's blow. Angered, Claarn swore, and struck again, but his attack still elicited no retaliation. The statue was focussed solely on Andra. It advanced within sword's reach, and swung, though

Andra easily ducked the glittering crystal blade, and sidestepped, avoiding its return swing. Marella hit the diamond warrior's back with all her strength, only to see her sword blade shatter across the hard crystal.

Unperturbed by the blow, the statue pursued Andra and attacked again. Andra parried with Abreotan's sword, and nearly had it knocked from his grip by the diamond warrior's strength, but he recovered, dodged another sweep, and scampered nimbly to the centre of the chamber. As the diamond warrior lunged, Andra stepped left, and brought his sword down on the warrior's exposed right shoulder. Abreotan's sword skidded harmlessly off the crystal.

Momentarily stunned by the sword's impotence, Andra narrowly avoided a killing thrust, but in leaping aside he tripped over a dracabeorn corpse and fell. He rolled left, to escape another thrust, and as he bounced to his feet he had to duck to avoid yet another sword sweep. 'Get everyone out of here!' he yelled to Claarn, as he drew the diamond warrior after him.

'What about you?' Claarn called.

'I'll survive. Just get everyone out.'

Tara defied Andra's order and let out a blood-curdling battle-cry, hacking at the diamond warrior's side as he stalked past her after Andra, but her unrestrained effort had no greater effect than any other blow made against him. Intensely frustrated, she threw aside her sword, gritted her teeth, and dived at the warrior's legs, wrapping her arms fiercely around his calves to bring him to the floor. It appeared her effort had succeeded, as the crystal being paused, but the diamond warrior stepped forward as if nothing at all held his legs, and Tara slid to the floor, rolling in pain, clutching her wrists. Claarn wrenched her rudely to her feet, and hauled her from the chamber despite her protestations, leaving Andra and A Ahmud Ki behind.

'Go!' Andra emphatically urged. 'Even my sword can't stop this magic.'

'Use your magic,' A Ahmud Ki prompted, seeking to test the enigmatic King's powers.

'I don't have any!' Andra responded, dodging another sweep from the diamond warrior's blade.

'Use the sword's magic then!' A Ahmud Ki ordered.

The words sparked Andra's memory. Through A Ahmud Ki he thought he heard Waeron Ardath's cryptic advice: What you will the sword to do, so shall it do. He was the sword. He only had to master his fears. He judged the speed of his crystal opponent and focussed into the sword. He wanted to destroy the crystal statue. The blade glowed with amber light, and the tingling along his arm intensified, becoming almost painful. He leaned back from a swinging attack and thrust the sword into the diamond warrior's chest. As the point bit deep, amber fire erupted along the blade, and it cut through the warrior like a hot dagger through cooking fat. The diamond warrior froze. The bright crystal structure rapidly lost clarity as spider web cracks appeared over the diamond surface, and when Andra wrenched his sword from the statue's chest, it shattered into a multitude of tiny gems that scattered across the polished floor of the chamber like solid raindrops.

A Ahmud Ki suppressed his wonder at the effect Abreotan's sword had on the crystal being, and bent to gather a handful of gems, which he slipped inside his silver robe. 'For a later need,' he said, with a smile when Andra raised a critical eyebrow. Then the Chancellor crossed the diamond-strewn floor and picked up the golden helmet. 'You've won the golden armour, my Lord,' he said, handing the prize to Andra.

The armour fitted perfectly. Though pieces initially seemed too small, or too bulky, magic within made the metal alter shape and size as Andra eased on each part. The breastplate expanded slightly, the gauntlets adjusted. No one needed to tighten or loosen strapping because the Dragonlord's golden battle suit moulded around the Guardian King as if it was made to order. Andra found it did not encumber him, such was the craftsmanship in the metal and the magic. He hooked the helmet onto the silver belt, and the scabbard fitted Abreotan's sword perfectly, a discovery that made him remember the suit depicted on Aian Abreotan in the tapestries. Had this been Abreotan's golden armour, and not the Dragonlord's? No, he reasoned. Impossible. This was the lair of Andrakis. But the suit was exact in detail to the one portrayed on Abreotan, even down to a detail on the helmet: a hole for a ponytail, or a braid. Yet, if it was Abreotan's mythical armour, he couldn't understand how or why the armour was hidden in Dragon's Tooth. Had Abreotan used Dragon's Tooth as his special storage after defeating Andrakis? If so, why were dracabeorn present? They were an anathema to Abreotan's principles. The more Andra reasoned the armour's origin, the deeper the mystery became. Perhaps an answer lay with the Dragonlord's army in the catacombs.

A Ahmud Ki smiled as he watched the Guardian King slip Abreotan's sword into the golden scabbard. One mystery was resolved. He knew the source of power for King Andra was the sword. Andra possessed no magical ability whatsoever, and that meant the human wasn't a threat to him without the sword in hand. When all this was over, he at least wouldn't have as much difficulty restoring control over the King, and therefore the Kingdom, because the King was a warrior, not a sorcerer.

There was still the matter of why the Guardian could wield the sword. Perhaps it was nothing but fortune. Liam, A Ahmud Ki's synthetic prophecy, perished, according to Peret's telling of the tale of Cennednyss, when he thrust his arm into a glyph surrounding the sword. Perhaps Andra's only unusual luck had been to grab the sword after the glyph burned out its power on Liam. Perhaps it was equally possible that he, A Ahmud Ki, could wield the sword. If he could, he'd have no need for a human King. He could become the Inheritor, the bane of Mareg, especially now that he was acquiring Andrakis' powers, and the Fifth Ki was at his fingertips. Soon he would know that answer too. For now, he had the King inside the Dragonlord's battle suit, and its magic would weaken his defence against A Ahmud Ki's influence. Each step in its turn, he reminded himself.

Claarn was angry as he glared at the black apparition following A Ahmud Ki, and silently cursed why he had not pressed Andra to slay the foul being. The Chancellor had plans of his own for their excursion into this Dragonlord's den. Claarn knew that. And, somehow, he knew the Chancellor intended to drag his friend under his influence, as he had Liam. He had to prevent that disaster occurring at all costs. He accepted it was inevitable there would be a showdown between A Ahmud Ki and himself. A Ahmud Ki was looming as a greater threat to Andra than the distant Dragonlord they were all meant to be united against. Claarn was determined he would not let A Ahmud Ki hurt his friend and King.

The descending tunnel spiralled into dark granitic rock that glistened with flecks of mica and silicon in the glow of A Ahmud Ki's light sphere. Unlike the crystal beauty within Dragon's Tooth, the lower tunnel was roughly hewn from solid granite, with sections unfinished and steps uneven in height. Progress was slow, cautious, until the stairwell ended in a tiny, low chamber that barely accommodated the party. In each wall, except the one through which they entered, a metal door barred further progress, exactly like the doors in the plateau fortress.

A Ahmud Ki studied the featureless doors and instructed, 'Search the walls,' and the search was fruitful because, like the fortress counterparts, levers behind craftily disguised wall panels operated the doors. One by one, the doors were opened, releasing stale, musty air. Stairways led down beyond each opening.

'Which one?' asked Claarn.

A Ahmud Ki studied the doorways, before turning to the party. 'It would be better if we searched in three groups to speed up time. That way, if anything is found, each group could return here and wait for the others.'

Marella and Claarn exchanged glances. 'What are we looking for exactly?' Claarn asked again.

'I'm not exactly certain,' A Ahmud Ki replied, 'but I suspect a glyph will be worth attention. And don't go tampering with anything you don't understand,' he warned. He created two additional light spheres to aid the separating parties in the pitch dark beyond the small chamber. By mutual agreement, Tara, and Ben took the left door, Claarn and Marella the central stairway, and A Ahmud Ki exited right, accompanied by Andra, Gerran and the shadowy dracabeorn.

In single file, King, Lord, Chancellor and dracabeorn silently descended the steps, until they stood on a landing, facing a blank wall, flanked by metal doors, left and right. Finding a panel to open each door was easy.

'Which way first?' Andra asked, as he rested his fingertips on the lever in the left wall, but before the Chancellor could reply, a piercing scream echoed through the tunnels. Andra forgot the lever, ignited Abreotan's sword, and sprinted back up the steps, as fast as his hunger-weary legs could move.

He met Claarn and Marella in the small chamber, and together they plunged through the third doorway where the others had gone. Only Andra's reflexes, and A Ahmud Ki's hovering light sphere created for Tara, and Ben, saved them all from injury, because halfway down the stairway, a gaping hole dropped into empty space where three steps ought to have been. 'Tara!' Andra shouted along the stairwell, 'Ben!' but he received no reply, only the echo of his voice from the pit beneath his feet. 'Watch your eyes,' he warned his companions, and concentrated on brightening the light from his sword until it was almost too brilliant for them to endure. He peered into the hole, holding the sword to illuminate the depths, and saw the grisly fate that had befallen the two missing warriors. Ten arm spans below, Tara's and Ben's twisted forms were impaled on iron-clad wooden spikes. He immediately extinguished the sword light.

'Traps!' Claarn hissed angrily.

'This place is riddled with them,' Marella agreed.

Andra checked if A Ahmud Ki had followed, but the Chancellor and Gerran were not there. 'We have to warn the others,' he said, realising the potential danger, and turned to ascend the stairs.

The orb above A Ahmud Ki revealed another gruesome vision as Andra, Marella, and Claarn approached the landing before the two metal doors. Gerran was lying on his back in a pool of blood, and the Chancellor was bent over the young Lord. The dracabeorn crouched in the dull light behind his master. Anguish thrilled through Andra as he descended the last steps to bend over Gerran's prostrate form. 'What happened?' he cried.

Gerran's eyes opened painfully at the sound of Andra's voice, and a faint smile touched the young Lord's lips as he mouthed, 'I think I saved you.'

Andra cradled Gerran's head on his lap and looked at A Ahmud Ki for an explanation. The Chancellor pointed to the lever on the left wall, and said, 'Watch.' He lifted the staff he carried and pressed the lever down. The instant it moved, two wickedly sharp metal shafts shot across the intervening space, to within a thumb space of the opposite door, bloodied points glistening in the magical light, and retracted, leaving no sign of their existence. To emphasise the point, A Ahmud Ki repeated the exercise with the right lever. Andra shuddered. He escaped Gerran's fate by sheer chance. He looked down at the young Lord's face. Gerran seemed no more than a youth. His smooth skin and pale complexion gave the dying Lord an ethereal beauty. He was watching Andra, the smile fading on his lips. Then his pale blue eyes stared at a spot beyond Andra's head, glazed over, and a nervous shiver rippled through the young Lord's body, forcing him to sigh once, deeply. Blood trickled from the corner of his mouth.

Three more dead, Andra pondered as they ascended the stairway to the small chamber. Gerran. Tara. Ben. Andrakis' cursed traps. The Dragonlord was killing in his absence. What kind of perverse mind created traps? He should have died before, not Gerran. A hand of fate guided him, protecting him from death's blow, but every time his safety came at a cost, a savage cost.

'This is the way down,' A Ahmud Ki announced, as they entered the stairwell Claarn and Marella had partly descended. 'I suggest you two lead because you've been down here.'

Claarn gave A Ahmud Ki a fierce grin. 'You're afraid you might get pricked by a trap,' he growled, and turned to lead, without waiting to gauge the effect of his bitter jibe.

A Ahmud Ki briefly considered letting Claarn discover how limited his warrior skills were by unleashing the dracabeorn, but he controlled his anger and followed Marella, walking beside Andra, casting sideways glances at the King's face to determine his frame of mind. Gerran's death clearly affected him. His weakness, his concern for those close, had to be exploited fully. A Ahmud Ki's immediate problem was to make certain the King was amenable to his influence in the presence of Andrakis' army. There were considerations essential to ensure that the army awoke and obeyed the substitute King in place of their old master, Andrakis. The golden battle suit was one.

At the foot of the stairs, Claarn proceeded slowly, using his drawn sword to test the granite floor for traps. The corridor disappeared into darkness, and their wary progress exaggerated its length, but they eventually arrived at a t-junction. Claarn peered left and right and saw the distant green glows of glyphs in both directions. He informed the others, and pressed the floor in the t-junction with his sword tip. A rumble made them step back, as the ceiling over the t-junction smashed into the floor, before recoiling, leaving a faint aura of dust.

'Well done,' A Ahmud Ki said, to which the red-haired giant responded with a curse.

The party avoided the trap mechanism by cutting the t-junction corner, and headed left, toward a shimmering glyph. Beyond the glyph, they saw a vast chamber spread ahead and left and right, infused by a dim yellow light reflected on thousands of suits of golden armour standing erect in uniform rows: an army of sleeping warriors, fully armed, faces hidden beneath golden visors.

'The golden army of Andrakis!' A Ahmud Ki announced, and turned to Andra, to add, 'Your army, my Lord. You are the Inheritor.'

'Look there!' Marella's warning drew their eyes to shadowy creatures becoming active at the rear of the chamber, and scrambling toward the glyph.

'More dracabeorn,' A Ahmud Ki observed.

'Eleven of the foul things!' Claarn growled, heaving his sword from its scabbard.

'There's no point, Claarn,' said Andra putting his hand on the warrior's weapon. 'Your sword has no effect. I have to fight them, alone. Too many have died to get here. This is my battle.'

'But there are eleven,' Claarn reminded his friend, thinking Andra's show of bravado foolish.

'Exactly,' Andra calmly replied. 'Now, take Marella and go back to the t-junction.'

'What if you are killed?' Marella asked, her concern mirrored in her tone.

'Then A Ahmud Ki is wrong about the armour,' he grimly replied.

Ignoring the Chancellor's glare, Andra directed A Ahmud Ki to dissipate the glyph separating him from the dracabeorn, crouched and hissing behind the glow, waiting hungrily for victims. A Ahmud Ki completed the task in moments, finding the glyph less intricately constructed than others he'd dispelled. As the glow faded, the dracabeorn attacked, their visages twisted with hate, their razor teeth and daggers intent on carnage. The first sweep of Abreotan's sword felled three, but the remaining eight immediately surrounded Andra, circling like a rabid wolf-pack.

Grateful to escape attention, A Ahmud Ki observed the unfolding drama. The amber glow from Abreotan's sword conjured memories of the Orb of Radiance. Does it share similar magical properties, he wondered? A dracabeorn seized the opportunity to jump at Andra from behind, but the Guardian cut the attacker down and balanced to ward the next attack.

Again, the pack circled. A Ahmud Ki studied the sword. The Orb of Radiance – the magic was familiar – Elvenaar magic, based on the Second Ki. The sword had Elvenaar magic wrought in it. If it was like the Orb, there were many ways to manipulate it. Another dracabeorn leapt and fell dead, writhing from the blade's fatal bite. What a waste of dracabeorn, A Ahmud Ki decided, and glanced at his servant lurking obediently beside him. If the sword was like the Orb, he had an answer. 'Lift the sword above your head!' he yelled.

Andra heard the order, saw the six surviving dracabeorn were reluctant to risk an attack, and carefully raised the sword, wondering why the Chancellor issued his instruction. Then he saw why. The silver-haired Chancellor weaved his hands in a fierce arcane ritual and turned his palms toward the sword. Though there was nothing visible, Andra felt a massive energy pulse through the sword, and rays of red light radiated from the blade, fixing each of the closing dracabeorn three paces from the Guardian. As he witnessed in the chamber with the diamond warrior, the faces of the dracabeorn melted into fearful shock, and they cringed from the sword's rays. The radiating energy diminished, and, as one, the six dracabeorn turned toward A Ahmud Ki and bowed, acknowledging their new master.

Andra lowered the sword, catching A Ahmud Ki's serenely confident face gazing back at him, as the dracabeorn moved to stand obediently behind the first one A Ahmud Ki had subdued. The Guardian's mistrust for the Chancellor was locked in a confusing struggle with his admiration for A Ahmud Ki's power, and his new puzzle about the sword's magic. The Chancellor had used it to amplify his spell.

No dracabeorn waited for intruders beyond the glyph in the second chamber where, in regimental rows, they found two thousand knights in suits of golden plate like the five thousand warriors in the first chamber, mounted on war steeds rivalling the best the Haardrishii possessed before the war.

Marella discovered a heavy door moulded from solid gold in the second chamber that led up a set of ivory stairs to a landing overseeing both chambers, and on the landing she found a ruby pedestal supporting a golden sphere. She led the others to the landing, and A Ahmud Ki stood before the golden ball, assessing its magical quality, while Andra, Claarn and Marella surveyed the vast golden army arrayed in the twin chambers.

'With this army, we will drive the Haagii out of the Kingdom,' Andra said, trying to come to terms with their discovery beneath Dragon's Tooth.

'I wish there was another way,' Claarn muttered.

'What do you mean?' Andra asked.

'I mean, my friend, this was once the army of a Dragonlord. I'm not so sure it is ours to control.'

'A sensible observation,' A Ahmud Ki butted in, as he joined the three at the edge of the landing. 'Only one person has the power to control this army. Andrakis.'

'Then we're wasting our time,' Marella said.

'No,' said A Ahmud Ki. 'We have Andrakis with us.' He pointed to Andra. 'If you tell them you are Andrakis, they will serve you. Your sword has the power to operate the golden sphere that will awaken the warriors and knights. Simple.'

'Too simple,' said Claarn suspiciously. 'What's the catch?'

'No catch, as you put it,' A Ahmud Ki replied. 'Andrakis relied on his traps, glyphs, and dracabeorn keeping intruders out. He didn't know much about Abreotan's sword when he created this army. Abreotan ambushed him in the plateau fortress, much later, then defeated and isolated him there, so he could never call his army to war. Abreotan probably never even learned of this army. That's why everything is still here and untouched. Abreotan and Andrakis are both dead, making this place the property of the Kingdom – which means it belongs to Andra. He's Abreotan's and Andrakis' rightful heir, under the circumstances.' A Ahmud Ki crossed to the pedestal supporting the golden sphere. 'Here is the lock,' he said, 'and we have the key.' He faced Andra and bowed slightly from the waist. 'This army will serve our King Andra.'

Nineteen

The water diversion was temporary. Although the shaft beneath the boulder consumed the bulk of water backflushed by the Haagii into the Deep Cave, it filled quicker than the defenders anticipated, and within a short space of time the level in the Deep Cave began to rise again. Realising the lower reaches were lost to the creeping flood, Guild Mistress Kara ordered the metal door sealed.

Tim kept watch over Sasha. She was alive, but unconscious, her breathing shallow, her pulse slow. She had all but drowned in attempting to shift the central boulder, and only Tim's desperate rescue prevented her from disappearing into the whirlpool. Two men perished, sucked into the watery vortex. There was little hope held by anyone that the female assassin would live long. Only Tim refused to believe otherwise, so he defiantly maintained his vigil beside her bed. He stared longingly at her dark lashes adorning her ashen cheeks, and her colourless lips over which the faintest of breaths crept, and prayed silently to the Aelendyell gods to sustain her against the touch of death. He smiled grimly at one stage, aware of the irony of his circumstance. Death's First Hand was trying to keep his love from Death. If that was to be, he would fight accordingly in his heart.

Milly came and went in silence, bringing water for Tim to drink. She, like everyone in the fortress, was growing weaker without food, yet she persisted with her tasks, finding things to do to stave off her lethargy. Hunger fascinated her. She passed beyond a constant gnawing need for food to an unexpected, peaceful emptiness in the ensuing days. The thought of food made her feel queasy, rather than famished, and she could imagine existing without food forever, sipping small amounts of water to keep her lips, mouth and throat moist. She overheard the priests talking, after prayers, about fasting, and its ability to liberate the soul, and though she didn't understand the soul concept she felt she could empathise with the free-body experience and exhilaration they claimed was gained from periods of intense fasting. Religion, she decided, was a strange experience if converts had to starve to be satisfied. She also overheard people arguing about eating the horses, and the war dogs, angrily complaining that people were dying, but the Haardrishii animals were protected when they could be a source of food. Out of fear for his safety, she retrieved Artega and took him into her quarters, and shared her water with him. Nevertheless, like the people, the dog was getting thinner daily, and she wondered if the animals would fare any better than the people.

She could see Tim loved Sasha. When she said so to Patti, the squat madam chuckled and hugged Milly to her ample bosom, telling her that love was the most potent force in the universe, only no one had learned how to harness it, except her girls. Milly heard sniggers from Jen and her companions, and knew there was smut associated with Patti's reply, but she also heard Patti's earnestness about love and inscribed the words on her heart. 'One day, my pretty little miss,' Patti said, ruffling Milly's hair, 'you'll find yourself a fine young man, who'll come professing his love for you, and then you'll understand what's in Tim's and Sasha's eyes when they look at each other.'

'She's already popular among the boys,' Jen quipped, and puckered her lips at Milly. The girl responded by poking out her tongue.

'Are you now?' Patti grinned, her cheeks crinkling into dimples and folds. 'And who's the luckiest boy of all?'

'None of the boys are lucky,' Milly retorted.

'Aaron,' teased Jen. Milly threw her a vicious glare and denied the accusation emphatically.

'No boyfriend?' Patti asked, feigning incredulity. Milly turned bright red, broadening Patti's smile. 'Then there is one, my pretty little miss, eh?' the rotund woman laughed.

'That's for me to know,' Milly replied, and trotted from the room before Patti or Jen could tease her further.

In the corridor, she paused to listen if the older women were discussing her list of boyfriends, but they turned to serious matters: talk of how much longer they could survive without food. She didn't want to hear a depressing conversation of dying, so she headed down the corridor, toward the chamber where Tim watched over Sasha.

She was annoyed for blushing in front of Patti. Aaron was a friend. That was all. She hadn't considered any other boy because she'd already pledged her heart to one. He didn't know yet, and she was frightened he never would know. But she was even more terrified he might find out how she felt. She idolised him. He took her heart with him when he disappeared, and now she didn't know if he was alive or not. No. He was alive. In her heart, she knew it. But she could never dare tell him how she felt. Not Andra. And she didn't dare risk telling anyone else. They would laugh at her – a kid with a King-size crush. She could already hear the teasing words.

Less than two days after Lord Rheims' death, more people started dying. High Lord Haephus' priests brought him word that hundreds were lying down to die, too weak from hunger to keep going, and the few with strength to rebel were angry, demanding the right to die fighting their enemy. The promised assembly in the Deep Cave was postponed by the flooding, but Haephus knew the committee and he could no longer avoid the issue. He sent word throughout the fortress that an assembly would be held in the upper chambers, to decide the last action they would take, and that all who were able to attend should do so.

Tim was reluctant to leave Sasha, but he acquiesced when Milly and Jen offered to take his place at her bedside, while the assembly decided the defenders' fate. He bestowed a gentle kiss on her pale, cold forehead before leaving, and whispered he'd return as soon as he could.

There were more at the assembly than Haephus anticipated, predominantly men, though a sprinkling of

174

women was scattered through the three chambers opened to the meeting. People spilled into the corridors, vying for their chance to see or hear what was proposed for the last days, and to hear what was decided. With Patti, Kara, and Tim, Haephus called for silence before he addressed the gathering. 'Blessings of Teka be upon you all,' he began, and heard a mixed response, some people accepting and returning the benediction, some bitterly cursing the religious reference to a goddess they believed long abandoned their hopes. He sensed the tension compressed in the assembly and could predict the outcome from the growing mood of discontent. 'There's little time for pretty words,' he said. 'I will bring us quickly to the issue. The facts are simple. We have no food.' Several men jeered.

'Eat the bloody Haardrishii animals!' a man yelled, and his angry voice was echoed by a host of others.

Haephus ignored the disruption, and waited for the noise to end, before he said, 'As we are, we will soon be dead from starvation, and I can do nothing to halt this happening. We could eat the animals, but how much extra time would that buy? Two days? Three? And then what?'

'We can fight!' a deep voice interjected from the centre of the first chamber. His shout was taken up by other voices, desperate, hoarse voices, weakened by hunger.

'Fight!'

'We won't die like rats!'

'Die like warriors!'

'Yes, fight our way out!'

'Like we should have done from the start!'

Haephus raised his hands to control the mob's angry outburst, but several moments passed before the interjectors let him speak again. 'I hear your voices. But listen. Listen!' he pleaded calmly, until a modicum of silence descended. 'That is a choice some of you propose,' he continued. 'To fight. I understand that desire. I have the desire nagging at me to doff my robes and take the sword against my enemy.'

'Do it, priest!' an angry voice shouted. 'Do it!' Others

175

added their support to the cry.

'Don't talk such foolishness!' Patti yelled above the babbling voices. 'The Haagii are waiting. They'll butcher every one of you, if you try to climb out the castle's ruins.'

'Better to die that way than starve miserably in here!' a tall, dark-bearded warrior yelled from the chamber doorway. Shouts of assent echoed through the chambers and into the corridor.

Tim watched and listened to the mood of the gathering. His friends on the committee couldn't prevent the inevitable. He glanced at Patti and Kara, and stood, climbing onto a chair to be heard and seen. 'Sit down, Tim Gaelus!' a voice roared. 'We know what you'll say! We aren't listening!'

'Don't tell us we shouldn't die!' another shouted. 'It's not a question of dying or not: it's how we die!' Another wave of approval washed through the crowd.

'Go,' Tim said, almost inaudibly above the din of voices. Faces turned toward him and peered. 'Go,' he repeated. 'Those who would fight the Haagii one last time, go and fetch your weapons and armour.' He caught Haephus' open-mouthed stare from the corner of his eye and continued. 'Meet me in the upper chamber, before the metal door, as soon as you can. Those who have goodbyes to make, make them now.' He paused in the stunned silence of the listening chamber and cast a searching eye over the faces. In every gaunt face he read the lines of death. 'Meet me in the upper chamber,' he repeated. 'When we leave there, we won't be returning. There will be nothing to return to.'

Exhaustion swept over him, and he swayed, before he stepped down from the chair, and pushed through the crowd. Some hands clapped him on the shoulder as he left, but most people stepped respectfully aside to let the weary Death's First Hand pass.

With Tim's withdrawal, the gathering dropped into quiet conversation, and people began to shuffle out of the chambers, their heads and hearts making decisions about their individual fates. Haephus, Patti and Kara remained in their wake, numbed by Tim's unexpected decision.

'If the Haagii come,' Tim instructed, 'use this as best you can.' He pressed a long-bladed dagger into Milly's palm. 'All the practice we've had has to be used now,' he added. 'You'll be fine.'

Milly rolled Tim's dagger in her hand, studying its finely-honed blade. Aaron would be envious that she received Death's First Hand's personal weapon.

Tim patted Artega's black snout, as he squatted beside Sasha's bed, where she was lying in her deep coma. He pressed her white hand tightly and placed a soft kiss on her left cheek. He bent closer to her ear, and whispered words Milly barely overheard. 'Hwaene we gemoetan eftsiththan sibb smolt swaes sinc,' he said, in a sibilant, lilting tongue alien. 'If she ever wakes before all this is over,' Tim said, turning to Milly, 'tell her I will always love her.'

'I'll tell her,' Milly promised, trying to hide her embarrassment, 'but I think she already knows.' Then her irrepressible curiosity got the better of her, and she asked, 'What did you say to her?'

Tim rose, approached the girl who'd learned to be an assassin under his training, and hugged her tightly. 'You have the ears of a born thief,' he said, with a grin, but his smile faded. 'I promised Sasha I'd be with her soon.'

'But in what language?' Milly insisted.

'My native tongue,' Tim replied.

'Please be careful,' she begged, as he released her, and took a short sword from Sasha's bedside to fit into his scabbard.

'As careful as always,' Tim replied, and he forced another grin, which made Milly laugh softly at the assassin's caricature. Tim opened the chamber door, pausing once to wink at Milly who fought back a tear. 'Wacor be, ond stercedferhth,' he said resolutely. 'Live long, my young friend,' and he left the chamber.

He counted two hundred and twenty-seven. Almost all the assembled warriors were men, and most untrained survivors who had not served in the Kingdom armies. The eighteen women were thieves and assassins. Two of Haephus' priests stood among the ranks, conspicuous in their yellow robes, and Tim wondered if Haephus knew his disciples were deserting their post. The number was far less than he anticipated from the earlier assembly's mood, but that made him happier. He guessed most people saw the futility in trying to break out, and had chosen to die in peace rather than in a fleeting, bloody battle.

After the last people arrived, his instructions were brief: a simple plan – a desperate charge to the outer gate, with a chance of breaking into the open countryside. He didn't dare consider what might lie beyond that: if they managed to get that far. 'On my order, the Guild members will unbolt and open the door. Those who choose to go first must be quick and committed. There's no turning back. Those behind will be pushing out so the door can be sealed a final time to prevent the Haagii breaking in.' He took a breath, and again searched the faces of those gathered. 'Make peace with whichever god, or goddess, you serve. We leave now.'

'It will be mid-morning outside,' a Guildsman, Ferris, whispered to Tim, as they waited.

'Time doesn't matter now,' Tim quietly replied. He motioned to twelve warriors, carrying light crossbows, to move forward, and form three rows, the foremost kneeling, the rear row standing full height, so all twelve crossbows could be fired simultaneously. 'Fire only if there are Haagii. Otherwise, step aside to let the others through,' Tim whispered. 'Good luck,' he added. He signalled to the doorkeepers.

Four startled Haagii reached for their swords, when the metal door swung open in the rubble of the ruined palace Royal Library, but they were cut down by a lethal burst of crossbow bolts. Tim ushered the first line of defenders into the bright sunlight, and followed, leading the larger body into the open air, for the first time in days.

The sunlight hurt their eyes, as they adjusted from the torch and lamp-lit gloom of the fortress, but they had the element of surprise and overwhelmed a squad of thirty Haagii stationed around the ruined walls and doorways of the inner palace. Eighty warriors, armed with bows and crossbows, turned to visible targets on the wall nearest the palace ruins, and loosed bolts and arrows, cutting down the shocked enemy.

Rattled by the defenders' onslaught, the closest Haagii retreated, but their shouts of alarm brought Haagii warriors pouring out of the old Haardrishii barracks and surrounding buildings. Hopelessly outnumbered, the archers abandoned their missile-fire for swords, pikes, and axes as the Haagii pressed the attack.

Tim used his small hand-held assassin's crossbow to deadly effect, reloading the thin metal darts the weapon fired with inhuman speed, until he found himself surrounded by too many enemies to use the crossbow. With a defiant yell, he tossed it aside, drew the short sword borrowed from Sasha's scabbard, and hewed into the Haagii. 'To the gate!' he yelled, above the din of conflict, and began a mad scramble around and through the warriors who lunged and swung at him, cutting down any who came within sword's length, as he dodged and weaved toward the open castle gate. Though he sensed movement all around him, in the chaotic turmoil of battle, he had no time to see how many others were moving with him. He felt stinging pain as Haagii swords found their mark on his exposed arms and legs, and one pike sliced across his forehead as he ducked too slowly, but he fought the pain, vowing he would not fall.

The gate tower loomed above him, but a wall of Haagii blocked the exit. The heroic charge was over. He heard a battle-cry to his left, and when he glanced sideways he saw twenty or more Kingdom warriors charge into the massing Haagii, forcing their way through the gate defenders by sheer determination. He moved to his left, and let himself be caught in their current, and a moment later they were outside the castle on Castle Road, in the open, with the

Haagii ten paces behind.

In the brief lull, he counted the survivors: eighteen, out of two hundred and twenty-seven. Still, he never expected to make it this far. He tasted sweat and blood pooling in the corner of his mouth, and every warrior with him was smeared in a brutal cocktail of their own and their enemies' blood. As he studied his hopeless situation, the Haagii coming like death out of the castle gate toward the decimated band, a thought made him grin. Claarn would've loved this moment. The red-haired giant always wanted to fight the last heroic stand. How he would scowl when he learned what Tim Gaelus had done in his place.

A howl from the Haagii broke his reverie as the enemy charged, bloodlust burning in their eyes. The exhausted and bloodied Kingdom warriors were overrun, and Tim plunged headlong into a brutal fight to save himself, despite the odds. He cut and swung, rolled, pushed, used every skill his weary, wounded and starved assassin's body could muster, but around him he heard the screams and groans of the dead and dying, and knew his was the fight of the cornered fox brought to bay by the pack of hounds. Determined not to die easily, he dealt out death freely, even as he felt the points of his enemies' weapons bleeding him too.

When a gap between the Haagii opened, he seized the opportunity, rolled, and scrambled to his feet at the edge of the road that dropped twenty arm spans to the next switchback section. He dodged a sweeping blow from the nearest Haagii, and struck back, sending his victim sprawling between his fellows, who turned as one to face the lone assassin survivor. 'So it ends here,' Tim muttered angrily, and tensed to meet their final attack.

Then the strangest thing happened. The Haagii turned their eyes from him, with a collective gasp of astonishment, and gazed past his shoulder onto the plain, pointing and gesticulating. Tim measured that something remarkable was happening from the awe and terror spreading across their leathery faces, and unable to resist curiosity he turned his head to see what was distracting his enemy – and stared incredulously.

At the edge of the ruins that had once been the Great City, a river of gold moved in a widening flood through the black Haagii army, drowning the enemy it swept over, leaving in its wake Haagii corpses. At its head rode a warrior in gold, bearing a shining sword of light, and beside him rode a red-haired giant, a dark-haired woman warrior, and a figure in silver robes, surrounded by dark shadows. Overcome with a pang of inner joy, Tim never saw the Haagii warrior who struck him from behind.

"Good defence is the first measure of strong attack."

"A Guardian learns to move with his enemy's blow and dull the force of its impact."

"Retreat is sometimes the most potent form of attack."

Anonymous, selected teachings of The Way

Twenty

'The plains are ours!' cried a Devi, as he reined in his black horse before the Golden King, and a dozen more Kingdom riders galloped to join the knot of horses on the rise before the opening to Central Gate. Above them, the Andrakian Mountains rose to their snow-tipped heights like ancient sentinels.

Andra saluted the Devi and dismissed the warriors. They wheeled their mounts and descended the slope toward the front ranks drawn up before the lower reaches of Central Gate. Their darker shapes skirted a thousand-strong phalanx of golden armoured warriors gazing silently toward the valley and old broken walls of the gate that once barred access to the plains of Ky. Even though the Kingdom's survival and resurgence depended on the ancient warriors of the dead Dragonlord Andrakis, the Kingdom warriors avoided the silent eternal golden warriors, fearing them more than the swarming minions of the living Dragonlord.

King Andra steadied his mount, and gazed into the hazy middle-distance, across the plains, as he assimilated the Devi's news. For three months, they harried and fought and drove the hosts of Haagii and Dark Warriors, and other enemy, back from the siege of the Great King's castle and the ruins of the Great City. For three months, the Golden Warriors and the Golden Knights, led by Andra and Claarn and Marella, and supported by the survivors from the fortress of Andrakis, wrought silent, lethal and methodical vengeance on the fear-driven Haagii. It took less than three days to rout the force around the castle plateau, but the Haagii armies separated, running west, north, northeast and southeast to escape their nemesis, and so Andra was forced to split his meagre forces, leaving Claarn to pursue the two groups heading north, and Marella to follow the southeast army. The bulk of the Haagii withdrew westward, and that was where Andra and the sword of Abreotan were most needed.

What started as a speedy campaign, bogged down when the Haagii resistance collapsed in terror at the seemingly invincible onslaught of the Golden Warriors, and the Haagii army fragmented into a hundred groups dispersing in every possible direction along the western section of the plains of Ky. No Haagii could be allowed to remain on the plains, no Dark Warrior spared, so while Andra and the main Kingdom force bottled the Haagii into Central Gate he coordinated groups to seek and destroy the fragments.

But he commanded an army full of dissension. The Kingdom soldiers, the few surviving Haardrishii, and the recruited warriors from all parts of the Kingdom, were eager and determined to rid the land of the Haagii menace and wreak the vengeance they demanded for the atrocities and defeats endured throughout the invasion in the past spring and summer, but they were uneasy, suspicious, and afraid of the Golden Warriors Andra led from Dragon's Tooth.

The Golden Warriors were neither alive nor dead. They said nothing, neither ate nor drank, and no one had seen them sleep. They were unnatural, the spawn of a Dragonlord. They acted as an extension of the Golden King's hand and mind, a form of Abreotan's sword – a killing machine. No warrior bond grew between them and the Kingdom's warriors. No such bond could be forged between the living and un-living. Only in battle did the Golden Warriors come alive, move of their own accord, so long as an enemy was near, and then they worked with uncanny coordination as an army, sensing pressure from dangerous quarters, responding to their needs as one organism, using the whole to protect the individual, the individual to protect the whole. The magic with which the dead Dragonlord had moulded them, turning them forever from life to un-life, was powerful beyond Andra's imaginings, and he began to understand the awesome threat the living Dragonlord, Mareg, posed to the people over whom he'd been made King. What mighty battles were fought in the past between

Dragonlords and their armies? he wondered.

The Golden Warriors didn't fight without loss. Though they were neither living nor dead, they could be beaten in battle, the magic binding an individual broken by physical force, but the handful who fell were overwhelmed by fanatical groups of Dark Warriors whose desperate efforts to break through the front ranks, early in the retreat from the ruins of the Great City, led them to isolate some Golden Warriors and cut them down. Mareg's strongest warriors struggled to bring down one golden warrior at a time, and when the full realisation struck the Haagii army they panicked and ran, scattering to escape the terror the Golden King with the fiery sword unleashed upon them.

Claarn's pursuit of escaping enemy took less time because his force outstripped the retreating Haagii, overtaking them to the west, and forcing the north bound army to turn east, away from Anedya Wood. A fierce battle, outside the ruins of Crystal, saw the Haagii defeated and a great many slain, but some escaped to join with a smaller band heading into the Valley of Rivers, and Claarn took a small portion of his Golden Warrior contingent in pursuit, while sending the main force to join Andra's army. That was four weeks ago. Most Haagii in the Valley of Rivers had been caught, but the last report Claarn dispatched by rider said there were pockets of Haagii hiding in the foothills of the Ureykyeu and Andrakian Mountains, and they were proving difficult to locate.

More serious news arrived from Marella that morning. Her army pursued the Haagii along the shores of the Lake of Peace, across Amat River, east as far as Vest, sweeping the plains free of the enemy, but there she met determined resistance, and even the Golden Warriors made little headway against significant odds. She was forced to take a defensive position at the base of the Dwarven Mountains to hold off the Haagii. Andra remembered a large Haagii contingent withdrew from the siege and headed east to destroy Targa. His personal force held the Haagii at bay in Central Gate, so he could spare the Kingdom warriors who bolstered his army to go to Marella's aid. And he would go with them.

Yellow-white fires crackled along the full length of the front ranks, lighting fifty paces into the night. Autumn's half-moon slid between invisible clouds, and red and gold sparks spiralled skyward, trying to imitate the bluer light of the stars before they winked out. Marella turned her gaze from the sky to study a knot of figures silhouetted by the flickering light of one fire and shivered as the cold air creeping down from the Dwarven Mountains bit her cheeks. Golden armour glinted at each fireside, and she wondered what kept the warriors alive, as she'd wondered every night since leading them from the castle plateau.

She didn't understand magic, and she didn't want to understand it. Like her compatriot, Claarn, she grew up in Tressel Deep, away from the world of magical power, and she distrusted it. The Royal Chancellor was a sorcerer, and everything he meddled with turned sour. He brought Andra and them all to Dragon's Tooth where the army of Golden Warriors was entombed, and he encouraged Andra to release them.

She'd never seen warriors like them. They were matches for anyone, even Claarn, she feared. Andra ordered her contingent to obey her every command, until he ordered otherwise, and they did: without question, without passion, without living, and that made her uncomfortable. Not one Golden Warrior perished in the constant skirmishes across the plains, while they mercilessly pursued the retreating enemy, up until the full Haagii force met them at Vest – and even in that battle their losses were minimal. For every Golden Warrior lost, five hundred Haagii fell. They didn't feel anything but a death blow. Their prowess over-awed Marella.

She pulled her hood over her long dark locks and moved to a fireside, near her tent. A dozen faces glanced up at her approach, but no one stood. She was in charge, but she told those who served her to never bow or acknowledge her rank, except to obey her instructions, so no one bowed to her, but the Kingdom warriors followed her with undisputed loyalty, respecting her warrior skill and her authority. 'How long before we can expect an answer from the King?' she asked a dour-faced Devi, who squatted beside her in the firelight.

He replied, 'Within a day. It's almost ten days since the messenger was sent.'

Marella cast a cursory glance over the faces at her circle. All had struggled through the siege, fighting the Haagii, hunger, and despair, but so few were left from the Great Armies Thana called into existence. Most warriors, who marched with her force, were survivors of the Haagii invasion: tough, hard-bitten, driven by revenge and desperation to drive out the enemy. She had none of the surviving Haardrishii, except two Devis, as her second-in-command.

Devi Erron sat opposite her at the fire. His face, like her leg and arm, bore a long scar from a Haagii sword, and seemed permanently set in a frown. She never saw the man smile. The other, Devi Tyrol, was a tall, athletic warrior who opposed the breakout attempt from the fortress of Andrakis on the last day of the siege. He was out in the night, watching over the army. He preferred solitude, except when he had to speak or lead as part of his duty. In battle, he was quick and ruthless. Marella admired his prowess with the lance, which he wielded with consummate ease and deadly precision.

For almost a month, the enemy checked her force at Vest. Eventually, conceding her army could not defeat the enemy because of the sheer number ranged in opposition, she sent for reinforcements. In the interim, she withdrew her soldiers to the relative safety of the Dwarven Mountain foothills, using inaccessible shale hillsides to hinder the Haagii. The Haagii tried several times to burst through the flat pass between the Ureykyeu and Dwarven mountains, onto the plains of Ky, to head for Central Gate and reunite with their comrades, but each time the Golden Warriors and the Kingdom soldiers held them back. Both sides settled into a long wait, and the longer they waited, the greater the advantage became for Marella's army, if Andra or Claarn sent aid. That was her main hope.

A figure in chain mail emerged from the darkness, and announced, 'The King is here.'

Twenty One

Milly watched the tall, silver-haired Chancellor walk between the rubble of the palace ruins toward the low wall that once formed part of the Royal Library. Three workers clearing stones stood aside as the Chancellor passed. He entered the opening, into the corridors of the fortress, and descended.

'I wonder where he's going?' asked fair-haired Aaron who stood beside Milly. 'That's the first time he's emerged from his tower since King Andra drove the Haagii away.'

'I don't know,' Milly replied absent-mindedly. She turned to Aaron with a serious frown. 'Find Patti and tell her you've seen the Chancellor heading into the fortress. Tell her I'm following him.'

As Milly went to clamber down from the shattered castle parapet, Aaron grabbed her sleeve. 'I'm coming with you.'

'No,' she hissed. 'Tell Patti. She'll know what to do.' She pulled her sleeve free, slid down the broken stonework, and scampered after the Chancellor.

Aaron watched her go and waited until she slipped into the entrance that led into the fortress heart before he slid down to find Patti. Milly was his best friend, and he desperately wanted to go after her, but if he did she would scold him with those big blue eyes, and he'd feel angry and foolish in her presence. She was clever, and quick. She learned assassin tricks quickly and easily from Tim, and thieves' skills from Patti and Jen, much more easily than he learned them, though he tried hard, and he did as well as anyone else in the fortress during the siege weeks. But Milly was different: she was smarter. He was glad she chose him to be her friend.

Milly ran on silent feet, along the sloping corridors and down three flights of steps, before she caught sight of the Chancellor's receding back in a pool of flickering torch light.

She slowed to follow at a respectable distance, aware very few people remained inside the fortress after the Haagii menace was removed. The Chancellor passed two old women, as he descended, and they glanced at Milly as she snatched a fresh torch brand and slipped by. Carrying a torch made it more imperative she maintain a wary distance from the Chancellor, but she guessed where he was headed: the Deep Cave. Why does he want to go there? she wondered.

The Haagii randomly destroyed everything they found in the Maze, and several upper corridors and rooms lay open and exposed to view since the Great City's devastation. The surviving thieves retrieved what they could from the upper sections and spent three weeks rooting out terrified Haagii who had retreated deeper into the Maze to escape retribution. Some lower sections, closer to the plateau, were flooded when A Ahmud Ki dispelled the glyph created to bar the Haagii from the Deep Cave. The Maze was no longer the secretive, all-hallowed place it had been before the war. Its mystery, a pervading sense of fascination and cause for fear even Milly sensed when Andra had taken her into its depths, was destroyed.

At the last metal door before the Deep Cave, she shielded her torch, and peeked into the dark, and shivered. The Chancellor's unerring ability to travel without light put her at an enormous disadvantage. She thought of Tim Gaelus' skill to see in the dark, and doubted she could ever become an assassin like him because of his natural ability. Not that killing people appealed to her, but she admired his dexterity, his precision, his timing, athleticism and intelligence. Or she had, she reminded herself.

Tim's disappearance, during the battle to retake the plateau, upset everyone. She helped in the fruitless search for him, among the corpses on Castle Road and in the rubble of the palace, but no one found him: only his dagger, and the sword he borrowed from Sasha, at the bottom of the plateau cliff. Tim had disappeared. Claarn and Andra reluctantly agreed he was most likely taken prisoner by the retreating Haagii forces, but though Andra's Golden Warriors routed many of the Haagii in the pursuit across the plains of Ky, and many Haagii prisoners were released or saved, Tim did not return.

Sasha took longer to recover, when she learned Tim's fate, and Milly noticed the dramatic change in the woman's attitude to everything. She was colder, distant, as if her spirit had dried up, and she spent much time alone, wandering the ruins, sword in hand, practising skills, not of an assassin but of a warrior, rebuilding her strength with silent, ferocious determination, and single-mindedness no one misunderstood. Milly tried to talk to Sasha, but the woman was unresponsive, even to Milly's charms, choosing to give brief answers, and avoiding laughter or happiness that Milly tried to evoke, and it made Milly sad.

Milly edged back, as a soft light appeared ahead, in the centre of the Deep Cave. Satisfied it wasn't coming toward her, she doused her torch and used the distant glow to creep along the corridor to the cavern entrance, where she spied the Chancellor standing beside the centre boulder. A small sphere floated an arm span above him, shedding a gentle glow, and his silver, braided locks glittered in the magical light. As Milly crouched to watch, he paused, frozen, like a tapestry she'd seen in Patti's rooms. He stretched his arms wide, and she heard the phrase, 'Staenan uphebban', in a language she didn't recognise, although it had a familiar lilt, like she'd heard Tim use when he farewelled Sasha.

To her amazement, the heavy boulder shivered, like a wild creature woken from a vast sleep, and gradually rose, revealing a circular, water-filled shaft. The Chancellor's hands indicated a direction left and the floating boulder moved that way, drifted to the ground and was inert, as if it had never been anywhere but where it now was lying.

Milly tried to hold her breath, fearing her heart was pounding loud enough even for the Chancellor to hear. She knew he had magical power, though, like so many people in the Kingdom, she wondered why he rarely exercised it, especially in the war against the Haagii where his magic was sorely needed.

The Chancellor was concentrating on the circular well. He wove his hands furiously, forming intricate patterns she couldn't follow, and he circled the well, mouthing words she couldn't hear, but his show fascinated her. The water in the well glittered with an inexplicable red hue and started rippling with life energy. It reared out of the hole like a liquid serpent, hissing and roiling along its tubular length, as it rose and arched toward the natural doorway leading to the lake from whence it had come in flood. Arm span upon arm span of glittering water, solid shape, liquid consistency, rose, twisting and coiling, toward the doorway, and disappeared up the stairs, while the Chancellor's hands worked through the arcane patterns and he whispered the words of magic to drive the water's force. The water python's tail vanished through the door, but the Chancellor maintained his concentration several moments more, slowing the spell-weaving, until he made a final, decisive cutting movement across the horizontal plane.

And Milly saw his eyes, burning red; bright, fiery red. Terror rose in her breast, as she fought her desire to scream, even though it seemed he was staring directly at her hiding place in the corridor. He'd seen her. She knew it. Her legs tensed to spring into running, but she was riddled with fear. Then the Chancellor turned away, and he wavered beside the empty shaft. As she swallowed, to fight the dryness of her mouth, he vanished, along with the light sphere, leaving the Deep Cave in darkness, as if there'd never been anyone there, as if Milly had woken in the middle of the night from a terrible nightmare.

A Ahmud Ki shook out his robes and blinked, letting his eyes adjust, his ears concentrate on sound. Beautiful silence. The light sphere brightened at his thought, until it lit the wall of boulders filling the central shaft and revealed the narrow crawl to his left. At his feet, was the bloated, decaying corpse of Peret. The Apprentices waited as he ordered. Such loyalty deserves a better reward, he thought, cynically, as he stepped over the body and moved into the narrow tunnel.

Outside the ornate golden door to Andrakis' tomb, he found five more Apprentice corpses. He edged them aside. All twelve, who faithfully followed him in, served their purpose because they opened the way to reach the Dragonlord's tomb, so he felt no waste, no remorse. All things to suit my ends, he reminded himself. For me, it has always been so, since Time's beginning, and will always be so for a Dragonlord. New Apprentices could be trained, if needed, after Mareg fell. He conjured a pass spell and entered the golden hexagonal chamber within.

The green glyph entrapping Andrakis Va'ristrin Nyavardenet's physical remains glowed as brightly as ever, adding lustre to the Dragonlord's golden armour. This is what A Ahmud Ki sought. He had everything else: the Dragonlord's knowledge and mind. With Andra wearing one set of golden armour, leading Andrakis' enchanted knights against the Haagii, it was necessary for A Ahmud Ki to be appropriately dressed, so he came to claim the last part of his inheritance, that which he'd left behind.

He detected subtle changes, not in the glyph but in its prisoner. The life was gone. The figure sagged, appearing to be held in place by external forces. The braided silver locks, identical to A Ahmud Ki's own, were faded to greyish white, and the face was decaying, its handsome strength sapped. Although he knew he was the cause of the change, the dead Dragonlord's appearance unnerved A Ahmud Ki. Immortality had finally escaped Andrakis. Will it also flee from me one day?

A Ahmud Ki snuffed his death-thoughts and focussed on the prize he intended to take. The armour looked as bright as the day it was forged, and the great battle-axe on Andrakis' belt gleamed. The body could rot, as far as he was concerned. He had his own, and Andrakis certainly had no more need of it. The real challenge was the glyph.

He studied the bright glow. What he gleaned from Andrakis' memory was that the sword of Abreotan created the imprisoning glyph. Aian Abreotan confronted Andrakis within the chamber, and used the sword's power to subjugate the Dragonlord, taking away his magic, and locking him in permanent stasis. Andrakis hadn't understood how that was possible – only that the sword nullified his magical strength.

A Ahmud Ki suppressed a smile. The Dragonlord was equally as staggered by A Ahmud Ki's imprisonment of his mind within the crystal pyramid. Andrakis was far more limited than he imagined himself to be: so much for the mighty Dragonlords. He, A Ahmud Ki, was already mightier. He held the Five Ki. The bearer of Abreotan's sword was his benefactor. He had drained the power and knowledge of the Dragonlord Andrakis. Who could boast as much?

He eased a step closer and focussed on the glyph's patterning. Like the one he deconstructed to unlock Andrakis' treasure hoard, this glyph was complex, woven with powerful magic. Its patterning felt familiar, but, as he probed into its fabric, he sensed subtler qualities, keys and locks with distinct variations on the other glyph, and he began to understand why Andrakis was unable to break free, despite his awesome Dragonlord abilities. The magic of Abreotan's sword was ancient, infused with hybrid elements drawn from the oldest Elvenaar knowledge, the strongest spells at the root of existence, power that spawned the first Dragonlords and gave them dominion over the world. It was a magic he was only beginning to understand, the magic of the Fifth Ki, the magic he sucked from the essence of Andrakis. Here indeed was a challenge he would enjoy. To have Andrakis' golden armour, and the battle-axe, he would need to be greater than any Dragonlord. A Ahmud Ki concentrated on the glyph with grim determination, and the red fire brightened in his eyes.

'Are you certain he saw?' asked Patti, bending forward from her chair, her ample body threatening to flow from her loose tunic.

Milly nodded. 'He was looking straight at the place where

I was hiding with bright red eyes. I thought he was going to cast a spell at me.'

Patti threw a quizzical glance at Jen, before she patted Milly on the shoulder and smiled reassuringly. 'You're a good little lass, my Milly. I'll look into what you've told us. Something about that Chancellor always smacks of wrong-doing.' Patti heaved off her chair, and ushered Milly out of the room.

Aaron skipped alongside, accompanying his friend, as she walked up the corridor, Artega padding silently behind. They clambered into the sunlight among the castle ruins. 'Did he really just disappear?' Aaron asked, full of wide-eyed curiosity.

'That's what I saw,' Milly replied flatly, annoyed with her friend's disbelief.

Aaron tried to change tack. 'I wonder why he's gone down there?

She shrugged, and squeezed through a gap in the old Royal garden wall, and waited for Aaron and Artega to follow. 'Tim never trusted him,' she said, as Aaron straightened. Artega trotted toward a broken statue.

'I think he's evil,' said Aaron. 'He's never around when the fighting's happening, and he hasn't gone off with the soldiers to fight the Haagii. He's probably a coward.'

Milly led the way through a clump of burgeoning green bushes, rare survivors of the castle devastation, onto the soiled gravel pathway that ran to the Chancellor's black tower. The imposing odour of decomposing flesh assaulted their noses, and they paused, staring at the tower. At its base, was the rotting corpse of a black dragon, on its side, the head keeled over and separated to the right in the dry foliage.

Aaron shivered, as if a cold wind breathed down his neck. 'It's creepy this place,' he whispered, staring at the tower. 'Everything else is wrecked, but there's not a single mark on that thing.'

'It's made of magic,' Milly replied, as if her simple explanation was all Aaron needed.

'It stinks of dragon,' he complained.

Despite the efforts of the defenders who remained to clean the debris and bury the bodies, after Andra, Claarn, and Marella led the armies in pursuit of the enemy, no one successfully removed the dead creature's corpse. It was too large to manhandle over the castle walls, and its scales proved too tough for the implements people brought in the hope of dissecting the beast to remove it. Many feared the Chancellor would order its removal at any cost, especially given the stages of putrefaction it went through in the ensuing weeks, but he hadn't emerged from his solid tower since returning with King Andra, preferring to remain locked inside with the shadows he brought from Dragon's Tooth.

Milly started toward the tower. 'Where are you going?' Aaron hissed.

She stopped to look over her shoulder at the boy, her brown hair sweeping around her cheek. 'Just having a look,' she answered.

'There's nothing to see,' he insisted, fear mounting. 'We've been around it lots of times. There's no doors, no windows, nothing.'

'I know. I'm just curious,' she replied, and turned toward the tower again. Artega emerged from the ruined garden and trotted toward the dragon corpse, nose inquisitively inspecting the stench.

Reluctantly, Aaron followed. This is really very silly, he thought. Sometimes he wondered why he was Milly's friend at all.

Twenty Two

The first winter snow clouds hung ominously over Central Gate, their powdery shapes illuminated by a full moon, and there was a sharp edge to the air. Winter was about to descend in its full fury on the Kingdom.

Andra shifted uneasily in his saddle. He was still uncomfortable astride a horse. He hadn't ridden a horse, until the Sisters of Veras gave mounts to Milly and himself to escape the Haagii advance on Spurl. He remembered the headlong scramble, the mad plunge down the hillside toward Bear's ferry, and how he clung desperately to his horse's mane, more afraid of falling off than of having to confront the enemy. Milly was unperturbed, being a competent rider, but the girl's heart was broken when she learned the Haagii slaughtered the horses outside Bear's hut. She loved them dearly. When all this madness is over, he decided, I will give her the best horse in the King's stables. He leaned forward in the stirrups, and patted his horse's muscular, scarred neck. 'Easy, Firebrand,' he whispered. 'Let's go to the top of the rise and see what the moon shows up.'

Four short months had passed since he acquired Firebrand. Claarn brought him the horse after they rode the Dragonlord's death-beasts out of Dragon's Tooth. Though the golden-armoured undead steed that carried the Dragonlord seemed immortal, Andra couldn't bring himself to ride it. He feared its unblinking gaze, its precise reaction to his thoughts, its unfettered strength.

'This is a real prize!' Claarn declared, as he led the grey gelding toward Andra, on the battlefield at the base of the castle plateau, after they drove the Haagii from the Great City.

As much as he disliked riding, Andra knew he had to persevere, and Claarn's offering rescued him from his greater loathing of the Dragonlord's horse. Firebrand was courageous, but he wasn't fearless, and that saved Andra in several scrapes, because the horse lunged away from the thickest knots of enemy warriors and the sharpest pike points. Andra's golden armour was stronger than standard plate, bonded with powerful magic, and it turned aside spear thrusts and a sword sweeps, but it still had joints where carefully aimed or probing points could bring him down. Had he not ridden Firebrand, the chances were he would have been cut down by overconfidence, unwary of unseen dangers, because the living dead creatures had no understanding of fear. The Dragonlord's horse was better carrying a Dragonlord warrior; undead aboard undead.

At the summit, Andra reined in and stroked Firebrand's ears. The biting air nipped at his cheeks and nose, as he stared across the moonlit plain, where dark patches, the ruins of peasant farms and tiny hamlets, marred the silvered stretch of earth.

In the near distance, he spied a large shadow; the ruins of Spurl. There were no survivors. The wooden palisade, hastily erected to keep out the invaders, was a charred line of ash around the town's perimeter. Every building had been destroyed. There was no trace of the convent. The Sisters of Veras had disappeared, wiped from existence, as if they never lived. Andra repeated Emiris' enigmatic revelation she delivered at their parting: 'The Sisters of Veras have a role to play, beyond the destruction of Spurl and the convent,' she said, 'but to play it, we must stay here.' It was like many prophecies he'd heard since leaving The Vale, its meaning obscure. He had hoped to find the Sisters hidden in the ruins, but search parties found no trapdoors and no living soul in the blackened ruins. Emiris' vision had failed her.

Beyond Spurl, a dark smudge marked the southern edge of Wynwuduholt. Andra knew that, in the fire-ravaged desolation of that great forest, Terath and Mirith, and the Elders of Wudufaesten, must have survived. Their magic was too powerful to fall to the Haagii. After his investiture, he would convince the Aelendyell to have faith in the rest of the

Kingdom. He smiled, wondering how Freyar, or Terath, or even Elder Tirenythlae, would respond to seeing the woroldbuend they saved from death return to them as King. He thought of Mirith, and his heart quickened at the memory of her softness and beauty.

To the south, he could see the fringe of Darken Wood, and beyond that darkness was Port, the second largest city in the Kingdom. What happened there? he wondered. Did the people find a way to survive? He wanted to go there, to learn the city's fate, but he'd seen enough to sicken his heart.

The battle for Axxon Plains was brutal. Surprised by Andra's force, the Haagii initially scattered, making the first encounter wholesale slaughter. So many Haagii fell at the hands of the Golden Warriors the earth ran red with their blood, and in the cool evening the plains steamed from the heat of dying bodies.

Andra led the push into Central Gate, where the Haagii planned to hold the Kingdom warriors at bay, until winter passed and they were strong again. Meanwhile, Marella coordinated her attack from the east, and the unfortunate enemy were trapped between two armies. The Haagii surrendered in hundreds, leaving a cohort of Dark Warriors to fight to the bitter end.

By the second day, the Haagii army on the plains rallied at Abreotan River and a protracted struggle began. Attack followed counterattack, the Haagii relying on sheer numbers to drag down their fair share of Golden Knights and Warriors.

On the fifth day, Claarn, Marella and Andra devised plans to hit and run at the enemy ranks, gradually encircling sections of the Haagii army to cut them off from the main body, until the Haagii were too depleted to resist a massed Kingdom force. The strategy was slow in operation, but it worked. The surviving Haagii were trapped in a tempestuous final battle on the tenth day, which saw them collapse and retreat northward, into the Kobold Ranges.

Eighteen thousand Haagii and other warriors in their ranks surrendered during the conflict. There were as many prisoners as there were Kingdom warriors by the end.

Claarn cursed their luck, complaining the Haagii had no guts for a good fight, and now the Kingdom was stuck with feeding them. 'What is the point of fighting an enemy,' he argued, 'when all you end up doing is caring for him? The Dark Warriors are better opponents,' the rankled giant concluded, as he stood to stretch his aching muscles. 'At least they fight to the death.'

Andra watched mist spreading across the earth, like fog rising from the graves, like creeping smoke from the pyres to burn the dead: so many dead. The Haagii suffered innumerable losses, thousands of their warriors falling like black chaff before golden scythes. But the Kingdom had its dead as well. Survivors of the siege – the warriors, farmers, hunters, trappers, merchants and thieves who escaped the Haagii invasion and joined behind the rallying cry of the Inheritor, King Andra, 'He Who Bears the Sword of Abreotan' – lay on the battlefields of Axxon and Spurt and in Central Gate in ironic celebration of the freedom they had won. And some of the Dragonlord's Golden Warriors had fallen, dragged from undeath to true death by a desperate and crazed enemy. The battle was won and lost, and neither side had cause to celebrate. 'Is this what a King must do?' Andra asked Firebrand's pricked ears. 'Must I bear a sword that cuts both enemy and wielder?'

The sunlight was brittle, the day cold. From the hillside overlooking the ash heap that was the town of Axxon, Andra watched the Kingdom troops assemble. He thought back to the last great assembly of the Kingdom's army, the fateful mobilization of Great King Thana's forces before they marched north almost two years ago. Then, twenty thousand eager warriors, the Four Wheels of the Great Armies, gathered to hear their King bid them bring glorious victory to the Kingdom in his name.

How the war had cut their numbers. The North and West Wheels no longer existed, massacred at the battle of The Rim

Shield, the South Wheel lost over half its contingent in the defence of Central Gate, and the East Wheel suffered major losses in the siege of the Great City. Many perished in the past four months. Of the original twenty thousand warriors of the Great Kingdom, a bare four thousand remained, and they were tired, hungry, ill and battle-scarred. Only their faith in a living prophecy, the sword of Abreotan, kept them going. Knowing they fought for him filled Andra with guilt. They fought and died because an accident made him King.

Andrakis' Golden Warriors numbered seven thousand in the catacombs of Dragon's Tooth, but almost two thousand were dragged down in the pitched battles with the Haagii forces. Nevertheless, over five thousand undead warriors were obediently serving their master, the newly reborn Abreotan, the Inheritor, King Andra. The Chancellor, A Ahmud Ki, had been right to release the Dragonlord's army from the catacombs of Dragon's Tooth. Without it, hope for the Kingdom would have disappeared, along with the people trapped in Andrakis' fortress.

But Andra remained uncomfortable in the presence of the unnaturally silent Golden Warriors. Their blank faces and colourless cold eyes gazed on a world that, for them, existed for killing. What would become of them when Mareg's forces withdrew, beaten – when the war was over for good – when there were no more battles to be fought, and no more killing to be done? Was there a way to return them to the depths of Dragon's Tooth and their eternal sleep? Could they be locked away again, like old armour, waiting to be dragged out in another time of need somewhere in the future? Who has that power? Andra wondered. The sword, or the Chancellor?

He searched the milling troops for familiar figures. Claarn was walking toward Marella, and she, on a black horse, waited for her companion. When he reached her, she dismounted, passing her reins to a nearby warrior, and the pair climbed the rise toward Andra. Through everything, the two warriors survived. Their friends, those dragged with them from their home in Tressel Deep by Thana's Haardrishii, were long dead, but these two, with giant hearts, endured. They defied the odds, even in the thick of battle. There was no denying their consummate warrior skills. Claarn's excessive size made him a man mountain, a brute tower of strength, and Haagii armour could not withstand a mighty blow from the giant's sword or axe. Marella's strength was enhanced by her speed and timing. What Claarn couldn't overwhelm, Marella could outsmart. Together, they were equal to anything Mareg might throw at them.

Seeing them approach, made Andra remember other friends, friends he met and from whom he parted, friends who had died. Alain. Stephen. Derik. Terath. Bear. Mirith. And Tim. He missed Tim Gaelus. Since his disappearance, Andra searched for the assassin in every Haagii camp, and in every pile of Kingdom bodies they stumbled upon. The retreating Haagii slaughtered prisoners, rather than abandon them, so he feared the worst for his friend, yet no one reported finding any evidence of his fate. So many had died – too many.

Claarn cleared his throat in an exaggerated manner, as Marella and he reached Andra. 'So,' he said, 'you tell me the Chancellor believes it is a good time for Your Highness' investiture. We have the Haagii army holed up in the Kobold Ranges, decimated, lacking the guts to resist us any longer, and this – this braggart, who calls himself Chancellor, dictates what the King should do? Come back and dress up in fineries for the people, he says. Forget the Haagii. They'll run home with their tails between their legs like the whipped curs they are. What good advice is this?'

Andra would have laughed at his friend's sarcasm, a day or two before, but he had pondered too long on the direction the war was taking and considered too deeply his responsibilities as King. 'Some of us are tired of the killing,' he said without looking up.

He didn't see the giant's startled face. Marella shook her head when Claarn went to argue the point, and the warrior acquiesced, seeing the past months of warring through different eyes. He held back his warrior's love for arms, and the struggle and glory of vanquishing a worthy foe. He had admired and envied Andra's new prowess, after his young friend came into possession of Abreotan's sword, but now he saw the responsibility of bearing the sword was taking a serious toll on the young King. He acknowledged Marella's tacit advice, and clapped a big, friendly arm over Andra's shoulders. 'Pardon my poor manners, Your Highness. You're right. It's about time we had a celebration about all this,' and he laughed. 'It's not every day I get to toast the health of a friend who is a King.'

Twenty Three

A Ahmud Ki studied the crystal pyramid with satisfaction. The final essences of Andrakis' mind were absorbed, dissolved, his. Nothing remained of the once haughty Dragonlord, except a rapidly decaying corpse, slumped on the cold stone floor, entombed deep in the bowels of the plateau. All that had been Andrakis was now A Ahmud Ki.

He turned from the pyramid to cast his eyes over the two golden suits of armour hanging in his chamber. There was little to differentiate them, except for the touch of cruelty worked into Andrakis' battle suit where its shoulders were curved into sharp spikes; small, but potentially lethal in close combat. The suit Andra wore from Dragon's Tooth was battle-scarred, with dents and scratches showing as duller patches, but in every other matter the two suits could easily have been forged in the one foundry by the same hands. There were mysteries about the ancients still eluding A Ahmud Ki's prying mind.

Getting Andra's armour wasn't difficult. Although it was closely guarded, whenever the King wasn't wearing it, the arrangements for his investiture meant it was necessary to have it cleaned and repaired. The armorer, selected to carry out the task, parted with the suit for a day and a night, in exchange for a little food. People in the city ruins were still starving, despite the Kingdom's liberation, and food was worth more than handfuls of gold. A Ahmud Ki needed only a short time to work a charm spell into the armour's structure. Using armour was clumsier than presenting the King with a piece of jewellery, like a neck chain, which he would wear all the time, but Andra was wary of gifts from A Ahmud Ki. He already refused one such offer, before the Haagii fury broke over the defenders in the siege, and A Ahmud Ki saw suspicion in the young man's brown eyes. Waeron Ardath was to blame for that seed of doubt, but

Ardath was dead, so Andra was A Ahmud Ki's for the taking. The charmed suit would serve to weaken the young man's mind, making control of him easy. The best King is a puppet ruler, A Ahmud Ki reminded himself, the Ithosen maxim coming to mind as he began weaving the spell into Andra's armour.

'I'm not wearing anything like that!' Aaron cried angrily, as Jen held up a clean brown vest and green leggings.

'What's wrong with it?' Jen asked, forcing her face into a serious frown, though she longed to laugh at the boy's indignant glare.

'It's got frills on the shirt bit for starters,' he answered.

Patti stopped folding bolts of silk cloth into her locker, and laughed heartily, before saying, 'An' it's a bit too clean for such a lad as you are, too, I bet!'

'I don't mind being clean!' the boy snapped, 'but I'm not wearing stuff that makes me look like-'

'Like what?' Jen asked.

'Like - oh, I don't know like what. I just don't like it.' Frustration forced Aaron into silence.

At that moment, the door swung open and Milly waltzed through in a heavy blue silk dress Patti had cut down to size for her. 'What do you think?' she asked, as she paraded across the centre of the room and curtsied before Jen.

Before anyone could answer, Aaron burst into a fit of giggles.

Milly whirled, eyes blazing. 'What's so funny, Aaron?' she snarled.

'You,' he said and snorted. 'In that thing.'

She hitched up the edges of the full skirt and advanced menacingly on the fair-haired boy. 'What's wrong with this thing, as you call it?'

Recognising danger, Aaron back-pedalled. An angry Milly was not a problem he wanted to face. It was only a silly old dress after all, hardly worth getting killed for.

'What's wrong with it?' Milly pressed, closing on the boy.

'Nothing,' he replied. 'It's-'

'It's what?'

'Different!' he blurted, lost for a safer word 'Different! I've never seen you in one of those things before.'

'This thing is a gown, Aaron. And just because you won't get dressed up doesn't mean we're all going to go as thieves!' Milly said icily, as she cornered him near the locker where Patti was bent over. 'You could at least look half-decent for Andra,' she advised, and fixed her friend with a look that dared him to defy her.

In the brief silence, both boy and girl became aware of other eyes. They turned. Patti and Jen were chuckling, and in the doorway behind them Andra, Claarn, Marella and Sasha, were laughing.

'Get the girl some armour!' Claarn roared with mock heroic rapture. 'At last we have found a warrior no Haagii would dare face in the field of battle, one whose glare would melt the golden armour off the Dragonlord's warriors.'

Milly was pinned by her own embarrassment. When she saw Andra smiling, she blushed and looked down, desperately wanting to leave the room. Her cheeks were on fire. Trapped, unable to rescue herself from her emotions, she spun from Aaron, pushed through the group in the doorway, and fled along the partially open-roofed corridor toward another section of the Maze ruins, the silk material whispering as she ran.

Andra turned to go after the girl, but Sasha caught his arm. 'Stay here,' the assassin instructed quietly. 'I'll go to her. She won't want to see you, of all people.'

Andra looked at Sasha in bewilderment, but she smiled, as if he should know what he didn't in the least understand. She released his arm and headed after Milly, leaving him confused among a grinning circle of friends. 'What was that all about?' he asked Patti, as he entered the room that sat below the cellar of the Guild brothel.

'She's a young girl, but a growing woman, that one,' Patti said, as she recommenced folding cloth. 'Time, straight soon enough.'

'That's an answer?' Andra asked.

'More answer than anyone should need,' Jen intervened. Everyone was grinning at Andra.

Andra looked at the boy, Aaron, who only shrugged to show he didn't understand them any more than Andra did.

'The arrangements are very simple, Your Highness,' Lord Haephus said, with a stately bow. 'Naturally, you appreciate that I, and my priests, would enjoy the opportunity to make greater pomp and ceremony than circumstances allow, but we have done our best to satisfy the traditional conventions of investiture.'

'I'm sure what you have arranged will be more than adequate,' Andra replied with a friendly smile. 'The bowing is unnecessary, Haephus.'

Haephus lifted his head and asked, 'If your subjects don't bow to you, how will you know they will serve you, Your Highness?'

'My Guardian Master told us, in the Teachings of The Way, that loyalty is always mirrored in the eyes,' Andra replied. 'I'd rather see your eyes than the top of your head.'

'You doubt my loyalty to the Inheritor?' Haephus inquired, looking as if Andra had ordered him to be whipped.

'I don't doubt your loyalty, Haephus. You've given me every reason to trust you. I just want you to understand what I mean.

Haephus automatically bowed, and said, 'Thank you,' and corrected himself, and looked directly, if uncomfortably, at Andra. 'I mean, thank you, my Lord King,' he said, with a nervous smile.

'I'm not King until you make me King, Haephus,' Andra replied. 'Just explain what it is I have to do tomorrow.'

A Ahmud Ki observed the High Priest explaining the ceremonial duties to the King-elect from the shadow of his black tower. In black robes, he blended into the wall so that only the keenest eyes could discern him. His metamorphosis to Dragonlord was complete, but the external changes were too prominent. He hated having to move furtively through the labyrinth of the fortress of Andrakis and the castle ruins, because it reminded him of his childling years, as a novitiate in Wynwuduholt, the years of angry impotence when he dreamed of becoming powerful, but he could never have imagined what he had become. Impotence did not restrain him now. No. What forced him to stay aloof, to avoid contact with anyone until after the investiture, was his burning potency, the legacy drained from Andrakis – his eyes of fire. He couldn't attend the investiture, wouldn't see the new King in his charmed golden armour, but that was no longer essential. The plans were made. The die was cast as he intended.

He studied Haephus. Of the original Lords of Thana's reign, only Haephus survived. The others met untimely fates. He engineered Laeowyth's and Nisus' ends, but the others were victims of Mareg's fatal touch – except the foolish Gerran, who found courage long enough to be impaled on one of Andrakis' traps. The only one he ever respected was the old idiot Ardath, but even he meddled in A Ahmud Ki's affairs in the end. If the accident hadn't taken the old Drycraefter, A Ahmud Ki might have enjoyed tussling in a magical confrontation with him.

The King's golden armour was collected from a pre-arranged room in the upper chambers of the fortress. The armorer could be trusted to keep his word: if he didn't, A Ahmud Ki would see he was visited by one of the dracabeorn. But there was no possibility the man would remember what took place. A Ahmud Ki erased the man's memory of the meeting and the armour's exchange with a simple Targan spell. As far as the man knew, he had worked on Andra's golden suit, as asked, and no one visited him.

The messenger summoned to carry A Ahmud Ki's apologies to Lord Haephus and Andra, to say he was very ill and couldn't attend the investiture, was a blind old woman. Her blindness kept his secret. That night, he would slip away from the plateau, with his dracabeorn for company, and head west. With the Haagii threat removed, he had a very old score to settle, before the new King came to full power. The opportunity was ripe.

Milly restrained Artega by his studded leather collar, and stared at the black tower she had grown to hate in the days since the Chancellor walked out and crept back in. No one saw him return, despite the surviving Eyes and Ears of the Guild's vigilance, but she knew he was in there. People were too busy to care about the Chancellor's movements. Working parties were preparing for Andra's investiture, or rebuilding the ruins, and everyone was involved in searching for anything to eat. There was so little food to be found on the plains. Haagii marauders ate or destroyed every stockpile of grain and food, moving like black locusts through the land, devouring everything. Meagre rations of fruits and seeds and nuts were being delivered from the lower mountain slopes and unburned forest fringes, but often what was brought to the plateau was insufficient to feed the hungry masses. The survivors slaughtered the pitifully few remaining horses, cattle, sheep and even pets. She saved Artega from that fate with Patti's help, but the dog was so thin his ribs rippled through his skin as he walked. A long winter and spring loomed, before crops could be coaxed from the soil. Many people were going to die in that time. The Haagii had withdrawn, but the war continued.

Milly was sure she could see someone leaning against the tower, not far from the dragon skeleton, but the figure was motionless, dressed in black, with a hood drawn. Intuition told her it was the Chancellor. Who else would be so near his tower? She followed the direction of his gaze, and saw he was observing the High Priest, in his fancy yellow and red robes, and Andra. The pair were talking and walking around the cleared square, where the palace and the Haardrishii barracks had stood, at the centre of which stood a stage, built from the rubble, for Andra's coronation. Milly checked

211

the almost invisible figure against the tower. He hadn't moved. What was he doing? Why was he still so secretive even with the Haagii pushed away? She knew the Chancellor meant no good to anyone, even though he had saved everyone with his glyph in the Deep Cave to hold back the Haagii. Her curiosity ached for an answer.

She returned her attention to Andra. He was handsome. Without the golden armour, his muscular frame was highlighted under the loose leather jerkin and trousers Jen had sewn. His dark hair had grown, and he let it hang loose, instead of tying it in a ponytail.

His arrival in Patti's room, catching Aaron and her arguing, startled her, and Claarn's oafish remark was too much. She did not want Andra to laugh at her, not when she was in a dress. She had avoided Sasha, even though she knew the assassin only wanted to talk and be a friend. She just didn't want to talk about it. Patti and Jen, and all the others, thought she was a little kid with a silly crush. Maybe it was a crush. Maybe it wasn't. But she wasn't a silly little girl. The little girl died with her father in their home village. She didn't have time to be a silly little girl.

Tomorrow she would wear the blue silk gown, and try not to look like an awkward, gawky thirteen-year-old girl-thief. Jen was going to braid her hair, but it wasn't long enough to be beautiful like that. She prayed he would see her. She was frightened he wouldn't. He couldn't do anything but see her. She was part of the King-elect's retinue. Tomorrow she could be a princess, if only for a little while, and she could stand near Andra, and imagine she was his princess, at least until they made him King. After that, she didn't know what she would be. She was scared she might cry. She didn't want to cry. She'd done enough of that. She didn't want to cry. She wouldn't cry.

Milly looked at the tower and squinted in the dull afternoon light filtering through the clouds. Shadows made finding the Chancellor's figure difficult, black on black. Then she realised he was gone, melted into the tower. What had he come to see? Was he spying on Andra? She peered at the

Chancellor's indestructible, impenetrable black tower, and felt a cold dread ripple up her spine.

She would tell Andra what she had seen – after the investiture, not before – after the investiture, when he was King, and she a mere servant of his Kingdom. She turned toward the square to catch one more glimpse of Andra, but the square was empty. Haephus and Andra were gone too, and she was alone in the silence, atop the rubble of the castle's western wall. She pulled on Artega's collar and withdrew.

Twenty Four

'Hold still,' Marella ordered. She tightened a buckle on his breastplate and tucked it neatly beside his underjerkin. 'There. Better?'

Andra stretched his arms, and walked to the mirror beside the door, to study his golden armour in the torchlight. Squinting, he imagined Abreotan as his reflection.

'Well?' Marella asked again.

'Perfect,' Andra answered, turning to her. 'Where's my helmet?'

Marella lifted it from the chair. 'You won't be wearing it today, 'she reminded him.

'I know,' he replied, 'but it's part of the suit, and I must keep it safe.' He clipped the helmet onto his belt. 'Fairlie, the armorer, did magnificent work to erase the scratches and dents.' He held out his armoured arms for Marella's inspection. 'Not a mark. I've never seen better,' he added with approval.

'It's like new. I wonder if Fairlie is entirely responsible, or whether the magic in the armour lets it mend itself?' she pondered.

Before Andra could consider her suggestion, someone knocked excitedly on the door, and when Marella opened it she met Aaron's beaming face. The boy was dressed exactly as Jen wished, looking every bit a pageboy, ready to serve a King. Marella cast an inspecting eye over the lad and grinned. 'The girls will want a man like this,' she said, winking at Andra. Aaron squirmed.

'Why are you here, Aaron?' Andra asked.

'The priest says it's time you came for the ceremony. Everyone's waiting.'

'Are you to lead me?'

'Yes,' Aaron replied. He paused, as if considering something important he'd forgotten, before adding, 'Your

Majesty.'

Aaron's postscript brought a broad grin to Andra's face. He reached forward and patted the boy's head. 'If it's to be Your Majesty, then I could find no better page than you, Aaron.' His compliment made the lad smile. 'We'd better go,' he added. He gave Marella a kiss on the right cheek, an action that startled her. 'That's for helping me get organised this morning, and for braiding my ponytail with so much patience.'

Marella coughed, nodded, and shifted to the door. 'Come on, it's time you became King officially,' she said hastily, and slipped outside so he wouldn't see embarrassment flooding her face after his kiss. She had no intention of displaying her reaction to him, or anyone else.

'We'd better go,' Andra told Aaron, shaking his head at Marella's departure. He lifted Abreotan's sword from the table and slipped it into the scabbard at his side. 'Now I'm ready,' he announced.

Outside the chamber, a Haardrishii honour guard was waiting, their black armour polished and shining in the torchlight. Great King Thana always kept two hundred Haardrishii in his service, but the war depleted the Haardrishii ranks to less than thirty. So much has to be rebuilt from the ruins in the wake of the Dragonlord's hordes, Andra mused. He saluted the ten warriors, as he passed between them, with Aaron leading along the corridor.

At the head of a flight of stairs, three priests of Teka met them. The priests bowed, and sprinkled sweet liquid fragrance over Andra, and the accompanying Haardrishii, and fell into line behind the party, chanting a soft mantra.

The entrance into the Great King's former Royal Library was swept of debris. It opened into daylight, and as Andra rose from the fortress of Andrakis he saw the gathered crowd awaiting him at the stone platform in the cleared ruins.

On the centre of the stage, High Priest Haephus stood, resplendent in his orange and gold livery, a tiny, peaked purple cap perched on his cropped head. Andra noticed the detail of Haephus' head above everything else. Overnight, the priest's head was shaved, his locks no longer hanging to his shoulders, and Andra wondered what ancient or religious significance existed in cutting the High Priest's hair.

As Andra walked toward the steps, he searched the crowd for familiar faces. Claarn stood at the head of a large contingent of Kingdom warriors, a frown stretched across his bearded visage. Marella and Milly waited at the base of the stage. Milly was wearing the blue gown he'd seen her in, before she ran off. Had Sasha spoken to her? He reached the steps, glanced up at Haephus, and stopped to let Marella and Milly follow Aaron, but Marella delicately indicated he had to go before them. Andra shrugged and ascended.

Haephus explained the whole procedure to him the previous afternoon. On the platform, Haephus would introduce him to the assembly, call down a blessing from Teka, lead him in swearing the Oath of Kings, add a final blessing, and crown him in the absence of the Lord Chancellor, who normally would perform the last duty. Then he would ride out of the ruined castle gates and descend Castle Road, where the people were gathered to wish him a long and prosperous reign as King. At the edge of Dragon River, he was to dismount, touch the waters and the earth with his crown, and swear allegiance to the land and his people. Finally, he was to order the celebrations to begin.

Andra peered over the assembly from the stage and a hush fell. He saw warriors, whose faces he recognised from battle in the past months, and many he didn't know. He felt a sudden need to see Aelendyell faces in the crowd, to know the Kingdom was whole again, but the hope was foolish since his army had not reached the edges of the forests, or communicated with the Aelendyell since the war broke out in all its fury. After this ceremony, there were old sores to heal, old friendships to re-establish, and new relationships to form to reunite the battered Kingdom.

A roar from the crowd broke into his consciousness and he was aware of Haephus staring at him. A voice in front called out, 'Hail the Inheritor! Hail the new King!' and a massed response echoed the cry 'Hail the new King!'

'Kneel,' Haephus whispered.

Milly was watching intently, so he winked at her as he knelt. Tim would have grinned, he thought, as his left knee touched the cool board lain across the stones.

'By all that is righteous,' the High Priest announced to the assembly, 'by all that is wrought by the gods and goddesses who watch over our tiny lives, I call you to witness the anointing of this new King under the benevolence of She who is our patron, She of holiness and purity, Teka, Goddess of All in this Kingdom, and this land.'

Andra let Haephus' litany drone above him. He hadn't realised how committed the High Priest was to his religious practices. He couldn't recall the priests having a high profile in the old Great City. There had been a stone building used for worship, near the Inn of Dragons, on the King's Way, but he'd never been inside it, and he didn't know anyone who had. The High Priest and his assistants were always in the Great King's castle, before the Haagii invasion, where they had private residences. What am I to do about the priests once I am King, especially if they don't serve any significant purpose? he wondered. Are there any gods? Is Teka real? He wanted to sneak another look at the assembly, but Haephus stood over him, touching the shoulder of his golden armour.

'Stand for the oath, my Lord,' Haephus whispered. 'Draw the sword.'

On cue, Andra stood and drew Abreotan's sword from his scabbard, and held the weapon with both hands, point upward, before his chest. The blade caught the dull light from the overcast mid-morning sky and shone with brittle beauty. 'Repeat what I say,' Haephus quietly instructed. The High Priest turned to the crowd and began the Oath. 'Hear me, subjects of the land, for I am your King.'

Andra followed Haephus' lead and repeated the Oath of Kings history attributed to the coronation speech of Aian Abreotan, after he defeated the last Dragonlord. Tradition required every successor to the throne to repeat Abreotan's immortal words, maintaining the link from generation to generation of kings over the thousand years. The Oath was a promise to rule fairly and firmly, giving all people the freedom to live and grow within the Kingdom in return for their loyalty to the throne. It was ironically, Andra noted, a promise to keep peace as King and promote peace between all peoples. The war with Uz Erhaag, the distrust between Aelendyell and human, were anathemas to peace. He felt he was lying, even as he made his Oath, and vowed silently to find other ways to solve disputes. And why hold a sword to make an oath of peace? he wondered.

Haephus passed a final blessing on Andra's head, wishing the new King vision to see clearly, the wisdom to rule with strength, and the humility to understand his weaknesses. He called Milly forward. Resting on a green and black cushion in her hands, she carried the gold griffin crown Thana had worn, and it sparkled as weak rays of sunlight caught a variety of inlaid gems.

Andra was amazed to see it. He assumed the crown was lost in the destruction of the palace and the Great King's castle, and that a new or makeshift crown would be used for the ceremony. Haephus must have rescued the original and hidden it for a time when a King would need crowning.

Then he noticed Milly. Her face was full of radiant concentration, caught in the sombre celebration of his coronation. He saw how she avoided looking directly at him, as she held the crown for Haephus to lift from its resting place. Her iceblue gown made her look more feminine than he remembered the child to be, and older than her years. She was growing into a pretty lady.

The High Priest raised the crown above his head, deliberately letting sunlight play over its jewellery, before he lowered it toward Andra's head, reciting a prayer to Teka to take this new King under her guidance so he might understand the nature of truth and wisdom, and lead his people with strength and fairness. Andra felt the crown press against his hair, and it didn't feel comfortable, as though it would slide from its precarious position. He wanted to hold it in place – even better, remove the clumsy thing, but ceremonial etiquette held him fast.

'Stand, Your Highness,' Haephus whispered.

As Andra stood, Milly silently withdrew, her eyes lowered. He wanted to reach for her hand to make her stay and celebrate his coronation, but he couldn't. He stood and regarded the throng gazing at their new King.

'All hail the Inheritor!' Claarn's powerful voice bellowed from the audience. 'All hail the King of Andrakis!'

'Hail to the King!' a thousand voices echoed. Their cries ran like a retreating ripple away from the square, through the remains of the castle's gates, down to the crowds lined along Castle Road.

Andra was lost in the moment, hearing the people's adulation. He was the warrior become King, who would drive the Dragonlord's servants back to their own lands forever. He would slay the dreaded monster to bring perpetual peace. He was King Andra, King of Andrakis.

Firebrand proudly carried King Andra down the narrow, winding Castle Road, as if he sensed the occasion's importance and was determined to impress the thousands gathered to watch the new King pass. Andra sat stiffly in the saddle, the offending crown constantly threatening to topple. People stared at his golden armour, as if seeing it for the first time, and he heard cries of 'Hail to King Andrakis!' and 'Long reign to the Inheritor!' mixed among the wider shouts of 'Hail King Andra!'

The first segment of the ride passed like a vision seen through the confusing mists of early evening, but as he neared midway he began to take in details that ate away the gloss of his coronation and made him sad, angry and filled with guilt. Behind the cheering and waving masks, he saw hunger gnawing at the people, their growing fear of the oncoming winter, and the lingering starvation the Haagii left behind to consume the sick, the old, the frail and the very young. Their celebration was not a victory celebration, but a plea, a cry for a miracle beyond a sword that could flame and behead dragons. The Inheritor's glory only placed a veneer over the reality of survival in a land ravaged and eaten bare by war.

Andra glimpsed tousled-haired urchins in dirty grey rags; parentless children like those he encountered in the abandoned warehouse the night Tim Gaelus led him into the Great City for the first time. Those remembered faces belonged to the waifs of the forgotten Aelendyell, half and quarter and eighth breeds who populated the thieves' quarters. Some survived the siege and stared up at him from the crowd. But there were other faces, faces of human children whose parents perished in the war and the siege, and they stared up at the new King on his fine steed in his golden armour, in awe of the wealth and power he held, but Andra could see they were tinged with doubt that what he was could change things for the better for them.

At the base of Castle Road, where the road swept in an arc to join the King's Way, a tall woman in black robes waited with a dozen other people Andra also recognised. He reined in Firebrand. The woman bowed and stepped forward. 'Hail to the Inheritor,' she said quietly, looking up at Andra with her dark eyes.

'Hello, Mistress Kara,' he replied.

She smiled at his polite greeting and put out one hand to gently stroke Firebrand's nose. 'Your Majesty may rest assured that his interests are the interests of the Guild, as far as the war with the Haagii is concerned.'

Andra nodded and replied with a gracious smile. 'The Guild Mistress may be assured the King will always remember what he honestly owes to the Guild and certain people in it.' Kara bowed again, and stepped back from Andra's horse, allowing the King and his procession to continue to the banks of Dragon River.

At the riverbank, Andra dismounted amidst the Royal party, which consisted of a squad of Haardrishii, Lord Haephus, Marella, Milly and Aaron. A space was cleared beside the partially dismantled stone bridge spanning the river, and a low platform leaned over the river waters. The crowd along Castle Road descended toward the river, like a human flood, pooling out from Andra in an ever-increasing lake, and he had to wait until the movement and the hubbub of voices ceased. 'It is time, my Lord,' Haephus whispered, as silence spread, directing Andra to the one task for which he was solely responsible.

Andra gratefully removed the irritating crown and stepped onto the wooden platform. The waters of Dragon River were running clear and deep, ignorant of the human misery clustered on its banks. Dutifully, he lowered the griffin crown, until it was submerged, held it as if to cleanse it of the touch of its former owner, then lifted it, dripping and sparkling, above his head. So many people were watching.

He remembered how the Chancellor, who was the Royal Advisor then, stood beside Thana when the Great King spoke to the Great Armies, and used magic to still the air and project Thana's voice to every listening ear. He could do with that kind of magical assistance now. He doubted those at the rear of the gathering would hear his words. He could only try. Word of mouth would repeat and transform the speech he made into the lore of the Kingdom. Who would record it the way Ardath the Drycraefter had recorded the reign of Thana? He needed a new Drycraefter. So much had to be replaced, rebuilt, and restarted.

He drew in his breath, saw Claarn's shaggy head above a knot of Haardrishii near the middle of the crowd, and relaxed.

'I bear a title I was never born to,' he began. 'Strange circumstance has led me here to be your King. I chose only to be a Guardian of the Vale, my home high in the Valley of Rivers at the foot of the Ureykyeu. I never sought a greater path than that. To me, it was the greatest path I could choose to follow.

I came here, conscripted into a war I barely understood. Yet, ages past, seers claimed another Abreotan would come to oppose the new Dragonlord. This prophecy was unknown to my people. Now, I am your King, and the inheritor of Abreotan's legacy. If that is what I have become, then it is The Way, my path, and I must follow it to its end.'

He searched the faces of the warriors, the soldiers, the children, the women, the old. Tired faces. He felt the weight of their weariness on his shoulders, and his nervousness wrenching his stomach. He looked up at the glistening griffin crown for inspiration and fixed his gaze on Claarn.

'The Dragonlord has come among us and brought death, hunger and ruin. The beauty of these lands, their people and their produce, have been scarred, laid to waste, burned and savaged. But no more. Now we rise from the ashes to defeat the hunger and rebuild our Kingdom. We will survive, and we will prosper. And above all other things, we will bring peace to this Kingdom, and forever lay to rest the fears that plague our hearts and our minds this day. This is my promise as King; that there will be peace once and for all from the terror of the Dragonlord. I, King Andra of Andrakis, have spoken.'

The people greeted his speech with spontaneous cheering, their spirits uplifted by his promise, and their unified voice echoed against the plateau cliffs like a triumphant roar. But Andra felt a cold breeze across the back of his neck, and he shivered, wondering how powerful his prophecy of peace would be, in the months and years to come.

The powerful are arrogant, the wise influential, the rich extravagant, the poor lucky, the honest lost."

a Targan maxim

Twenty Five

Vukaat Argaa bowed respectfully, as he walked between the double ranks of Dammeraag warriors on guard in their ebony armour, outside the Eternal Palace. He had a terrible foreboding about the afternoon, a fear his life was in imbalance, at risk, now it was no longer his. He glanced apprehensively at the slate clouds perpetually roiling above the Eternal Palace's Central Dome, as he climbed the jade steps leading to the entrance archway, glimpsing in their violence the potential wrath awaiting him within the Palace. He was met at the top of the steps by Dammeraag warrior guards with crossed pikes.

One blond warrior glared with deep blue eyes and demanded, 'State your rank, name, and business!'

Vukaat felt ice in his veins at the tone of the warrior's voice, and bowed his head low, as was always required of one of lesser rank before a Dammeraag warrior. 'If it pleases, I am Vukaat Argaa, official messenger for Dragon-General Klatt Ur Yemeg. I bear an important report for the Lord of Many Peoples.'

The warrior's handsome features were impassive. 'Give the message,' he said, holding out his left hand.

Vukaat bowed more deeply. 'With the greatest of respect, most noble of guardians, but General Yemeg instructed I must deliver the report in person to The Great One.' Vukaat half-expected a blow to fall on his vulnerable head, and awaited it, but all he heard was the Dammeraag warrior mutter, and a muffled reply from his companion, before the curt instruction, 'Pass,' was given. Without risking raising his eyes, Vukaat shuffled through the arch into the Palace.

As he passed through the Hall of Visitors, he was surprised by the empty marble expanse. It was true no one visited The Great One, except officially, and then reluctantly, but he had expected to find someone, guards, within the Hall, and great luxury, but there was no one present, and the interior was plain and empty. The roof arched thirty arm spans above him, and he guessed the Hall stretched fifty paces. The marble walls were etched with dragons and dragon riders subjugating hordes of peoples of different races, the people running in terror from the laughing warriors riding their fearsome beasts. No doors led from the Hall of Visitors; only an obsidian stairway descended into the earth at the furthest end.

At the stairway head, he paused, and gazed into an amber glow issuing from far below. He heard rumours that The Great One's chambers were constantly bathed in amber light, a bizarre concept to Vukaat, an eccentricity his mind rejected as impractical and ostentatious. He chastised himself for being foolish and arrogant to have such thoughts in the very Palace of The Great One. He heard other rumours too, the darker ones that The Great One could peer, any time, into his servants' minds and unravel their deepest secrets, as easily as peeling skin from ripened fruit. He shivered. Why General Yemeg passed the unpalatable news to him he could not imagine, except that he, Vukaat, was Yemeg's highest official messenger remaining in Uz Erhaag, while the General led his army south, against the barbarians. Promotion had its costs.

Vukaat descended and entered a chamber glowing amber from crystals orbiting an arm span below the ceiling. The crystals fascinated him so much he was unaware of another presence, until a spear point pressed against his neck from the left, and a harsh voice hissed, 'Your purpose?'

He didn't quite know what to do. He immediately thought to bow, as was appropriate protocol, but the spear point threatened to pierce his carotid artery if he so much as flinched. He drew a short, nervous breath, and answered, 'I seek your pardon, but General Yemeg sends me to report an urgent matter to the Imperial Lord of All Nations,' using one of the multitudinous titles The Great One invested himself.

'Your rank?'

'Off-official M-messenger t-to General Yem-em-eg in Uz Er-erhaag,' Vukaat stammered. He imagined the spear pressed harder, but the pressure was released, and he bowed his head again, too afraid to look his aggressor in the face.

Heavy booted footsteps receded, and he heard a door open. Voices whispered in echoes from his left. When he saw the amber glow against the marble floor turning red, he imagined it to be the colour of his blood. Taking word to a Haagii chieftain is child's play compared to this, he decided. The Kreerg chieftain, Murgash, briefly immersed him in a nest of storm ants to test his stamina and grit, and that was the most fearful moment of his career as Yemeg's messenger. But that agony paled in comparison to the cold fear he felt, awaiting a remote chance of an audience with The Great One. He'd heard The Great One kept messengers waiting for days, and then sent them away without hearing their messages. Others were left to their fates at the ruthless hands of the merciless Dammeraag warriors who guarded the outer premises. He saw the grisly head of one unfortunate displayed on a pole outside the Eternal Palace. Now Yemeg sent him. What wrong had he unwittingly committed against the Dragon-General to deserve this?

The heavy footsteps returned. Black boots, topped with metal armour strips, appeared in the field of his lowered vision against the floor's amber background. 'Keep your unworthy face lowered, messenger,' a guttural voice warned. He That Is Everything has decided that a brief hearing will be allowed. Follow in obedience. Lift your eyes but once, unless bidden, and you will see the dark shadow of eternity.'

Vukaat's heart raced. An audience with The Great One! Not since his great-grandfather defeated the Desert Haagii had such honour been bestowed upon his family's name. He was certain to become the hero of a fire-song to be sung through the coming generations around the home hearths of Uz Ekraal, his birthplace.

Then he felt the emptiness in the pit of his stomach, only

the greatest fear engenders, as he followed the black-booted heels. His message would enrage The Great One's heart. He, Vukaat Argaa, was the bearer of the worst news General Yemeg could send. Whatever glory he might've drawn to his name, by entering the inner sanctum of The Great One, would be dissipated as desert sand before the great east winds when he delivered his report. His fate was pre-written by a cruel god and sealed by a thankless master.

After three golden doorways, and one set of opal stairs, the black boots halted, and Vukaat stopped. He did not raise his eyes. The black shadows of eternity remained distant. He was the victor. He focussed on the tiled patterning that supplanted the marble of the other chambers and corridor, trying to determine what image formed beneath his feet, but his ears caught distracting sounds, as if the space where he stood with averted eyes was full of people. Voices whispered in alien tongues, and footsteps hastily came and went, right and left of him. He heard the commanding voice ahead and above. Its bass tone thrilled his spirit, touched his heart with vague terror, and numbed his mind, as if it washed through his ability to think and rendered that capacity impotent. 'Let the messenger from Yemeg advance and gaze upon my face,' the voice said.

'You,' the black boots hissed. 'The Eternal Master gives you an unsurpassable honour. Obey his words.'

Caught in a dream and a nightmare, Vukaat shuffled forward, until his feet rested against a diamond plinth, where he lifted his eyes slowly, carefully, unsure of what he was about to see, terrified the vision would strike him down with its magnificence. Never had one of Yemeg's messengers gazed upon The Great One of Uz Erhaag, the Eternal Ruler, whose reign began with the unification of the Thousand Tribes into one nation, and who struck fear into the hearts of their enemies. He, Vukaat Argaa, was first.

At the head of five diamond steps, on an emerald throne carved with unfathomable skill into the abstract form of a rearing dragon, sat Mareg Dru'artha Sutnavanistra, Dragonlord of Uz Erhaag, wearing a silver breastplate and black robes, his silver-grey hair braided into a dozen warrior's knots beneath his gold dragon claw crown. Mareg gazed down on Vukaat Argaa through burning red pupil-less eyes that glowed with absolute malice and unfathomable power. Vukaat felt the ice of fear in his stomach turn to water and run into his legs, making him weak and giddy. The One Eternal Lord was smiling at him, from a handsome yet cruel face. Beside the throne, a black creature stirred, opening green slit eyes to stare at Vukaat. Its unmistakable feline form identified it as a night tiger of Uz Ekkutz, or perhaps it came from within the Fire Mountains of Uz Erhaag. Vukaat had heard tales of the legendary and fearsome creatures, and their insatiable appetites for flesh, and now he found himself staring into the limpid green pools of a night tiger's eyes, and only the Dragonlord's voice dragged his attention from the creature. 'You appreciate Reshka's beauty,' he said, more statement than observation.

Automatically, Vukaat bowed his head, and averted his eyes from Mareg. 'I have never seen such a magnificent animal, O Eternal Lord,' he replied, as courteously as he could muster, hoping his response was appropriately expressed for Mareg.

'You have a message from Yemeg. I have been awaiting this news. The barbarians are crushed?' Mareg asked, with the bored confidence of one who expected no surprises and enjoyed being right.

Vukaat wanted to retreat inside his heart and hide there from The Great One. He hesitated, sweat beading on his brow and in the palms of his hands. Why had Yemeg chosen him to deliver the report? What wrong had he done to the General?

'I'm awaiting your report,' the forceful voice called from the dragon throne.

Death is the doorway to eternal shadow, Vukaat reminded himself. Death is the night without end, the sleep without waking. Why had Yemeg chosen him? He shuddered and lowered his head further. 'O Lord of All People, I bring news from Dragon-General Yemeg that is unworthy to repeat to your ears,' Vukaat uttered reluctantly. He felt a chill descend in the throne room, but he dared not lift his eyes.

'Repeat your news,' the voice commanded.

Vukaat heard the subtle change in tone, the metallic edge in the Dragonlord's voice, prefacing anger. He had no road to follow, but the cruel and fatal one he'd been ordered to walk. 'General Yemeg bids me inform the Lord of All People that he has failed his duty,' Vukaat explained. 'The barbarian Kingdom has a new King, who bears a sword of fire and leads an army of Golden Warriors who do not fear death. This new King has driven General Yemeg's army from the plains back into the valleys and mountains. General Yemeg's Haagii contingent is decimated.'

Vukaat knew his fate was sealed. Vulnerable, trapped, pinned by the extended silence, he was seized by a compulsion to lift his eyes again, to gaze into the face of the Eternal King of Uz Erhaag, the Dragonlord, but he dared not. To do so now would surely mean death: certain death. Why was it so silent? Why didn't the Eternal One speak? Then he heard a low rattle, a deep-throated growl that seemed far off and yet he knew was close.

Against his fears, Vukaat raised his eyes, until he was staring into a pair of narrowed green feline eyes set in darkness. He opened his mouth to scream, but the night tiger had already leapt, fangs gleaming.

General Yemeg saw the elongated shape sweeping through the cloud-ridden skies toward the Kobold Ranges, and his heart filled with the usual passion of elation and dread at the vision of a dragon in flight, the same passion he experienced ever since the One Lord of All Lands rose to power over Uz Erhaag. The Master had sent reinforcements. This brash new human King with his sword of fire and Golden Warriors would feel the fire of a dragon's breath and know the taste of defeat.

Yemeg hated humiliation. From childhood, he vowed to

never yield to anyone. He learned to fight hard and long, until he won the fear and respect of every warrior in his tribe, and he carried that glory into every skirmish with other Haagii tribesmen – until the ascension of the One Lord. That the One Lord chose him to command the Armies of Death against the barbarian humans seemed right and inevitable. He was the best Haagii warrior in all Uz Erhaag. No one dared dispute his claim. When the Dammeraag warriors and the Yaki Bowmen, and even the One Lord's Shakan, his sorcerers, came to bolster the Armies of Death, Yemeg bowed to no one. All obeyed his orders, because his orders were the Will of the One Lord.

The dragon circled the Kobold Ranges, spiralling lower and closer, until the Haagii on the barren hilltops could see the rider clinging to the gigantic beast's back. The creature altered the angle of its giant wings, fluttered to hover, and settled atop a large hill several hundred paces from Yemeg's position.

Yemeg turned to three Dammeraag warriors and ordered them to greet and fetch the rider. As the Dammeraag warriors moved through the narrow ravine connecting the two hills, he appraised them. Fearsome warriors, their skill, and black plate armour, made them formidable foes and welcome allies in the war, easily a match for the barbarians' black warriors. The One Lord brought them from a place to the far north of Uz Erhaag, a Kingdom vaguely referred to as Nefrar, where all the people were tall and blond-haired. Nefrar lay beyond the deserts of Azig, which no Haagii crossed, except a handful of foolish traders who as often perished in the deserts as returned with the distant silks and metals they sought. The Dammeraag warriors were aloof, arrogant, and Yemeg always felt they, of all who served under him, were the most likely to threaten his command. He admired their fighting prowess, but that was all.

Four figures returned. The Dammeraag warriors walked a respectful distance behind the one they escorted to the General, deference they normally didn't accord anyone, Yemeg noted, and as the leading figure approached, he thought he recognised familiarity in the man's walk and the slight stoop of his shoulders, despite the unfamiliar black garb. Dragon riders were creatures with whom no one, but the One Lord, was familiar. They were neither living nor dead, beings the One Lord chose to ride his dragons because life and death were nothing and the same to them. They were dispensable.

When the figure halted before the General, and drew back his cowl to reveal an emaciated face, traced with deeply gouged claw marks, and one lustreless eye staring from its torn socket, Yemeg froze with fear. He stared into the living dead face of Vukaat Argaa. He did not fear death. He had stared into its eyes more times than any Haagii General, especially since the barbarian King drove his army out of the heart of the Kingdom, but to see death before him, with a supercilious grin ripped across its visage by an unnameable terror, sapped his spirit. He could not fight the trembling beginning to ripple through his body like silent, wicked laughter. He tried to gather composure to speak with a modicum of strength to the gruesome apparition, but when his words came they were half whispered and full of fear. 'What - is - the Master's Will?'

Vukaat's face shuddered, and the lone eye brightened and focused on Yemeg. As from a great distance, a hissing, rasping voice issued from his bloodied lips, though the lips barely moved. 'You failed me, Yemeg. I gave you power and you wasted it with your cowardice and stupidity. You have not completed the simplest task. I have no further need of you.' Then Vukaat threw back his head and laughed with an insane wheezing cackle, revealing the serrated gaping wounds to his throat.

An awful rush of numbness sank through Yemeg at the sound of the dragon rider's laughter. The dragon rose, and was on him, the shining talons of its left claw closing like iron around his body, crushing breath from him, before he could scream, or make a futile gesture of defiance. Clutching its limp trophy, the dragon swept north from the Kobold Ranges, toward Uz Erhaag, gaining velocity with powerful beats of its massive wings, becoming a dark receding dot.

As the dragon faded from view, Vukaat Argaa's tortured corpse shuddered and toppled, rolling down the slope of the hill past the feet of stunned Dammeraag warriors, and Haagii who witnessed the grisly spectacle.

Twenty Six

The eagle banked above the dark green forest, descending on air thermals toward the treetops, where it seemed content to glide into the luxuriant tree cover, but it dipped its wings in alarm and rose furiously, levelling out high above the forested area, circling, as if searching. Then it turned and swept toward the ash-blackened forest perimeter and landed. A Ahmud Ki shook himself, as he resumed his true form. Of all the magic he learned, Seralinna's remained his favourite.

The ash under foot was harsh and dry, and a desolate landscape of twisted, charred roots and tree trunks, protruding grotesquely from the blackened earth, stretched north and south. The Haagii torched huge tracts of forest in attempts to burn out the Aelendyell defenders in Wynwuduholt, sometimes with success, sometimes without, and what was once a long, broad forest, taking at least ten days' walking to cover from north to south, was reduced to outcrops and patches of green islands in a sea of ash.

A Ahmud Ki had surveyed the ruin from his vantage in the sky. One large circle of green survived near the centre of Wynwuduholt, a strong Aelendyell tun encircled by a very powerful glyph. He'd nearly flown into the glyph, only sensing its scintillating and deadly energy as he was about to drop into the tree line. If time permitted, he'd visit it before returning to his business with the new King, but a small, ragged clump of forest, in the northern portion of Wynwuduholt, marked the village that was his childling home, and it was at the edge of this green island he landed.

He approached the fringe, avoiding tripping on corpses littered everywhere. The corpses were well decayed, some even burnt, reduced to little more than bone fragments, melted armour and distorted weapons, suggesting the defence of the small, forested piece had been fierce, but ended months past. The ragged forest edge suggested it was created by fire and firefighting and wasn't guarded by a glyph. Nevertheless, A Ahmud Ki tested the air for magic, and when he was satisfied he could walk forward with impunity he entered the forest.

He found scorched sections beyond the fringe where fires had been started but extinguished, and more signs of battle – abandoned and broken weapons – but no more bodies. He discovered the presence of Aelendyell minds when he cast a searching mind spell and knew Aelendyell eyes were watching him. Tempted as he was to expose his shadowy observers, he chose to ignore them, and pressed toward the heart of the forest, searching for familiar paths and landmarks.

There had been a lot of change since he lived there. Trees were taller. Bushes had sprouted. Bird song had disappeared, and the forest was quieter than he remembered. The paths weren't altered. He recognised the route to the Meeting Stone amphitheatre when he reached it, and knew he was on the village outskirts.

He passed the point of greatest familiarity, the camouflaged entrance to the path to his sleeping place as a youngling, and wondered if it was still there, the tree with its woven cover and secret niches where he hid stolen parchments long ago in his first thirst for magic. He doubted it. The Elders would've taken everything, having pronounced him an outlaw and a murderer. They always sought reasons to hold him down, and push him away from what was his, because he wasn't pure. Sired by rape: that's why they cursed and conspired to keep him from his destiny. That's why they kept the Lore Book from him and forced him to steal it to satiate his hunger to learn magic. That's why they isolated him with an Aelendyell foster family, and why he had to kill Elder Laeocwyddyn when they tried to stop him leaving the village. They were jealous of him, of his potential, of what he might become. He laughed. Now they would all learn what he had become – a bearer of the Five Ki – more powerful than any Aelendyell could ever dream of becoming.

They must have known all along he could become so great. Perhaps the Chanter and the Elders feared that from the outset.

Two Aelendyell Weapon Bearers appeared from the underbrush, bows loaded and aimed, and A Ahmud Ki smiled. He expected them to stop him before he reached the village. 'Who are you to enter our village uninvited and alone?' the shorter Bearer asked in his Aelendyell tongue.

A Ahmud Ki turned the red glow of his pupil-less eyes on the speaker, who saw the Dragonlord's eyes for the first time and stepped back. A Ahmud Ki appreciated his response, as he framed his reply to the question. 'Inform your Elders that Terin of Solweonyn has returned.'

'Why are you here?'

A Ahmud Ki gazed around the empty amphitheatre ringed by the forest. The last time he stood before the Elders, they were sentencing him to his fate for stealing the Lore Book. He returned his attention to the questioner. The Aelendyell's silver hair hung free to his shoulders, but the face was unfamiliar. 'I come to claim what is rightfully mine, and to repay an old debt.'

'The name of Terin of Solweonyn has been long forgotten,' another Elder said. A Ahmud Ki met his stare. Twenty years was a very long time, but he felt he should recognise the features. 'I would not have known you either,' the Elder said, as if guessing A Ahmud Ki's question. 'You were long considered dead.'

A vague memory stirred in A Ahmud Ki's mind. He saw a face leading other Aelendyell younglings in a chase after Terin through the forest. The Aelendyell were pitching stones at the fleeing child, teasing and laughing. 'Laefstrael,' he said, without emotion, though hatred burned in his heart. 'I remember your friendship. I'm flabbergasted to see you an Elder so young.'

The Aelendyell nodded acknowledgement of A Ahmud Ki's recognition. 'Much has changed since Terin of

Solweonyn walked these forests,' the Aelendyell said quietly. 'Many you knew are dust and sad whisperings through the silent forest of our ancestors.'

'Very lyrical,' A Ahmud Ki noted. 'I'm touched.' His sarcasm shocked the Aelendyell, and he sensed the antagonistic edge in their combined stare following his words, and it made him feel better. Sympathy wasn't what he came for.

'To what do you lay claim?' the Elder at the centre of the seated seven asked.

He was the successor to the Chanter A Ahmud Ki had known, the same Chanter he slew atop his black tower, the day the Aelendyell unsuccessfully tried to return the Orb of Radiance to Heolstorcofa. 'The Book of Lore stored in the Chanter's Well.' He heard the sharp intake of breaths saw the odd mixture of shock, anger and disbelief in the faces of his audience. The seven Elders exchanged quick whisperings and shook their heads.

The Chanter glared sternly at A Ahmud Ki. 'Your request is absurd. Terin of Solweonyn has no claim to the Book of Lore, either as Aelendyell, or in any capacity.'

'I've come for the Book of Lore, and I will take it, if it is not freely given,' A Ahmud Ki said, with confident assurance, and a shrug.

His arrogant statement threw the Elders into a second flurry of quick exchanges, after which Elder Laefstrael stood. 'While there is still some composure in your presence,' he began, directing his words at A Ahmud Ki, 'what debt are you here to repay?'

A Ahmud Ki grinned. 'I return to repay the Aelendyell for all they did in raising me among them with such care and kindness. And you, Laefstrael, would be one who would understand that.'

Laefstrael hesitated, but the Chanter stood. 'Hear me, for my word is law in this place. I am Elder Sybbanel, successor to Elder Iranyth, who was Chanter before he was called to the ranks of the Ieldran. I, Sybbanel, forbid your claim to the Book of Lore. Know that the name of Terin of Solweonyn was recorded in our lore as maegslaga, and the bearer of that name may never again walk the paths of this village. Terin of Solweonyn is dead, a shadow memory only.'

A Ahmud Ki listened patiently to the Chanter's decree, and, as the Aelendyell Elder finished his pronouncement, he began to laugh, shaking his head slowly. 'It seems my Aelendyell brethren still do not understand what is happening,' he said, and chuckled, as he turned his eyes to glare at the seven Elders. 'You're right about one thing though, Sybbanel. I'm no longer Terin of Solweonyn. I am A Ahmud Ki. The Terin you speak of perished a long time ago. He was just the poor little Aelendyell bastard who was exiled in his village, chased, teased, hounded, pelted with stones, wasn't he Laefstrael? You denied him his birthright, kept him from learning the magic he so desperately wanted to learn, pushed him away, and forced him to do what he didn't want to do. You're right, Sybbanel. Terin is dead. Just his pain and his shadow linger.'

Laefstrael's eyebrows were raised. Then the Elders saw the burning red fire in A Ahmud Ki's eyes and they froze with dread. A Ahmud Ki heard one Elder whisper the word, 'Chancellor.'

'Yes,' he said with satisfaction. 'I am A Ahmud Ki, Chancellor to the new King of Andrakis, the human King of these lands. I am the one who took the Orb of Radiance from the heart of Heolstorcofa, and it was I who sent a dozen of the Ieldran to walk the forests of their ancestors when they were foolish enough to doubt my power. You speak of Iranyth. Go send for your old Chanter. Call him from the Ieldran. He will not hear you. He came, like an old fool, to take the Orb from me, and now he watches life from the shadows of the Silent Forest. I am A Ahmud Ki, and I am more, much more than you dare to imagine.'

He paused, letting the impact of his revelation settle on the Aelendyell Elders. Two more stood, as if compelled to respond to A Ahmud Ki's speech, but, like their fellows, their dread held them fast, and they stared with disbelief at A Ahmud Ki's red eyes. 'The Book of Lore is mine to take,' he concluded, no longer hiding his threatening voice, 'and take it I will.'

As he turned with absolute disdain from the Elders, he glimpsed Laefstrael's hands begin to weave a magic pattern. Reacting, he made a single motion with his right hand, and Laefstrael stiffened, eyes bulging with shock, hands rigid in mid-spell. He staggered forward three steps, gurgled, as if he couldn't breathe, and toppled face down on the cold, hard surface of the granite Meeting Stone.

A second Elder was conjuring. A Ahmud Ki raised his left hand and a short burst of energy pulsed in a white light straight through the chest of the Aelendyell, killing him. The Chanter and another Elder blinked out, but A Ahmud Ki knew where they had gone. With a precautionary glance at the remaining three Elders, who were keeping perfectly still, lest they draw the visitor's wrath, he turned and walked out of the amphitheatre, heading for the village.

The arrow glanced his cheek. He rolled into the bush to his right, and concentrated, until he located the thoughts of three archers, perched in an elmoak above the village entrance. The disadvantage of mind spells was their ability to affect only one mind at a time. Though he couldn't see the archers, from where he crouched, he used his spell to target them. He recalled a spell, from the First Ki, which he magnified many times and cast it at the tree crown. The crown erupted in a ball of flame, as if a dragon had swept through, and three screaming archers tumbled to fiery deaths.

The village was empty, as he expected. The tree he set alight was crackling high to his right, but there was other fire damage scattered through the village trees, burns, and ash from older Haagii attacks. The Spell Grove, where trees once arched to form a natural hall for the Novitiates to study the art of the First and Second Ki, was destroyed. He had no intention of avoiding the village, though he kept his mind tuned for independent thoughts of other archers. He tracked through frightened and curious childling and youngling minds, adult Aelendyell crouched in their tree homes with weapons in case the stranger in their village turned their way, but he sensed no direct danger to himself; except from a group gathering at the far end of the village.

When he approached the path that led beyond the Spell Grove to the Chanter's Well, a dozen armed Weapon Bearers stepped out to bar his progress. Behind them were eight Lore Bearers. The Elder, who disappeared with the Chanter, stood at the head of the group. A Ahmud Ki halted. 'No further,' the Elder warned. 'Already you've forfeited your life. The Book of Lore is not yours to have.'

A Ahmud Ki assessed the numbers and flexed his fingers. 'More Aelendyell blood on my hands means little to me,' he said quietly. 'If you're so keen to leave this life, stay where you are. Whatever you plan to do, I am going to the Chanter's Well, as I intend.' He took a step forward, motioning lightly with his hand as he advanced. Bows thrummed in unison, and a dozen arrows bounced harmlessly from his chest. As his fingers finished patterning, the eight Lore Bearers collapsed, writhing with pain from a spell affecting their ears. He untied the silver cloak from his shoulders, and threw it aside, revealing a suit of bright gold armour. He unhitched an enormous battle-axe from its belt. 'This is something new,' he said aloud to the shocked Aelendyell Weapon Bearers who drew their swords to meet him.

'Dracafeond!' the Elder hissed, a greater terror seizing him.

The moment of terror was all A Ahmud Ki required. He heaved the heavy battle-axe around in one sweep, smashing through a sword thrust forward by a Weapon Bearer in a vain attempt to block A Ahmud Ki's blow, and cleaved through the chest of the Elder. The effort nearly caused A Ahmud Ki to overbalance, and he barely avoided a cutting lunge by a second Weapon Bearer. He brought the battle-axe up, and chopped his attacker's sword arm cleanly off at the elbow. Fighting with weapons was not his forte. Realising the danger the pressing Weapon Bearers presented, he tossed the battle-axe aside and dodged into an open space to cast one final spell. The Weapon Bearers were set upon by a rabid pack of wolves that materialised inexplicably in their midst, and while the Aelendyell struggled with the confusion his illusion created, A Ahmud Ki strolled toward the Chanter's Well.

The Cover Stone was still in place beneath the Chanter's tree where Sybbanel was waiting, his green Aelendyell robes drawn out in preparation for a magical confrontation with a Dracafeond. He watched A Ahmud Ki's arrogant approach. Writings of the Lore described Dracafeond: the Dragonlords the Elvenaar often fought in the ancient times. Now Sybbanel faced an incarnation of the most feared and powerful beings described in the Lore. He understood, at last, what controlled the Haagii hordes, who came plundering the forests in the past months. This was not Terin. He trembled. Whatever resistance others had made, between the Meeting Stone and here, mattered little to such a being. Sybbanel's resistance would matter even less. Only his sacred oath as Chanter, to keep the Book of Lore safe, held him in place before the tree. So much he wanted to run, to escape the fiery eyes of death glaring at him from across the Cover Stone.

A Ahmud Ki stopped and glanced down at the Cover Stone, opening his senses to the binding magic there. Sybbanel had reinforced the locking spells, forming a complicated pattern reminiscent of a minor glyph; quite an accomplishment for a young Chanter with only the First and Second Ki to work on in a short time. 'I'm impressed, Sybbanel.' A Ahmud Ki said, and smiled as he looked up at the Aelendyell. 'You have more talent than Iranyth.' He concentrated and passed his hand over the circular Cover Stone. The massive slab groaned and floated to the right, uncovering the well containing the Book of Lore. 'But you see,' A Ahmud Ki said, his face becoming harder, 'you waste your energies trying to oppose me.' Another twist of his left wrist, and the Book of Lore levitated from its locked storage casket, out of the well, and into A Ahmud Ki's hand.

Sybbanel started weaving his hands, conjuring his most

potent trapping spell, while A Ahmud Ki appeared distracted, but the Chancellor lifted his eyes and glared at the Chanter. 'Don't be so stupid,' he warned sharply, and pointed his right hand toward the Aelendyell.

Sybbanel faltered and collapsed to his knees in despair. He knew he couldn't stop a Dracafeond.

'There's no shame in realising the limits of your power,' A Ahmud Ki offered, as he nonchalantly thumbed the edges of the thin vellum pages containing the collective wisdom of ancient Elvenaar and Aelendyell lore. 'In fact, you show greater wisdom than many others. Confrontation with me would only lead to your needless death. There's no other outcome possible.'

He flicked through the pages, feeling the teachings of centuries weighing down the light volume, knowing the secret of the text without having to read it. He finally held the text he longed to possess, the Book of Lore he grieved over in dreams, and periods of waking, which tormented him with such fierce passion it drove him back on a vengeful path to the ruined forest. Now he held the prize, he was empty. In the intervening years, he outgrew the Book of Lore, having learned its secrets in acquiring the Five Ki, and learned much more beyond its limited text.

He closed the Book of Lore, placed it gently on the Cover Stone, and stepped back, studying it one last time, noting the detail in its soft green leather cover.

Sybbanel watched, wondering why the Dracafeond was returning the text. Had his Aelendyell heritage won out? Then his face flinched with horror as the Book of Lore erupted in a bright blue flame that sparkled and spat with pent-up energy. The burning text grew, as it was consumed, page after page appearing and disappearing in rapid succession, tongues of vivid blue flame leaping through the pages with insane hunger to consume and destroy every word, every piece of history, every name, from Elvenaar to Aelendyell, from the beginning of the records to the most recent, consuming everything of the village's history, its ancestry, its origins, even its name. Sybbanel reached for the book, but intense heat forced him back. As the last pages flared and disappeared, the whole Cover Stone burst into a ball of brilliant green light, blinding him.

When the light died, and he could see again, he was alone at the foot of the Chanter's tree. The Dracafeond was gone. Close by, he heard screams of fear and pain of his people, and fires raged through the heart of his dying village.

Twenty Seven

'And I say we take no more from this intruder! There is time for vengeance in our hearts!' The Elder's eyes flared to mirror the intensity of his passion, and he clenched his fist before his face. Around him, the circle of the Ieldran, his colleagues, remained impassive. The Elder's anger hung above them like a shadow over reason.

'Elder Theran is correct to vent his anger,' an Aelendyell, to the Elder's right, quietly asserted. 'He only says what we all feel in the deepest part of our hearts.'

The quiet Elder stood slowly, and Theran acceded the right to him to speak by sitting in his accustomed place in the circle. 'We shared our anguish when we heard Elder Sybbanel's news. We share the pain and horror of his village. When it seems the Ealdfeond are withdrawing from laying waste to our forest homes, another comes and destroys what remains. And we ask ourselves when will it all end? When will we be left in peace?' He paused to let the common question be acknowledged by all in the circle. 'I hear Theran's cry. Within me I hear a voice that says no longer endure, Farynyael, you are Aelendyell. You are one of many descendants of the Elvenaar, the fairest of people who once ruled a vast forested world, before the Dracafeond came. I hear that voice, and part of me says, no more. The Aelendyell will be avenged. No more will you endure the suffering the Ealdfeond and the humans have forced upon you. Rise and take what is yours!'

'And we shall do it!' Theran interjected. Heads nodded and voices muttered agreement.

'No,' Farynyael argued softly, shaking his whitened locks of flowing hair. 'No.' He moved toward the centre of the circle and raised his hands, palms outward. 'Passion must never rule over logic. I learnt this lesson a long time ago, from Chanter Leafthalyon. You all learned this lesson. It is at the heart of everything we become. It is why we sit here, as the Ieldran. If I followed my deepest passion now, I would tear the last Aelendyell people apart, and throw them on the merciless spears of the Ealdfeond, and the hatred of the humans the Ealdfeond war on. I would kill my people. I cannot follow passion. I must obey logic.' Having spoken his turn, Farynyael bowed his head and moved to the edge of the circle to resume his place.

Above the solemn gathering, in the heart of Elvenaar Forest, wind whispered through the dark tree canopies, and higher still, like ancient diamonds scattered on black velvet, stars winked between smudges of cloud gliding through the skies. The mortal world bathed in the artificial light of thirty light wands inverted in the earth at the inner edge of the Ieldran circle. Silver light played on silvered and white locks and green robes, making them glow with the lustre of a dream. Aelendyell minds pondered the fate of their existence.

A tall Elder swayed to his feet and took two steps into the circle, his hand cupped around his chin, revealing the depth of his thought. He seemed initially oblivious to the others, or even to his movement. The circle patiently waited for him to share what he considered. When he spoke, his voice had the brittle quality of trembling breezes over thin reeds. 'Elder Sybbanel tells us this renegade has the great power and has no qualms about using it. These are facts we know. He desecrated, and sealed from our hearts, the Elvenaar shrine at Heolstorcofa. He slew brothers of our sacred circle who went to take back what he had stolen. He struck down Iranyth when he tried to return the Orb of Radiance to its rightful place. He has defied the Elders in Sybbanel's village, the renegade's birthplace, and slain others. He deliberately destroyed the copy of the Book of Lore there. His power is greater than any Aelendyell has wielded since the beginning of our people's time. His evil is greater. Sybbanel tells us he moves and looks as if he was a reincarnation of a Dracafeond. Why, then, must we let this – this unnatural beast shelter in the world of men, and wait in fear, or in hope, he will slink back among our people again to work more of his evil on us?'

As the tall Elder sat, another rose. 'Heaothana has a point,' he said, and gently cleared his throat. 'We can't wait for him to come to us. He may never come. What has he to gain from us? He wields more power than all of us could muster. Not one of us has anything he seeks. As far as he is concerned, we are nothing, dust in his tracks, a bitter memory. Perhaps we need never fear him again.'

'You are a fool, Erinthyll!' Theran growled. The circle turned as one toward Theran, eyes castigating the Elder for his undignified interruption. Theran turned his eyes down and bowed his head in humility.

Another Elder stood in the soft light of the circle and waited for Erinthyll to sit. 'There will not be a decision tonight. This we all know,' he stated simply. 'But I ask that you let me invite one to our assembly who can tell us more about the Great King's Chancellor and what is what in the affairs of the humans. He is not an Elder, though he is known to some of you, as he is to me, and he has seen much more of the human world than any of us. Perhaps his words and his answers will lead us to a decision on the path of logic that Farynyael correctly reminded us of.' The Elder cast a glance around the circle and noted approval for his suggestion. No one objected. The matter was resolved. Satisfied, he moved to the edge of the circle and sat, patiently awaiting a new speaker to lead the Ieldran into discussion of a different topic, talk which would take the assembly deeper into the evening. The issue of the Chancellor would be broached the following meeting.

Pain dogged him in his right leg. The sword cut the Haagii dealt left a permanent limp because the severed muscle tissue hadn't knitted cleanly, despite healing Aelendyell powders and poultices. He was conscious of the limp, even imagined dragging his semi-useless right leg along like unnecessary baggage, reduced to the penury of a beggar, unable to work an honest, or even dishonest, living because of it. The leg injury irritated him more than the loss of his right eye. An eye could be covered with a patch to hide its failing. A dragging leg was a blazing sign to everyone here was a cripple ripe for pity or ragging. The leg stopped him from plying even the simplest aspects of his trade.

Still, he had a lot to be grateful for. He was alive. For days, he thought otherwise, mercilessly dragged behind a Haagii cart, rusted chains and manacles cutting into his wrists, chafing his skin, until his arms were bloodied from shoulder to fingertips. And there were constant beatings and abuse. He lost count of how many times the Haagii sank their rugged boots into his stomach, spat on him, urinated on his head, punched him in the face. He moved through cycles of bright, pain-wracked consciousness, and long stretches of blankness, remembering nothing of his captors' movements, waking brutally sore and bloody from being dragged in his unconscious state, along rough earth, across the plains of Ky, and over shale and rocks through Central Gate.

He remembered begging for death. He swore once, a long time ago, that he would never be humiliated into begging for mercy before an enemy, but that oath dissipated in an ocean of agony, pounding on the shore of his senses, as the torturous journey passed moment after pain-ridden moment. He begged for them to slit his throat and be done with him – not once, but at least three times. And he endured their guttural laughter, their jeering, leather faces, as they spat on him, and kicked him in the groin in response to his begging. And he hated himself for failing so miserably. Humiliation, not physical punishment, scarred deepest.

They took his eye well into the journey. He had no clear sense of time, but he remembered being shaken into consciousness, beyond Central Gate, by an ugly brute of a face that stared at him with one dark eye. Where the Haagii's right eye had been, a deep ragged scar furrowed, running from centre forehead to below his right ear. He wondered how the Haagii warrior survived such a horrendous blow, and why he was showing so much interest in him. Then the

Haagii wrenched back his head by the hair, pressed down on his eyeball with his thumb, and ripped it from its socket. The pain flooded out the world. But he didn't pass out, though he wished he had, because when he forced open his remaining left eye he saw the Haagii playing with his disgorged eyeball, pretending to place it in his hollow socket.

Elder Keryl's formal request that he attend the evening's assembly of the Ieldran was unexpected, so he dutifully followed the Elder along the narrow trail to the Sacred Circle. Keryl explained he was to be asked about the human Kingdom, what he knew of it before his capture, and especially what he knew of the Chancellor. As to the Ieldran's reasoning for the interview, Keryl hadn't enlightened him. He could only surmise that the Aelendyell were seriously contemplating rekindling their liaison with the Kingdom. With Andra as the new King, that could only be good for the war against the Haagii.

He owed the tattered remnants of his life to these people. Broken, bloodied, unconscious, an Aelendyell war party carried him from the carnage of a chance battle between the Haagii and the Aelendyell on the charred edges of Elvenaar Forest and brought him into the forest to be healed. They nursed him slowly back through the thick veils of pain, until his will to live returned, and oversaw his convalescence as the days became weeks, and late summer drifted through autumn into winter.

Though he was only quartercast by birth, raised as an orphan in Patti's brothel in the Great City, he held a powerful affinity for his Aelendyell heritage. Whenever he stumbled upon a plan of Great King Thana's that might affect the Aelendyell, he sent information by secret channels from the heart of the Thieves' Guild to the Ieldran, to warn them, or at least guide their negotiations. More than any member of the Guild, he understood why the Aelendyell had nothing to do with Thana's assassination, and he knew Andra's recovery, after disappearing in the dust of Dragon Breath Plains, eventuated from Aelendyell intervention, even without Andra's possession of an Aelendyell Weapon

Bearer's prized bow. He was no stranger to the Aelendyell, and when they established his identity beneath the blood, the dirt, the bruising, and the healing scars, he was welcomed home among the people of the forest as though he'd always been one of their family.

Elder Keryl led Tim into the silvery light of the Sacred Circle where the Ieldran gathered and motioned for him to sit beside him. The gathering was silent save the gentle sounds of individuals entering and joining the circle. No one spoke.

Tim had never witnessed a gathering of the Ieldran, the wisest Elders, drawn from every Aelendyell village and tun throughout the forests. Few Aelendyell were ever so privileged, and outsiders never received an invitation to the Aelendyell council of high Elders. Ceremony held little interest for him, but what he saw in the formal gathering of the Ieldran spoke unpretentious majesty and grace. Every member had long silvery-white locks, carefully brushed or braided, and their flowing green robes and cloaks that in daylight blended artfully with the forest's hues shimmered in the incandescent light dotted around the circle's perimeter. Nothing he experienced in the Guild came close to comparison. There, ceremony was brief, unadorned, the antithesis of the Royal ceremonies Thana promulgated in the name of his monarchy. Here, in the Sacred Circle of the Ieldran, all else seemed remote and intransient.

Although there was no cue, no call to order, he heard a curtain of silence press down on the gathering, and Elder Keryl rose, unannounced, and stepped into the circle. He paused to gaze up at the cone of night sky, framed between leaves and boughs, far above the Sacred Circle, and lowered his face toward the assembly.

'So, the circle is completed one more time and we are here,' he noted in a mild voice, and his simple opening statement was greeted with tranquil nods of affirmation. 'So, we again can speak our honest hearts freely among friends,' he added. His formality set the tone. Keryl took several more steps to the circle's centre before speaking again. 'Last night, we heard Sybbanel's words, and we spoke of their meanings to us, and the people, for a long time. You gave consent to bring another here to speak on this matter, and this I have done, for in the Sacred Circle sits one who has seen the workings of the one who calls himself the Chancellor and brings death and bitter vengeance to our people. To him I give my right to speak.'

Aware he was invited to enter the circle by Keryl's manner, Tim rose awkwardly and stepped self-consciously forward, as Keryl took his seat in the circle of Ieldran. Eyes sparkled in the soft glow of the light wands, eyes watching him patiently. He had no idea what they were seeking, why they waited for him to speak, but they mentioned the Chancellor, and he heard the whisperings among the Aelendyell during the day since Sybbanel's arrival. 'I am Tim Gaelus,' he tentatively began. 'How can I serve the Ieldran?'

An Elder, to his left, rose to speak. 'You are welcome among us, Tim Gaelus. Whatever we ask of you in the Sacred Circle is not meant to compromise your welcome. But we would appreciate your honesty in answering questions about the human Kingdom, and its people, and its policies. Will you speak to us freely, as we will to you?'

Tim reflected for a moment. There was nothing about the Ieldran suggesting anything but pure trust. 'I'll answer what I can,' he replied.

The initial questions were polite, concerning Tim's health, and how he was captured. Once he began to detail the siege of the plateau, the utter destruction of the Great City, and the heroic endurance of the people encircled by the vast Haagii army, the Ieldran listened intently, and their questions became steadily more specific.

'Tell us what the new King is truly like,' Farynyael asked, standing at the edge of light in the circle.

Tim hesitated, caught in the web of fond memories of his friendship with Andra. He remembered the raw young Guardian in the Great King's camp, fighting beside his friends against impossible odds, and the final vision of Andra the King-elect, in golden armour, cutting a swathe through the enemy army, before the Haagii cut Tim down on Castle Road. 'He's the one true successor to Aian Abreotan,' he answered.

An urgent whispering broke out among the Ieldran following his statement, and Elder Ithanyryll tottered to his feet, squinting at Tim in the glimmering light. 'Does he bear the mark?'

'Yes,' Tim replied, 'and the sword.' More whispering erupted, and Tim heard references to the sword, the orb, and Abreotan from every point of the circle. It was as if they temporarily forgot his presence. His voice cut across the general hubbub. 'He has the sword,' he affirmed, 'but the Orb of Radiance is destroyed.'

Theran pushed to his feet. 'That cannot be! The Orb is a sacred relic from the lost days of Elvenaar magic. There is nothing that can touch its power; nothing – except the sword.'

Tim heard the shock and passionate anger in the Elder's voice, the unsubtle accusation of the wielder of Abreotan's sword. 'The Orb was destroyed by the Dragonlord's people,' he explained.

An eerie hush descended on the circle. Theran remained standing. 'Are you certain this is true?'

Tim nodded. 'It's true. I was in the Great City when it happened. I saw the bodies of those the Dragonlord sent to destroy the Orb. The Chancellor had mounted it, as you know, on his tower to ward off the dragons, so the Dragonlord had it removed. That's why the dragons came.'

Another Elder stood. 'Tell us what you know of the Chancellor.'

Tim sensed the undercurrent of hatred in the Elder's request, despite the Aelendyell's attempt to disguise his emotional judgment of A Ahmud Ki. He knew the Chancellor meddled often, and maliciously, in Aelendyell affairs, and was not liked by these people. He marshalled his thoughts, and said, 'He has secrets about his Aelendyell birth right that I'm sure you already know. Where he came from, no one in the Kingdom is certain, though there were rumours in the Great City that he came from the neighbouring land of Targa.

He sets his own laws. He revels in the human game of politics, with little regard for others, unless they suit his plans. He wants to hold power over the whole Kingdom, from the lowest to the highest. He made Great King Thana, and Orrin of the Guild, his puppets, and now that they're gone I know he'll try to reassert his power over others. He wields greater magic than anything I've ever seen - except the sword.'

'He is the enemy of the Aelendyell,' the Elder said with venom.

'He is the enemy of many things,' Tim added. 'In the Great City, we've been caught between two evils – the one without, brought by the Dragonlord, and the one within, that is the Chancellor. I have no love for him.' He broke off, remembering his suspicions of A Ahmud Ki's plot to implicate the Aelendyell in Thana's assassination, and the Chancellor's role as the Shadow's Voice in the Guild.

'I say we must find a way to strike at this evil in the heart of the land!' cried Theran, who was on his feet again. 'We must make this ecg-bana feel justice!' Three more Elders rose to join Theran's call.

Tim watched the unexpected surge of hatred ripple through the circle and wondered what other evil A Ahmud Ki had perpetrated against these people.

'Peace! All of you.' Elder Keryl moved into the circle's centre, near Tim. 'We have heard what we knew, and suspected was true, about the Chancellor. But we did not hear what should be heard.' He turned to Tim. 'Tell us of the new King, the one you say bears the mark and the sword. Will he shelter this Chancellor from us, like the last Great King did? Or will he listen to us, and work justice, like the One King our great ancestors revered enough to work their strongest magic for in the Dragonblade?'

Tim barely hesitated in answering. 'Andra will listen to you. He's walked with Aelendyell and keeps their secrets. I know, because he carried a Weapon Bearer's bow and a healing powder pouch when he returned to the Great City.'

An Elder stirred at the fringe to speak. 'I know the

worold-buend you speak of. He came to Wudufaesten, many cycles ago. He carried an Aelendyell talisman even then, and he was lucky to live. The Elders of the tun saw the mark on his cheek, and before the Ealdfeond fell upon them, they sent word to me of his arrival. We spoke of this strange event, but we did not see the outcome it might bring.' Murmurs crept around the ring.

'How can we be sure he's not already a pawn of the Chancellor, like the others?' Theran coldly asked.

'Because he's strong,' Tim answered, 'and he's the successor to Abreotan. As much as I doubted prophecies before, for once I believe what I've seen. I know this man. He no more trusts the Chancellor than does anyone here. Go to Andra. Tell him the crimes the Chancellor's committed against the Aelendyell. Ask him for justice. He's the one human you can trust to restore the Aelendyell to their rightful place in the Kingdom.' He bent his head, as the silent evening crowded around his words, then looked up again and caught Keryl's steady gaze. 'Of all people I know,' he added, 'I'd trust Andra first with my life. He is hondgesella.'

Twenty Eight

From the ruined gate tower, Andra watched the low veil of rain sweep across the southern plains, angling from the Lake of Tears toward the Andrakian Mountains. All morning, intermittent showers came and went, leaving the earth moist, and cooling the air.

Movement directly below along the King's Way caught his eye, as a rickety cart lurched along the road, away from the plateau, drawn by four people. The cart was lightly loaded with salvaged fragments of wood and stone, intended for building.

The Great City remained a shadow of its former self. Many siege survivors settled inside the plateau's catacombs, certain the war with the Haagii was far from over, but others persisted with their former lives, returning to the city's ruins to scrape together ramshackle shelters, or reclaim allotments to build on, before the bitter wet weather of winter descended. Frail fingers of smoke rose from rough buildings clustered along Dragon River.

These were Andra's people. Always at the edge of starvation, food supplies scarce since the Haagii invasion and devastation, they were determined to endure against the odds and the enemy, most believing he was their saviour from the threat of the Dragonlord ensconced in Uz Erhaag. He held their trust and their hopes.

Andra descended the steps from the gate tower to ground level, where two Haardrishii dutifully waited, and headed for the fortress entrance with his retinue in tow. The ever-present Haardrishii guard, since his coronation, quietly annoyed him, though he couldn't refuse Claarn's insistence that, as King, he had to be protected. He personally perceived no immediate threat. The Haagii were driven out of the main part of the Kingdom, and the coming winter would keep them at bay for at least two or three months.

Where else could a threat emerge?

At the entrance, two more Haardrishii bowed their heads, as he passed with his personal bodyguard. He descended the angled corridor and, at a junction, turned right, toward chambers designated as King Andrakis' personal quarters. King Andrakis – the title still fascinated him. The people latched onto the title from his coronation, turning King Andra of Andrakis into King of Andrakis, and finally into King Andrakis, in a matter of days. He accepted it as appropriate, especially as he was not only Abreotan's inheritor but also the inheritor of the realm that had belonged to Dragonlord Andrakis. So, he was King Andrakis to the people.

Lanterns burned along the corridor, and he was acutely aware of oily smoke as he passed. When winter was over, and the people could begin to plant the first batch of new crops, he would order the reconstruction of the castle. He'd spent too long in the old Maze of the Thieves' Guild not to fully appreciate outdoor air and natural light. A short distance along, he paused at a door, before another pair of Haardrishii. One immediately turned and opened the door, and Andra quietly thanked him.

The room within had a low ceiling, and was hazy from vapours drifting from wall lanterns, and people rose from their seats as he entered. He recognised Claarn's red hair, and Marella beside him. Guild Mistress Kara stood opposite, one seat down from Lord Haephus, who was still resplendent in his red and orange robes. Beside Mistress Kara was Sasha, newly named as Tim's successor to Death's First Hand in the Guild. Seven places, including his at the head of the carved stone table, were empty. The Chancellor was notably absent.

Andra strode to his chair, facing the only visible entrance to the room. There was another – a carefully concealed door in the right wall, which led into the adjoining chamber marked as the King's Private Study. Sasha found it when she was asked to search the room, two days before Andra's coronation, and Kara, Claarn, Andra and she were the only ones privy to its existence.

'Be seated,' Andra said, gesturing with his right hand, and took his place, as the others followed his suit. He looked about apprehensively, smiling at Claarn and Kara, and nodding acknowledgement to each of the others. 'I'm not used to whatever ceremonies Great King Thana brought to such meetings,' he began apologetically. 'All I ask is that whatever is spoken here between us is spoken honestly. In my home village, people who entered the Hall of Council had to swear an oath. Its words were something like I enter here with peace in my heart and the needs of the people in my thought. Truth, above all things, is valued here. Truth,' he emphasised, 'is what I value.' He paused to watch the faces of those gathered. Heads nodded agreement.

'Then let us make such an oath,' Haephus suggested, 'for each time a meeting of the King's Table is called. And it can carry the blessing of Teka.'

'Yes,' Kara added in support. 'Haephus can write an oath for us all to learn.'

'So long as it's simple,' Claarn warned, with a wry smile at Haephus. 'I like the simplicity of Andra's -' He paused to bow his head at Andra. 'Of King Andrakis' oath.'

Before Andra could chide the giant for his mock politeness and use of title, the door to the chamber swung open, and the tall form of A Ahmud Ki entered. Everyone saw the Chancellor's silvered cloak glitter in the yellow light as he bowed. A dark shadowy being slipped in behind him and took a position to his right. 'I wish to ap-' A Ahmud Ki began, but his words were cut off by a burst of rage from Claarn.

'Get that filthy black thing out of here!' the giant bellowed, and he pushed away his chair, drawing his sword. Marella joined him, and they glared at A Ahmud Ki. Haephus' eyes were riveted to the black humanoid lurking against the wall.

'You've nothing to fear from my dracabeorn,' A Ahmud Ki calmly replied to Claarn's protest. 'He's my servant, totally obedient to me.'

Claarn advanced threateningly on the Chancellor. Behind the Chancellor, the two Haardrishii guards holding the door open silently drew their swords. 'That thing doesn't belong here,' Claarn growled.

A Ahmud Ki slowly lifted his right hand. 'Claarn!' Andra cried, stopping the warrior at the end of the table. Claarn turned his head very guardedly toward the King. A Ahmud Ki's hand drifted back to his side. 'As your King, I order you to return to your seat.' Claarn hesitated, but he heard the resolve in Andra's voice and obeyed, reluctantly, muttering something to the Chancellor as he turned that didn't carry to Andra's ears.

'Your Majesty,' Haephus began. 'I also object to the presence of this evil being. What right has the Chancellor to bring it here?'

Andra cast a glance toward the shadow skulking behind A Ahmud Ki and said, 'Your servant has no place here.'

A Ahmud Ki remained still a moment, and Andra sensed defiance, but then the Chancellor made a simple motion with his right hand and the dracabeorn slipped into the corridor and was gone. The Haardrishii sheathed their weapons and closed the door. A Ahmud Ki moved to the table, and stood beside his seat reserved nearest the King. His demeanour suggested he was unperturbed by the incident, but Claarn sat opposite him, glowering.

'I trust you've recovered from your illness?' Haephus asked A Ahmud Ki.

'Yes,' the Chancellor replied. 'Well recovered.' He turned to Andra and bowed his head, as he had upon entering. 'I wish to apologise for failing to attend Your Majesty's coronation, but the illness I contracted was surprisingly difficult to shake.'

'I accept your apology, Lord Chancellor,' Andra responded. 'Please be seated.'

A Ahmud Ki sat, as Andra composed his thoughts. He'd tried to prepare what he wanted to say at the first meeting of the King's Table, but the role of King was new. On the battlefield, against the Haagii, he could delegate leadership, and he could relate to the warrior's experience when making a King's decisions. This gathering, to talk and make decisions around a table, was an entirely different affair. He was acutely conscious of his role as mediator and final law, and he was uncertain he could fulfil it like the inheritor of Abreotan's legacy should.

He breathed deeply before recommencing. 'Today, I begin my apprenticeship as King. Though I'm your master and ruler by decree, you are my masters-in-training, charged with helping me to become a good King. Therefore, the first task I undertake is to share responsibilities. Each of you must be my right hand in these matters.' He paused, unsure if he'd said what he wanted to say. The others sat, watching, waiting for more, so he pressed on. 'First, there are the people of the Kingdom. I've decided their representative here will be Mistress Kara.' Everyone turned to the raven-haired lady who held the highest place in the Guild of Thieves.

A Ahmud Ki raised one eyebrow in question of Andra's choice. 'She oversees the thieves,' he politely objected.

'There are no thieves in Andrakis,' Andra calmly replied. 'Only hungry survivors. Before the Haagii came there were rich and poor, fat and hungry, landed and homeless. That's no longer true. There are only people now, and many already belong to the Guild. I think Mistress Kara understands what I mean. I need someone who can reach the people and help them work together to rebuild the city. She has that talent.'

Kara bowed her head, before lifting her dark eyes toward Andra, to say, 'As my King requests.'

'Thank you,' Andra said, and added, 'Lady Kara.' Kara smiled at hearing her conferred title spoken. 'Then there's the army,' Andra continued. 'That's already in the hands of Claarn,' and he grinned, and followed it with, 'or should I more correctly say Lord Claarn?' and fixed the giant with a beaming smile.

Claarn responded by bowing his head deeply toward the table, then lifting his head to respond. 'Lord Claarn accepts King Andrakis' most high favour, and I will conduct my duty with honour in your Royal Highness' service.' His tongue-in-cheek vow ended in a bubble of laughter from Marella, and

Andra and Sasha grinned at their horseplay, until Andra reasserted control.

In turn, he accorded responsibilities to the others: Haephus to oversee his religion and to work in conjunction with Kara where needed; Sasha the unexpected role of seeing to his personal security and matters pertaining to the running of the fortress; Marella was entrusted with reforming the Haardrishii, and training elite corps in the new army, working closely with Claarn.

Lastly, he turned to A Ahmud Ki. 'For the Lord Chancellor, there will be a change, especially since Lady Sasha has the most immediate role in the fortress. You have two tasks. First, I ask you to become my direct ambassador in re-establishing relationships with neighbouring lands. Our Kingdom can't survive, alone, against the Haagii. When winter's over, we must be organised enough to meet the enemy with combined forces. I want you to invite representatives from other peoples to the Table.' Andra let his specific instruction sink in and ignored questioning glances coming from Haephus and Claarn. 'The second task is equally important. As little as I know of it, what I do know is that the task once undertaken by Lord Ardath must be continued. I charge you with chronicling what happens here, and rebuilding the King's Royal Library. You must fulfil the Royal Drycraefter's role, either personally, or by overseeing it.'

A Ahmud Ki bowed his head, before making a query. 'And my role as your Advisor, Your Highness?'

Andra looked at A Ahmud Ki. The facial changes in the Chancellor were so evident, though slight in nature: beardless, cheekbones higher and slightly more prominent. He had so much Aelendyell in his features, and yet he was more strikingly handsome. And his piercing oval eyes, grey as they were, had a mysterious red hue in their depths. 'I consider truth my advisor, Lord Ki. And since every person at this table will swear a binding oath to speak truth, then every person here is my advisor.'

A Ahmud Ki bowed again to demonstrate obedience. 'As

you wish,' he answered quietly.

A Ahmud Ki waited for the others to withdraw so he could speak to the King privately. He ignored Claarn's suspicious glance and the giant warrior's reluctance to leave the chamber. When Andra approached, ending his short conversation with Sasha, A Ahmud Ki lowered his head respectfully and asked if he could have a brief audience. He cast a mild glance at Claarn and the two Haardrishii in the doorway. 'Alone, if Your Highness will,' he added.

Andra saw Claarn's eyebrow rise. 'What's on your mind?'

A Ahmud Ki shrugged. 'As you might guess, Your Highness, it's a delicate matter, one I'd prefer to share with you before anyone else.'

Andra motioned to the Haardrishii, who withdrew. Claarn hesitated, to show Andra he didn't approve of his decision, before he followed the guards into the corridor.

A Ahmud Ki eased the door closed. 'Your Majesty,' he contritely began, moving back to the table, 'do you remember I told you there was a Dragonlord's fortress in the plateau?'

'Yes,' Andra replied, bemused by the Chancellor's self-evident question. 'That's why we're here.'

'Of course,' said A Ahmud Ki, 'but I only revealed half of it. The chambers in the plateau are just the upper portion of the whole fortress. Beneath the Deep Cave, there's much more – the heart of Andrakis' fortress, in fact.' He saw Andra's astonishment at his confession and inwardly enjoyed the reaction.

'Go on,' Andra instructed, moving to the opposite side of the table to face the Chancellor.

'Beneath the Deep Cave lies the old dragon chambers where Andrakis stabled his pets. And Andrakis' personal chambers are there, still intact in the main.'

'How do you know this?' Andra asked.

'I've been there.'

Andra held A Ahmud Ki's gaze and saw flecks of red light

glint in the Chancellor's eyes. 'Why have you waited until now to tell me this?'

A Ahmud Ki broke the gaze, and gently snorted. 'There wasn't time until now. Too much has been going on. The Haagii were pressing us daily, and I was pursuing other matters. Besides, getting into the lower chambers is especially difficult without magical spells. The ways were sealed a long time ago.'

'By Abreotan?' Andra asked.

'Almost certainly,' A Ahmud Ki agreed. 'Andrakis was never meant to return from the tomb Abreotan created out of his lower chambers.'

Andra shifted toward the further end of the table where his Royal seat was positioned, and ran his fingers along the smooth stone, savouring its cool touch. 'And what did you find?'

'Not a lot,' A Ahmud Ki replied, 'but I found Andrakis.'

Andra was alert. What new horrors had the Chancellor stumbled upon or meddled with? 'The Dragonlord? He's still down there?'

'Of course,' A Ahmud Ki said nonchalantly, as if the presence of a Dragonlord meant little to him. 'But very much dead, Your Highness - very much dead.'

Andra breathed an audible sigh of relief. One Dragonlord was going to be enough to deal with as the Inheritor. The prospect of warring against two was beyond comprehension.

'But that's not why I tell you all this, Your Highness,' A Ahmud Ki continued. 'I've brought something out of the lower chambers.'

'What?' Andra asked.

'A golden suit of armour - Andrakis' armour.'

Andra cocked his head and squinted quizzically at the Chancellor. He already had the Dragonlord's armour from Dragon's Tooth.

'I see you understand my dilemma,' A Ahmud Ki smiled, taking a friendly step toward the King. 'To whom did the suit of armour we secured from Dragon's Tooth belong? Or did

Andrakis have two suits? I've wondered too. That's why I'm telling you what I've found. I'm curious to discover what similarities or differences exist between them, but I need your assistance.'

'So how can I help?' Andra asked, although he tempered his enthusiasm with a faint glimmer of distrust that A Ahmud Ki read clearly.

'Will Your Highness humour me by wearing your armour to my tower so we can compare your suit of armour with the one I've unearthed?'

Andra heard the Chancellor's invitation, expected it, and paused to make his decision. He knew Claarn and the others would object. The Chancellor was no longer trusted by anyone. The Guild members and Lady Kara believed Tim's assumption that A Ahmud Ki and the Shadow's Voice were one and the same. Sasha informed him of Milly's trailing of A Ahmud Ki to the Deep Cave, so part of the Chancellor's revelation was already known to him, but if A Ahmud Ki had found another suit of armour, one identical to his own, he had to know its value. Perhaps Claarn or Marella could wear it and receive the protection such a suit offered the wearer.

The war was far from over. Andra could see long battles with the Dragonlord's hordes raging to the north, once winter passed and the isolation of snow-bound and flooded valleys disappeared. He had the power of the sword. It enabled him to enter the Chancellor's tower once before, defying A Ahmud Ki's resistance, so if the Chancellor was plotting something, Andra was certain the sword would be more than ample protection against A Ahmud Ki's magic – at very least, it was a key out of the tower.

A Ahmud Ki watched the young King contemplate his invitation. For reasons he couldn't decipher, the charm spell he worked into the King's golden armour before the coronation had failed, and the King seemed less willing to listen to him than ever. What had he got wrong in the spell? He needed the King to accept his invitation so he could determine how the spell failed and rectify the matter. He knew the King wouldn't accept an invitation alone, under the circumstances. His friends had planted too many seeds of suspicion in his mind. Naive as Andra might be, A Ahmud Ki conceded he was at least intelligent enough to heed advice. Perhaps he should force the King to obey him with magical persuasion. No. The larger plan needed subtlety. So, he played his final gambit. 'Your Highness, I think it would be good if you brought along someone worthy of the armour, if it proves useful. Perhaps the giant warrior? Or another?'

Andra was pleasantly surprised by A Ahmud Ki's unexpectedly open invitation. He knew how little the Chancellor and Claarn tolerated each other. A Ahmud Ki was making a genuine concession by inviting Claarn to accompany Andra into the tower. Under those conditions, he saw no further reason to refuse A Ahmud Ki's offer. 'I'll come tomorrow morning,' he said. 'With Claarn and my inevitable bodyguards,' he added wryly.

A Ahmud Ki grinned in appreciation, and moved to open the chamber door for his King. 'I'll prepare for your visit, Your Majesty,' he said warmly, and bowed as Andra passed into the corridor to join his waiting retinue.

Twenty Nine

'Whatever your reason for coming here, you know how much I distrust this infernal Chancellor. Once inside his tower was once too often already,' Claarn grumbled, as he walked with Andra, hand resting on the hilt of his sword. A Ahmud Ki's black tower loomed ahead, darker than the rain-bearing clouds hanging low above the plateau. A brisk, chill breeze bit at their cheeks.

'Heavy rains are coming,' Andra said, looking up, and wistfully added, 'The Valley of Rivers will be flooded soon.'

'The Chancellor awaits us,' Claarn intervened, drawing Andra's gaze to the base of the tower.

A Ahmud Ki, in his silver and black robes, holding an amber pyramid, watched the party of four approach. 'Greetings,' he said, with a brief bow. 'Thank you for honouring my invitation, Your Majesty.'

'What's that?' Claarn abruptly asked, pointing to the pyramid.

'A key,' the Chancellor politely replied. 'It will allow you to enter my tower.'

'We didn't have much difficulty last time,' Claarn reminded A Ahmud Ki.

A Ahmud Ki gave a strained smile in reply, before saying to Andra, 'I'd prefer you didn't tamper with the fabric of the tower. The last time was expediency, Your Highness, I understand that, but your sword could cause irreparable damage to the spells holding the structure together. Besides, such crude power isn't necessary. This crystal alters the wall so you can pass through without harm. Please.' A Ahmud Ki waved a welcoming gesture, and placed the crystal on the ground at the base of the tower, whispered a foreign word, and indicated Andra, Claarn and the accompanying pair of Haardrishii should step through the wall.

The stark white marble interior hadn't altered since their

hurried escape into the tower from the Haagii. A Ahmud Ki stepped through after them, carrying the pyramidal crystal key, and asked them to follow him up the steps to the chamber Andra recalled was a library. He also remembered there were no ladders, steps or openings leading to the upper tower levels, a fact that fascinated him. Though magic had rapidly become a major facet in his life, since leaving The Vale, through the sword, and through the Chancellor, the Aelendyell, and the Dragonlord, it continued to mystify him.

When they entered the chamber, Andra observed a large crystal sphere resting on a pile of books on a central table. Other books were scattered about, opened. Then he was aware of dark shadows moving around the perimeter of the room and his hand moved to his sword.

Claarn and the Haardrishii had already drawn their weapons. 'What trap is this?' Claarn snarled, glaring fiercely at the Chancellor.

A Ahmud Ki sighed deeply and waved his left hand. Immediately the dark shapes, six in all, skirted the extremities of the chamber and descended the steps to the lower level. 'There. Gone,' he said with a casual air. 'They're as harmless as house pets.'

'Where's the armour?' Andra asked, relaxing his guard.

'I've stored it in the upper levels. For safety,' A Ahmud Ki replied, as he moved toward the central table. At the table, he passed his hand over the crystal sphere, and it began to glow with a soft amber luminescence. 'Here it is. You can see it,' he said, indicating the sphere. Andra moved to stare into the sphere. In its depths, he thought he could see something glimmer with a golden sheen, and he was aware of a sudden rush of light that swept past and around him with unexpected fury.

Do you know who I am?
    No.
    I am Berak N'eth, God of Power. You are my servant.
    I don't serve you. I serve the people.

You serve me. I am the source of all that you are. I give you your power.

The sword is my power.

I am the sword. The sword is part of me. You are merely its servant. You are my servant.

Andra fought through the confusion whirling in his mind. I am the sword. Ardath told me so.

Ardath was a misguided old fool. He never understood power. He never came to me.

Then why haven't you spoken to me before now?

Because you were not ready.

Ready? Ready for what?

Ready to serve. Ready to wield the sword's true power. Ready to be a strong King.

Amber mist swirled. The voice came from beyond the mist. Andra tried to push through to find the source of the voice, but the mist thickened, threatened to choke him. Why do you hide in the mist?

I am your master. Were you to gaze on my face it would destroy you. The mist protects you. No one gazes on the face of Berak N'eth, God of Power, and lives. Andra relented. The mist thinned a little. Good. You must learn to obey me.

Did Abreotan serve you?

All who wield power serve Berak N'eth.

A Ahmud Ki eased his concentration on the King's prone figure stretched on the circular mat in the centre of his Prayer Room, golden armour reflecting the soft amber glow of the spinning pyramids. On the King's ring finger, a fine platinum ring glittered, set with a fragment of amber crystal. A Ahmud Ki had bestowed his coronation gift. He had no explanation as to why the spell in Andra's armour failed to charm him. When he pried the magical aura surrounding the King, he found a confusing pattern of energies operating that didn't resemble the fabric of the spell he created, though he recognised fragments of it in the aura. Something disrupted the spell patterning – perhaps the sword. The ring on the unconscious King's finger was infused with much greater power than the simple charm spell he'd worked into the armour. It would allow him to penetrate Andra's mind at any point, and communicate freely, making the King a puppet to manipulate at his whim. He needed a little time to test whether the sword would interfere with the ring's working.

He was astonished to find a determined degree of resistance to his magical influence in the young King's mind when he entered with a mind spell. The King had strong moral beliefs in honesty and trust, for someone so young, and Ardath obviously made a bigger impression on Andra than A Ahmud Ki expected capable of the old Drycraefter.

And there were other sources, a broad range he stumbled upon in his guise as the god Berak N'eth. There were Aelendyell influences embedded in the King's memory, a discovery that astonished him. When had Andra spent time with the Aelendyell?

And he discovered the foundation of the young warrior's beliefs: the lessons of The Way. In time, he'd unravel the sources and secrets underlying these memories wrapped inside the King's mind. For now, control was paramount.

He made a wise choice, adopting the role of the god, because he realised, if he entered Andra's mind as himself, he would have failed, such was the level of defence the King had built against him. He tripped over a web of suspicions and theories about himself, in the process of convincing Andra that Berak N'eth was his true master, so tangled a web that it was highly unlikely he ever could achieve control of the King, except by brutal means. Subtlety was better. The result would be more enjoyable, more effective.

He expected the sword to interfere with his attack, but it didn't. Its magic was clearly limited to whatever the user manipulated from it. It wasn't an entity in its own right. Another of his concerns was allayed. But then, he mused, if it is only a magical object, then there is the possibility anyone can wield it.

Curiosity awoke. A Ahmud Ki released his mental hold on the unconscious King, entering the aura of light in the chamber's centre where the handle of Abreotan's sword glittered in its scabbard, and stared at the sword, his hand breaking into a cold sweat at the prospect of possessing the most powerful object he'd ever seen. He surmised it was even more powerful than the Orb of Radiance, being more versatile, more deadly in its uses, and with its undeniable ability to multiply and magnify his magic he could become the ultimate master, more potent than any Dragonlord, the embodiment of Abreotan's legendary power and everything the Dragonlords mastered. Who could oppose him? Who would dare? He tentatively stretched his hand toward the hilt, and, with a determined rush, he wrenched the sword from Andra's scabbard.

As he grabbed the weapon, amber fire burst along the blade and raced over his arm toward his head. He screamed, intense pain searing through his rigid limb, and he tried to free the sword from his hand, but his fingers were magically welded to the handle. He wheeled, amber flames writhing around his entire body, and conjured a desperate spell of release, despite the agony pulsing along his arm, shrieking his arcane words, until unconsciousness swallowed him.

The chamber, bathed in amber light, was entirely unfamiliar when Andra opened his eyes. Lying on his back, on a rug, his first thought was to reach for Abreotan's sword, which was securely strapped in its place by his side. Fragments of a fantastic dream flitted through his mind. He imagined A Ahmud Ki was stealing Abreotan's sword, and laughing, because he was powerless to stop him.

He sat up and surveyed the chamber. Strange pyramids of amber light circled at four points, suspended by their own volition. Magic was everywhere. His eyes rested on a suit of golden armour, like his own, standing against the wall to his right. He rose to his feet unsteadily, but the movement sent sharp pain stabbing through his head, and he clutched his temples. He remained immobile, until the pain subsided to a dull throb, and when he could finally refocus he took a step toward the armour.

He heard a groan to his left, and turned to discover a crumpled figure curled into a foetal position: A Ahmud Ki. He crossed to the Chancellor and kneeled to see what had happened. His headache pounded as he bent his head, and he felt as if he was going to pass out, but he steadied and rolled the Chancellor over. A Ahmud Ki moaned and rolled away, clutching his right hand.

Andra stood again, gingerly nursing his aching head, and searched the chamber, his hand steadily drawing Abreotan's sword from the scabbard, trying to identify the source of danger that rendered him unconscious and so effectively disabled the Chancellor. Nothing was obviously about to attack. No one else waited in the chamber. Then he remembered the pulse of light from A Ahmud Ki's sphere in the library. What caused that? Had the Chancellor triggered the wrong spell? Where were Claarn and the Haardrishii? Where was he?

Another groan rose from the Chancellor, and when Andra glanced down he saw A Ahmud Ki's damaged right arm extend and retract. The cloth was burned away, and the flesh was scalded. What in Teka's name happened? He knew he was in another chamber of the tower because of the size and circular nature of the chamber, and the presence of the second suit of armour confirmed his assumption, but there were no visible openings, no doors or stairways up, out, or down. A Ahmud Ki used magic to get them here, and something had gone horribly wrong.

He bent over the Chancellor again, his throbbing headache fading. 'Lord Ki? Can you hear me?' he asked. The Chancellor's eyes remained closed, his breathing rapid and shallow. Andra recognised the strangling grip of shock. The Chancellor hung on the edge of death.

Alarmed at the seriousness of A Ahmud Ki's injury, he left the sword beside the Chancellor and searched for a secret exit, but he found nothing. Trapped. Without A Ahmud Ki's magic he couldn't escape or get help – unless he used the sword. He'd broken through the magical fabric before to get into the tower. He could use it to escape. Then he remembered A Ahmud Ki's warning the sword might permanently destroy the tower's structure. Worse, he had every reason to believe A Ahmud Ki had shifted them high into the tower, which meant it wasn't simply a case of forming a hole in the wall to leave. He had to get himself, and the dying Chancellor, down, as well as out. A Ahmud Ki groaned again, and shivered violently, uncontrollably. Sweat beaded on his contorted face. There was too little time. He'd seen the signs of death often on the battlefield. Without the Chancellor's magic, the battle with the Dragonlord would be even more difficult in the coming months. He had to do something.

He summoned Abreotan's sword into his hand with a thought. What are the limits of the magic of this sword? he wondered. Can it heal as well as kill? Ardath unlocked the key to it for him. You are the sword. What you will, so will it do. He placed the point of the blade against the Chancellor's forehead. The unconscious Chancellor winced and shuddered at its touch, but Andra ignored his reaction and focussed his desire into the weapon, willing it to heal. The blade began to glow white, forcing back the amber radiance of the pyramids, and the glow steadily spread from the sword tip, along the length of A Ahmud Ki's body, until he was enveloped in a white halo. The Chancellor's involuntary shivering subsided, and as the glowing light faded and dissolved, he let out a deep sigh, before slipping into the steady breathing rhythm of sleep.

Andra relaxed and lifted the sword tip from the Chancellor's forehead, sheathed the weapon and squatted wearily against the amber-hued wall to wait, feeling the dull ache of his headache return with renewed vengeance, but he allowed himself a tired half-grin as he wondered how impatient Claarn would be downstairs with the Chancellor's dracabeorn lurking on the floor below.

A Ahmud Ki opened his eyes. He was lying against the curved

270

wall of the Prayer Room. The sword: he glanced at his right arm. The silver and black material was shredded and burned from his skin, but there was no burn on his arm, only the outline of a faint scar stretched across his wrist to his elbow. Healed! How? He sat up and glanced around the space. The King wasn't lying in the centre of the prayer mat.

'How do you feel?' Andra's quiet voice startled A Ahmud Ki, who jerked to face the young King seated against the wall. 'You nearly died.'

Andra's matter-of-fact statement amazed A Ahmud Ki. He clambered to his feet and asked, 'What do you mean?'

'When I came to, I found you in shock. The burn on your arm was as nasty as I've seen. I healed it with the sword.'

A Ahmud Ki stared at his arm again. The sword caused the injury in the first place. Now he owed his life to it? 'Something must've gone wrong with your spell.' Andra suggested.

A Ahmud Ki looked back at Andra, who was also getting to his feet. How long had he been unconscious? What had the King been doing? 'Yes. It appears so,' he mumbled absently. He glanced at the armour.

'It's identical, except for the jagged additions,' Andra said, moving toward the point of A Ahmud Ki's gaze. 'I'd say this is Andrakis' battle-suit. It's like the armour the Dark Warriors wear. You were right to bring it from Andrakis' tomb.'

A Ahmud Ki nodded, still gathering his senses. 'Thank you, Your Majesty,' he said.

'The problem is deciding what to do with it,' Andra continued, running a hand across the breastplate of the hanging suit. 'It wouldn't fit Claarn. Too small for him. And it's not exactly proportioned to fit Marella either.'

'If Your Majesty would consider my proposal?' A Ahmud Ki asked, moving toward the King.

'Well?' Andra asked.

'It fits me perfectly.'

'You've worn it?'

'Yes.'

271

Andra toyed with an unusual scabbard at the suit's belt. 'Is there a weapon to fit this?'

'There was a battle-axe,' A Ahmud Ki explained, 'but I discarded it. It was too heavy to bring from the lower levels.'

'Any chance of retrieving it?' Andra asked.

'I doubt it. I had enough difficulty getting in and out last time,' A Ahmud Ki replied, trying to direct Andra's interest from the battle-axe he'd thrown away, outside his Aelendyell home.

'Pity,' the King said, shaking his head. 'It might've been a useful weapon.'

'I'm certain it was only decorative,' A Ahmud Ki suggested.

Andra moved from the armour toward the centre of the chamber. He could see little harm in letting the Chancellor keep the armour. There was no one else he could imagine it fitting without radically altering it in a forge, and that process might destroy the armour's beauty and qualities. 'It's yours,' Andra said, 'if you tell me where we are.'

A Ahmud Ki gave a courteous nod. 'Thank you,' he said. 'As to where we are, you stand in my Prayer Chamber.'

Andra turned to A Ahmud Ki. 'You pray to Teka?'

'No, Your Highness,' the Chancellor replied. 'To the Ithosen god, Berak N'eth.'

Andra felt a flicker of recognition. He was familiar with the Ithosen god's name, yet he was certain he never heard the name before. How could that be? 'I think it's time we returned to Lord Claarn,' Andra suggested, satisfied that the issue of the armour was solved. 'He'll be concerned for my safety, being gone so long.'

'As you wish, Your Highness,' replied A Ahmud Ki. 'It's essential you hold onto my cloak as we descend,' he explained. 'The spells only work on those casting them, and what they carry or touch.'

How did we ascend? Andra wondered. A Ahmud Ki weaved his hands in a short, precise pattern, uttered several obscure words, and the pair passed through the floor, and each of the tower's levels, until they stood in the library again.

For a moment, Andra thought Claarn and the two Haardrishii were in a trance, but as he went to speak Claarn flung up his arm to shield his eyes and cried 'Look out!' A Ahmud Ki laughed at the giant's reaction, laughter which brought Claarn's scornful anger to the surface as he lowered his arms. 'What stupid magical prank is this?' he growled.

'No prank,' Andra answered. 'I've seen the armour as promised.'

Claarn looked bewildered. 'When?'

'While you waited here.'

'That quick?'

Andra was amused by Claarn's sense of time. 'If you consider that as quick, I guess so.'

Claarn shot a stern glare at A Ahmud Ki. Something was amiss, but he couldn't figure what it was. The Chancellor seemed content. That wasn't a promising sign. Claarn and the Haardrishii followed the King and Chancellor downstairs, where the leading pair paused at the wall. Claarn kept a watchful eye on the dracabeorn crouching near the stairway.

'This is a gift in return for the armour,' A Ahmud Ki said, and he extended his hand. In it, he cupped a pyramid crystal key to the tower.

So that was it, Claarn decided, as he watched Andra accept the crystal and practise the Ithosen word to activate its magic against the wall. The Chancellor had the right to wear the armour. How had he convinced Andra to give him the armour?

'Come on,' Andra called to Claarn, as he stepped through the wall. Claarn gave another sharp glance at A Ahmud Ki, who stood with an enigmatic smile watching him depart, before he stepped through the wall.

In the cleared space that had been Thana's Royal Gardens, rain poured out of the darkness, and as the group hurried across the open ground toward the fortress entrance and shelter Claarn was sure something was wrong with the world. It was much darker than he expected for mid-morning, even given the rainstorm. Once he conducted

Andra to the relative safety of his rooms, he returned to the Haardrishii stationed on watch near the fortress door. 'What time of day is it?' he asked one warrior, as he shook the water droplets from his red mane.

'Gone nearly third watch, Lord Claarn,' the Haardrishii respectfully replied.

Claarn stopped shaking and stared at the man. Third watch. No wonder it was dark. Night was approaching. That was what he sensed. In the tower, they lost the good part of a day, yet he missed only a moment from the flash of light in the sphere to Andra's re-appearance. Something was indeed very wrong.

Thirty

Milly watched glistening water trickling from a hole in the earth above her, and spiral through the semi-darkness to flow into a puddle at her feet. Artega was lapping at the water, red tongue the only visible element in his blackness. The rain outside was falling steadily, not heavy, showing no sign of abating. It had rained non-stop for five days, after the storm clouds swept in from the southern lakes and the Endless Sea.

She crouched against the earthen wall of the ruined section of the Maze, listening to the steady hiss of rain on the earth above, and fixed her eyes on the patch of grey wintry light illuminating the hole in the tunnel's ceiling, remembering how she used to watch rain fall while her father filed horseshoes near his forge. The room was always lit by the red glow of the coals, and their warmth kept out the biting cold. She remembered how her father's rough hands smoothed her hair, or brushed her cheek, their broad backs hairless from constant exposure to the forge's flames, and the ever-present smell of smoke from his clothing when he hugged her and told her stories. He always told stories about horses, about wild steeds racing across the vast plains of the Kingdom, defying warriors to ride them because they were free, and stories of horses that were courageous, and beautiful, and faithful to their owners. She heard descriptions of black Haardrishii stallions, long before she ever saw them in the Great City, and her father pictured Great King Thana's wonderful creatures drawing his ceremonial carriage in such detail that she remembered lying awake at night imagining the grace and elegance of horses that drew a King behind them. Though horses were uncommon in the Kingdom, her father always promised her one, when she was old enough to handle and care for it. She dreamed of being a princess, dressed in white and turquoise and yellow, mounted on her pure white horse, parading through the shallow valleys toward her village, the people gathering to watch her arrive, and her father proudly gazing on the whole scene from the peak of the nearest hill, smiling as she waved to him. She dreamed it whenever she could, before the Haagii came – before they killed her father.

A dark shape obscured the hole. She tensed, but Artega's tail wagged reassuringly. Aaron scrambled through the opening, and slid down beside her, brushing water droplets from his face and hair. 'Why are you hiding here?' he asked, as he patted Artega's welcoming snout.

'I'm not hiding,' Milly replied coldly. 'I might just as well ask why you're running around in the rain.'

'I've been helping Taggart fix a leak on his shelter. He wanted me to fetch mud and straw from the riverbank.'

'I thought there'd be enough mud at his feet in this weather, without getting it from the river,' she responded, unimpressed with Aaron's explanation.

'It's not clay like at the river,' he said, ignoring her disdain, 'and you still didn't say why you were here.'

'It's quiet,' she answered. 'You're wet.'

Aaron shook his hair, sending droplets spraying over her, so she cursed and hit him squarely on the arm. He rubbed the sore spot, muttering, 'Thanks a lot. I needed that.' She grinned at his hurt look, and he relented by laughing. Then they both laughed. 'Patti's been looking for you,' he said, as his mirth subsided.

'Is that why you're here?'

'Partly,' he replied. 'I just wanted to find out where you were.'

'Why?'

Her question made Aaron turn away before he answered. 'Because - well because I just did, that's all,' he said shyly.

She wondered at his shyness. Since the siege, she sensed something had changed in his attitude to her. She wasn't sure whether she liked the change or not. 'And what's Patti want?' she asked.

'Don't know. She just said if I saw you today to ask you to see her as soon as possible.'

'Then I better go.' She began to merge into the darkness of the Maze. 'Coming?'

Artega's ears pricked expectantly, and Aaron nodded. Then he noticed the suspension of expression on Milly's face as she stared past him. He turned to look up through the opening into the grey light, as she scrambled by. 'What is it?' he asked, confused by her action.

'Dragon,' she hissed, and used her arms to pull herself out of the Maze into the dull rain. They emerged in the debris of a shattered building that hid one of hundreds of secret trapdoors into the Guild's Maze, Aaron and Artega in tow of Milly, whose eyes were fixed on the low, grey ceiling of sky, searching, waiting.

Aaron peered into the rain and saw nothing beyond the grey wall. 'Are you sure you saw a dragon?'

'Sure,' she half-consciously replied, without diverting her eyes from the heavens. Long moments dragged by. Rain soaked inside Aaron's clothing, and he shivered. He began to doubt her word. Then she pointed. 'There!' Low on the horizon, a dark smudge on the tapestry of rain, a winged shape drifted down, momentarily visible between sky and earth, before being swallowed in the shifting shades of grey. 'Did you see it?' she asked, fixed on the distance.

'Uhuh,' Aaron muttered, and he shivered again, no longer cold from the rain, but touched with different fingers of ice.

Andra leaned the sword in its scabbard against the earthen wall of his private chamber and stood on the rough rug in the centre of the floor. He stared at the gilt handle and the rune-marked blade, its wickedly serrated and curved adornments breaking the straight lines of its cutting blades, memorising its physical attributes. He glanced at the door to make certain no one was coming in. The Haardrishii posted outside were under specific orders to admit no one, until he

277

countermanded those orders personally.

He returned his attention to the sword. The magical potency of Abreotan's legacy had hardly been touched. He concentrated, willing the sword to his hand. An instant later, he felt its familiar texture in his grip and the scabbard was empty. He looked away from the scabbard, imagining it in his mind, and willed the sword to return. Weight dissolved in his grip, and when he turned to face the scabbard the sword gleamed in place, as if it had never moved. He willed the sword to rise from the scabbard and hang in space. The sword responded, levitating an arm span above the floor, spinning to point upwards. He silently ordered it to flame. Light leapt around the chamber walls from amber tongues of fire, illuminating his desk and a handful of books A Ahmud Ki passed to him from the tower collection, books that had belonged to Waeron Ardath. He dissolved the flames and moved his eyes to the wooden door. Like an arrow, the sword streaked to the door, burying its point into the spot where he focussed. Satisfied, he recalled it to his hand.

Its weightlessness belied its proportion. If it weighed what it ought by what anyone could see, the weapon was only ever likely to be clumsily wielded in two hands by a warrior at least the bulk and strength of Claarn. Yet, for Andra, it was never heavier than a solid dagger. He stared at the long blade and willed it to become invisible. The blade dissolved before his eyes, until only the handle was visible. He reached out his free hand gingerly, testing for the presence of the blade, and his fingers found the cold metal edge. He brought the sword back into sight and restored it to its scabbard.

He was certain he only knew a fraction of the sword's powers. He knew it could heal. A Ahmud Ki owed him his life for that. It cut through dragon scale, as easily as an oar through water. It could provide light in a variety of intensities. It flamed. It created holes in physical and magical constructs at his will. It focussed and enhanced magical energy, as it had for A Ahmud Ki in Dragon's Tooth. Strangest of all, it made him feel he could grow in stature and strength to be the physical equal of a dragon, as it had outside A Ahmud Ki's tower during the siege of the fortress. Yet he knew, instinctively, it could do more, a great deal more. Finding the key to its secrets was the mystery. He was the sword.

Andra loosened the Guardian circlet securing his ponytail and ran his fingers through his long locks as his freed hair fell to his shoulders. Magic. His whole world was ensnared in it. A long time ago, in The Vale, he remembered sensing the faintest touch of magic in the wizened stare of old Master Geat, but he hadn't understood it because The Vale had no need of magic. But the world revealed more and more magic the longer he lived in it – the Aelendyell, the Dragonlord, A Ahmud Ki, the sword – everything was touched by it, in ever-increasing degrees. He shook his head, as he sat at the chair by his desk. Then a fleeting image of a pair of dark eyes triggered his thoughts: Berak N'eth - God of Power. Unconsciously, he rubbed the platinum band on his ring finger as he struggled with his memory. Abreotan had served Berak N'eth. He served Berak N'eth. When did he learn this?

'You can't enter. The King has expressly forbidden anyone to disturb him,' the guard coldly confirmed, his hand resting menacingly on the hilt of his sword. He stared at the black war dog and boy accompanying the girl.

'I'm not just anyone,' Milly replied. 'I've got to see him now.'

'You have no business with the King that can't wait,' the Haardrishii warned.

'But it's urgent!' Aaron blurted. 'He's in danger.' Milly wrenched at Aaron's arm in anger, but the Haardrishii was already bending forward.

'What sort of danger?'

'That's for the King to know,' Milly interrupted, frowning at the guard.

'I can't see any danger here,' the Haardrishii said, with a knowing wink to his companion, 'but I'll inform the King of your concern when he countermands his order for privacy.'

Milly spat, and turned on her heels to walk off, Aaron and Artega following in her wake. 'Where are you going now?' Aaron asked as he caught up.

'To find Sasha,' Milly scowled.

The Sharvan assassin crouched at the muddy base of the plateau, and watched rain pock the grey surface of Dragon River. A shadowy figure cowered beside him, featureless in its own darkness, except for a sensation of glittering eyes and ragged teeth. He hated the dracabeorn as much as he feared the awesome power of The One King he served, but he had no choice except to forebear the shadow's presence.

He had a matter of great importance and honour to complete. The One King had chosen him, Terag Ni Yerval, to assassinate the human King, and carry the sword of fire to Azikhaag, as a gift for his master. In choosing Terag, The One King elevated him to the highest rank among his people and brought supreme honour to his family and his village. Should he return successfully, as he was certain he would, he would be known to the whole world of Uz Erhaag, and singers would praise his name for eternity around the hearths of his people. He would set the path for victory; he, Terag, the Sharvan who rode a dragon on his quest. If this was his death-journey, he would be no less the subject of many a song. His honour and name were assured by The One King's choice, and in that knowledge he had no fear of death. But he would not die.

He glanced at the lurking dracabeorn and crept to the riverbank. The constant rain was an excellent ally, driving the Kingdom barbarians under shelter so they couldn't watch for trouble. Terag checked his black dagger was secured in his belt, and slipped into the waters, heading for the opening in the plateau base from whence the river flowed.

'Milly!' Aaron whispered. 'Come back!'

'Shut up, Aaron!' Milly hissed. She crouched at the junction of corridors, and peered into the darkness to her left, listening. Sasha and The Hand assassins melted into the tunnel. 'Can you smell them?' she whispered to Artega. The dog cocked his head.

'Milly,' Aaron wheedled, edging closer to her. 'You heard Sasha's instructions. She said keep out of the way.'

'We are,' Milly retorted.

'Then let's go back to the hearth room and wait like we're supposed to.'

She snorted at his suggestion, and moved into the left corridor, holding Artega's collar, so Aaron sighed with reluctant resignation, slid his makeshift assassin's dirk from his belt, and followed, squinting to catch a glimpse of anything in the uncomfortable dark.

They passed three closed doors before reaching the next intersection on the sloping corridor. Steps dropped deeper into the earth. Artega sniffed the floor and looked disinterested, so Milly decided Sasha's group must've moved well ahead. She considered which direction to take and headed right, along a narrow corridor that cut back below the upper chambers where many of the Kingdom warriors bunked. Burning torches hung every ten paces to light the way, illuminating doors into storage rooms and chambers used as animal pens during the siege.

Halfway along, Milly froze, wrenching on Artega's collar, and the dog's hackles rose as he growled viciously. Aaron, following in her wake, nearly blundered into her. On the floor, at the next junction, an arm flopped from the corner and quivered. A maroon stain spread across its palm. Milly slid her dagger from its sheath and backed into a door recess beside Aaron.

A shadowy figure appeared at the corner, crouching warily above the outstretched arm, and hastily glanced left and right. Glittering eyes fixed on Milly and Artega. Caught by the creature's steady stare, Milly shivered, as though someone trickled ice down her back. With a sibilant screech, the black creature leapt.

281

Before Milly could move voluntarily, Aaron wrenched her arm, pulling her and Artega through the door he opened, and slammed it shut. Inside, they pressed against the wood, desperately barring entry to the shadowy being, Artega growling and snapping at the plinth. Something thumped against the door, and scratching and brutal pounding started, accompanied by harsh, low hissing sounds. Milly wondered how long the door would hold against the battering. Then the noise ceased. Artega growled and began sniffing harshly at the door. Milly could hear the rush of her heartbeat, and Aaron's rapid breathing beside her in the darkness. 'Is it gone?' she asked.

'I don't know,' Aaron hastily replied. 'And I'm not looking to find out either.'

Terag wiped the blood from his havek dagger, the black blade curved like a serpent and serrated for eight thumb spans midway along one edge, and let the soft body of his victim slip to the tunnel floor. He listened, before he crept to the intersection to decide his next move. Voices. He crouched in an unlit corridor, and edged back to the body of his victim in the darkness. Five people crossed the lighted intersection: three old women and two old men, carrying material and wood.

He waited for the sound of their chatter to recede, before moving up to the intersection again. The cursed dracabeorn had slipped away in the darkness, somewhere beyond the large cave they entered after swimming the underground lake. It had its own purpose for certain, The One King would've given it a mission, and so long as it didn't interfere with his task Terag wasn't going to waste time worrying where it was. Still, he wished it hadn't come in with him. The corridors ahead were all lit. He had to move with caution and intelligence. He crept back to the body and dragged the tunic and trousers from it to slip over his black garb. In Kingdom clothing, he could bluff his way to the chambers of the King he was meant to kill.

As he began to pull on the rough cloth trousers, a noise stopped him. Lantern light spilled across the intersection. He let the trousers fall and spun on the spot, his two throwing daggers instantly to hand. A woman and three men were staring at him, tiny assassin dart bows armed and pointed. The woman said something in her alien tongue. In a blur of action, Terag threw his daggers simultaneously, a skill perfected from his forefathers who were Sharvan assassins. If the daggers found fatal marks, he never knew. Four darts hit him squarely in the chest, unbalancing him, and, caught in a tangle of trousers around his ankles, he pitched backwards toward the hard floor, falling, but never feeling its solidity.

Thirty One

Claarn shifted uncomfortably in his chair and glared at the Chancellor who was sitting too close, for his liking, to the King. He still hadn't resolved the loss of time on their visit to the Chancellor's tower, and he had far too little opportunity to pursue the matter with Andra because of the necessary and time-consuming duties of reorganizing the army. He was especially suspicious of the Chancellor's latest gift to the chamber of the King's Table: a thin slab of stone, set into the wall, that glowed dull yellow and gave off heat, like a hearth. He appreciated the warmth, like everybody else, but why did have to come from magic? Worse, why from the Chancellor?

'The plans have been presented to me,' Andra was saying. 'Whilst the people can choose to rebuild from the ruin of the Great City, it makes far greater sense to furnish the fortress of Andrakis. The plans detail what ought to be done and where in the fortress.' He nodded to Kara, who deftly unrolled a parchment on the stone table. Under the light of one of A Ahmud Ki's floating spheres, the members of the Table leaned forward to study the suggestions.

'Who drew this?' Marella asked, leaning back.

'I did,' A Ahmud Ki quietly answered, 'with some suggestions from the King and Lady Kara.'

'This includes space for a temple to Teka?' asked Haephus with raised eyebrows.

'Space for Teka and Berak N'eth,' A Ahmud Ki replied.

Haephus' eyebrows knitted. 'What sacrilege is this?' Claarn and Sasha looked up with the others, hearing the challenge in Haephus' words.

Surprisingly, the Chancellor leaned back and allowed Andra to respond to the High Priest. 'No sacrilege. Teka may well be the preserve of the people who lived under the past kings, but Berak N'eth is the true God of Abreotan, and is the living force in the sword and me. There will be a temple to

Berak N'eth.'

Haephus went red in the face, flustered by the unexpectedly lucid and firm argument from Andra. 'But this is not the province of another god or goddess. Most Holy Teka has presided over the Great City and Kingdom for as long as there have been priests. Her dominion stretches back long before Aian Abreotan wrestled the throne from the Dragonlords. I cannot allow you to present a usurper to her power.'

The longer he spoke, the more flustered he became, until Andra cut across his speech. 'You cannot allow? You? Do you dare to question the promise and piety of your King?' Andra stood over, daring the High Priest to argue.

Haephus faltered, glancing left and right at the others, who stared open-mouthed at the confrontation. He seemed poised to plunge into debate, but his eyes rested again on the King, standing threateningly at the end of the table, and he bit his lip. 'I beg Your Highness' pardon,' he said in a humble manner, and bowed. 'I forgot myself under the – unusual circumstances.'

Andra smiled. 'You're forgiven, Lord Haephus. Times have changed. The old gods and goddesses are powerless. Berak N'eth protects us where Teka could not. Outside are the ruins of her world. In here are the seeds of Berak N'eth's world.'

His explanation failed to placate the priest, but Haephus restrained his hurt and anger, and avoided further eye contact with the King, out of shame and frustration.

Andra waited for order to settle at the table and continued. 'Part of the plan is to refurbish the King's chambers and main rooms in the upper section of the fortress. Work on the reconstruction of the castle, and the new buildings within, will commence tomorrow. Lord Ki will oversee the work. Lady Kara will coordinate labourers to help. The Kingdom warriors will be released from duty temporarily, and the security of the plateau placed under the sole jurisdiction of the Golden Warriors – who are to be called Andrakian warriors hereafter. Only Marella's

285

Haardrishii will continue their normal duties and training.'

When Andra paused, Claarn shifted uneasily in his seat. The former warrior of Tressel Deep was suppressing his rising anger. Something was dreadfully amiss with Andra's decisions, but he couldn't rationalise the problem to voice it. Before he could ponder further, the King continued to detail the plans in hand for the winter, and early spring, while the central plains of the Kingdom were beyond the reach of the Haagii and the Dragonlord's army.

'Lord Ki has also organised an embassy to Ranu Ka Shehaala, our western neighbour, seeking their aid in providing food, supplies, and soldiers for the next phase of war, and he will begin reforming his Apprentice Guild, selecting worthy participants from the children in Andrakis.'

Claarn saw the hurrying rain clouds scudding across the low, gloomy sky from the east toward the plateau, and descended from the ruined gate tower to shelter. At the bottom, he found Marella huddling from the brisk breeze, in an alcove formed by a portion of the ruined wall. When he saw her, she shook her head as if she understood his confused state. 'What is happening?' the giant asked. 'What has changed?'

Marella shrugged, her dark locks shuddering, and she stared into the empty space beyond the alcove. Three Haardrishii moved like fleeting shadows across the plateau, through the heaps of stone and rubble piled in past efforts to tidy the ruins left by the Haagii army's assault, seeking shelter from the approaching rain. 'He is not Andra,' she said.

Claarn put a big hand on her shoulder and turned her gently to face him. 'You heard it too? You saw it.' She nodded. Claarn grunted in despair and disgust. 'The things he said. They were not words Andra would use. He spoke like another person, said things from the mind of another, not from his heart.'

Claarn struggled with his explanation, desperately trying

to voice the turmoil within, but Marella put a finger to his lips. 'You heard and saw what I heard and saw. Something has changed,' she reassured him. 'Did you see how little the Chancellor had to say at the Table?'

Claarn recalled the meeting. A Ahmud Ki said very little. He sat quietly away from the table, near the King, and remained uninvolved, except to make supportive statements at Andra's request. That was unusual. The Chancellor normally tried to manipulate everything to suit his ends. 'Then we must do something.' he decided. 'I don't like what I see and hear, since the Chancellor returned after Andra's crowning. I will find a chance to speak with Andra, as a friend.'

'I'll come with you,' Marella said, 'because I think I fear Andra will need help from both of us.'

Milly and Aaron's news that a dracabeorn was loose in the fortress set everybody on edge, but despite extra caution no one sighted the creature. It was as if the shadowy being melted into the darkness. The body of the Sharvan was removed and buried, and Sasha stepped up security to counter the Dragonlord's revival of attempts to assassinate Andra.

The longer the dracabeorn remained hidden, the greater became the unease among the warriors and people inside the fortress. Knowledge that ordinary weapons had little effect on dracabeorn rapidly spread, and even Marella's Haardrishii began to experience the uneasy vulnerability of the exposed and hunted. When the first three bodies of the dracabeorn's victims were found, hideously slashed about the face and throat, dissension among the warriors threatened to break down the fortress' security. Sasha and Marella moved to allay their fears, but many of the fortress' inhabitants chose to evacuate and seek refuge among the new building on the plateau, or down in the shelters rising along Dragon River.

'The intruder has to be found,' Sasha informed a select

group of The Hand assassins. 'We'll coordinate a search from top to bottom, through every corridor and chamber, until we corner it.'

'And then what?' asked a short, thin-faced man nicknamed Ferret by the others. 'Ask it to leave?'

'You know we can't kill the thing,' another assassin cut in.

Sasha needed no reminders of the dracabeorn's deadly magical defence and efficient killing skills. 'All we have to do is locate it,' she explained. 'Once we know where it is, King Andrakis will destroy the creature with his sword.'

A Ahmud Ki smiled at the black servants ranged before him in the tower library. He enjoyed their unquestioning obedience. They reminded him of Ranu women, shrouded in black, eternally serving their men without ever considering why. A Dragonlord held supreme sway over everybody and everything, and dracabeorn and undead warriors were his ultimate followers. How Andrakis and Mareg, and their kin, must have revelled in the power they wielded. He laughed. That power was now his.

He beckoned to a shadowy figure, and it approached the centre of the chamber near the reading table where he made it kneel. He pointed his right index finger at the figure and mouthed words in an ancient tongue, the forgotten language of the Dragonlords, a silken smooth litany forming the fabric of a shaping spell. As he moved into a soft chant, his pupils glowed with a red light that spread until his entire eyes burned with scarlet fire, like the eyes of Mareg burned in the Inner Sanctum of Targa. The dracabeorn cowered, shivering beneath his spell, and its shape blurred and altered in the wash of words, until it transformed, taking on colour and texture.

When A Ahmud Ki finished the spell, kneeling before him in the dracabeorn's place was a naked, white-haired elderly human. 'Oh Master, bless you, bless you,' the old man stammered, as he looked up. 'A thousand times bless you.'

A Ahmud Ki allowed himself a faint smile of appreciation. Then he beckoned to a second dracabeorn and waited until the shadowy creature kneeled beside the transformed first.

King Andrakis stood beside the growing wall of stone marking the building site for Haephus' new temple to Teka and watched the flurry of activity spreading across the plateau. Priests worked side-by-side with the men, women, and children who were asked to help in the construction. He enjoyed watching people labouring, because he sensed purpose returning to the former castle ruins that his predecessor, Thana, ruled so ineffectually. Repair of the castle outer walls was proceeding rapidly, it being done by Kingdom warriors overseen by Claarn.

Andra knew Claarn disapproved of his method, but he had his reasons. With the war in recess because of wintry conditions, the warriors needed a challenge to maintain their fitness. He remembered Trainer Murdok pushing his friends and him, despite lulls in the early weeks of the war, making them run at every opportunity, to maintain their peak conditioning. He was certain Claarn could see the reason.

The second reason nagged at him. With each passing day, his mind was filled with an ever-increasing desire to be a King in a mighty fortress befitting his status. He was Abreotan's successor. Yet the desire confused him, because another voice inside his head interfered, reminding him a Guardian was humble; that there were more important things than building a monument to satisfy personal desires. He still suffered from headaches. Some mornings he woke and couldn't focus his eyes. By nightfall his head pounded. Was it the pressure? he wondered: the irreconcilable contradiction he struggled with daily?

A brief shower swept across the castle grounds, but very few people ceased working. Andra left the temple site, acknowledging Haephus' wave, and walked toward a second building being erected closer to A Ahmud Ki's black tower, another temple: to Berak N'eth. Kingdom warriors were busy fitting precisely chiselled stones to form the outer temple wall, keying each to match its neighbours, disguising the joint lines. No mortar was used. The weight and keying held the components of the temple accurately. A stonemason A Ahmud Ki found among the survivors of the Great City was overseeing the building with a meticulous eye for detail. If anything didn't meet his approval, the work was dismantled and replaced or reworked.

Andra felt Berak N'eth lurking at the far reaches of his mind, waiting to be acknowledged. As much as he tried, he couldn't remember how or when he first became conscious of the god's presence. The sword had to be the connection. He was the sword. No. Berak N'eth was the sword. More confusion. Why?

Food was still a problem in Andrakis. No one was outright starving, enough basic food being collected and transported by a network of gatherers and carters from Anedya Wood to the north, from parts of the plains, and from the lakes and ocean to the south, but the spectre of hunger hovered in everyone's bellies. What Andra feared most was that the Kingdom wouldn't be prepared for a resumption of war without adequate food supplies. The constant work to rebuild the castle fortress was risky because it placed a physical demand on the people to replenish their energy through eating, yet Andra wanted that work done. He was King. A King had to have a secure and impressive castle.

'Oh, in Holy Teka's name,' Gareth whispered, and he crept backward, out of the chamber, trembling with terror. His left hand, shaking furiously, grappled with the door handle. His companion, Jon, a stocky youth with a shock of blond hair, peered around the partially open door to see what prompted his cry of shock, and in the flickering torchlight saw two bloodied corpses pressed against the far wall, their throats ripped open, and torsos disembowelled. A vague shadow shifted to his right. Gareth pushed past and wrenched the door shut, nearly catching the youth's face. 'Get Sasha!' he hissed, and his knees buckled.

Jon lunged at the torch in a desperate effort to catch it before it burnt out against the floor, but in his haste he fumbled and it rolled out of reach, and died. The rush of darkness unnerved the youth. 'Gareth,' he whispered. 'Gareth.' He reached blindly down to shake his friend. As his hand touched Gareth's chest, he felt a warm, sticky substance ooze between his fingers. Blood.

Seized by a renewed wave of fear, Jon straightened and tried to run blindly along the corridor, but his foot caught the dead torch, as he rushed forward, and he sprawled onto the floor. He rolled against the wall and struggled to his feet in panic, in time to catch a glimpse of another torch passing across a junction forty paces away. He summoned his strength and screamed. 'Here! Here! In pity's name!' The torchlight receded, ignorant of his plea for help, plunging the corridor into utter darkness again. Behind him, Jon heard the door click open.

'These are the rods you assemble in the centre of the great hall the Ranu call Kal E'haruk Ka Irandu. The letter I've given you must be delivered directly to Leiksha Ithrandyr Shehaal, no one else. Understood?' A Ahmud Ki's three servants nodded. The white-haired elder, attired in an ill-fitting red robe and holding a staff marked with rune patterns, bowed respectfully. 'What is it?' the Chancellor asked.

'Master Ki, how will you know when it is time?'

A Ahmud Ki held out his right hand, moved his left across the open palm, and a tiny silver ball appeared. He passed the object to the old man. 'If you hold this before you, and concentrate on my face in your mind, the ball will expand, and you will see my image and hear my thoughts. When the portal is ready, and Shehaal present, call me.' The white-haired servant bowed. 'And you will need this, Saleem,' A Ahmud Ki added. He held up a silver chain with a figurine attached: a distorted shape of a woman, her outline and

291

features heavily blurred. Saleem allowed A Ahmud Ki to place the pendant around his neck. 'Ranu language is very different to the old tongue of the Kingdom. The pendant has a translation spell worked into it, a very common piece of magic among the Ithosen of the Ranu Ka Shehaala. It will allow you to understand and speak their language. The figurine is their Goddess Fareeka. Be respectful to the pendant. Your life will depend upon that respect.' Saleem nodded. 'Everything has been arranged. Speed on your journey.'

Saleem bowed low and turned to the horse awaiting him inside the castle gates. One Haardrishii assisted the old man aboard his horse, whilst Saleem's two companions, a tall, sandy-haired warrior in chain mail and a dark-eyed archer, mounted their steeds. The small embassy, accompanied by a half dozen Haardrishii, rode out of the gates to journey west to the barbarian land. Immediately they departed, the Chancellor headed toward his tower, though he paused to admire the structure of the temple being built in honour of Berak N'eth.

Claarn observed the proceedings from a respectable distance, atop the western parapet. He stroked his red beard and spat, as A Ahmud Ki returned to his tower. Nothing was as it seemed. He still hadn't found an opportunity to speak to Andra. No. Not true. There were opportunities. He knew he only had to go to his chambers, or approach him, and the Guardian King would listen. Or would he? Every time Claarn saw the young man, he was brooding, or solemn, or lost in thought, or directing reconstruction. Claarn was unsure of him. Was he afraid of the dracabeorn lurking in the fortress? Or had the role of King perverted him? No. Not that either. What nagged at Claarn was a constant belief the Chancellor had a hand in Andra's change, ever since the day he, Claarn, had been stupid enough to allow Andra to enter the Chancellor's tower.

He peered over the edge of the wall and caught sight of the tiny band of horses and men heading west, along the outward road, toward the ruins of Ky. The giant warrior understood the need for diplomacy and help from the western barbarians in the war with the Haagii, the Kingdom's army being significantly depleted, even with Andra and the ghostly golden Andrakian warriors, but the embassy puzzled and annoyed him. From where had the old man who led the mission come? Claarn couldn't recall any similar person living in the Great City, or the fortress, during the siege. For that matter, his two protective companions were strangers, appearing to carry out the Chancellor's tasks as if they were his long-time servants. There were too many mysteries again. The unanswered questions aggravated his hatred for the Chancellor and heightened his suspicion that something very sinister was brewing in the heart of the Kingdom.

Thirty Two

The ships raced toward Kenton out of the teeth of a thrashing gale, their ragged sails all but torn apart by the wild winds driving them across the white-capped Lake of Tears. By the time word of their arrival reached Andrakis, the former Great City of Thana, a vast storm front raged across the plains of Ky, thunder and lightning rending the dark skies, and rain flooding the earth, trapping every living creature inside available shelter.

For three days, the storm raged across the Kingdom. Patti, and older survivors in Andrakis, claimed they'd never witnessed so violent and prolonged a storm in their memories, and the rumours among the gossips and pessimists was that it was the work of the Dragonlord, venting his pent-up fury on the Kingdom for driving out his army. Haephus and his priests offered prayers to Teka, to quell the ferocity of the wind and rain, more to settle agitation and unease among the people than in sincere belief their goddess would interfere in the natural processes of the world, but the storm did not relent.

The morning after the storm dissipated, the people of Andrakis awoke to a cold, grey world, beneath a cloud-strewn sky. Dragon River was swollen to flood level, water lapping over its banks and running along the streets and paths into new dwellings and buildings. The earth was drowned, saturated by broad mirror-grey puddles.

News of the ships' arrival awakened A Ahmud Ki's interest. The Kingdom had no large sailing vessels, the technology of large shipbuilding having never been deemed important. Only Targa had ships, but the Dragonlord's armies destroyed Targa, unless the people escaped into the ocean. The possibility some sorceresses survived the brutal invasion attracted A Ahmud Ki, who pressed the King to travel south, to Kenton, as soon as the storm ceased.

Andra had no objections to A Ahmud Ki's request, and arrangements for the journey were made. Marella's Haardrishii were initially ordered to provide escort, but Andra altered his decision in favour of a squad of Andrakian knights.

Then Sasha was informed she wouldn't be required to provide the normal security cordon to protect the King. The man who brought the message to her chambers was a stranger. His long blond hair was plaited in a ponytail, and he wore loose dark green and black garments of the kind she associated with the defunct Royal Assassins of Thana's court. 'Who gave this order?' she asked, scrutinizing the blond stranger before her.

'The King,' he replied, dark green eyes narrowing.

'And who are you?' she asked, suspicious of his unfamiliar face.

'You can call me Sarcen,' he replied coolly.

Sasha made a barely perceptible gesture with her right hand to three Hand assassins stationed across the corridor from her door, in a dimly lit alcove, and saw a flicker in the eyes of one indicating they understood and were prepared for trouble. Her face remained impassive, but she was certain she read the faintest recognition in the stranger's eyes, meaning he also saw her signal. 'I don't remember your face,' Sasha calmly asserted, ready to expose a threat to Andra or the fortress' security.

Sarcen smiled faintly. 'I am a servant of Lord Ki.'

His answer made the skin crawl on her neck, though she had no logical reason for her feeling, except her strong dislike of the Chancellor, but the stranger seemed far more threatening. 'Where did you come from,' she asked, 'before you began serving him?'

This time Sarcen's smile became a short, cold chuckle, a response that heightened Sasha's feeling of dread about the stranger. 'Lord Ki forbids me to tell anyone, my Lady. Perhaps you should ask him yourself.'

The touch of impertinent arrogance made Sasha want to slit his throat, but when she looked into his eyes she saw him daring her to do just that. She closed her door in his face, without further comment, but she knew she had to talk to Andra.

When she reached the King's chambers, she discovered other changes had occurred in the interim between the morning posting of the guards and her arrival. There were no Haardrishii warriors present. Her assassins were lounging in the nearby corridor. Outside Andra's door, two golden Andrakian warriors stood on duty. 'What's going on?' she demanded of the three assassins she assigned to security.

The woman of the group answered. 'Humble apologies, Death's First Hand, but the King countermanded your order for us to keep an eye on things. He told us we weren't needed any longer.'

'No explanation?'

'None,' a man muttered.

Sasha glared at the assassins, who shifted uncomfortably under her gaze, but relented, aware they weren't negligent in their duties or responsible for Andra's decision. 'Go then,' she instructed, 'for now. I'll speak to the King to find out what's brought this on.' The assassins nodded and drifted gratefully into the shadows of the descending corridor to their quarters.

Sasha headed for Andra's chamber, but when she reached the door the Andrakian warriors moved to confront her. Their empty, emotionless eyes stared through slits in their helmet visors. She remembered they were souls trapped in limbo by a powerful spell their former Dragonlord master invoked centuries ago to create his private army of fearless warriors, and that memory engendered in her the same deep discomfort as had Sarcen's laugh.

Before she could address the warriors, an angry voice erupted beyond the door, a voice she recognised – Claarn. 'By all that the Goddess Teka blesses, you're mad!' she heard him bellow. 'Why must you trust the word of this walking evil? What has he done to you?'

Sasha assumed Andra replied to Claarn's rage, but the intervening door muffled his voice. 'Let me through,' she ordered the twin guardians. Neither warrior relented. She assessed her chances of forcing them to shift. 'I demand you let me in!' she repeated. It appeared they were determined to keep her out, but they shifted their weight, making a passage to the door.

Sasha's attention flicked to a shadow she sensed further along the corridor. A figure was obscured from the lantern light by the entry to an alcove, where her assassins normally took their post, and she was acutely aware the strange figure had signalled to the Andrakian warriors, which brought their change of attitude. She paused, considering approaching the figure, to see who lurked in the shadows with so much authority, but another outburst from Claarn changed her mind. She opened the door.

'Have you forgotten what he has done?' Claarn yelled. 'Have you forgotten the blood on his hands? The tricks? The way he's avoided pulling his weight?' The giant warrior stood in the centre of the room on a ragged rug, his shoulders bunched as though he was locked in a wrestling match, his fists waving and clenched so tightly they were white with his anger. Andra was watching Claarn, his gold plate armour flecked with flame from a burning hearth, and, directly opposite, Marella was leaning against the wall. As Sasha entered, Claarn turned to her, his face lit with fury. He dropped his arms to his side with a huge sigh, and gave her a comical look of appeal, and if she hadn't understood his reason for frustration she would've laughed at the image. 'Sasha,' he begged. 'Make this fool, who would be a King, see the trap he's walking into. He won't listen to us.'

Claarn's expression told her talking with Andra was going to be futile. Something significant had changed in the past days. She acknowledged Claarn, before approaching Andra. The King was smiling, but she recognised the false smile that promised no friendship, no familiar welcome. 'Why did you dismiss my people?' she asked.

Andra's polite smile disappeared. 'There's no point them attending me,' he answered coldly.

'What made you change your mind without talking to me

about it? I thought you appointed me to see to your safety,' Sasha reminded him.

'I did,' he glibly replied. 'But you can't do that, can you?'

Her eyebrows shot up at the suggestion she was failing him. 'What do you mean by that?'

Andra squared up to the assassin who loved his friend Tim Gaelus. 'I mean, you and your assassins aren't good enough to keep the minions of Mareg off my back,' he bluntly stated, 'but my Andrakian warriors won't fail me.'

Claarn scowled in the background and banged his fist against the wall. Sasha's anger rose. 'The Sharvan is dead -'

'But the dracabeorn isn't,' Andra cut in, 'and your assassins can never kill it, can they?' He shot a spiteful glance at Marella and at Claarn. 'None of your pathetic people can stop it. They don't have the power.' Abreotan's sword materialised in his hand, and amber flames flashed along the blade. 'You need power to defeat Mareg,' he reiterated. 'You need magic to kill a dracabeorn. What magic do you bring to protect me? My Andrakian Warriors will stop the dracabeorn when it comes skulking here. If I relied on your assassins, or the Haardrishii, to protect me, I'd be left to defend myself, while your people lie dying at my feet. I'm doing you a favour by dismissing them. Now they don't have to die pointlessly.'

The King's unexpectedly spiteful tirade astonished Sasha. She backed away from him, and looked to Marella for support, an explanation, anything, but the warrior shook her head, as if she no more understood the cause of Andra's anger than Sasha. His manner and tone made it abundantly clear arguing further was pointless.

Claarn lumbered forward and kneeled before Andra. 'I swore to serve you as my King when the crown was placed on your head. A warrior of Tressel Deep honours his lord. So, I honour you.' He lifted his head, stood, and drew up to his full height. 'But before you were my King, you were my friend,' he said, his deep voice softening. 'You and I were warrior brothers. We have faced death together many times. We share the blood bond.' A rapid knocking sounded at the door. Claarn ignored it. 'I am still Claarn, Andra. You have honoured me with the title of High Lord, but I am still Claarn.'

The door burst open, and three Andrakian warriors entered, led by a man in black robes. Neither Marella nor Sasha recalled seeing his dark bearded face before, but he addressed himself directly to Andra, cutting across Claarn's plea, as he bowed low and spoke. 'Lord Ki says it is time, Your Highness. The horses and escort are ready.'

Andra extinguished the flames along his sword, sheathed it, picked up his helmet as he headed for the door, and left without further comment to his dismayed friends who watched him go. Claarn felt as if a hand reached inside his chest and was squeezing life out of his great heart.

Three ships rocked on the churning swell in the bay, their single main masts drawing aimless patterns across the low ceiling of grey cloud scudding seawards across the lake. Andra reined in Firebrand, as the Royal party crested a rise, overlooking the ruins of Kenton and the grey expanse of the Lake of Tears, and silently gazed at the anchored vessels. Ships – curious wooden craft built to travel over the mysterious blue depths of the oceans, moving at the whim of the winds. He'd never seen a ship. He ran his eyes along the low-slung, sleek hulls, taking in the little detail he could gather at so great a distance, assessing the mast height, and wondering how the ships floated being obviously heavy in construction.

'They fascinated me when I first saw them,' A Ahmud Ki intruded.

Andra saw the Chancellor was also staring at the ships. 'Have you ever sailed on one?' he asked.

'No,' A Ahmud Ki replied flatly, and spurred his borrowed Haardrishii stallion forward, leaving Andra to follow down the gentle slope toward Kenton with his entourage of Andrakian warriors.

Like every other Kingdom settlement, Kenton was devastated by the invading Haagii the previous summer, but many people used their small fishing boats to head for safety, from the enemy, out on four tiny islands. No dragon visited the town, which was a blessing, but the Haagii vented their frustration at losing the pleasure of killing most of the townsfolk, by destroying every structure, as they had in the Great City.

When the Haagii withdrew, driven out by Marella's liberating force, the surviving townsfolk returned and began rebuilding the town from the ashes before winter settled. Though only a shadow of its former comfortable, if ramshackle, appearance, Kenton boasted taverns and workshops and business houses and residences. Even the old town stone wall, built to protect the town from marauders a century after Abreotan's death, was partially restored and strengthened. The Royal party entered a re-born community, who turned out to see King Andrakis the Inheritor and his fabled Andrakian Warriors parade the main street to the waterfront.

Andra was pleased to see the faces of the people, especially the children, were far less haggard in Kenton than in Andrakis. The fishermen fed well off their fish and water plant diets. He was surprised to see a herd of sheep, and another of goats, tethered near the lakeshore, as his entourage approached a large inn. He presumed, from his own experience at the siege of the Great City and the fortress, that all Kingdom herd animals were slaughtered to feed the ravenous invading Haagii armies. Perhaps the town folk of Kenton were smart enough to take their stock with them to the islands, foreseeing the threat of famine lying in wait after the departure of their Haagii enemy. Small as the two flocks appeared, they provided hope. They could form the foundation of new herds and help start the slow process of rekindling the agriculture destroyed by the Haagii.

'You've a much sharper mind for important matters than your predecessor,' A Ahmud Ki offered, as Andra's horse approached the inn. 'The sheep and goats,' he prompted. 'I'm curious to know how they survived too. But I don't think the local people own them.'

'Why do you say that?' Andra asked, as a tousle-haired

boy took Firebrand's reins, and two Andrakian knights dismounted to assist their master.

A Ahmud Ki flicked back the cowl of his black cloak, revealing the intricately braided silver hair of his Aelendyell heritage, and slipped down from his horse, before answering. 'Some things I know,' he replied with the faintest touch of a bow.

Andra studied the Chancellor, as A Ahmud Ki spoke briskly to the innkeeper before entering the building. The Chancellor had an increasingly uncanny ability to predict his thoughts, almost as if he was thinking identical ideas. Coincidence? Or more of his magic?

He dismounted, allowing an Andrakian warrior to assist him, and headed for the inn's entrance. Above the door, he noticed a fire-blackened, battered sign proclaiming the establishment 'The Fisherman's Dream' and it was illustrated with an ale tankard full of fat fish, one of which was a buxom girl with a fishtail. Andra thought the design was absurd, but his thought was disturbed by a scuffle, and when he turned he saw an Andrakian warrior throwing a small child back into the throng of onlookers who'd gathered to see their King. The warrior's rough action brought an outburst of dismay and abuse from the crowd, and three fishermen started arguing heatedly. The child got up and looked with bewilderment at the warrior who treated her so roughly. Andra felt a strong surge of concern, a desire to go to the child and cuddle her. He thought of Milly.

You are a King, the familiar voice said in his head. Show a King's strength. Andra stared at the child. She needed help. You are a King, the voice repeated. Berak N'eth was speaking. You hold power. Never give it away for trivial reasons. The child is your servant. The warrior is your servant. They obey you. Without question. So, too, do you obey me. Your destiny is inside the tavern, not at the feet of one foolish child. Go inside. Go inside as a King should go.

Andra turned from the child, who was swallowed in the crowd, and entered the inn, unconsciously rubbing the platinum ring, studded with its amber gem.

301

Inside, he was faced with a large, open room, warmed by a huge blazing hearth. Low ceiling beams traversed the airy space under a shingled roof, and a magical glow hung between a pair of beams. The comforting aromas of broth and stew, smells rare in Andrakis, permeated the air, inviting him in, and setting his hunger juices flowing with expectation.

A Ahmud Ki was directly ahead, near the low bar for serving, talking to two women, and a heavy-set man whose thick face bristled with a black beard. One woman appeared old and frail, though she held her head proudly erect, and her eyes shone with confidence. The second was younger, with brown hair, perhaps in her mid to late thirties, attractive, despite her face being lined with hard use. A Ahmud Ki turned to Andra, as he entered, and with an uncommonly generous sweeping gesture of introduction he drew the three strangers toward the King. 'Your Highness, King Andrakis the Inheritor,' A Ahmud Ki announced with a self-satisfied smile, 'I present Lady Fay, Captain Nathaniel, and Lady Jasmin. Of Targa.'

'The dragons swept across the city in the darkness,' explained Jasmin, 'lashing buildings with flames, until it seemed as if the whole world would be lit by the fires raging in Targa. The air was thick with screams of dying people and choking smoke, and above everything we could hear the keening cries of the brutish beasts, as they circled and dived down to burn.'

'No one, and nothing in the city, was safe,' Lady Fay cut in, her memory jogged by the scenes of destruction.

'The fires leapt from building to building,' Jasmin continued, 'fanned by an incredible wind that seemed to grow of its own accord along with the fires, hand in hand, destroying all Targa with wanton abandon.

No one expected dragons. They came out of the night, setting the city ablaze so rapidly that very few people had time to prepare to defend or escape. Lady Corinna summoned as many of us in the Order as could portal to the city, to help battle the creatures when the attack started, but even so we could do little. The dragons seemed immune to our magic, and those who arrived knew nothing about fighting dragons.

In the confusion, we tried to make our way, by underground tunnels, to the port, when we realised Targa was lost. Finding safe passage through the fires was almost impossible, because of the heat, even below ground, but we managed to clamber aboard ships. Most captains immediately put to sea when the dragons came, but a handful remembered their allegiance to the Order and waited until Lady Corinna was safely aboard a vessel, before getting underway.'

'The sea glowed from the light of the fires,' Captain Nathaniel interjected. 'I was afraid our ship was as visible to the dragons as a moth against torchlight, so I headed for the pall of smoke that was spreading low in the cold air across the southern end of the bay.'

'It was a thankful strategy,' Jasmin said, and sighed, 'because the dragons did come in search of our ships.'

'It was more horrible than the city burning,' Lady Fay rasped from her dry old throat. 'People were leaping out of their boats into the sea, all on fire.'

'I saw ships explode in balls of flame as the dragons passed,' Captain Nathaniel said, with a sorry shake of his head.

'I counted eighteen ships on the water,' said Jasmin. 'Three made the cover of the smoke and escaped to the south. The rest were consumed. Less than six hundred people escaped the city. And only two of us from the Order have survived.'

'So where did you escape to?' Andra asked, curious to learn about the unknown world beyond his Kingdom these survivors of the burning had escaped to.

'To Em Basa,' Jasmin replied. 'It's a nation on the northern tip of the Great South Lands, eight days sailing from Targa.'

'We traded there,' Nathaniel explained. 'Some spices, ochre, powders, metal, wood.'

'You travelled eight days, across the Endless Seas?' Andra asked, trying to comprehend the concept of sea voyaging, having only seen an ocean from a distance. This was stranger than magic.

'Eight there, eight back,' Nathaniel confirmed.

'So why come here?' Andra was aware of A Ahmud Ki watching him when he asked his question of the Targans. What had he said wrong?

'We wanted to see if the Dragonlord had taken over our land, or whether we could return home to rebuild.'

'The Dragonlord's armies have been driven back,' A Ahmud Ki explained, before Andra could answer. 'Targa is safe again.'

'So we learned,' Lady Jasmin replied with a smile directed at A Ahmud Ki. 'But we have another boon to ask,' she continued, redirecting her attention at Andra.

'Ask,' the young King instructed.

'We need wood for our buildings, a lot of wood. There are no more forests in Targa for us to use, and Em Basa is a long sailing trip, with only three ships to carry cargo. We want to trade whatever we can for access to wood in your Kingdom, so Targa may live again. We want to use your forests.'

Thirty Three

'You all fully understand why you are here?' A Ahmud Ki studied the fifteen men and five boys, as they nodded silent affirmation. They were essentially a rag-tag lot, ill dressed and dirty, but hungry men were desperate men, and that's exactly what he needed. He turned from the small group to his assistant, waiting behind and to his right.

The sharp-eyed young man, his long blond hair tied back and plaited in a ponytail, bowed deeply out of respect when he saw A Ahmud Ki's eyes on him, and shifted to stand beside his Master, facing the gathering. He drew a dagger from a scabbard secreted within his dark green tunic, its hilt fashioned in the shape of a dragon's bead, and held it directly before his face, his green eyes fixed on the gleaming, wickedly sharp blade. 'This,' he said, and grinned, lifting his eyes toward the audience, 'is your badge of office.' He stared and became solemn. 'By it, you will live.' He grinned again, as if emotions were fleeting through his face at whim, and he adopted a serious, almost bitter expression. 'But cross me, or our Lord and Master, and I promise you, on the breath of Berak N'eth, that, by it, you will die.'

A Ahmud Ki watched several men shuffle nervously upon hearing Sarcen's cold oath, and focussed on memorizing their faces for later observation. No weakness would be tolerated. He beckoned Sarcen to his side, out of the rabble's earshot, and said quietly. 'Your task isn't going to be easy.'

Sarcen bowed politely. 'No, Lord Ki.'

'Nevertheless,' A Ahmud Ki added, 'you will train them efficiently and quickly. And ruthlessly. The King must have his Royal Assassins. Am I understood?'

'It will be done, My Lord,' Sarcen responded, bowing.

A Ahmud Ki placed his hand on Sarcen's shoulder, in a gesture of unexpected friendliness that made the assassin wince. 'Yes,' the Chancellor emphasised, 'it will be done.'

A Ahmud Ki left Sarcen and his apprentices to begin their secretive training in the lower chambers of the plateau, and he commenced the long walking climb, through the corridors, to the upper levels. As he walked, he sensed eyes watching him pass, and he grinned with smug approval at the aura of respect and fear his passing engendered in the people of the Kingdom. He turned to see a boy scamper away, a young lad who was trailing him, and laughed aloud, his laughter echoing along the corridors. They were afraid of him, as they should be. True power is generated by your enemy's fears, he reminded himself.

Further along, he passed a familiar girl, lounging in a doorway, with a Haardrishii war dog sitting at her feet. Contempt filled the girl's eyes. He read it, and chose to ignore it, but several steps on he stopped, and turned back to the doorway, nagged by a warning there was more to the child's contempt than dislike for his presence – but she and the dog were gone.

Then he remembered her – the girl Andra favoured – Milly. He stood in the corridor, considering her potential to be a threat to his plans. She had Andra's trust, but so did that irritating warrior with the red hair, and his companions, and they were more likely to cause trouble than anyone. Besides, the girl hadn't been allowed near the King for weeks. She was a child, barely reaching an age to make her an idol of the King's passion, so that absurd possibility could be dismissed. He knew she had connections with Lady Kara and the Guild, but then so did most urchins in Andrakis, and the King's rather useful decision to dissolve the need for a Thieves' Guild, because of the necessities and deprivations of the war, eliminated a threat of insurrection from that quarter. He shook his silver locks and laughed at his overcautious zeal in considering a child a threat to his supreme power. He was A Ahmud Ki, Dragonlord. Who would dare oppose his might in the days to come?

He emerged in the newly constructed atrium of the Upper Palace, that was situated above the entrance to the fortress, where the old King's Royal Library stood, and stopped to admire his design. The interior walls would be lined with polished white marble, and the roof would be filled with glass panels, after the fashion of the Great Hall of Light in Yul Ithrandyr. He borrowed much from his memory of that beautiful city's architecture. The Upper Palace would stand in marked contrast to the dark, enclosing quarters of the fortress, and it would shame the shabby interiors of the old palace the Haagii destroyed. The new fortress of Andrakis would outshine that of the human kings since Abreotan, and it would surpass the former glory Dragonlord Andrakis Va'ristrin Nyavardenet wrought into the heart of the plateau. A Ahmud Ki's future subjects would come to stand in awe of his castle, his palace, his fortress, and wonder at the power of the mind that created such a prodigious structure.

There was a lot to do. He needed craftsmen and artisans to take over where the current brute building in stone being carried out by Kingdom people and Haagii prisoners would leave off. He needed stonemasons to revive the ancient craft of their ancestors, and Ranu glaziers to mould and blow glass. He needed Targan carpenters to construct beams and furnishings. He needed time.

From a window overlooking the shaft, he paused to watch a Haagii work gang heaving another massive boulder, used to seal Andrakis' old dragon lair, from its resting place. Manipulating the King's thoughts was uncommonly easy, he quietly noted, and grinned. The ring, with its amber jewel emanating the necessary control spell, and the sliver of communication crystal enabling A Ahmud Ki to contact and communicate his thoughts to Andra over any distance, were working wonderfully well. He'd created his puppet in every sense of the word, the strings fully in his hands to operate at his whim. What he, A Ahmud Ki, wanted set into law, Abreotan's Inheritor initiated, accepting A Ahmud Ki's thoughts as his own.

The dragon shaft was being excavated, the new palace constructed. Lady Jasmin, and the surviving Targans who miraculously escaped Mareg's marauding dragons, were already rebuilding Targa from its ashes, and shipping precious food supplies, and other goods from the southern lands across the Endless Seas, in exchange for Aelendyell forests. He enjoyed that ironic twist against the Aelendyell, more than the revenge he exacted on his old village. No doubt there would be an outcry when the Aelendyell started killing Kingdom woodcutters sent to fell the forest for the Targans. What a pity for all concerned the new King would side with Targa's request and expel the Aelendyell from the borders of the Kingdom. Who could argue? The god Berak N'eth instructs Abreotan's Inheritor. Who would dare argue with a god?

'So, I find you here, gloating.'

The intrusion of Haephus' voice startled A Ahmud Ki, but he masked his reaction by turning to the High Priest and five of his yellow-robed followers with his left eyebrow raised. 'I have reason to gloat, as you put it,' he said with a charming smile. 'My work is beautiful.' He spread his arms to indicate the sweeping atrium.

'That temple is an abomination,' Haephus coldly replied.

'Your temple to Teka could be rebuilt better than it is, if you desire,' A Ahmud Ki offered.

Haephus' expression became fierce. 'I refer to the blasphemous temple you've ordered built for the foreign and false god you've convinced the King to worship.'

'I've convinced the King of nothing,' A Ahmud Ki said. 'He worships Berak N'eth because it's his duty.'

'The duty of the King is to lead worship of Teka, Goddess of the Kingdom,' Haephus argued, enraged by A Ahmud Ki's unruffled composure. 'Every King since Abreotan has worshipped Our Holy Lady! She is the Keeper and Protector of the Great City!'

A Ahmud Ki laughed with deliberate amusement, goading Haephus. 'I've heard this foolish argument before, priest. Remember? And you were asked to explain how your precious goddess protected her city when all that we witnessed was its destruction at the hands of the enemy? Remember, priest? Where was your precious Teka? I'll tell you.' A Ahmud Ki paused for effect, his lunge at Haephus' vulnerability determined to be fatal. 'She's a fake.'

The sharp intake of breath from the six priests was an audible hiss in the vast airy structure of the atrium, and Haephus' face turned scarlet. 'Blasphemer! Heretic!' he screeched. 'May Teka curse and blight you for your foul tongue and evil lies! May you rot in the eight hells, until you beg Teka a thousand times for her mercy!' A Ahmud Ki's eyes sparkled at Haephus' vituperative outburst, and he broke into mocking laughter. 'Laugh, you unholy bastard!' Haephus scowled, regaining control of his voice. 'Laugh and be damned!'

All six priests began a complicated series of gestures with their hands A Ahmud Ki initially thought were arcane, but the pattern was unrecognisable and he relaxed, sensing the futility in the priests' ritualised actions. 'Do as you please, Haephus,' he said, and laughed contemptuously. 'Call on your goddess to strike me dead. Curse me. I'm not afraid. You're wasting your time. Teka is dead. She never lived. She's nothing more than a false idea created by your predecessors to keep the people in line for the kings, and the priests in a job. Call on her now, if you truly believe. Do it Haephus. Do it or be damned yourself.'

Haephus tried concentrating on his prayers and cursing incantation, but A Ahmud Ki's constant taunting kept breaking through his barriers, provoking his anger and his dignity. Teka is real, he reminded himself. Teka is my life and my worth.

'Let's prove once and for all whose god is real!' A Ahmud Ki roared in challenge. 'Come on, priest. Prove Teka is real. Prove Berak N'eth is not!'

Haephus looked to his followers. Their faces were focussed on him. Jani, his successor and confidante, was shaking his head very gently, his face white with fear. The rest were watching, waiting, wondering. Behind them, people were gathering, hearing the eruption of angry voices and running to witness the confrontation. He felt the circle closing, leaving him at its centre, the representative of Teka left to face the heretic and false god. Was he trapped? Or chosen?

A Ahmud Ki watched the High Priest's indecision with cold pleasure. Without his engineering, he'd brought the fool into a trap from which escape would mean humiliation and the dismissal of the priests. Even better, the outcome lay in the hands of the gods. What happened now was not his doing, nor his responsibility. 'Admit Berak N'eth, and renounce Teka,' A Ahmud Ki said slowly. He projected a calculated thought at Haephus. I am with you, my servant, a soft voice whispered inside Haephus' mind. I am with you and in you. Destroy the infidel. The startled expression on Haephus' face told A Ahmud Ki his thought projection was effective.

Haephus' confidence grew, and the High Priest waved his hands in an ancient ritual of cursing. 'For your heresy and your false belief,' Haephus intoned, 'I curse you to die in a sea of boils and carbuncles. May Teka have mercy on your soul beyond the shores of the eighth hell.'

A Ahmud Ki casually raised his arms and awaited the affliction of the curse, while the watching crowd hung silently on the scene, wondering at the High Priest's anger and the rage of Teka, curious as to why the Chancellor stood passively in the presence of the goddess' awesome wrath. Nothing happened. Haephus was dumbfounded. He repeated the cursing ritual. Nothing changed. Murmurs rippled through the gathering. The priests stared open-mouthed at each other. Haephus fixed his eyes squarely on the Chancellor.

In an open display of boredom, A Ahmud Ki let his tired outstretched arms fall and grinned at Haephus. 'Slow worker your goddess, isn't she?' he laconically commented. He raised his right arm and muttered under his breath, words Haephus couldn't quite catch, and the watching audience barely noticed. Aloud, A Ahmud Ki called upon Berak N'eth. 'Oh God of gods, teach these unbelievers the power of your Will.' Haephus jerked to attention, his body wracked by a powerful spasm. His eyes widened with fear and his mouth opened to scream the agony clutching at his heart, but only a high keening emerged, a sound that reminded the witnesses of a dragon's cry. Haephus' rigid body ignited in a fierce rush of green flame that consumed the priest, leaving a scorched shadow on the stone floor of the atrium and a distinctively pungent sulphurous gas cloud floating in the air.

Above the cries and gasps of astonishment and terror, following Haephus' dramatic combustion, A Ahmud Ki called for order, and when the hubbub settled the five remaining priests were slumped on their knees, their heads bent in prayer, their hands shaking, faces white with terror. The crowd stared at the spot where Haephus had stood in challenge of the new god. 'Let word of what you've witnessed be spread among the people. Berak N'eth calls on you, as his people. Berak N'eth tolerates no other gods, for he alone is the One True God of Power.' He smiled and headed for the exit to his tower.

By the next morning, the temple to Teka in the castle grounds was pulled down, and her priests vanished into hiding.

Thirty Four

With the portal's red haze shimmering in the tower chamber, A Ahmud Ki passed his hand over the communication crystal, letting it fade in luminescence and shrink, until it was a silver ball on the pedestal. He checked his black and silver cloak concealed his gold plate armour, before stepping into the red glow.

He emerged, not in the Kal E'haruk Ka Irandu of Yul Ithrandyr but in a foreign antechamber. Not that he was surprised. The palace of Leiksha Ithrandyr Shehaal, Lord of all Ranu Ka Shehaala, was reputed to have a thousand rooms, so it was possible Shehaal varied at will where he chose to meet people. The room was lushly decorated with hanging screens of rainbow silk and the walls were the familiar polished marble that adorned most palace rooms.

A Ahmud Ki had forgotten the opulence abounding in Shehaal's palace, having spent so much time surviving in the catacombs of the Andrakian fortress and the austerity of his black tower. This is at least the minimum inspiration that must bedeck the new palace of Andrakis, he thought, as his eyes roved over the bright colours.

He became aware of the people prostrated before him, their foreheads pressed against the cold marble floor in customary Ranu Ka Shehaala fashion for inferiors before a superior. He studied their backs, relishing the domination the rulers in this land took for granted from every citizen, a presence of power he would soon wield over his servants in the Kingdom. One figure was wrapped in the smothering red robes of an Ithosen, a Holy man with magical powers and the status to sit in audience before Shehaal. The other three wore light chain mail corselets, and purple undershirts and leggings in the manner of palace guards. 'Anye ne salett,' he ordered, the familiar words rolling like honey from his tongue, and the four attendants rose obediently.

312

The guards stepped back, avoiding A Ahmud Ki's gaze, but the red-robed Ithosen bowed his head in courtesy, before greeting him. 'Irand shadu arat shehaal.'

A Ahmud Ki returned the formal greeting, as was customary, and waited for the Ithosen to introduce himself.

'I am Salamin. The Most Holy Lord of Light has instructed me to bring you to him, the moment you arrive. Please come with me now,' the Ithosen said, and with that he turned and led A Ahmud Ki to an obsidian door, which a guard opened.

They travelled a long, wide corridor that A Ahmud Ki recognised. He spent a long time as a teacher in the Palace Irandu Shadu, under Shehaal's protection, as a favour for saving Shehaal's life from an assassination attempt, and he was free to roam through much of the palace in his search for learning. The room he arrived in was unfamiliar because it was one of several chambers that hived off the corridor that led toward the Kal E'haruk.

His escort halted before a pair of carved ivory doors. A Ahmud Ki studied a bas relief decorating the centre panels of an indistinct, grossly exaggerated female figure, Fareeka, mother of all Ranu Ka Shehaala, and consciously patted his cloak, feeling his holy Ithosen talisman of Fareeka hidden inside; the one his mentor, Karrilyon, gave him during his apprenticeship and learning of the Third Ki. Salamin bowed respectfully, and asked A Ahmud Ki to wait patiently while he entered the Kal E'haruk to inquire if Leiksha Ithrandyr Shehaal was ready to speak with him. A guard opened the right-hand door, and Salamin went through, the guard closing the door behind.

Not much has changed in Ranu Ka Shehaala during my three-year absence since portalling out of the Sands of Fire, thought A Ahmud Ki, while he waited, though it was over twelve years since he last stood in the palace, after being sent into temporary exile by Shehaal. The Lord of Peace and Light found A Ahmud Ki's hunger for power distasteful, threatening, and sent him to the most unpleasant place in his domain, the desert the Ranu called the Sands of Fire, where daytime temperatures were often unbearable, expecting him to learn humility. Instead, he only succeeded in fuelling A Ahmud Ki's passion to acquire even greater power, and his isolated, uninterrupted studies led him to experiment with portals. When he escaped from Ranu Ka Shehaala through a crude one-way portal to Targa, he deliberately left witnesses, including a fat-bellied Murzat Ka Shet named Jezarba, to inform Shehaal of what they'd seen. He was probably a legend because of his dramatic, magical disappearance.

The ivory doors swung wide, and he stared past his three guards at five more Ranu warriors in purple plate armour – Shehaal's personal guards. Salamin was beckoning to A Ahmud Ki to enter the Great Central Hall of Light, and he bowed low, the guards following suit, as A Ahmud Ki walked between.

The doors opened into the Kal E'haruk from the left, near the very front, where a raised stage thrust into the hall. Daylight spilled from glass panels high overhead, and the brilliant marble gloss of the hall reflected and enhanced the patterns formed by the windows, lending the entire structure a light, airy aspect. Magical light spheres floating between ceiling and floor added lustre.

A Ahmud Ki was aware of the red-robed Ithosen audience on the marble bench tiers on the main walls, at least two hundred on either side of the hall, far more of them than he expected, watching him as he approached the base of the steps that led up to Shehaal's throne on the marble proscenium. When he gazed up, he saw Shehaal standing before the marble throne, wearing his customary white robes and turban, flanked by his official party. Two guards, huge men, reminding A Ahmud Ki in their stature rather unpleasantly of the foolish Kingdom warrior Claarn, stood beside Shehaal, daring anyone to threaten their Holy Lord, and three men stood behind and to the left of the throne: one wearing the red of the Ithosen, one the purple hue of the warriors, and the third in black robes proclaiming him as Shehaal's Advisor.

There was something aesthetically pleasing about the

splashes of colour against the white marble background, A Ahmud Ki decided, as he studied Shehaal's retinue, something that added to the man's charisma, and his ordered empire. The Kingdom of Andrakis was too messy, too dull, too much of a patchwork of muddied colours and designs to appeal. That had to change in his new regime.

Shehaal raised his right hand slightly, and the Kal E'haruk became mobile, as the Ithosen audience, and Shehaal's party on the stage, all dropped to their knees, and placed their foreheads against the floor as a sign of submission before their leader. A Ahmud Ki suppressed a smile and remained upright, as he always had in Shehaal's presence, sustained by his intention to never kneel before anyone, sustained by his arrogance and his hidden power. 'Irand shadu arat shehaal,' Shehaal said, in greeting.

'Irand shadu arat shehaal,' A Ahmud Ki politely replied, and waited.

'I see the Seeker of Power has not yet learned the value of humility,' Shehaal observed.

'Humility is only of value to those who cannot wield power,' A Ahmud Ki replied casually. 'Servants must be humble to their masters. Masters serve no one, but themselves.'

'Perhaps,' said Shehaal, 'but who is the master here?'

'We are all masters of our own destiny,' A Ahmud Ki answered, 'unless we choose to give away that responsibility to others.'

'And are you the master of your destiny?'

A Ahmud Ki began to levitate toward the proscenium without invitation. 'I am the master of many destinies,' he said, 'exactly as you are.'

Shehaal watched A Ahmud Ki approach and recognised danger in his brazen manner. The arrogant stranger who aspired to the rank of Ithosen so many years ago hadn't changed his unfortunate attitude, but something had changed significantly, because the person ascending his steps came with the easy diffidence of one used to power beyond the reach of mortals, and with the casual air of

315

authority only a Leiksha could afford in Ranu Ka Shehaala.

There was something else he noticed, as A Ahmud Ki reached the top of the steps and faced him. He saw a youthful handsomeness in A Ahmud Ki's features that was incongruent with his age. It was at least twelve years since he last saw A Ahmud Ki's face, that fateful day when he exiled him to teach him the necessity of humility, and yet A Ahmud Ki seemed no older than he remembered then, indeed fresher, more charismatic. And he could see fire burning deep in the recesses of the visitor's eyes, an all-consuming fire that glowed red behind the grey, an alarming energy.

A Ahmud Ki smiled as he stood before Shehaal. The Holy Lord of Light and Life looked less imposing than he remembered. He still had the same green piercing owl eyes that were determined to peer inside a soul, but the bushy eyebrows and tufts of beard at the edges of the turban and face shroud were greying, and the man's face was creased with age. The intervening years had been unkind to the leader of the Ranu. No doubt his successors among the hopeful Ithosen were already squabbling.

Shehaal ordered the assembly in the Kal E'haruk to rise, and muffled outcries of consternation greeted the realisation the visitor had dared ascend the proscenium steps unbidden. Shehaal's guards were particularly miffed, having failed in their duty to protect their Lord. 'Your purpose in coming here has partly been explained by your servant,' Shehaal began, as the Ithosen in the hall resumed their seats. 'He spoke of the Dragonlord, and the war, and the new barbarian King who bears a sword of fire.'

'All these things are true,' A Ahmud Ki explained, smiling at the way the Kingdom people and the Ranu saw each other as the barbarians. The truth is they are all barbarians, he thought. Only he understood the future. 'The new King is called Andrakis, after the fortress and dead Dragonlord who once held it. There are prophecies that say he will slay the living Dragonlord.'

'This Dragonlord - what is his name?'

'Mareg Dru'artha Sutnavanistra.'

'Find what you can,' Shehaal instructed the black-robed Advisor, who bowed deeply and withdrew.

To the library no doubt, A Ahmud Ki decided. What do the Ranu know of the Dragonlords? His experience in researching in Shehaal's massive library reminded him how extensive the Ranu library was. There was every possibility their records might unearth details he hadn't accessed in the Targan and Kingdom libraries, or through absorbing Andrakis' memories and power. He doubted that. 'I take it the Dragonlord's armies haven't marched against the Ranu Ka Shehaala?' A Ahmud Ki asked.

'They did. In the summer,' Shehaal replied, 'but the tribal riders drove them back into Murkaatz from Batt Ji'Nya. You are surprised the people could drive away the enemy so easily, when the same enemy laid waste to the Kingdom of barbarians?'

A Ahmud Ki smiled. Shehaal's uncanny ability to read the emotions of others hadn't waned with time. No doubt the Leiksha would try mind-reading next. He was due for an interesting surprise if he did. 'To a degree,' A Ahmud Ki answered.

'There is no secret,' Shehaal replied, and beckoned to the purple-robed member of the party. 'Keraam can tell you what happened.'

Keraam bowed deeply, before looking A Ahmud Ki directly in the face. The man had the common dark eyes, tanned skin, and heavy eyebrows of the Ranu, but the exposed portion of his right cheek displayed a broad white scar, obviously earned in battle. His voice was deep, gruff, commanding. 'The barbarian hordes came, like a river flood, through the Fez Arik from Murkaatz into Batt Ji'Nya, burning and killing. They swept away Tul Maheem and Tul Haruk, Tul Ira and set upon Tul Kareb before the people could mobilise against them. We sent out riding bands to hit and run, and break up the barbarian army. You see, they have no horses, except for a handful for the ones in black armour, and they are not true riders. We struck swift and hard, day and night,

317

until they could take no more punishment. When they began to retreat, we hit at them faster and harder still, until their morale shattered like a wooden spear on a metal shield, and then we washed the plains of Batt Ji'Nya with barbarian blood to cleanse it of Ranu deaths.' Keraam bowed again, and stepped back behind Shehaal, his duty completed.

A Ahmud Ki nodded respectfully. 'I'm impressed,' he said to Shehaal. 'Mobility and speed – and obviously no dragons.'

'No dragons,' Shehaal confirmed. 'Your Dragonlord was more intent on securing the eastern lands before seriously attacking us.'

A Ahmud Ki considered Shehaal's explanation of Mareg's movements. If the Dragonlord's armies were, on a larger scale, limited in number, then he'd have to be careful in laying his tactics and avoid overstretching his resources.

'So why have you returned, Seeker of Power?' Shehaal asked.

'To seek your help against the Dragonlord,' A Ahmud Ki replied. He recognised Shehaal's shift in concentration, as he began an attempt to probe A Ahmud Ki's thoughts. The Chancellor smiled and responded with like concentration. There's no point interfering in my inner self, A Ahmud Ki projected, as he felt the gentle touch of the Ranu Lord's psyche. Shehaal's probing spell recoiled, and A Ahmud Ki saw astonishment register in the Leiksha's eyes, so he projected at Shehaal's consciousness, The Ithosen you banished to the Sands of Fire was subsumed long ago. I am much more than you can imagine, much more than your simple spell can discover. He realised there was a risk of frightening Shehaal and ruining his plans by making a pretentious response, but he also knew the Ranu Lord was not easily disturbed. Indeed, it was better Shehaal knew at once he was no longer dealing with an inferior. That would ensure the discussions to come were honest, even blunt if necessary.

Shehaal was shocked by A Ahmud Ki's impudent mental invasion, and the ease with which he cast aside his attempt to test the truth behind the Chancellor's words, but he quickly regained his composure before his attending guards and advisors noticed a hiatus in the discussion between the two. 'Much must be spoken between us,' Shehaal said, his green eyes narrowing with suspicion, 'since much has changed.'

'The only constancy in all creation is change,' A Ahmud Ki replied with a courteous smile. 'That is one Ranu proverb I've never forgotten.'

Shehaal bowed his head to acknowledge A Ahmud Ki's apparent respect of the Ranu culture. 'And how can Ranu Ka Shehaala help the Murkaatz?' the Holy Lord of Light and Life asked.

'Too many mysteries,' Sasha said despondently.

'You have to admit he is no longer Andra,' Claarn argued. Everyone nodded. 'He hasn't been the same since I let him talk me into accompanying him into that infernal black tower!'

'You couldn't stop the Chancellor's magic,' Patti said.

Claarn clutched the hilt of his sword. 'I could have stopped the cursed Chancellor though!'

Marella crossed to stand beside the red-haired man. 'I've watched him goad you before, Claarn,' she said gently. 'He'd like you to try just that. You heard what he did to Haephus.'

'And he claims the gods were asserting their authority. Where was Teka?' Claarn asked.

'There are no gods,' Patti asserted, and chuckled. 'The Chancellor killed Haephus. I'll bet my virtue on it.' Smiles spread around the room.

'You have no virtue, madam,' Kara retorted, and laughed, and Patti broke into a broad grin of admission.

'No, I don't, that's to be certain enough. As much as there are no gods either.'

Only Claarn refrained from laughing at Patti's humour. Instead, he moved to the hearth and squatted, staring into the flames, as he often did of late. 'There must be a way, some way of breaking whatever hold it is the Chancellor has

319

over Andra. There must be a way.'

'We need more information. We need to talk to Andra,' Kara suggested.

'How?' asked Sasha. 'The King is virtually under lock and key when he's not surrounded by the Chancellor's Andrakian Warriors. And we can hardly get inside the Chancellor's tower.'

'No,' Kara replied, 'but I've learned the Chancellor's reforming the Royal Assassins. We could get someone inside them.'

'It'll have to be someone we can trust thoroughly,' Marella said.

'I have an idea of someone. But he's young,' Kara ventured.

'Aaron,' said Patti.

Kara glanced at the chubby madam. 'Yes. How-'

'He learned a lot from Tim during the siege weeks. He knows the assassin's craft. And he's reliable. And he won't look too suspicious,' said Patti with a knowing grin.

'But he's a mere lad,' Claarn growled.

'All the better,' said Sasha. 'He's less to consider a threat.'

'I don't like it,' the giant warrior muttered, and turned away.

'And there's another way in,' Kara continued, turning her attention to the others at the table. 'I know the Chancellor is keen to recreate a Royal retinue of page boys and serving girls around Andra to give him the aura of great Royalty before the war begins again.'

'The lass Milly will leap at that opportunity,' Patti said. 'She's desperate for a chance to be with him. She's tried a dozen times to trick the golden guards into letting her into Andra's quarters.'

'We couldn't have a better contact close to the King,' Kara added.

'Won't the Chancellor recognise her?' asked Sasha.

'Perhaps,' Kara replied. 'Perhaps not. He wasn't present at Andra's coronation, and he's even less likely to consider a young girl a threat, under the circumstances.'

Claarn strode to the table and stood towering over the women. 'And if all this gathering information comes to nothing, what then?' he asked, anger rippling in his voice.

'Then we look at other possibilities,' Kara coolly replied.

Claarn muttered and strode toward the door, opening it as he arrived. 'What happens, happens. Play your women's games,' he growled, glaring back at the group at the table in the small chamber. 'But if the Chancellor harms Andra, or anyone else in this Kingdom, I'll deal with him the only way I know how.' He exited, slamming the door to emphasise his frustration. Kara turned to appeal to Marella to soothe the giant warrior's anger, but the woman was already on her feet, heading for the door and Claarn.

Thirty Five

Late winter storms swept across the plains of Ky incessantly, flooding Dragon River and preventing even light work on the Upper Palace buildings or outer walls. The people, squatting in their half-built hovels and shelters at the plateau base, gradually abandoned their makeshift homes and sought refuge from the fury in the fortress catacombs, and although the storms lacked the intensity of the one that carried the Targan ships into Kenton several weeks earlier their constancy made them more dangerous.

As Kara predicted, the Chancellor organised urchins and older children to learn, or in some cases re-learn, the crafts of page and servant appropriate for waiting on the King and his retinue. Milly mixed with others who sought employment in the King's service, and soon earned enough recognition from the three young ex-servants of Thana's palace to be nominated as suitable to directly attend the King. A Ahmud Ki had no immediate contact with the apprentices in the early stages, so Milly ran no risk of discovery as she trained.

Aaron sought the lower chambers where the Chancellor's assistant, Sarcen, conducted recruitment and training of the new Royal Assassins. The Eyes and Ears of the supposedly defunct Guild provided Kara with information, enabling Aaron to find Sarcen's squad.

Sarcen was initially suspicious of Aaron, especially as the boy found the secret chambers very easily, so much so that he started wondering if A Ahmud Ki arranged for the boy to check up on his training progress. The direct result of this assumption was that Sarcen made a special effort to pay close attention to Aaron's learning in every training session, attention which made the boy very nervous, and nearly resulted in Kara calling the plan off during the first week for fear of Aaron's safety.

The Chancellor instituted one major change in the

Kingdom during the time of the storms. From thin air, an embassy of eight Ranu barbarians, clad from head to foot in red robes, their faces hidden so only their dark eyes were visible, briefly appeared in the fortress for three days. The incident set tongues wagging, and minds speculating, as to how and why the Ranu were present, but no one provided answers, and, as mysteriously as they came, the Ranu disappeared before the storms blew over. Not by coincidence, fresh food also became available: Ranu grains and meat, and milk, food scarce among the people in Andrakis.

Once the storms blew out, the people emerged, and began the long and messy task of mopping up the damage. The common belief was they'd sat through the last true storms of winter, and by the reckoning of the calendars it was less than twelve days to spring. That knowledge, together with the fresh supplies of food that kept appearing in increasing amounts, fostered a festive atmosphere throughout the fortress, and talk of the first Spring Celebration since before the war buoyed the workers' spirits, as building recommenced.

A Ahmud Ki issued orders, on behalf of the King, to Marella, Claarn, and others that there would be an important meeting of the King's Table, within three days, to prepare for the coming of spring and the certain return of the Dragonlord's army. On the agenda would also be the necessity to appoint a new High Priest over the temple of Berak N'eth to fill the vacancy created by Haephus' unfortunate death.

Claarn organised the Kingdom warriors; firstly, preparing equipment by taking stock of what remained, what needed repair, and what needed to be forged by the smiths who set up new foundries in chambers within the plateau.

Marella concentrated on the Haardrishii, especially continuing the rigid training of the volunteers recruited after the siege. The Haardrishii were a different force from the one that served Thana. A central core of experienced black knights remained the backbone of the regiment, but they numbered less than thirty of the original two hundred. The rest were warriors with a desire to wear the black plate armour that represented honour and status in the old Kingdom; volunteers untrained in the traditional Haardrishii code and fighting skills. Marella assigned five recruits to every experienced Haardrishii, to maximise the efficiency of training and minimise the time required to complete it, but she begrudgingly accepted the new Haardrishii were a shadow of their predecessors.

Both Claarn and Marella ignored the army of golden Andrakian warriors and knights who waited silently within the fortress for the war to recommence. Though Claarn was officially High Lord of the armies, he knew full well A Ahmud Ki controlled the Andrakian warriors, and was glad to leave it that way, disgusted at the magic keeping what should be dead moving.

Work on the Upper Palace resumed fully by the third day after the last storm. Haagii prisoners continued to haul great boulders from the increasing depth of the central shaft, and artisans chiselled blocks in the cool morning sun that topped the eastern Ureykyeu Mountains. Cirrus clouds dappled the pale blue sky, promising everyone a fine day, and on the plains the few surviving farmers commenced the task of seeding the earth, and teaching those who would learn from them how to till and harvest the soil. The planting was late, and the coming harvest in late summer would be scanty, but it was a fresh start for the new Kingdom of Andrakis.

The dark dot on the northern horizon appeared over the spur of the Andrakian Mountains, and Marron, who was on watch in the newly completed northern tower, stared with disbelief as the dot grew steadily, heading directly for the plateau. He felt acid in his stomach ripple with fear. They're coming too soon! We aren't ready, he found himself thinking, as the dot resolved into the fearsome shape of a black dragon, its wings moving in slow deliberate rhythm. We aren't ready. 'Dragon!' he screamed from the tower to the workers milling below and pointed north where the beast raced in on extended wings.

Claarn heard the warning cry where he was assembling a pile of broken and battered shields in the northwest corner of the palace grounds. He glanced toward Marron's tower, searching for the threat, but the dragon's angle of approach hid it from his view. 'Get the garrison up here at once!' he commanded a warrior who was helping him, and turned to a second, and said, 'Tell the King.'

As the warriors ran to their duties, a dark shadow flitted over the palace grounds and Claarn looked up to see the dragon's dark grey underbelly sweep over, its huge wings extended full length to catch the natural updrafts generated by the plateau. The black creature passed, and with a dozen steady wing beats, it ascended toward the clouds.

Wanting a clearer view of the creature, Claarn sprinted up a set of stone steps to the parapet and searched south in time to see the massive creature wheel to its right, and begin a slow glide toward the plateau. As much as he hated and feared the beasts, he was numbed with admiration for the majesty and power the approaching creature displayed in its ease of flight, and he remained watching the dragon as it swept over the plateau a second time, the rush of air around its scaled body filling his ears with a sibilant whistling as it passed low and fast, turning him with its motion.

'Lord Claarn?'

He turned to the voice. 'What?'

A blond-bearded warrior he knew as Hart stood on the parapet, asking, 'Your orders?'

Claarn remembered what a dragon attack meant. 'Tell everyone to use bows and spears, but only when the creature isn't headed their way. When it faces them, tell them to hide behind the wall, or get cover as best they can. There's no dishonour dodging dragon flame. Understood?'

A wry smile crept along Hart's lips. He also remembered the dragon attacks in Central Gate. 'Yes, my Lord.'

'Lord Claarn!' Claarn looked down at the warrior calling to him, as Hart withdrew to spread his orders; the same man he ordered to inform Andra of the dragon's arrival. 'Lord Claarn, I couldn't reach the King.'

'Why in Teka's name not?' Claarn yelled.

'The Golden Warriors wouldn't let me pass,' the warrior explained.

'Damn them!' Claarn spat. He looked to the north, to see the dragon circling, gaining altitude above the plains, and swore. 'The King will know what I want him to know!' he roared, and he leapt down the steps from the wall, heading for the atrium and fortress entrance.

In the corridor leading to Andra's chambers, Claarn confronted two Andrakian warriors on silent guard. He spat and began to walk between them, but the warriors shifted to bar his entry. 'I am Lord Claarn and I come to see the King!' he bellowed, but the warriors remained impassive. 'So be it!' he growled. He turned, as if to depart, then whirled on his heels and caught a warrior under the jaw with his extended arm. The blow spread-eagled the warrior against the corridor wall, and he slid to the floor. Caught unawares, the second guard drew his sword, but Claarn had the advantage and pushed the warrior aside with a sharp punch to his visor, then strode toward the door.

The searing sword cut caught him unawares. He stumbled face forward to the floor, and only his instinctive roll to the left saved him from a fatal blow, the sword blade intended for his neck striking harmlessly against stone. As he lumbered to his feet, his uninjured victims closing on him, weapons weaving menacingly, he realised his mistake. 'Curse the sorcerer who ever gave the dead life!' he scowled, and he wrenched his sword from its scabbard.

The Andrakian warriors hampered each other's movements in the corridor, giving Claarn an edge in the ensuing fight, but the brutal blows he struck seemed ineffectual. 'The dead can't die,' he wheezed, parrying a thrust from the nearer opponent. 'So, I have to cut you apart like the Dark Warriors do.' He dodged, and used his greater strength to kick the first warrior off-balance, and as he ducked under the second's sweeping blade he swung his heavy sword and decapitated the fallen enemy. 'One of you cursed beings!' he grimaced, but winced as the second warrior's blade slashed his cheek open. 'By all that smells of death!' he roared, and swung down with all his strength, cleaving the golden helm and the warrior's head to the neck. To Claarn's amazement, the warrior remained upright, sword arm twitching, as if the horribly mutilated Andrakian warrior wanted to continue the fight, but the body shuddered and toppled over at Claarn's feet. The corridor went silent. 'So be it,' he breathed with relief and exhaustion.

He turned to the King's door and swung it open. He hadn't expected to find A Ahmud Ki staring directly at him, let alone come face to face with a red-robed Ranu barbarian in the chamber with Andra.

The Chancellor raised a questioning eyebrow as Claarn tried to take stock of the situation. 'You have an annoying habit of blundering into things, don't you,' he commented.

Claarn heard the bitterness in the Chancellor's words and straightened to full height. 'I've come to speak to the King.'

'Is it that urgent?' A Ahmud Ki asked, feigning boredom.

'How urgent would you consider a dragon?' Claarn replied.

The Chancellor's face registered shock, which he covered quickly, but Claarn saw enough to satisfy his anger. 'Where?' A Ahmud Ki asked.

'Outside,' Claarn answered.

The room became a flurry of activity as Andra summoned Abreotan's sword and buckled on his golden armour, while A Ahmud Ki led the Ithosen through a side door that Claarn thought was meant to be a secret entry and exit point only known to Andra and his trusted friends. 'What was the dragon doing?' Andra asked, as Claarn helped him tighten the breastplate.

'It's flown over twice, circling.'

'Has it attacked?'

'No.'

'Odd.'

Not as odd as the scene I've witnessed in here, thought Claarn. Where do these Ranu barbarians keep coming from? And why?

Claarn followed the King from the fortress into the atrium, where they were greeted with the mystifying news the dragon had landed in the northern area of the grounds, near A Ahmud Ki's tower, on the desolated space of the old Royal Gardens. The creature made no attempt to attack, only breathed flames to keep the Kingdom defenders at a respectable distance. Two dragon riders had dismounted. 'Go rouse a squad of the Andrakian warriors,' Andra ordered Claarn.

'Why?' Claarn asked. 'We can protect you, my Lord.'

Andra whirled to face the giant, staring up at him with cold brown eyes. 'Do as I say.'

Claarn nodded obediently, and headed into the fortress to begrudgingly do as his King ordered.

Andra followed the noise toward A Ahmud Ki's tower. The brutish, ugly reptilian dragon's head loomed above the near-completed outer buildings of the Upper Palace, and as Andra approached he wondered what purpose Mareg had in sending another of his creatures to Andrakis so early, before the armies of either side could be mobilised. A show of strength? Perhaps. He knew A Ahmud Ki had taken the Ranu ambassador to the safety of his tower through the portal constructed in the chamber set aside for meetings of the King's Table. That was the plan for the scheduled meeting – to reveal to the others how the portal was linking the several lands – Targa, Ranu Ka Shehaala, and Andrakis – to prepare for the renewed war against Mareg, and to provide the Kingdom with constant supplies. The Chancellor's plan was increasingly brilliant, Andra believed, and none of the others had even begun to achieve what A Ahmud Ki was achieving.

In the space where the dragon rested, its neck bent so that its golden-green slit eyes could study Andra's approach, its scaly tail shifting slowly back and forth on the earth, like an angry cat, two figures waited, watched by a crowd of Kingdom onlookers.

One figure Andra recognised – a dracabeorn, distorted and recreated by Mareg to ride his dragon. It lurked near the dragon's grey-black belly, as if it was afraid to venture further than necessary.

The other figure was imposing. At first Andra thought he was a Dark Warrior, his black metal armour, all wicked spikes and sharp edges, shining despite the dull sunlight, but as he closed the distance he could see differences. The warrior was as tall and broad as Claarn, taller, and he leaned on the pommel of a broadsword that looked in every shape and form the twin of Abreotan's sword, only larger. The warrior's face was hidden behind a heavy visor and full helmet. His plate armour was studded with short spikes in every conceivable place. Even the warrior's gauntlets gleamed with brutal stud spikes, on the back of the hands, and around the wrists. He presented a formidable opponent, if opponent he was destined to be.

Marella marshalled her Haardrishii in readiness to defend the King and the people. Sasha organised a squad of archers along the nearby wall. Claarn would no doubt soon arrive with the Andrakian warriors. The odds were set against the stranger, dragon or no dragon. Abreotan's sword ensured that. Besides, a single warrior had little hope against an army – but a nagging doubt plagued Andra's confidence. There was something wrong. He approached the warrior, and sternly demanded, 'Who are you?'

The voice in response that issued from the warrior defied Andra's ears. It was harsh, deep, and manifold, as if more than one person spoke from beneath the visor. 'I come to kill the King who claims to bear a sword of fire.'

'I am King Andrakis. I bear Abreotan's sword,' said Andra.

'Then I come to kill you,' the warrior replied. He hefted his huge broadsword above his head, chanted a string of guttural words, the blade burst into dark amber flame and he swung down at Andra.

Seeing the arc of fire, Andra rolled and came to his feet with Abreotan's sword magically appearing in his hand. Too slow. The flat of the warrior's sword smashed against the shoulder of his armour, fire searing under the edge of his helmet, sending him sprawling across the ground toward the dragon's twitching tail. Abreotan's sword cartwheeled from his hand. He shook his head in amazement and rolled again to avoid the downswing of the warrior's flaming blade. As he got to his feet, a volley of arrows clattered harmlessly against the dragon warrior's black armour, and the warrior laughed. 'What can arrows do against a dragon's hide?'

The distraction and boast turned to Andra's advantage. He summoned his sword to his hand and willed it to flame. *So, the armour is dragon hide. No matter. Abreotan's sword can slice through it with ease.*

The dragon warrior advanced, closing to strike again, and this time Andra met his sweeping blow with Abreotan's sword. *Mistake.* The dragon warrior's superior strength was obvious the instant they connected. Andra was sent sprawling again, though this time he held onto his sword and rolled quickly – but not quick enough to avoid the sharp blow the dragon warrior dealt across the back of his armour. He kicked away in the opposite direction, predicting his opponent's downswing, and pushed to his feet.

Gaining a brief respite, he concentrated on the sword, and the surrounding crowd gasped as Andra grew until he towered over the dragon warrior, standing almost as tall as the dragon watching proceedings impatiently like a hungry pet. To Andra's dismay, his opponent mimicked his action, until they faced each other as lethal giants in a very small arena. Seeing the imminent danger, the crowd scrambled to the safety of the nearby buildings and cowered. 'At least we're equal this way,' Andra said, with an uneasy shrug.

'You are not my equal,' the dragon warrior replied, and lunged.

They traded blow for blow with sweeping swords of fire, each searching for a weakness in his opponent's defence; finding none, showing none. Andra was tiring for the first time in combat since acquiring Abreotan's sword. *Was his opponent tiring?* He had other possibilities with the sword – invisibility – the bolt of energy he called upon to slay the first dragon at Cennednyss, if necessary.

No, a familiar voice said. Fight as you are.

Why? he thought, and slipped, taking a savage blow to the side of his helmet, a blow that made him reel and lose ground. People scattered from his feet, as he trod back on a low wall and crushed it.

I am your god. Trust me.

Andra recovered, forcing the dragon warrior back two steps toward A Ahmud Ki's tower, but as he did he glanced down, distracted by movement behind the dragon at the tower base, where A Ahmud Ki, in the golden armour he retrieved from Andrakis' tomb, was conjuring. His glance earned him another powerful blow, this time across his left knee, and Andra slumped, seeing his golden armour crumple under the force of the sword edge. Pain ripped through his body.

Get up! ordered the voice in his head.

He saw the killing swing coming from the dragon warrior and called on his Guardian training. Roll with the force. As if in slow motion, he began to roll as the sword edge contacted the underarm of his breastplate, and he let the force throw him carelessly aside, like a child's rag doll. He felt the bruising pain, but no cut as he landed heavily against the castle wall, from where he heard his opponent's mocking laughter believing he'd slain Abreotan's Inheritor. Andra let the sword's magic, sustaining his giant size, dissipate, to add to the illusion of defeat.

Gloating with victory, the dragon warrior returned to his natural size, and swaggered toward Andra's slumped figure, sword burning maliciously. 'Watch as your master's servant takes the head of this false King!' the dragon warrior bellowed, as he turned to the crowd.

Claarn pushed forward, wielding his sword. 'You have one more opponent to fight before you claim any heads here, you demon from the eighth hell!' the High Lord yelled in fury, and he strode toward the dragon warrior.

'I don't mind light entertainment,' the dragon warrior chortled with bloodthirsty delight at the twist in events, and he squared up to face the oncoming warrior whose mane of red hair flared like the flames on the dragon warrior's blade.

As Claarn approached, A Ahmud Ki's hands weaved at blinding speed, breaking down the remaining binding spells holding Mareg's magical construct together. The flames along the giant broadsword winked out and a strange blue halo enveloped the dragon warrior. Claarn stopped several paces short of his target, staring with bewilderment.

Strike now, the voice in Andra's head ordered. Abreotan's sword flamed to life, and Andra pushed to his feet, lunging up and deep into the middle of the dragon warrior's exposed back. The burning sword punched clean through the warrior, and the air filled with a cacophony of screaming voices; voices crying in agony, voices dying: the black armour shimmered inside the blue halo and disappeared with it. Impaled on Andra's sword was a thin, naked wretch that defied description as a human being. Andra slumped to the ground again, stunned, and in pain.

Claarn, Marella, and others ran toward Andra, but only Claarn reached the King. The others froze in their tracks, as the dragon at the tower turned its brutish head malevolently. They all saw A Ahmud Ki behind the cruel, scaly creature, babbling in an ancient, unrecognizable tongue. The Chancellor was crooning to the beast, coaxing it. What madness finally possessed the Chancellor? As if in answer to their fears, they saw the dragon turn its pendulous head toward the Chancellor, its great golden green reptilian eyes assessing him. A Ahmud Ki continued his incantation, moving his hands gently through the air, in long sweeping patterns, and slowly, ever so slowly, the dragon lowered its head, until one eye sat level with A Ahmud Ki, and its lower jaw rested softly on the ground, as if it wanted the Chancellor to stroke it, like a dog bowing its head to its master for a long-awaited pat.

And then came the most wondrous and fearful moment anyone witnessed on the plateau since Abreotan sealed Andrakis Va'ristrin Nyavardenet in his tomb a thousand years before. A Ahmud Ki, golden armour glinting beneath his silver-black robes, silvered locks braided and shining, climbed triumphantly onto the neck of the submissive dragon.

"Like twin heroes, like gods of old,
They stood and fought the golden foe,
With bow and sword and courage bold,
A ruined cottage sought to hold,
And traded blow for mortal blow,
Till breath was wind and blood was cold,
And spirits leapt where legends go."

excerpt from 'The Ballad of the Red Giant and the Quick Thief', Anonymous

Thirty Six

The snows in Central Gate thawed quickly in the lengthening days of early spring, and the floodwaters in the Valley of Rivers reverted to pebble watercourses in a week, leaving the way open for Mareg's assault on the Kingdom to recommence in earnest. Watchers searched the skies above the plains of Ky from the vaulting palace towers, and their counterparts gazed north and west from the craggy lookouts above the western end of Central Gate, waiting for the first view of Mareg's armies, or his dragons heralding the war, but they watched in vain. No army came. Scouts sent to the edge of Dragon Breath Plains reported no activity northward, and the remnant of Haagii survivors that wintered in the Kobold Ranges was dormant, hiding, unwilling to emerge onto the plains of Axxon, or attempt to escape to their homelands. The Dragonlord was mysteriously quiet.

Work on the Upper Palace of Andrakis raced to completion. The Haagii prisoners dragged the last boulders from the central shaft within days of the battle between King Andrakis and the dragon warrior, opening for the first time in a thousand years the ancient lair deep in the heart of the plateau, and already a dragon nested there: the personal pet of A Ahmud Ki. The excavation revealed the radial pattern of corridors and tunnels in the plateau, all running from the central shaft. There were galleries, at the inner end of each corridor, looking out and down into the centre of the plateau, galleries where before only solid stone sealed the openings, and people came to stare and wonder at the architectural vision of the Dragonlord who created the fortress.

Access to the lowest chambers, the rooms and library of Andrakis Va'ristrin Nyavardenet, was denied because the shaft in the Deep Cave remained sealed by a massive boulder, a secret entrance only A Ahmud Ki knew, and Milly and others guessed at, and the only other entrance was in the dragon's lair, that no one dared enter. Rumours spread quickly that not all the fortress was opened, because a lower ledge and gallery and the metal door into the sealed chambers of the dead Dragonlord were visible from the upper galleries, but A Ahmud Ki let it be known that horrors still lurked in the deepest recesses of the old fortress, and that only fools ignored the ancient warnings of Aian Abreotan who sealed the old Dragonlord in those chambers.

The warnings were readily heeded. Those few prisoners with masonry skill were set to work on the interior of the Upper Palace, carving walls and placing marble fascia in position, according to A Ahmud Ki's directions, under the guidance of Ranu masons. The Upper Palace outer walls began to adopt ostentatious curves, and spiky sweeps of stone vaulted toward the sky, making the palace resemble, as Claarn muttered to Marella one morning, the shoulder spikes on the armour of the Dragonlord's Dark Warriors.

The King rarely emerged from his underground chambers, and when he did it was to inspect the building progress, or attend the temple of Berak N'eth in the company of the Chancellor, a dozen Andrakian warriors, always at least two or three Ranu Ithosen, and six or seven other individuals who spoke to no one and kept near A Ahmud Ki.

Marella recognised Sarcen, the man responsible for training the new Royal Assassins, but the others were strangers – unaccountable strangers. Neither she, nor Claarn, nor anyone could get close to Andra since his battle with Mareg's dragon warrior. Claarn carried the weary and sore King to his Royal chambers, cradling him like a child in his great arms, but once there the Chancellor ordered them out so he could heal the King's injuries. She barely prevented Claarn from making a very foolish mistake, as he turned to confront A Ahmud Ki, but her giant friend was too tired to argue when she called him aside, too disillusioned, too confused when he saw the man he most hated bending to heal the one he most loved. He followed her out of the chambers like a dejected puppy, and went back to his duties, without speaking again of the whole incident, as if he refused to admit what had happened, or how he felt.

The only time they could talk to the King was at the assemblies of the King's Table, briefly and officially. The meeting following the arrival of the dragon warrior shocked them all. When Marella and Claarn entered, they saw a weird shimmering red glow at the far end of the chamber, a magical light fixed between two upright ebony poles the Chancellor explained was a door to other places. Marella had seen one before, in the Chancellor's tower at the height of the siege, when they travelled to Dragon's Tooth, but she hadn't expected to see another outside the tower, let alone at the King's Table. That was from where the Ranu Ithosen, or holy men, came. A Ahmud Ki had established a magical link with the barbarians, and another with the eastern land called Targa. Their ambassadors could come and go at will. Supplies of Targan and Ranu food could be portalled into the Kingdom.

Despite the unnerving fact that the Chancellor master-minded the scheme, Marella couldn't help but see the possibilities the portal connection offered the Kingdom in future conflict with the Dragonlord's armies. When the Chancellor intimated he was preparing a larger portal to allow whole Ranu cavalries through to help in the battles against the Dragonlord, the gathering at the King's Table was impressed, except for Claarn who remained silent. He refused to tell Marella after the meeting why he disapproved of the portal. She assumed his hatred of the Chancellor no longer allowed him to accept any positive possibilities from him, but, to her, the portal system seemed good.

The following meeting of the King's Table revealed another twist. Andra presented Haephus' successor, as High Priest, though Marella had never seen the white-haired old man who hobbled into the chamber. Like the retinue accompanying the King, there was no explanation as to from where High Priest Argwyllyn came. He certainly wasn't in the fortress during the siege.

When Marella asked Kara, after the meeting, if the Guild knew of Berak N'eth, or Argwyllyn, Kara replied in the negative, equally curious as to where the old man had sprung from. They agreed, though, that too many mysterious people were beginning to surround Andra, and the Chancellor, and hoped either Aaron or Milly would soon have answers, before the war became their singular focus again.

He was attracted to the fluctuations of light emanating from the communication crystal. Of its own accord, it altered from a silver ball to a full crystal sphere. Normally, when either Jasmin in Targa, or Saleem in the Palace Irandu Shadu, wanted to contact him, the silver ball glowed with an intense light. The current phenomenon was unexpected, and fascinating. As he peered into the crystal, the light pulses ceased, and the sphere became brilliantly clear, charged with energy that made the loose wisps of his silvery hair spray outward. A Ahmud Ki knew who was summoning him – his enemy, his brother: Mareg. A chill passed through his body, but it was an adrenalin-pumping mixture of fear and exhilaration, fostered by a cold destiny being fulfilled, exactly as he dreamed it would be. For so long, he'd worked toward this second confrontation, a chance to show the Dragonlord he was no piffling pretender to be brushed aside: that he was a master of the Fifth Ki, a master of all magic.

Red eyes burned in the crystal's centre, and around them, Mareg's cruel, handsome features materialised: his almond-shaped eyes, prominent high cheekbones, and flowing mane of silver hair. Like staring into a mirror, thought A Ahmud Ki. He is my brother.

Don't dare consider me your brother, the deep, resonant voice echoed inside A Ahmud Ki's head. A Ahmud Ki smiled, a touch of nervous arrogance sprinkling through his thought, which caused the Dragonlord's red eyes to flare like pools of fire. You consider yourself my equal, Mareg sneered. But I know who you are, pretender. We've met before.

Good, thought A Ahmud Ki. You've remembered. He felt a stab of anger from Mareg.

You call yourself the Seeker of Power in the tongue of the wretched Ranu, Mareg announced. A Ahmud Ki. I thought I crushed you out of existence the last time you interfered on the Sphere of Thought.

A Ahmud Ki laughed again. You tried, Mareg. But you failed. He sensed a ripple in the fabric of magic binding them, a mind-threatening surge of energy like the one Mareg sent on the first occasion they crossed paths in the crystal, and responded, summoning the lessons he eked from Andrakis' memories to smooth out the rippling effect.

Mareg projected his frustration at A Ahmud Ki's unexpected response. Clever. Especially for a pretender.

You no longer deal with a pretender, A Ahmud Ki stressed, his confidence growing. I am as powerful as you, Mareg, perhaps even more so.

Mareg's expression shifted from annoyance to a vague glimmer of curiosity. His eyes narrowed. There is familiarity here, he mused. Perhaps you are more than you seem.

I have your dragon, Mareg, A Ahmud Ki informed him.

Mareg's curiosity disappeared, replaced by his piercing glare of anger. I grow weary of your King and his sword of fire!

No, Mareg, not the King, A Ahmud Ki corrected. I have your dragon. As a pet.

Mareg's eyes widened enough for A Ahmud Ki to see his revelation brought Mareg to an understanding of what had happened: what was happening. Andrakis?

Is dead, A Ahmud Ki bluntly stated. I killed him. No. More than that. I've made him serve my need. The challenge was made. Mareg's eyes gleamed with fire. A Ahmud Ki knew his eyes were burning in the same fashion, the raw magical energy of his Dragonlord powers building and surging within to maintain the balance, the status quo, between Mareg and himself in the communication crystal.

Mareg's face twisted in a sneer, and the Dragonlord tipped back his head and laughed, loud and long, babbling like a mad being between the laughter. Andrakis is dead. Andrakis. The idiot. Caught in the web of that meddlesome Abreotan's sword, and sucked dry by an upstart who fancies himself a Dragonlord. Still. He never was enough of a realist, was he? Lacked the inner strength, the vision. The fool. The poor, mad fool.

A Ahmud Ki observed the Dragonlord's outburst with utmost caution, and his vigilance saved him from a sudden attack as Mareg abruptly broke his laughing spree to cast a sharp pulse of energy through the crystal link. A Ahmud Ki concentrated, met the energy surge with his own, and imagined the silent explosion as the two forces met and dissipated in a shower of iridescent lights on the Sphere of Thought connecting him to Mareg. As he relaxed and opened his eyes, he saw Mareg's visage grimacing.

There can only be one of us.

Of course, A Ahmud Ki answered. There will be one master.

Mareg smiled hideously. Then let's settle it in the crystal.

A Ahmud Ki suspected a trap, so he held back from using his spell to portal into the magical realm within the crystal, a spell and knowledge he acquired from Andrakis' memories, until he saw Mareg's face disappear. He had his chance to finish it for good. He grabbed the crystal sphere and threw it against the wall, but to his astonishment the ball bounced harmlessly off the wall and rolled to the floor, still clear and glowing.

You pathetic fool, Mareg laughed. A true Dragonlord knows well enough you can't shatter a magical item protected by a Dragonlord's spells. Do you think I'd be so foolish as to enter the crystal and trust you? Now enter and face your destruction as the charlatan you truly are. Or are you a coward?

Mareg's taunt angered A Ahmud Ki, but he controlled his emotion and concentrated on entering the sphere. One thing Mareg would learn, now and forever, was that he was no faker when it came to spell casting.

He felt a sharp shift in place and time, the rush of air

filling a vacuum, as he finished reciting the short phrase for the spell, and he stood on a vast, level, grey plain beneath a vaguely blue, cloudless sky. The air was still. The only break across the vista of the plain were isolated, twisted, dead white trees, jutting out of the greyness like skeletal hands, and on the distant horizon he could see a long dark smudge rising. A cliff? Hills? His memory stirred at the vision. He gazed on a place like this a very long time ago, as Terin.

'Welcome to Se'Treya,' said the voice, no longer in his mind.

A Ahmud Ki spun to face Mareg. The Dragonlord was grinning, and though his head was uncovered he was wearing the ebony armour A Ahmud Ki remembered him wearing in the Inner Sanctum of Targa the day he inadvertently released Mareg when trying to rob the Dragonlord's powers. He was dressed as a warrior, not unlike the dragon warrior he created and sent against Andra. Hanging from his left hand was a black battle-axe like the golden one that had adorned Andrakis' armour.

'You know what Se'Treya means, don't you?' Mareg asked.

'The Death Place,' A Ahmud Ki replied, translating the old language. 'I understand the Ancient Tongue quite well. Well enough to speak and read it.'

Mareg nodded wisely. 'Perhaps there is a touch in you of a Dragonlord,' he condescended with a shrug. 'You've obviously meddled with too many things you haven't understood.'

'Like you are now?' A Ahmud Ki asked, answering the Dragonlord's goading with a barb of his own.

'I don't meddle with anything,' Mareg acidly replied. 'I take, give, change, create, destroy as I please. That's one of the minor benefits of absolute power.'

'I know,' A Ahmud Ki replied.

Mareg smirked, as he unhitched his battle-axe with nonchalant ease and rested it in his hands. 'Enough pleasantries,' he said.

A Ahmud Ki was perplexed by the Dragonlord's intention

343

to use the weapon. Did Mareg so terribly underestimate his opponent's power? He was so amazed by Mareg's apparent stupidity, he had to leap backwards to avoid the first vicious sweep of the Dragonlord's battle-axe.

'At least fight,' Mareg growled, and closed the gap.

A Ahmud Ki focussed his concentration. He would destroy the Dragonlord as quickly as he could with a crushing spell on his heart, the same spell he used to kill the idiot Haephus. Mareg's axe swept down as A Ahmud Ki launched his magical attack, but he barely escaped a fatal blow, the axe shredding through his cloak, as he threw himself backwards into a cloud of swirling grey dust that erupted as he landed heavily.

Coughing, he scrambled to his feet, bewildered by the failure of his spell. Mareg lunged again. Without armour, he was just able to dodge Mareg's flurry of blows, enough to put several paces between the Dragonlord and himself, gaining time to conjure a second spell. He concentrated on a ball of fiery energy that would rip through Mareg's armour and mortally wound him. He uttered the arcane words and thrust his hand toward the Dragonlord.

Mareg broke into a broad smile. 'You are a novice,' the Dragonlord chuckled. 'One who learns the truth too late.' The axe flashed up and Mareg leapt.

A Ahmud Ki dived aside, calling on all his former Aelendyell agility to save him from the deadly blade, and when he made his feet again he tried to run – only to discover how chokingly thick the dust at his feet was. It swept around his ankles, growing deeper, slowing him down.

Mareg's flowing laughter came closer. 'You can't run away here,' the Dragonlord told him. 'That's part of the rules we created, a long time ago. Search Andrakis' memories, since you claim to have them. He knew how to play the game. We had many a good joust on Se'Treya. But you have to be a true Dragonlord to appreciate that.'

There wasn't time to search Andrakis' memories, A Ahmud Ki decided. Mareg had caught him in a trap, a clever one, but there was one way out. He concentrated on escaping the crystal's magical world. 'That won't work either,' Mareg sneered as he confronted A Ahmud Ki, axe poised to strike a fatal blow. 'Two or more Dragonlords have to agree to leave Se'Treya before one can go. That was another of our rules. Like it?' He laughed with manic delight, and swung the axe, precisely as A Ahmud Ki disappeared.

He looked at the shredded mess hanging over the stool in his study that had been his favourite silver-black cloak, and felt death's icy touch caress his throat. Mareg nearly killed him – all because he was too eager to prove his right to Dragonlord status. He hadn't considered all the possibilities before leaping recklessly into the crystal. He acted like a fool. 'Power never lasts long in the hands of a fool,' he chided himself. He'd written that in his notes, and today he nearly proved the truth of his own adage. In his desperation to acquire all the magical power from Andrakis Va'ristrin Nyavardenet, he ignored the Dragonlord's warrior attributes. He ignored the balance.

There was a reason the Dragonlords wore armour; a purpose to the brutish battle-axes that hung at their belts. They were warriors, proud warriors, powerful warriors who could wield a weapon, as easily as ride a dragon or cast a spell. Their magic was a portion of their whole being. And all he knew was the magic. Mareg trapped him and could've killed him.

He saved himself by a sheer stoke of fortune when Mareg broke the secret about two Dragonlords needing to agree to leave Se'Treya. Andrakis saved him. In the moment of spell casting, he drew on Andrakis' memory presence, as well as his own, weaved them together as separate entities, joining two minds to break the lock that would otherwise have bound him to Mareg's will, and to his death.

At least he would've left a seed of doubt in Mareg's mind with his escape, enough to keep Mareg guessing, but now he understood why the prophecies claimed a warrior like Andra would slay the Dragonlords. Mareg could match most other spell-wielders spell for spell, negating the power of magic in a final conflict. In the end, it would come down to a physical confrontation. Warrior skill would decide the outcome – and he, A Ahmud Ki, had no such skill.

Thirty Seven

Milly bowed to the golden guards when she reached the doorway to the King's Royal chamber, and waited politely while one guard opened the door for her. She smiled sweetly, hiding her revulsion at the thought the man who held the door was neither alive nor dead, and couldn't think for himself beyond what another directed him to do, and entered the fire-lit room, bearing her golden platter of sweet meats and cake for the King.

Andra sat on the edge of a chair, watching her enter, and, as usual, he was in the company of a red-robed Ithosen, and the blond man who was training Aaron to be a Royal assassin. Four other men lurked in the shadows, at the far end of the room, wearing the green tunics and black leggings of the new Royal assassins. Milly set her platter on the table, at the room's centre, curtsied as she'd been taught, and waited in the hope Andra would ask to speak with her.

'That will be all,' the blond man said, dismissing her.

Milly hesitated, her eyes appealing to Andra, but the King turned his attention back to the Ithosen. Disappointed, Milly curtsied again, and withdrew.

Having done her morning's duty, she was free to go her own way, until the King's midday meal was due to be served, so she followed the corridors to the lower chambers, where she hoped to find Aaron. He was sitting in a corridor, when she reached him, flicking a dagger backwards out of his hand, over his shoulder, and catching it in front by the hilt. 'That's an old trick,' she said.

He looked up and laughed, and threw the dagger to her. 'You do it then.'

Milly caught the dagger hilt cleanly, spun it to hold the point, and neatly tossed it from behind her back over her shoulder, catching it as Aaron had been practising. 'Well?' she asked.

'Show-off,' he scowled. 'You should've been doing this instead of me. Tim taught you better.'

'I learned better,' she replied with a giggle, and tossed the dagger to him. 'And I couldn't do this because they don't want girl assassins in the Royal assassins.' She sat beside Aaron. 'What've you found out?'

He glanced conspiratorially left and right, before he led her into a small chamber along the corridor. Inside the chamber, they scrabbled among the odd collection of metal and wood, until she found a battered, but working lantern containing a residue of oil. Aaron moistened the wick and lit it. Yellow light spread in a small pool, revealing they were in a storage chamber. 'Siege equipment,' he noted, glancing around. 'I've still not been in every door on these lower levels.'

'I bet the Guild has,' she asserted. He nodded, as he sat on a wooden beam. Milly sat against the door. 'So, tell me,' she said.

'Well, I told Patti and Kara all this, this morning,' he began in a semi-whisper. 'All us assassins had to swear a blood oath two days ago. That means if anyone even suspects any of us is telling secrets about the Royal assassins we'll be killed by the others. No questions asked.' She gave him a look of concern. 'Kara warned me to be more careful than ever,' he continued. 'She said I could get out now, if I wanted, and the Guild would hide me. But I want to stay.'

'Why a blood oath?'

Aaron became perceptibly nervous. 'Sarcen said we had a hit to make, a very big hit. He said only the four best assassins would be chosen. And the blood oath makes sure none of us will blab who the hit is. Or that a hit's being made.'

'And who's the target?'

He shook his blond head. 'Only the chosen four will know that. They go tonight. We don't even know who's been chosen. Sarcen will tell them privately, so only they will even know who their companions are.'

'I saw them,' she said, remembering the four strangers in

348

the shadows of Andra's chamber.

'Where?'

'In Andra's chamber, with Sarcen.'

'Can you remember what they looked like?'

'Roughly. They were in shadows,' she answered. She gave Aaron the details she could remember, and the youth's face lit up.

'We've got to tell Kara. She's desperate to know who it is they're going to hit. I think she'll get The Hand to capture one of them so she can find out what's going on.'

Harlin glanced at his companions and shook his head, before he turned to Sarcen and bowed, his temporary red-robed disguise rustling. 'I've no idea what's happened to Forge. He only went to get his gear,' he said.

Sarcen stared at the door to the King's Table chamber, his face and blond ponytail lit by the portal's red glow, scowled and swore. 'We can't wait any longer for him. You three will have to do the task. Forge is my problem. He may be the first example for all of you that the blood oath's a serious matter.'

Harlin and his companions exchanged a brief understanding. 'We don't need him, Master Sarcen,' Harlin said, his face twisting with contempt. 'He were too cocksure of himself, as it were. We'll do the job without him.'

Sarcen turned to his three Royal assassins and checked their Ithosen robes. 'Make certain you do. You know what failure will bring.'

All three nodded understanding. There would be death tonight – if not their target's death, then their own.

Sarcen cast a final glance at the door, decided Forge's fate, and motioned the assassins to the portal. 'Go.' Harlin pulled up his red face cloth and led his companions into the shimmering glow.

Once they were gone, Sarcen paced uneasily toward the door. Forge's failure to appear was an unnecessary complication. When Lord Ki learned of it, he would be angry.

The Lord hated loose ends. Sarcen had to deal with Forge immediately. He opened the door, bowed peremptorily to the Golden Warriors, and headed deeper into the fortress, toward the assassins' quarters. A blood oath was a blood oath.

Sometimes he felt as if he was a stranger, outside his body, but looking down on himself, watching what was happening around him, and listening to what he was doing and saying from someone else's viewpoint. At other times, the world seemed incredibly lucid, bright; so bright it hurt his eyes to stare at objects, or people, for too long.

Then there were the terrifying times, the moments when everything would fade, lose sharpness, become distant and fuzzy, as if he was trying to see through a fog, but couldn't move to see more clearly. Those times frightened him most of all, because he felt alone, terribly alone. If it wasn't for Berak N'eth's reassuring voice, he would find a way to die, to escape those moments of vague horror.

There was the sword. When he held that, he could see the world so brilliantly he felt like weeping with wonder and joy. He felt he ought to hold the sword forever, because it drove away the confusion and the mist – but when he did, his energy drained, flowed from him, until exhaustion drove him near to collapse. He couldn't hold the sword forever. He was too tired.

Faces came and went every day: strange faces, new faces, faces he couldn't recall from the muddled morass of memories. There was the Chancellor. He knew him. He was the rock in the surging sea of confusion. He always hovered near.

And another came and went, a blond man, who promised to protect him as a King should be protected. Why? Who threatened him? He knew he was never alone, because the faces kept coming back, and voices whispered in the shifting patterns of light and dark.

There were times he couldn't remember anything, when

he struggled to remember his name. Was it Andra? Was it King? Was it Andrakis? Someone kept calling him my Lord. Another called him Leiksha Andrakis. Was that his true name?

When he held the sword, he knew he was Andra. No. He was King Andrakis the Inheritor, Abreotan's successor, the King destined to slay the Dragonlords – when he held the Sword.

He vanquished a giant warrior in black armour. That hung clear in his mind, but it was confused with another memory of a giant warrior carrying him like a child away from battle, a giant with his hair aflame. When had that happened? Who was the giant warrior?

Voices other than Berak N'eth's whispered in the darker recesses of his memory. Names flashed like fish in Dragon River, silvery scales sparkling briefly in the light, before disappearing into the flowing depths. Who was Claarn? Or Tim? Or Mirith? He had a mother somewhere. Who? Anedra? Sasha? So many names.

The brown-haired girl, who came to his chambers, kept giving him odd looks. She seemed to want to talk to him. Her eyes were intensely bright blue and very familiar. Serving wench? Did he bed her? No. Too young. Maybe. She seemed so familiar, but her name wouldn't come from the murky waters of confusion. And why should it? What was a serving wench to a King?

And there were so many dreams. He dreamed of fiery swords cutting through bodies, through trees, through mountains. Dragons. Draca. Odd word. Where did he learn that? No worold-buend would know it. Words and dreams; dreams out of the mist in the utter blackness of midnight. He wielded his sword, and always he cut down everyone who approached him – everyone – whether he wanted to or not. The arm and the burning sword swept through everything, and he could do nothing. He could do nothing.

'Are you sure that's the name he gave you?' Kara asked.

The sandy-haired Hand assassin nodded. 'He had trouble enough admitting it through his broken teeth, Your Ladyship, but that's what it sounded like. Shehar.'

'And tonight?'

'Yes. That's a certainty,' Glyn confirmed.

'Alright. You'd best give him peace,' Kara said, and she turned to Sasha and Patti.

'Right enough, Your Ladyship,' Glyn solemnly replied, and drew his dagger from its sheath. 'For a newie at this trade, he was pretty tough to get answers from. Bit of a waste really,' he added, as he slipped out the doorway.

Kara sat at the table deep in thought. 'Shehar,' she mused aloud. 'Who is Shehar?'

'The name means nothing to me,' Patti said. 'No one in the Guild, or in Andrakis, has that name.'

'It's got a foreign ring to it,' Sasha suggested. 'Is it one of those Ranu strangers?'

Kara stood up, her face pale. 'Shehaal,' she breathed. 'Ranu Ka Shehaala. That explains the red robes.' She spun towards Sasha, and shouted, 'We need to know more! Stop Glyn!'

Sasha bolted from the room, leaving Patti staring at Kara in bewilderment, heading for the chamber where The Hand interrogated Forge.

'I don't get your meaning, lass,' the pudgy-faced madam said.

'Ranu Ka Shehaala,' Kara explained. 'It's the barbarian land. We know the Chancellor's been there. He speaks the language fluently. He's behind the Royal assassins. And Shehaal's the name of the King, or emperor, or whatever they call their leader.'

'But I thought he was trying to get help from the barbarians? Through that portal of his.'

'He is. But he's hungrier than that. I'm just afraid our Chancellor's got bigger plans in mind.'

'Then we better stop him,' Patti said.

Sasha thrust the door open, breathing heavily from her sprint, and shaking her head. 'Too late, Kara. Glyn's already dispatched him.'

Kara shot a sharp glance at Patti. 'Then we're already too late to stop the hit,' she muttered, shaking her head ruefully. 'Let's pray to Teka my guess is wrong.'

A Ahmud Ki set down his quill and pushed the parchment aside to dry. He glanced at the communication crystal on its pedestal. No word from Saleem yet. Shehaal was alive, though not for much longer. His assassination was well planned, and unfortunately necessary – necessary because Shehaal was reluctant to lend his vast army to march against Mareg under King Andrakis' and A Ahmud Ki's command. Shehaal, and a number of Ithosen, believed they were better defending Ranu Ka Shehaala, if and when Mareg decided to launch his offensive. The assassination was unfortunate because he would've preferred to confront Shehaal personally to repay him in kind for the exile thrust upon him twelve years beforehand.

To get control of the Ranu military resources, he needed a political change; a new Leiksha, from the Ithosen ranks, ambitious enough to risk an assassination bid for his rise in status. Saleem found several individuals willing to sacrifice personal life to gain the ultimate rank in Ranu Ka Shehaala, and A Ahmud Ki finally settled on an Ithosen named Harrudin. He had the greatest support among the dissatisfied Ithosen who sat in the Kal E'haruk Assembly to succeed to Shehaal's post, and he had the strongest personal hunger to be Leiksha at any cost. Harrudin had already portalled into the Kingdom, been formally introduced to King Andrakis, and was wearing a platinum chain imbued with a spell, a very special gift of trust between himself and A Ahmud Ki. Harrudin would serve A Ahmud Ki's plans well.

The communication crystal flooded the chamber with amber light. A Ahmud Ki shifted from his stool to the crystal. Saleem's face materialised. Irand shadu arat shehaal, Great Master Ki, Saleem's projecting began.

And? A Ahmud Ki demanded, foregoing the formalities.

There has been a terrible tragedy, Master. The Ranu Lord of Light and Life is dead.

A Ahmud Ki's frown became a satisfied smile. Are you certain?

Most certain, Master. I witnessed the murder as Leiksha Ithrandyr Shehaal was walking with ambassadors through the Gardens of Peace. Three assassins, dressed as Ithosen, approached him and struck him down with poisonous darts before his guards could react.

And the assassins?

Unfortunately, they were slain by Shehaal's guards, before they could escape.

Good. No loose ends.

There is concern the assassins are not Ranu, but look like barbarians from Murkaatz, Saleem hesitantly admitted.

Then do something about that immediately, A Ahmud Ki ordered. Get rid of the bodies and spread the counter truth that Shehaal's Advisors are trying to shift the blame for his murder from themselves. That should add to the confusion. What's Harrudin doing?

He's taking responsibility for overseeing the month of mourning that will customarily follow the Leiksha's untimely death.

Excellent. That will gain him widespread status among the people, and almost assure his election to Leiksha when the mourning is completed. Anything else?

No, Master.

Then you're dismissed. Report again, tomorrow, at this time.

Saleem bowed and his face faded. The amber light receded, leaving a featureless silver ball on the pedestal.

A Ahmud Ki relaxed and returned to his stool. The parchment he'd been writing on was already dry, ready for his next entry, so he picked up the quill, dipped it in ink, and bent to his writing.

'The beauty of puppets,' he wrote, 'is in the uncanny way they can mimic reality without minds of their own. The power of the puppeteer lies in being able to make the puppets dance - to any tune he chooses to sing. And, soon enough, the puppets believe in the illusion, believe they created the dance themselves.'

Thirty Eight

The Dragonlord's silence broke at the end of spring, as the fresh crops struggled out of the warm earth, and the first-born animals imported from Em Basa and Ranu Ka Shehaala gambolled on the plains of Ky near Andrakis. Northern scouts reported a vast army moving across Dragon Breath Plains, heralded by a wall of grey dust hanging like a curtain across the horizon.

High Lord Claarn initiated military action by leading a Kingdom force into the Kobold Ranges and flushing out the starving and despondent Haagii holed up after their last defeat. He regrouped the army and prepared to march north to meet Mareg's soldiers on the edge of Dragon Breath Plains, but on the morning his army began the march he was ordered by the King to turn his command over to Devi Erlan and return to Andrakis. No explanation came with the herald who brought the message. Infuriated, and close to ignoring the order, Claarn saddled his horse, disdaining escort from his troops, and started the six-day return ride, anger raging like fire in his stomach.

When he reached the ruins of Axxon below Central Gate, early the third morning, he saw a party of people winding toward the first of the rebuilt defensive walls in the mountain pass. Distracted by curiosity, recognizing the party as neither military nor merchant in nature, he spurred his mount on, and caught them when they reached the first gate in the pass. They were Aelendyell.

Claarn reined in as he drew alongside. The Aelendyell were technically outlaws in the Kingdom, officially held responsible for the assassination of Great King Thana. They withdrew to their forest homes, while the war with Mareg raged before the winter, and no one had sighted them since. The sound of a horse, and the arrival of the red-haired warrior, brought vigilant glances from the Aelendyell. Then to Claarn's amazement a familiar voice hailed him. 'Claarn! Claarn, you bearded rascal!'

He stared hard at the Aelendyell, who broke from the others to approach with extended arms. Recognition flooded in. 'By all the holy gods there are!' he roared and swung down from his tired horse. 'Tim! Tim Gaelus!' The pair embraced, the giant hauling the thief into the air out of joy, laughing heartily at their unexpected reunion. Then Claarn set Tim down, and held him at arm's length, studying his scarred face. 'But we'd given you up for dead,' he said, shaking his head.

'I might as well have been,' Tim replied. 'The Haagii did everything but cut my throat. If my people hadn't come, I would long ago be feeding the earthworms.'

'No,' Claarn laughed. 'Never you. You've the cursed luck of Teka. No Haagii could kill you.'

'They tried,' Tim said.

'And now where are you going?' Claarn asked, looking over Tim's head at the band of Aelendyell who were patiently waiting.

'To the King,' Tim answered. Claarn frowned. 'Why? What's wrong old friend?'

'The King is – he's no longer Andra.'

'What do you mean?'

Claarn searched for an explanation, an easy way to describe the changes he witnessed, his anger, his frustration. 'If you insist on going, then you will see for yourself, but the Chancellor has too great a hold on the King. Our friend isn't himself anymore.'

'Perhaps he's just adjusting to his new position,' Tim suggested. 'It would be hard to be a young warrior finding himself supreme ruler over a Kingdom.'

'I wish it was that easy to explain,' Claarn muttered.

An Aelendyell voice interrupted. Tim nodded, and told Claarn, 'Elder Keryl reminds me we must pass through the mountains before nightfall. Our problem is the human guards at these gates refuse to let the Aelendyell pass. One's claiming he can earn a handsome reward for arresting us and taking us to the King.'

Claarn scowled. 'I'll change that idiot's tune.' He strode toward the large iron and wood gates barring the road into Central Gate, and when he hammered on the gate two heads appeared in the gate tower window. 'Open this infernal gate for the Aelendyell now, or I'll have you whipped and forced to eat horse dung for a week!' he bellowed, arms akimbo. The heads retracted, the guards recognizing the High Lord of the Andrakian army, and the gate creaked open to allow the Aelendyell through. An honour guard stood on the inside, out of respect to their High Lord, and as Claarn passed through, last, leading his horse, he grinned and complimented the guards on their efficiency.

As always, the Aelendyell walked. They had no use for horses in their forested homelands, and while they revered the creatures as beautiful very few Aelendyell knew how to ride. Claarn walked beside Tim, listening to his tale of capture, torture and escape, leading his horse, which received many gentle pats and cooing words from the Aelendyell party. 'You speak of the Aelendyell as your people,' Claarn said after they passed through the middle gate in the mountain pass.

'They are my people,' Tim replied. 'I'm part Aelendyell by heritage, and I owe them my life. I'd much sooner live among them than return to the life of an assassin. Wouldn't you, if you were in my place?'

Claarn shook his red locks and grinned. 'I could never play the assassin,' he admitted. 'Or run through the trees. I'm a warrior. Always will be. Even pretending to be a High Lord is too hard for me. But the more I think of you, my friend, the more fitting it seems that you should run off to the forests.' Claarn made a playful cuff at his friend, and they laughed as they led the Aelendyell band along the well-worn road toward the third Central Gate wall.

That first night, they camped in a small copse, off the road, a thousand paces from the eastern entry to Central Gate. There were no inns or villages, only ruins from the previous summer that hadn't been reclaimed, or rebuilt, but the Aelendyell were deliberately avoiding human contact, preferring the familiarity of trees to the makeshift shelter of rubble. Claarn wondered whether their caution was through fear of retribution for the alleged assassination of Thana, or simply so they could arrive unheralded in Andrakis.

Out of respect for the giant warrior, the Aelendyell built a small fire, and Claarn appreciated its friendliness and warmth. There was little risk of hostile discovery since the Haagii were defeated, and very few travellers were yet willing to venture along the roads at night. He couldn't understand the Aelendyell conversations as he shared their meal, and Tim made no effort to interpret for Claarn, since no one, apart from Tim, tried to communicate with the human. He found the whole circumstance uncomfortable, feeling alone despite the company.

When the meal was completed, the Aelendyell Elder, Tim identified earlier in the day to Claarn as Keryl, nodded to Tim, and the entire Aelendyell party stood and drifted away from the fire, leaving the ex-assassin and Claarn to talk in private. 'Where are they going?' Claarn asked, watching the last figure disappear into the moonless darkness.

'To chant,' Tim replied. 'It's an Aelendyell custom, for Elders when they're away from their forest homes, to go over poems and songs and tales that remind them of their heritage.'

Claarn drew a long draught from his waterskin, enjoying the pleasant freshness of icy water running down his throat, and edged nearer the small fire to study Tim's disfigured face again, imagining the agony the assassin endured with the Haagii. 'Why do the Aelendyell go to see the King?' he finally asked, when Tim looked up.

Tim used a short twig to prod an unburned stick into the flames as he explained. 'Two reasons: to try to re-establish diplomacy between the peoples, and to exact justice on the Chancellor.'

Claarn's eyebrows raised. 'Why the Chancellor?'

'He's a morthorwyrhta – maegslaga – a killer of his own people.'

'The Chancellor is Aelendyell?'

'Surely you can see the signs?'

Claarn felt foolish. He sometimes considered the possibility, but the idea the Chancellor hated the Aelendyell because he was Aelendyell made little sense to him.

'He's half-blood,' Tim explained. 'His mother was an Aelendyell, but his father was human. That accounts for the physical discrepancies. He was raised in an Aelendyell village in Wynwuduholt. You know it as the Border Woods. He killed an Elder and disappeared. No one seems to have seen him for years, until he popped up as Thana's Advisor and started his malicious attack on his people. The Aelendyell didn't kill Thana. The Chancellor arranged it, through The Hand.'

'I wouldn't put it past the cur,' Claarn growled. 'But how do you know it's true?'

'I was one of the assassins chosen for the hit on Thana. But I had a feeling something was wrong. So did Kara, so I refused the job. The ones who hit Thana are dead.'

'Can you prove this?'

'No,' said Tim with a shake of his head. 'It would be my word against the Chancellor's.' He stoked the fire again. The flaring flames lit his scarred face, and the one remaining eye glittered with the old humour Claarn remembered separated Tim from other men he knew: gave Tim the spur to act and keep acting. He decided it was probably even at the root of Tim's survival in the Haagii hands. 'But we've got proof of a more horrendous deed the Chancellor's committed,' Tim continued.

'What?' Claarn asked, eager to hear of any chance to destroy the person he held most responsible for the Kingdom's woes.

'A golden axe he left behind in Wynwuduholt just before winter.'

'What was the Chancellor doing there? And with an axe?'

'Killing. And stealing.'

Claarn was puzzled. The Chancellor was no warrior. Everyone knew that much.

'He skulked back to his old village and took revenge for

something that happened fifteen years ago by most people's assessment,' Tim explained. 'The Elders know the tale better than I, but I was told he killed Aelendyell indiscriminately, and destroyed a village even the Haagii and their dragons hadn't reached during the war. He's deliberately alienated the Aelendyell from the Kingdom.'

'The miserable bastard!' Claarn swore and spat.

'In every way,' Tim bitterly agreed. 'But he made a very stupid, arrogant mistake. He left witnesses. And he left behind a rather ostentatious battle-axe, wrought from gold, and bound with magical spells to enhance its effectiveness as a weapon. I know that, if I can show this proof to Andra, the Chancellor will be forced to justice, and the truth brought to light.'

Claarn's face became despondent at Tim's mention of hope and justice. He flicked a fragment of wood into the dying flames of the fire, and watched the wood consumed. 'I fear you've come too late, my friend,' he said, when Tim saw the change and pressed him to explain. 'Andra is not who you think he is. He serves the Chancellor's will.'

'Why do you believe that's so?'

Claarn's anger surfaced. 'Would Andra excavate a stinking Dragonlord's lair? Would he build a fancy palace out of the sweat and blood of others? Would he refuse to see or speak with his friends if he was Andra still?'

Tim was dismayed. 'This can't be true.'

'I have seen these things. He does what the Chancellor bids be done. And he expects us to serve without question.'

Movement beyond the firelight perimeter distracted the friends. The shadowy outlines of the Aelendyell reappeared, and as Elder Keryl approached, his normally white hair glowing gold, Tim stood respectfully and addressed him in Aelendyell, which caused the Elder to stare at Claarn, his concern clear. He made a quiet reply, before withdrawing into the darkness. Tim's remaining eye fixed Claarn. 'There's little doubt then the Chancellor holds Andra under a spell. You and I both know Andra would never do these things you describe. Elder Keryl says he and the others will find out what they can about it, if we can gain an audience with him.'

'You'll get an audience,' Claarn vowed. 'On my life, I'll see that it happens!'

A Ahmud Ki was furious. The idiot High Lord Claarn brought a stinking pack of Aelendyell with him to Andrakis, and demanded an audience with the King. He dared to defy A Ahmud Ki. He was tempted to have King Andrakis refuse the audience, brand the High Lord a traitor for bringing rebels to the city, and call on the Andrakian warriors to cut down the Aelendyell dogs at the palace gates. Who would question the King's decree? Or maybe he could summon the dragon to attack them and claim it got out of control?

No, he remonstrated himself, clumsy idea. He must control his impulses. He had nothing to fear so long as he held King Andrakis under his influence. Play puppeteer. Let the foolish Aelendyell make their petition to the King and learn how their forests were already forfeit to the Kingdom's needs and Targa's.

He relaxed, casting a sideways glance at the King who sat motionless on his new throne in the freshly completed Upper Palace. Working the high back of the new throne into the shape of a rearing dragon, its wings stretching toward the heavens, made it an impressive replacement for Thana's old throne destroyed in the fires. The throne room was faced with pure white marble, with only five steps leading to the platform supporting King Andrakis' throne, and the use of Ranu glass panels in the roof duplicated the airy, light atmosphere created in the Kal E'haruk. Gold doors opened into the space from outside, and from the adjoining atrium, and A Ahmud Ki had arranged for servants to hang purple and gold silk in long strips from ceiling to floor as decorative additions. A dozen Golden Warriors stood at silent attention along each wall. No seating was provided, bar the King and his retinue on the dais, and the floor was smooth, cold marble, and bare of embellishment, a harsh, uninviting floor: very apt for a figure of absolute authority, the Chancellor considered.

When Claarn led in the Aelendyell, A Ahmud Ki fixed the High Lord with a deliberate, spiteful glare, an expression Claarn enjoyed because his bringing the Aelendyell had ruffled the right set of feathers. Smiling, he approached the steps to the throne, and bowed his head before the King. 'My Lord, I bring an old friend,' he said, and looked up into Andra's passionless brown eyes.

The King nodded, and replied, 'Thank you, Lord Claarn. You may leave us.'

Claarn continued to stare at the King, trying to read whatever emotion was hiding in his dull brown eyes. 'Your Highness -' he faltered.

'Leave us!' Andra instructed.

Claarn straightened. 'As you order, Your Majesty.' He shot a murderous glance at A Ahmud Ki, who smiled in return. Recognizing the wheels of control in the room had changed momentarily in the Chancellor's favour, Claarn turned on his heel and marched out of the throne room, heading for the atrium and the lower chambers.

'I will kill the arrogant bastard!' Claarn swore. 'He has Andra in his thrall, and he goads me with it!'

'If Tim's plan is as you say, the Chancellor's time has come,' Kara said, reaching to wind the lantern wick higher. 'How can anyone deny the truth?'

'I just can't believe he's still alive,' Sasha said, as she paced to the door for the countless time since Claarn brought her the news of Tim's return.

'Patience, child. In good time, you'll see him,' Patti consoled, smiling wickedly. 'He has important business to attend first. Then you can renew the paths of lovers.'

Claarn saw Sasha's radiant, expectant face, so changed from the harsh, serious expression that afflicted her from the day of Tim's disappearance, and he felt a pang of guilt that he hadn't told her how disfigured her lover's face was from the Haagii torture. How could he tell her? The door opened and Milly skipped in. 'Is it true Tim's back?' she eagerly asked.

'True enough,' Patti answered, before the giant warrior could respond to her question. 'The lad's back and doing us all a greater service than ever.'

'What is it?' Milly asked, her curiosity rising.

'You wait 'n see, my knowin' lass,' Patti said with a teasing wink. 'Wait 'n see.'

'How long has it been?' Sasha asked, as she moved back to the table where Milly sat to challenge Patti to a quick game of thimbles.

'Long enough,' Kara replied.

'Long enough to damn Berak N'eth himself!' Claarn growled. 'I'm going upstairs to see what's happened.'

Just as he moved, they heard a frantic knocking, and the door burst open. Aaron stood in the doorway with Tim. 'I wasn't sure where you'd be,' Tim said, catching his breath. 'Lucky I spotted Aaron in the lower chambers. He led me here.'

'What's wrong?' Sasha asked, moving toward him, overjoyed to see her lover, but shocked by his scarred and breathless appearance.

'The King rejected our claim for justice.'

'By the infernal hells no!' Claarn roared, smashing his fist against the wall.

Tim turned to him. 'You warned me, old friend, but I didn't want to believe it. Even when I saw what was happening, I couldn't see past Andra's face. The Chancellor was laughing at us all the time.'

'Did you show him the battle-axe? Did you tell him what you told me?' asked Claarn.

'Everything,' Tim replied, 'but he didn't hear a single word. He ordered us to turn over the battle-axe to his guards, reminded Elder Keryl the Aelendyell were outcasts in the Kingdom, and further infuriated the people with a proclamation that the forests were to be cut down at the King's whim to foster building and trade with Targa. It was all I could do to restrain the Aelendyell from trying to kill

Andra and the Chancellor there and then.'

'You should've let them!' Claarn growled.

'Not Andra!' screamed Milly, pushing to her feet.

'You did well to stop them,' Kara interposed while Patti restrained the girl. 'The Chancellor has the powers of a Dragonlord.'

Tim's good eye focussed on the former Death's First Hand, whom he served in The Hand and the Guild. 'So we've learned. The Elders' worst fears were confirmed by this visit. They headed away at once to prepare their people for a disaster they feared since this degenerate half-breed bastard destroyed his home village. That's why I can't stay. I have to follow them immediately.'

Sasha's face paled and she clutched his arm. 'You don't leave me behind this time.'

Tim hugged her and smiled. 'There's too many risks – ' he started to argue, but she cut across his excuse.

'Don't dare patronise me, Tim Gaelus. I'm as good an assassin as you, better now by the looks of your eye and leg, and it's just as dangerous living under the shelter of the Chancellor as it is escaping it. I'm coming with you.'

Tim grinned, hugged Sasha warmly, and told her to fetch her gear, the bare requirements. She kissed him and hurried out.

'That lass loves you badly, Tim, my lad. You take good honest care of her,' Patti said waggling her pudgy finger. 'Or you'll be havin' me to deal with.'

'Care, yes,' he laughed. 'Honest? Now that's a different matter.'

Claarn's bulk ranged between Tim and Patti, interrupting their by-play. 'You told me on the road here there was a chance the Elders could work out what spells the Chancellor's using on Andra. Did they?'

Tim glanced at his companions, a solemn expression returning to his face. 'Elder Keryl had Elders Charwyllyth and Shanallynn study the Chancellor and Andra closely as the interview took place. They risked a spell, when the mood became heated, and did all they could to mask their intentions. The news isn't good. The Chancellor is using a spell on Andra that's more powerful than anything the Aelendyell understand. It seems to emanate from a ring on the King, but even that's not certain because the aura of energy surrounding Andra ebbed and flowed wildly, and they were conscious the Chancellor also knew they were casting a spell, despite their precautions. Elder Shanallynn said he saw the Chancellor about to conjure a spell in return at them, so they ceased scrying to avoid conflict. The worst of the news is that the spell binds the ring or whatever it is causing the evil magic to Andra.'

'What do you mean 'binds it to him'?' Milly asked.

'He'll never remove it as long as the Chancellor wants him to wear it.'

'Then we've lost Andra,' Kara said. The room pitched into a well of silence.

Sasha appeared in the doorway. 'What's wrong?' she asked.

'I've got to go,' Tim said, ignoring her question. 'The King gave the Aelendyell five days to be out of his Kingdom, or face the penalty of outlaws and be hanged.'

'Then Teka travel with you,' Claarn said, and embraced Tim and Sasha.

'Can I go with you?' Milly pleaded. 'I missed you.'

Tim hugged the girl. 'No,' he told her. 'Stay here. Andra needs you more than ever. Perhaps you'll find a way to remove the ring or break the spell.'

Milly kissed Tim on the cheek, hugged Sasha, and ran from the chamber to hide her welling tears. Aaron chased after her, but she easily lost him in the corridors, wanting to share her grief with no one, but herself, and when she was certain no one else followed, she slowed to a walk, heading deeper into the fortress where few people bothered to go.

She missed Tim so much, believing, like everyone else, he was dead, and to have him return, so briefly, only to go again, and take Sasha with him, made her miserable, because she was losing two people she considered important friends. But to learn, above everything else, that

366

Andra, the man she loved more than anyone in the world, was ensorcelled by the Chancellor, so deeply ensnared in his magic that not even Tim could think of a way to save him, ached her heart to despair.

She stumbled, sobbing, into a disused storage chamber off a lower corridor, closed the door, and poured her grief into the darkness, until she fell into a deep and exhausted sleep. When she finally emerged, and wandered back to Patti's chamber, she found the room empty, the lantern dying, and Tim and Sasha long gone.

Thirty Nine

The voices were there again, echoing through the mist; odd voices, new voices, familiar voices. Someone called his name, his old name, Andra. Why his old name? The mist was encroaching. Berak N'eth's voice broke in. These people despise you.

Do they? Why?

You are what they fear. The One King come to restore his rule on the Kingdom. You are Abreotan's Inheritor.

But why do they fear me? I don't want to hurt them.

They fear your power. They know they have no choice but to serve you. As you serve me.

I don't understand.

But you do. They are too proud to serve you as they should. Listen to their voices. They ask you to give back their forests and let them rule themselves. They don't accept your supreme right to rule.

Is that wrong?

Yes. Very wrong. A divided Kingdom cannot defeat the Dragonlord. They must agree to serve you.

And if they don't?

Then the Chancellor will know what to do. You are King. Tell him to deal with them. Trust him.

He should summon the sword. That would clear the mist. He could see the faces attached to the voices. With a thought, the familiar hilt rested in his right hand.

The chamber snapped into sharp focus and he could see the bright purples and golds spiralling from the opaque ceiling. The chamber was washed in white. He liked the new throne room. A Ahmud Ki had a sense of beauty.

'Andra, you must hear our appeal.'

He shifted focus and stared at the talking figure in green robes beside two others, also dressed in green. They had hair like the Chancellor's. Silver-grey. And white.

'Andra, it's me, Tim Gaelus.'

I know you, Tim, he reflected. Of course I know you. But you're dead. You don't look the same. You're different.

'Have the decency to address His Royal Highness by the appropriate titles.' That was the Chancellor. But he heard Berak N'eth inside his head again.

They murdered Thana rather than accept his rule. No human King can trust them.

But I know Tim, Andra insisted.

An assassin.

A friend.

An assassin. Here with your enemies.

The Aelendyell. I remember now. And then the mist came again. He held the sword, but the mist was descending. The faces blurred.

Tell them no.

Why?

Because I, Berak N'eth, command it. As I commanded Abreotan.

He said no. To what? He couldn't remember, but he said no. There was talk of a battle-axe: A Ahmud Ki's battle-axe. He remembered one came with the Dragonlord's armour and it belonged to A Ahmud Ki. Why did the Aelendyell have it? It wasn't theirs. They stole it. But why? Then there were accusations. Harsh words. Strange words. Syruwrenc. Morthorwyrhta. Ecg-bana: Aelendyell words of hate. Terath spoke them in Wynwuduholt. Haagii spears and fire. But Terath wasn't there. Was he? And Mirith?

They will kill you, Berak N'eth warned.

Berak N'eth help me.

Drive them out of your Kingdom. Banish them.

I can't think. The mist. Help me.

Banish them. Drive them out. You are the King!

I am the King!

The Inheritor!

The King!

Banish them forever! Crush them!

369

'I swear I heard the order given, Lord Claarn. The new Devis rode out with sixty of those dead knights, and I was on duty at the gates with Durdan,' the Kingdom soldier said.

'How long ago?' Claarn asked, his eyes bright with anger.

'Not long,' the dark-haired soldier called Durdan replied. 'But they were set for some hard riding.'

'A thousand pox scabs on them!' Claarn growled. 'Fetch my horse at once. And a dozen javelins. Have them ready at the gates when I get there. And don't tell a soul.'

The giant warrior stormed toward his chamber in the fortress, pausing once to glance along the corridor leading to the King's rooms, and spitting. The Golden Warriors on duty didn't move. Inside his own chamber, he slipped on his mail corselet, and hauled an oilskin bundle from under his bed to unwrap his favourite broadsword. He slipped it inside its scabbard and belted the weapon to his side. There was no time or place for other armour. He'd be riding as fast and as light as possible. Even though he had the tallest and strongest mount in the Kingdom, his size made him a heavy prospect even for the best horse. When he was prepared, he headed for Kara's chambers.

'What's wrong?' she asked, as he burst into her room.

'The bastard double-crossed Tim!' Claarn said. 'He sent a squad of those cursed Golden Warriors to ambush him and his Aelendyell friends. I'm going to add a twist to that tale.'

'Not alone,' Kara argued. 'You know how the Andrakian warriors fight. They're protected by magic.'

'No time, Kara. If Marella gets back from the Valley of Rivers before I return, tell her – tell her – I was sorry she wasn't here to come too,' he said, and grinned. 'And when I've sorted this mess out, I'm coming back to do what I should have done to that blasted Chancellor a long time ago.' With that, he turned and strode from the chamber.

Claarn's horse was waiting at the gate, as he ordered, but four others jiggled impatiently, their riders mounted. 'What in Teka's name is this?' he demanded, as he swung into his saddle and glared at Durdan who was mounted nearest.

'The only horses we could find, High Lord.'

'And why are you mounted?'

'Because it's poor protocol to send a Lord riding without an armed escort,' Durdan said, and he patted his crossbow. 'So we're coming too.'

Claarn considered Durdan's bold move, nodded, and grunted approval. Then he threw back his head and laughed. 'Open the gates or be damned!' he roared, and the tiny party galloped out and down Castle Road.

The afternoon sun slanted low above the Andrakian Mountains as they rode, and Claarn felt blood singing in his veins like the wind rushing through his mane of red hair and bushy beard. He muttered a prayer to Teka that he wasn't too late to reach Tim and the Aelendyell, but as the moments passed and the road rolled under their horses' pounding hooves his fear grew that he wouldn't reach his friend in time.

They crested the first ring of hills surrounding the plains of Ky, five thousand paces from the plateau, before they saw a pall of dust that had to be the Andrakian knights, and when they closed rapidly, Claarn realised the dust wasn't moving but was stationary beyond another low crest. The golden knights had already caught the Aelendyell. He spurred his horse on, pulling ahead of his companions, and unsheathed a javelin as he rode over the low hill.

The battle was raging a hundred paces off the road to the left, around a low wall and the ruins of an old stone farmhouse. Coming from behind, Claarn startled his enemy. He swept two Andrakian knights from their horses with his javelin, and crashed through their line, heading full tilt for the farmhouse. Twenty paces from it, he heard a shout from within and an arrow whistled by his left ear. 'It's Claarn!' he bellowed, and kicked his horse forward, leaping the low wall, and dismounting before the horse came to a stop.

A dozen stunned Aelendyell stared open-mouthed as Tim Gaelus hailed him from the doorway of the farmhouse. 'By the sons and daughters of the Elvenaar gods! Claarn! What are you doing here?'

Claarn clasped Tim's arms, as four more horses pounded over the low wall, and their riders dismounted to Aelendyell cheering. 'A couple of lads said there was a good fight brewing, and I said I'd hate to miss out on the fun.'

Tim threw a glance at Claarn's four companions. 'Seems they didn't want to miss out either.'

'Bloody disobedient lot, my soldiers,' the giant cursed and grinned.

While the soldiers tethered the horses, Tim led Claarn into the farmhouse. The interior was dark, even though the much of the roof had been burned away during the Haagii raids, and rubble covered the floor. Near a hole in the wall, where a window looked toward the road, Tim kneeled beside Sasha, who greeted Claarn and continued bandaging the shoulder of an Aelendyell Elder. Claarn kneeled with Tim. 'Anyone else hurt?'

'Two Elders dead on the road. Three warriors badly cut,' Sasha informed him.

'So that leaves fourteen of you, and five of us, if we count the injured.'

'Yes,' said Tim.

'Good odds,' Claarn declared joyfully. 'There are less than sixty of them.'

'Where did they come from?' Tim asked. 'The Chancellor's creations?'

'No,' Sasha explained, as she tied a knot in the bandaging. 'They were the private army of the Dragonlord that lived under the plateau where the palace and the old castle sat. We found them in the catacombs of that place to the north called Dragon's Tooth. The Chancellor knew about them and led Andra there to release them.'

'They fight as though death means nothing to them,' Tim said.

'It doesn't,' said Claarn, and he spat in disgust. 'They're not really dead or alive.'

'Onscuning,' the Elder whispered. Claarn caught the old Aelendyell's brittle stare.

'He said they're abominations,' Tim translated.

'You have to cut them up to stop them,' Claarn added.

'Or use drycraefting – some magic,' Tim replied. 'The Elders have a few tricks yet.' He peered out the window at the troop of Andrakian knights encircling the ruined farm. 'No doubt the Chancellor sent them,' he muttered. Claarn nodded. 'I'm glad you're here, old friend,' Tim said, with a warm grin.

'So am I,' Claarn replied and chuckled. 'So am I.'

The Golden Warriors closed the circle around the farm, and sat on their horses, patiently watching the sun dip behind the Andrakian Mountains and the shadowy fingers of dusk reach eastward. Claarn stationed his four soldiers with crossbows on the inside of the farmhouse, at the top of the crumbling walls, where they could get the clearest shot at the riders. Tim's Aelendyell Weapon Bearers, eight archers and swordsmen, crouched at the wall, and Sasha took station at the farmhouse door. The remaining Aelendyell, Elder Keryl, and Shanallynn whose shoulder was injured, and two Lore Bearers, stationed themselves inside the farmhouse in a circle, facing outwards. 'What are they doing?' Claarn asked, when he saw the Aelendyell.

'Preparing to work a little magic for us,' said Tim. 'Keryl can weaken the strength of the Golden Warriors, give them a little more life than they might necessarily want.'

'You mean make them easier to kill?'

'Apparently,' Tim answered with a smile.

A jingle of riding tack drew their attention. The Andrakian knights were closing the circle at a steady walk on their mounts. 'They're coming!' Sasha yelled.

Inside the farmhouse, Claarn heard the Aelendyell begin chanting in their lilting language. He hefted a javelin and loosened the hilt of his sword. 'Teka guide your hand,' he said to Tim.

'And Wynowyth yours,' Tim answered, calling on his newly adopted Aelendyell goddess.

The knights broke into a charge, the rising crescendo of thundering hooves bearing down on the defenders subsuming the Aelendyell chanting. Claarn waited, until a horseman singled him out in the mad charge, and Claarn hurled his javelin with all his strength. It punched through the rider's plate armour and sent him cartwheeling over the horse's rump. Claarn wrenched his sword from its scabbard in time to swing up at a second knight who bore down on him and knocked the rider's spear from his hand. Two more riders tumbled from their horses to his right, hit by metal quarrels from Durdan's crossbow, but he had to spin left to face a pair who dismounted to single him out. He met the lusty swing of the first with his sword and sent him sprawling. The second lunged, catching the giant's thigh with the edge of his blade. Claarn retaliated with a brutal sweep, decapitating the luckless knight with a single blow. The first Andrakian knight waded in, flailing his sword with vicious precision, and Claarn parried five blows that would've beaten an ordinary warrior, before he caught the upswing of the sixth and punched the golden warrior in the exposed throat with his left fist. As the warrior staggered back, Claarn spun full circle and caught him with all his powerful momentum under the breastplate. His sword split the golden armour and ripped through the knight's mail, mortally wounding him. He collapsed to his knees, and toppled over, clutching his bloodied left side. Claarn wrenched his sword free and turned to assess the tide of battle.

The settling darkness made it impossible to see who in the melee was who, but there were far too many golden knights: too many for the small band to ever hope to overcome. Durdan and his companions dropped into hand-to-hand fighting at the single door to the farmhouse, and Claarn recognised he was in danger of being isolated from them. With a bellow, he plunged into the knot of struggling men, hewing and slashing at their exposed backs, until his presence forced the Andrakian knights to turn to face him or leap aside. He charged headlong at the others, and crashed through, into the ruin, with a triumphant roar.

He barely had time to breath before a section of the old farmhouse wall collapsed inward and four enemy breached the gap. He blocked their entry, lunging and parrying, ignoring cuts and welts blades inflicted on his unprotected skin as he forced the enemy back, step by step. The last daylight was all but gone so he hit at sounds – spurs against stone, metal chinking – hit out like a berserker, hitting and hitting and hitting, hitting, until Tim's shouting brought him to a standstill.

'Hold, my friend! Enough! You're hitting the wall!' Tim teased, and laughed as Claarn lowered his broadsword. 'They've retreated. They can't see any better than you in this moonless sky. They're not Aelendyell. Not when the spell binding them is affected.'

Claarn glanced around and could see nothing in the inky blackness of the ruin. The gaps through the wall and door appeared only a shade lighter, enough for him to know they were gaps. He sighed, and relaxed, and eased gingerly onto the rubble, feeling the exhaustion of battle settling on his bones, and the throb of wounds.

'Hold still,' Tim muttered, as he began dabbing at Claarn's arm and face. 'This one on your cheek's a recent wound re-opened.'

'You can see it?' Claarn asked in astonishment.

'Be quiet and let me apply a herb to it that Genythlyll is offering,' said Tim nonchalantly.

Claarn wanted to ask Tim how he could see, how anyone could see in darkness, but he acquiesced to his friend's request and let his wounds be tended, asking instead how they fared in the battle.

Tim sighed, before answering. 'Badly. If it wasn't for the luck of darkness, we'd be tending each other's wounds in the Afterlife. Counting you, me, and Sasha, old friend, we're nine in number. And only Keryl, Genythlyll and your friend Durdan escaped serious wounding.'

'There's nothing serious about my scratches,' Claarn asserted.

'It's as well you can't see in the darkness,' Tim retorted.

Claarn accepted a handful of Aelendyell berries and seeds to eat, and a swill of honey mead from Tim to wash them down. His eyes slowly adjusted to the lack of light, but he couldn't understand how Tim or the remaining six Aelendyell could see so well when he couldn't. They talked in low whispers about the old times for a short while, keeping their minds distant from the encroaching sickly smell of blood and death piled on the earth around the ruined farmhouse, until Claarn could no longer fight off the exhaustion pouring down on him, and he drifted into a fitful sleep, dreaming of The Rim Shield and Dragonlords with swords of fire.

The morning was bitterly cold for summer. As soon as there was enough light for the humans to see, Tim woke Claarn and Durdan to relieve the Aelendyell watch. Sore and irritable as he felt, Claarn could see, from the darkness under his eyes, that Tim hadn't slept throughout the night. He stretched his aching arms and legs and studied the deep cuts. Had it not been for the Aelendyell herbs, he knew the wounds would've normally left him in enormous pain, but this morning they only ached and looked fearsome. He moved to the window to start watch. Barely thirty paces from the ruin, he saw the golden Andrakian warriors standing silent guard, their horses hobbled further back.

'I counted twenty-six,' said Sasha, leaning against the window gap beside Claarn.

'Plus their two Devis,' added Tim. 'We accounted for more than half their force last night. I'd say we've got every chance of coming out of this little fracas alive,' the assassin grinned.

'Perhaps,' Claarn nodded, as he agreed, 'but take away your four magicians in here, and that leaves six to fight twenty-six. Plus their Devis.'

Tim grinned, and carefully slapped Claarn's back to avoid hurting any of the giant's bruises. 'I like gambling. Always did. Part of being a thief, I guess.' He edged between Claarn and Sasha to stare out at the silent line of Andrakian warriors. The first hint of sunlight graced the brilliant blue sky opening to the east above the distant Ureykyeu. Without the touch of the coming sunlight, the warriors' armour looked tarnished, faded. 'You know,' Tim confessed quietly, 'on the day I led that suicidal charge out of the fortress, the day you returned from Dragon's Tooth with Andra and these Golden Warriors, I understood what it was that drives you. I laughed in the middle of the fighting because it was you, Claarn, not me, who should've been there, playing legendary hero in a final pitched battle against impossible odds. I thought, then, that if ever I was meant to die in a hopeless situation it had to be with you beside me. Because I finally understood what it felt like. You know, I think I cursed us both that day.'

Claarn cocked his head toward Tim, gave him a bitter smile, and cuffed his ear. 'If we get out of this infernal rock heap alive,' he growled, 'I'm going to give you a thorough thrashing, Tim Gaelus. That's no curse, it's a promise.'

'They're coming,' Sasha said casually, hefting her crossbow to the window ledge. 'I'd appreciate a little of that Aelendyell chanting about now,' she added with a toss of her dark hair, and took aim.

'Just remember I love you,' Tim said, moving from her to take up a position at the breach in the wall.

She laughed softly. 'I'll believe you when you tell me after this little fight is over,' she said bitterly.

'You can bet I will,' Tim replied with a wink. 'Wherever we are.' He settled into the breach in the wall, unsheathing his sword and twin daggers, and studied the line of Golden Warriors advancing on foot toward the defenders, swords drawn, walking steadily, deliberately, silently, like hunters stalking their prey. 'I think it's to the death this time,' he said and whistled through his teeth. 'I'd give anything for my right eye right now.'

'How about your left one?' Claarn scowled. He unhitched his scabbard and leaned his broadsword against the wall where he could easily reach it when hand-to-hand fighting started. The giant flexed his muscles and cursed the fact he'd ridden to this fight without proper armour. But what did it matter? A good fight was a good fight in any circumstances, and at least he was free to move. He shook his fiery mane of red hair and breathed in the freshness of the growing morning and watched the sunlight spilling across the distant purple peaks.

Elder Keryl joined his three companions in their spell circle, but as he moved past Claarn he turned and said something to the giant warrior that sounded like 'Maegencyning', before he sat and began the chant to cast the unbinding spell. When Claarn glanced questioningly at Tim, Tim grinned.

'He just paid you the highest compliment an Aelendyell warrior could hope to receive, let alone a lowly human like you. He said, if the paths of life were true, you should've been a mighty King.'

'I've seen what happens to mighty kings,' Claarn grumbled cynically, as he loaded a discarded crossbow. 'I think I like it as it is. There's more honour this way.'

Tim chuckled, as he prepared the only arrow shaft he'd have time to release before the closing Andrakian warriors poured over the outer stone wall. 'I just hope the cursed bards get our names right when they make up the hearth songs about our last battle.'

Forty

The war reached stalemate on the edge of Dragon Breath Plains after nine weeks of bitter fighting. High Lord Lori, appointed by A Ahmud Ki on King Andrakis' behalf, after the unfortunate murder of High Lord Claarn at the hands of rebel Aelendyell, awaited the King's orders. Mareg's army retreated across the grey desert and waited at The Rim Shield for the Kingdom's army to march into a trap, as it had two years earlier. The status quo between the two forces was re-established by the same hostile natural barriers that kept the Kingdom and Uz Erhaag separated for a millennium. The cost in blood, in those short, desperate weeks of fighting, was high. Across the plains of Axxon, and the northern hills east of the Border Woods, funeral pyres lit the nights, until the air of the western portion of the Kingdom was permanently tainted with death's ashen smell.

As in the first summer of the war, the Haagii swept south across Dragon Breath Plains in immeasurable numbers, overwhelming the Kingdom army Claarn dispatched from the mopping-up operation in the Kobold Ranges, and marched again toward Central Gate, but the new High Lord of Andrakis rode out to meet the enemy, reinforced by Andrakian warriors on foot and horseback, leading a contingent of Ranu riders and soldiers A Ahmud Ki had successfully portalled from the western barbarian nation through a massive magical gate constructed in the grounds of the Upper Palace. Leiksha Harrudin Shehaal, successor to Ithrandyr Shehaal, was extremely willing to place the forces of Ranu Ka Shehaala at King Andrakis' disposal, and there was more than rumoured speculation that, in time, Abreotan's successor, King Andrakis the Inheritor, could well rule two nations, such was the honour and power accorded him by the new Leiksha of Ranu Ka Shehaala.

The presence of the almost invincible Andrakian knights

and warriors, the superior riding mobility of the Ranu horsemen, and the sheer number of Ranu soldiers sent to support the dwindling army of Kingdom warriors, swung the battles in the Kingdom's favour, and the Haagii army began a slow and bloody withdrawal to the Kobold Ranges. There, the armies fought a protracted battle for three bitter weeks, the Haagii and their cohort of Dammeraag or Dark Warriors refusing to yield.

In the end, King Andrakis rode from his fortress with his sword of flame, and his arrival on the field turned the tide for the Kingdom, as he cleaved through enemy ranks to slay the Haagii General. Inspired by the vision of their triumphant King, the Andrakian and Ranu forces descended like summer reapers on the overawed Haagii and drowned the earth beneath an ocean of their blood, exacting brutal vengeance for the horror and devastation they visited upon the Kingdom and its people the previous summers.

Defeated, without the aid of Mareg's dragons, the Haagii retreated to the devastated edge of Dragon Forest and spur of the Abreotan Ranges, on the brink of Dragon Breath Plains, where they halted again to welcome reinforcements from the north and three of Mareg's flying reptilian pets.

The presence of the dragons chilled the morale of the Kingdom army when they drew up before the Haagii, even with King Andrakis and the sword of Abreotan at the front line. The Ranu soldiers and riders had never seen the fabled beasts, and their horses were skittish at the distant smell of the fearsome creatures. The Kingdom warriors knew what awesome destruction dragons were capable of. Only the Andrakian warriors and knights were impassive, surrounding King Andrakis like a defiant golden sea.

When the two armies joined battle, neither held sway. While Andra's presence, along with the troop of golden knights, swept the Haagii before him on one portion of the field of battle, the dragons circled and swooped elsewhere, their fiery breaths burning and scattering Ranu and Kingdom warriors in fear, letting other Haagii contingents hew through the Kingdom's forces. King Andrakis drove toward the dragons, determined to slay them, and they moved uncannily away, avoiding his fiery sword, while they lashed the luckless warriors with their tongues of fire. The conflict became a swirling maelstrom of fire and panic and death, sweeping everyone into whirling confusion for three days, until the Haagii and humans began collapsing on the field from sheer exhaustion, while the tireless dragons and Golden Warriors battled inexorably, sustained by their binding magic. Nothing suggested a conclusion would be reached – just absolute annihilation of both forces.

The King's exhaustion was the most terrifying of all to the Kingdom troops. Though he carried the sword, trying to rally his human troops against the relentless dragons, he became desperately tired, his energy sapped by the mist constantly enveloping his mind, and time and again he swooned, was carted from the midst of the raging battle by his concerned soldiers, they afraid the Inheritor and their Kingdom's one hope against the Dragonlord had perished, only to reappear, plunging into the thick of the conflict, as though nothing had happened. Yet, to those closest to him in the fighting, his power seemed less invincible, limited by time.

The turning point came on the dawn of the fourth day. From over the shining peaks of the Andrakian Mountains, a dark shape swept toward the carnage, a dragon flying from the east instead of the north. The news and sight sent a widening ripple of dismay through the beleaguered and exhausted Kingdom army: a fourth dragon. Three had failed to succeed – just. A fourth would be the end. Coming from the east also meant one thing – the Valley of Rivers was breached by another arm of Mareg's forces. The central region and the plains of Ky were being overrun.

The dark creature circled, calling to its brethren, hunkered at the western edge of the battlefield eating cattle carcasses, before it dipped and landed in the middle of the Kingdom army. At the point between neck and powerful shoulders, ahead of the creature's folded black wings, sat the black shadow of a dracabeorn – and A Ahmud Ki, in his golden armour, secured by a tackle of belts and rope, sat

381

directly behind the dracabeorn. The Chancellor had come to join in the war for the first time.

Mareg's three dragons finished their fresh meat, and preened themselves, which gave the Chancellor a little time to hold audience with the King. Having spoken briefly, he signalled to the dracabeorn, who guided the dragon back into the morning air, while he strode to the front, pushing through the line of Andrakian warriors to face the enemy. He wove his fingers through a complex web of arcane patterns, and used low, commanding alien words. The front Haagii ranks saw the golden magician's eyes glowing red, like the terrible eyes of their Dragonlord master, and they cowered, afraid of what might eventuate from what they were witnessing.

Mareg's dragons responded to the keening of A Ahmud Ki's dragon and beat their wings, lifting off before their dracabeorn riders could clamber aboard. They rose, closing the distance, as A Ahmud Ki's dragon circled south and swept back low toward the Kingdom armies. As the rider-less trio angled, and dived toward the lone dragon circling beneath them, King Andrakis seemed to grow in stature, as he had when he fought the dragon warrior, his sword glowing but not aflame, and he clasped the weapon in both hands directly over his head.

When it appeared the King was going to meet all three dragons head-on, A Ahmud Ki pointed both hands at the sword and shouted another string of alien words. A bolt of radiant blue energy shot from his hands into the sword of Abreotan, and three rainbow rays emerged, striking the swooping dragons simultaneously. Stunned and disoriented by the infusion of magic, the dragons rolled, crying with shock as they flapped their massive wings and tried to climb.

A Ahmud Ki's dragon seized the moment, while the Haagii army stared in disbelief at the attack on their dragons, and stooped into the heart of the enemy, gushing fire over a tight knot of Haagii warriors who writhed and screamed in agony as a yellow ball of flame enveloped them.

Panic spread like dragon fire. Those near where the

dragon struck dropped their weapons and fled for the forest and the hills. Those in the front ranks near A Ahmud Ki followed their example, convinced another Dragonlord faced them. The Dammeraag warriors responsible for the Haagii army shouted and flailed their swords in a desperate attempt to restore control over their demoralised troops, their violent bids forcing the warriors furthest from the points of attack regrouped, cursing and spitting at their wide-eyed fellows who ran in wild panic for acting like Kingdom cowards. Then they looked up at the circling dragons and began to rue their resolution to stand.

A Ahmud Ki's dragon climbed to join its brethren and marshalled them into a tight diamond formation. The foursome circled to the north and stooped, levelling low over Dragon Breath Plains, sweeping in fast, heading south to pass over both armies, the Haagii army first.

One Dammeraag warrior, the man who obviously took over command from the Haagii General slain in the Kobold Ranges by King Andrakis, stood in his stirrups, haranguing his troops excitedly, pointing at the dragons and the Kingdom army, exhorting them with the promise the dragons were united and going to punish the enemy. As the dragons closed the distance, the Haagii around their General began beating their shields, taking up the eerie rhythm they played during the siege of Thana's old castle.

Dragon fire burst over the Haagii ranks in four brilliant flaming streams, the light making the golden armour of the warriors in the front row of the Kingdom army glow. The same rush of light bathed A Ahmud Ki's face, lifting his silvery hair in a soft halo, as though he was a god descended to bring justice on the realm of mortality, and he broke into a loud peal of laughter when the four dragons passed overhead and climbed to prepare for a second pass.

The Dammeraag warrior, rallying his troops in the mistaken belief the dragons were still under Mareg's control, teetered on his unfortunate horse, supported by the shrouding flames, then both toppled like discarded toys as the terrified Haagii army broke and poured northwards, like water released from a dam.

The Kingdom army stood rooted to the earth in disbelief at what they witnessed. The dragons made another fiery pass over the fleeing enemy, before wheeling and settling on the ground near the Chancellor, bowing their heads to him to be stroked like house cats. Spontaneous cheering broke across the knots and squads of warriors, as they realised the fortunes of war had dramatically changed. They no longer needed to fear the Dragonlord or his hordes. They had a Dragonlord of their own. And they had Abreotan's Inheritor to slay Mareg.

When the troops turned to share their moment of triumph with their King, voices raised in joy and relief, a shockwave pass outward from their stunned centre. On the ground, where his image had towered over them to help A Ahmud Ki subdue the dragons, King Andrakis lay in a crumpled heap, clutching Abreotan's sword, babbling incoherently. The magic was too powerful. The King had gone mad.

'It's all lies. Everything's a lie!' Milly cried. Kara gently stroked the girl's brown hair. She felt sorry for the child whose personal world had disintegrated. 'Can't anyone else see what's happening?'

'Plenty of us see it, lass,' Patti's homely voice chipped in, 'but there's nothing we can see to do about it. The Chancellor holds all the strings.'

Milly sat up and stared at the two adults. Apart from Marella, who was in the Valley of Rivers with her Haardrishii, holding back the Haagii, and Andra, who wasn't Andra anymore, Patti and Kara were the only survivors, the only ones who knew the truth about the Chancellor: who knew he murdered Claarn, and Tim, and Sasha, and Teka knows who else. Yet they were too scared to stop him, too powerless to rescue Andra.

'Milly,' Kara said quietly. 'We've got to be patient. We must keep searching for a weak link, a way to get at the

Chancellor, or get to Andra, without getting anyone killed. We have to outsmart him, but we have to get him to show us the answers we need. That's why what you and Aaron are doing is so important.'

'But that's too slow,' Milly complained.

'Better slow than dead,' Patti said, with a bitter smile on her thick lips. 'As much as I admired our red-haired warrior friend, he was never going to get to the Chancellor. He was too blustery, too eager to stir up the watching dragon.'

'Don't say that about Claarn!' Milly protested, glaring with eyes full of disgust at Patti for speaking so dishonourably of the murdered warrior who was her friend.

'Patti's not being unkind,' Kara intervened, trying to calm Milly. 'It's just that the Chancellor set a trap for Claarn because he knew Claarn would try to fight him.'

'Then what about Tim? And Sasha?' Milly argued, tears brimming.

Kara swallowed and looked away. When she turned back, her eyes were watery too, and her face lined with tiredness. 'Milly, we've got to be patient,' she repeated. 'Please understand.' Milly rose, and headed for the door.

'Where are you going?' Patti asked.

'Nowhere. Just to find Aaron.'

'Be careful,' Patti reminded her. The door closed.

'Am I wrong to worry about her?' Kara asked, turning to Patti.

Patti shook her head, the wattles under her chin rippling. 'No. The lass is always scheming something. Tim used to say she was the best apprentice the Guild could've gotten, after Andra brought her here. She's got a talent and a mind that's hers and hers alone. And she's set on Andra too.' Kara sighed and stared at the closed door.

Milly cast another pebble into the pool's crystal waters and watched ripples oscillate on its surface. 'There has to be a way we can help Andra break free of the spell,' she said.

'You said Tim told you to take the ring off him,' Aaron

replied, tossing another pebble into the water. 'Isn't that supposed to break it?'

Milly nodded absently. That's what Tim said, she remembered, but he also said he wasn't sure. She picked up her dagger and spun it lazily through her fingers. 'The problem is, Aaron, he won't take it off by himself. It's got to be taken off him.' Aaron whistled, the dying note echoing softly in the low chamber housing the pool. 'There's got to be a way of doing it,' Milly mused, as she stuck her dagger in the ground. 'There's got to be a way.' She reached for Artega's ears and rubbed them, and the dog's tongue lolled from his jaw in appreciation.

'It's hard enough getting near him as it is,' Aaron reminded her. 'His guards don't let up for a moment. And Sarcen's always there. That's not likely to change when he comes back from the war.'

'No,' Milly mumbled. She picked up her dagger again and rolled through the burgeoning ideas in her head as she flicked the dagger, tip to hilt, several times, catching it cleanly each rotation. 'Let's suppose,' she said solemnly, staring at the water. 'Let's suppose we were going to get the ring from Andra. How might we do it?'

Aaron ran a hand through his shock of blond hair, and leaned back on his other hand against the cold cavern wall to consider the possibilities.

Something was going wrong, despite his careful planning. The King's unfortunate collapse after the battle was completely unrehearsed. He oversaw his temporary recovery on the field, ordered his dracabeorn surrogate High Lord Lori to maintain the status quo at the edge of Dragon Breath Plains, and arranged Andra's immediate return to the palace. Once there, he had his dracabeorn servants take the semi-conscious King to his tower where he could study what was happening to him.

The diagnosis was painfully obvious. The ring he placed on Andra was at odds with something else. The sword? No.

It often counteracted the ring's magic, giving Andra too sharp an insight on occasions, A Ahmud Ki noted, but it didn't seem to oppose the ring's presence. The armour? Even when it was removed, Andra fluctuated through vague moments, threatening to pass out, before snapping into reality.

In a last attempt to decipher the riddle, A Ahmud Ki concentrated on the young warrior's memories, searching through the mist and confusion, but eventually he had to relinquish that method of searching because of the increasing disorder bordering on insanity spreading through the King's mind. His puppet was falling apart, and he couldn't determine why. The ring's controlling magic was sending the King mad.

That had to be it. The King wore no other visible sources of magic. Should he risk removing the ring? No. If he ever removed the ring, Andra would remember everything, would know Berak N'eth was a lie, would understand that he, A Ahmud Ki, was manipulating him to make decisions and do deeds he would never countenance under his own volition. Released, he would exact revenge with Abreotan's sword because the sword protected him, and as much as A Ahmud Ki hated to admit it the sword was the one enigmatic source of magic he couldn't control. It nearly killed him in the tower when he tried to steal it. He had a problem he couldn't solve, and it frustrated him.

But did he need an answer? Did it matter if the magical conflict occurring in Andra's mind slowly destroyed Andra? All A Ahmud Ki had to do, after all, was to keep the King alive, and under his control, long enough for the final confrontation with Mareg. The sword's ability to enhance A Ahmud Ki's magic and multiply his power would give him the final advantage over his Dragonlord rival, would allow him to weaken and humiliate Mareg, until Andra could strike the death blow as the prophecy promised. After that, it didn't matter if the King was sane or not.

Forty One

A Ahmud Ki clicked his fingers, uttering the magical Targan command 'Haeraeni' Seralinna taught him, and red shimmering light rippled between the three-arm span tall ebony rods in the open parade ground as the portal crackled into life. A Ahmud Ki opened his hands, revealing a glowing orb into which he spoke. A moment later, a horseman burst out of the portal bearing a purple Ranu banner, followed by a troop of six hundred soldiers filing through in rows of five, all wearing the purple and silver heraldry of the Imperial Ranu army. They bowed respectfully to the Chancellor and King Andrakis as they passed. 'That, Your Majesty,' A Ahmud Ki informed Andra, 'is the first of ten such cavalry units Leiksha Harrudin Shehaal has promised to send to support our push north across Dragon Breath Plains and into Uz Erhaag. In total, the Leiksha has graciously committed eighty-five thousand Ranu riders and foot soldiers to the war against Mareg.'

To the King's left, Sarcen watched the response, and turned to his companion, Helix, the dracabeorn A Ahmud Ki caught in the fortress and restored to his assassin human form. 'Our Master's pawn is losing his senses too quickly,' he asserted with a shake of his head.

Helix cast a searching glance at Andra and grunted his disgust. 'To think my former keeper, Mareg, was foolish enough to consider him a threat at all.'

'He has the sword,' Sarcen reminded Helix, whose dark eyes shifted to the golden handle of Abreotan's sword jutting from its ceremonial scabbard on the King's belt. 'One touch of that cursed thing is enough to kill a dracabeorn, let alone we mortals.'

'I begin to wonder whether I was better off in the state Mareg trapped me,' Helix said, rubbing the stubble on his pointed chin.

That's a very stupid thought.

Helix winced at the unexpected intrusion of A Ahmud Ki's voice inside his mind. He glanced at the Chancellor, saw A Ahmud Ki's angry glare, and bowed at the waist until his forehead rested against his horse's mane. Seeing Helix's reaction, Sarcen automatically followed suit.

If you really want to return to dracabeorn status, it can be very easily arranged, A Ahmud Ki warned.

The assassin remained suppliant, afraid his new master would punish him. Being restored to human form meant he could die from the strokes of ordinary weapons, but at least he could think for himself, enjoy the pleasures of the flesh, eat, drink, and make love. A dracabeorn's magical near-immortality had a high price. The victim was a single-minded servant of his master; unfeeling, unthinking.

'Remember it,' A Ahmud Ki added in person as he passed his servants, heading toward the portal. 'Accompany the King to his chambers and see that he is fed and prepared for a meeting tonight, at the King's Table, with our guests.

Milly paused at the t-junction and waited for Aaron. 'Where have you been?' she hissed.

Aaron caught his breath. 'Master Sarcen insisted we had to take watches around the perimeter of the palace grounds as security against the Ranu riders. I'm supposed to be with Josh on the eastern wall, but he's covering for me.'

'You didn't tell him anything?' Milly asked.

'Of course not,' Aaron replied and grinned in the lantern light. 'I told him I was onto a certainty with a girl in the serving quarters.' Her eyes narrowed, which made him suppress his grin. 'I was only making up an excuse, Milly,' he quickly explained, in a clumsy attempt to appease her.

Milly peeked around the corner. She turned back to Aaron and handed him the silver platter of food and the mead jug she was carrying. 'There's no one coming. Hold these for a moment.' She undid the lacing on her overshirt and pulled it deftly over her head, revealing a thin cotton cloth that made him stare because he could see her breasts through the white cloth. She noticed his expression. 'There's no need to stare,' she said. He blushed and turned his head away, while she undid her belt and slid off her trousers. 'There,' she said, as she straightened. 'Do I look right?'

Aaron didn't know what to do. He was afraid she'd scold him for ogling, if he looked again, but he wanted to look, and she had invited him. He cast a cursory glance over her attire. Even with the flimsy dress covering her body, she might as well be naked, he considered, caught between appreciation and embarrassment. He wanted to tell Milly he loved her, because she was the only girl he knew well enough to like, but he never imagined her standing before him like this.

'Well?' she asked, irritation rising.

'Oh. Fine,' he answered absently, and controlled his confusion to reply, 'Great, actually.'

'Give me the platter and jug,' she instructed, 'and take the dagger out of my breeches.'

He handed over the crockery and rummaged through her discarded trousers until he extracted a short, broad-bladed dagger.

'Put that in here,' she told him, indicating the jug. 'Blade first.'

Aaron placed the dagger in the jug and asked, 'Is it razor-sharp?'

Milly nodded. 'Of course.'

'What if he's wearing more than one ring?' he queried.

'Andra didn't wear any rings,' she replied, annoyed with his question.

'Yes, but he's a King now. They always wear lots of rings, to show they're rich.'

'He won't be,' she angrily insisted. 'And if he is, I'll face that when it happens.' She peeked around the corner a second time. 'You know what to do?' she whispered, as she ducked back.

Aaron nodded solemnly. 'If Sarcen and the others in the room don't come out, I come down.'

'And don't wait too long,' Milly added. 'I'm freezing in

this silly stuff.'

Aaron had a sudden urge to reach out and cuddle her to warm her, but he knew she'd belt him for it, so he nodded dumbly and tried not to stare at her goose bumps. She winked nervously, stepped into the empty corridor, and headed up the gentle slope toward the King's chambers.

At the junction leading to Andra's door, she saw two shadowy figures lurking. Conscious of her skimpy outfit, she hurried past, but she couldn't avoid one man's face leering out of the shadows, or help overhear his lewd comment to his assassin companion. Sarcen was obviously being extra careful about security, she noted, and hoped Aaron's Royal assassin comrades wouldn't hinder his passing if she needed his intervention.

At the doorway to Andra's chamber, she bowed to the pair of Andrakian warriors, but they remained motionless, as if totally unaware of her presence. Because she brought serving trays frequently to the chamber, they were conditioned to let her through without question. She placed the jug on the floor so she could knock. 'Who is it?' a voice asked from within.

'The King's chambermaid,' she replied, trying to disguise her increasing nervousness at the crazy risk she was taking. 'I have food, mead, and a special gift from the Chancellor.'

A key rattled. Yellow light spilled from the chamber into the corridor. Sarcen's blond hair gleamed around his shadowed features. Milly saw a lurid grin spread across his lips. 'Aha!' he said with wicked delight. 'A banquet for the King's pleasure!' Instead of letting her enter, he blocked her path, and she felt the horrid touch of his eyes roving over her body. Then she realised the chamber light splashing across her thin garment gave Sarcen a clear view, and she felt sick in the pit of her stomach when her eyes caught his again to find he was smiling knowingly. He stepped aside, at last, and bowed as she slid by. 'Your Highness,' he announced ostentatiously, 'a most pleasant meal is served with a very tasty dessert.'

Milly walked straight to Andra's side and placed the

platter on a low table reserved for his meals. She looked at him, as she bent over, and to her horror noticed that he was slumped in his chair. Asleep? She reached out to nudge his arm, though protocol wouldn't normally allow her to do such a thing.

'You're wasting your time, pretty lady,' Sarcen said from behind.

Milly whirled to face him, and for the first time she noticed two more figures in the room, sitting near the low hearth which glowed with red coals. One was High Priest Argwyllyn. The other was dressed in the green and black garb of a Royal assassin, like Sarcen.

'The King's not up to the kind of entertainment you were sent to provide, my love,' Sarcen continued as he advanced. She sensed the heightening danger the man presented and clutched the jug with the dagger close to her breast. 'You're very young to be entertaining a King, aren't you?' Sarcen asked.

'The Chancellor doesn't seem to think so,' Milly retorted, hoping that invoking A Ahmud Ki's apparent involvement would dampen the assassin trainer's interest.

'Careful, Sarcen,' warned the second assassin, as he turned to study Milly. 'Master Ki might not like us messing with something he's prepared for the King.'

Sarcen stopped, and tilted his head toward Helix, grinning. 'Master Ki doesn't care much for women or girls. You know as well as I that they're only good for one thing. Besides,' he said turning back to Milly, 'this one's not even ripe enough to be picked by the King. I think we should make the fruit a bit more edible. He doesn't look very hungry anyway.' Sarcen's banter, as he closed on Milly, brought chuckles from his companions, and the High Priest turned to watch the interlude with carnal interest.

Milly backed against the wall. You better not let me down now, Aaron, she thought, as she slipped her hand inside the jug and clutched the hilt of her dagger. She assessed her odds of killing the head assassin and his offsider. Poor. Her plan was stupid.

Sarcen moved quicker than she anticipated. He grabbed her arms and swung her away from the wall before she could wrench the dagger from its hideaway. Caught in his vice-like grasp, she found herself staring into his cold, hard eyes as his heavy breath enveloped her senses. 'What were you going to do with the jug, my little bird?' he asked and grinned evilly. 'Wash me in mead?'

Come on, Aaron, damn you, Milly prayed.

Sarcen pulled her into his enfolding embrace and eased the jug from her grip. 'You might be a little bird just out of your nest, my love,' he chortled with delight, 'but today I'm going to test your wings and teach you all about flying with an eagle.' He ran his left hand over her shivering thigh and up her waist, until he squeezed her tiny, right breast. Then he ripped open her fragile garment. Milly screamed. The door to the chamber burst open, and Aaron dived into the room, pursued by the Andrakian guards. Sarcen released Milly, pushing her away against the wall, and turned to the source of the intrusion.

'Master Sarcen!' Aaron gasped, as one golden warrior lifted his sword to strike.

'Hold!' Sarcen ordered. The Andrakian warrior paused. 'What's the meaning of this intrusion, boy?' Sarcen demanded.

Aaron scrambled to his feet and bowed. 'Master Sarcen, there's been a terrible disaster. Someone's tried to kill the Chancellor, Lord Ki. You have to go to him quickly!' Aaron blurted, saw Argwyllyn and Helix and added, 'All of you!'

Sarcen glanced at his companions, startled by Aaron's news, ran his eyes over the slumped figure of King Andrakis and muttered under his breath, before turning to Helix and saying, 'Come on. This is more than serious.'

'What about him?' Helix asked, indicating Andra with a jerk of his thumb.

'He's not going anywhere. These blasted Golden Warriors can stand watch.'

Aaron saw Milly crouching against the wall in the shadows, her dress in tatters, and forgot his purpose, moving

393

toward her to see if she was hurt.

'Boy!' Sarcen yelled. Aaron froze, scared his ruse was exposed. 'Get that half-grown wench out of here before I come back,' the assassin trainer ordered at the door. 'And if you've got any interest in it, have some fun with her,' he added with a sly chuckle, as he led the Andrakian warriors and his two companions out.

After the room emptied, Aaron stooped to Milly and put an arm around her shoulder. She shivered and looked up balefully with tears staining her cheeks. 'What took you so long?' she sniffed.

'The Golden Warriors wouldn't let me pass,' Aaron explained. 'I had to dodge and jump around, to get past them, and I nearly didn't make it. Are you alright?' Milly said she was and tried in vain to cover her breasts with the shredded top of her dress. She gave up in disgust and stood, searching the room. 'What are you looking for?' Aaron asked.

'The jug. My dagger.'

'What's wrong with him?' Aaron asked, bending over Andra's unconscious form, as Milly found the jug and removed her dagger, glistening with mead.

'I don't know,' she replied. 'Look for a ring.' They lifted a heavy hand each, and she discovered a ring on Andra's left hand: a platinum ring set with an amber crystal. 'This the only one?' she whispered.

He nodded. 'Uhuh. There's no rings on this hand.'

'Then I hope Tim was right, Andra,' she said as she placed the King's left hand on the chair's armrest. 'I pray to Teka Tim was right.' She took a firm grip on the ring and pulled at it. It didn't budge. She wrenched harder, nearly pulling Andra out of his chair, Aaron only managing to stop the King's dead weight from toppling by pushing against Andra's chest. 'It won't come off,' she gasped.

'You told me that,' Aaron replied.

'I know,' she said, catching her breath, as she twisted her dagger in her right hand, 'but I had to make sure before I tried this.' She returned Andra's hand to the armrest, took a deep breath, and lifted her dripping dagger directly above Andra's ring finger. The precision-honed blade gleamed in the golden lantern light.

'Hurry up,' Aaron whispered urgently.

Milly frowned at him, swallowed, and directed her full attention on the ring finger. 'I love you, Andra,' she whispered. As she spoke, Andra's eyes opened and stared at her. She screamed and struck.

Voices faded in and out. The mist was thicker than ever, crowding in, blocking even the voices. He remembered a fluttering purple banner and riders. Someone was guiding him to his chamber. He didn't want to go there, but it didn't matter. At the edge of the mist, he heard a girl whisper. Then, somewhere, far away, too far for him to reach, he heard her scream. It might not have been the same girl. It might have been. How could he tell beyond the mist? The strangest sensation was someone pulling at the fingers on his left hand. How could he feel the pulling and not see who was pulling?

He tried to climb out of the confusing mist to see what was happening, forced his defiant will against it; after all, wasn't he King? Even mist should obey him. And it did. He pushed through. He was sitting in his chair, in his chamber. Someone, a girl, was whispering that she loved him. When he turned to her, pushing away the last vestiges of mist, he saw she was half naked, familiar. She was holding a dagger. She was going to kill him.

With sudden fear, he summoned the sword, just as a sharp flash of pain seared through his left hand and arm and exploded in his head like dragon fire. He dropped Abreotan's sword, and clutched his head in both hands, staggering in agony up and out of his chair, screaming. His whole body shuddered, until his knees buckled, and he fell helplessly.

Memories, faces, places, events flooded like shining light into the dark well of his mind, blinding his consciousness with piercing clarity. He saw Claarn begging on his knees to him, Tim Gaelus, scarred and disfigured by some horrid accident, standing with a group of Aelendyell Elders and asking him for leniency, A Ahmud Ki aboard a dragon, laughing at him, as he signed a document giving over Kingdom trees for Targan building, and the strangers stared at him; strangers in red robes, strangers in golden armour, strangers in purple garments on horses, staring at him. The piercing light intensified until he couldn't bear it, or the images it conjured. It enveloped him, like a raging fire, and he screamed, until a black wall flooded over.

She was calling, begging him to stand, pleading for help. He could hear her. It was the girl who whispered to him, the girl who screamed, the girl who held the dagger – Milly. Milly was pleading for him to help her. He forced himself to his feet and focussed on the room. Two Golden Warriors were closing on someone trapped near the wall, a boy with blond hair. Aaron. He remembered the lad. Two more figures circled to the right. They wore green and black robes. Thana's old Royal assassins wore robes like that. Milly was crouching beside him.

'Relax, Your Royal Highness,' an assassin said. 'We'll get rid of these nuisances.'

Andra summoned Abreotan's sword. The weapon glowed with a soft amber radiance and its appearance startled the assassins. 'Leave the girl alone,' he warned. Hearing Andra's threatening tone, the assassins took a wary backward step, staring at each other.

'Help!' Aaron cried, and he dived past the legs of a Golden Warrior whose sweeping sword caught the lad across the back. Aaron yelped with pain and rolled under the central table. Both Andrakian warriors lunged at the boy, but Andra's sword intervened, turning their blades aside.

'Enough!' he ordered. 'Return to your posts.' The Golden Warriors sheathed their weapons, turned, and obediently marched from the chamber. Amazed by the unexpected turn in events, the assassins darted out before Andra could question them.

'Aaron's hurt,' Milly called.

Andra crossed to the huddled pair by the chamber wall and bent to see. A raking cut scored the lad's back, bleeding heavily. Milly was desperately mopping up the wound, and Aaron was breathing erratically.

'Don't be silly, Aaron,' the girl whimpered. 'You're not allowed to die.' She turned her blue appealing eyes to Andra. 'He's not allowed to die, Andra. Not after all the help he's given me.'

Andra studied the wound and the boy's pale cheeks. Aaron was in severe shock and close to death. 'I learned something very important about this sword in A Ahmud Ki's tower,' he said slowly, as he turned the handle in his right hand. 'I can't think of a better time to use it.' He asked Milly to step away from Aaron, before he placed the tip of the sword's glowing blade on the edge of Aaron's wound, closing his eyes to will the sword to use its energy on the boy, focussing inward and channelling it so it didn't exhaust him, like it had when he revived A Ahmud Ki. Aaron's wound stopped bleeding, and, to Milly's astonishment, an amber haze flowed along the gaping cut and fused the torn skin.

'How-?' she tried to ask, unable to frame the words.

'I don't know.' Andra replied, relaxing his concentration. Tiredness in his arms combined with a vicious throb from the ring finger of his left hand. 'All I know is if I want the sword to do something, I only need to think of it happening, and usually −' He held up his left hand to study the reason why his ring finger hurt so much, and discovered the finger missing, its severed stump bleeding. He felt queasy at the sight and remembered his vision as he broke through the mist. He stared at Milly. 'Did you-?' he began to ask, leaving the question hanging like his hand before Milly's face.

Milly paled. 'I had to, Andra,' she said. 'The ring was evil. The Chancellor was using it to control you. Honest. It's true. He gave you the ring, and it made you do horrid things. Tim said that was why you changed.'

'Tim?' Andra interrupted at the mention of his friend's

name. 'Tim told you this?'

'Yes,' said Milly. 'He told us just before -' She stopped, remembering the lies the Chancellor spread about Claarn and Tim's deaths.

'Just before what?' Andra asked.

Voices echoed along the outside corridor. Milly glanced at the open door in alarm. 'Andra, you can't stay here,' she hissed.

'Why not?'

'Because the Chancellor will kill you,' Milly said, as she helped Aaron to his feet. The lad lurched groggily. 'He'll kill us.'

'I won't let him.' Andra said, with authority. The voices outside dropped to harsh whispers and Andra heard the familiar rattle of weapons being drawn. They wouldn't dare harm him. He was the King.

'They won't kill you straight away,' Milly argued, 'but they'll try to kill us. We know too much.'

'I won't let them,' Andra repeated.

'But the Chancellor had Claarn and Tim killed, and no one can prove anything,' Milly blurted, realising Andra was not going to be easily persuaded. 'We'd be no challenge to him. And then he'd just put you back under the spell, and there'd be no more Kingdom.'

Milly's half-confession about Tim and Claarn's fates shocked Andra. They were dead? Both dead? And Milly was claiming the Chancellor engineered their deaths. Tim? And Claarn? How could A Ahmud Ki kill them? Why? The memories drifting through the swirling confusion of his mind sparkled with abrupt clarity. He, Andra, sent Tim and the Aelendyell away. They came to speak with him and he ordered them to go. It was his fault.

Before he could consider his actions, a figure appeared in the doorway, an assassin with an arrogant face, dark glittering eyes, and a long blond ponytail. He held a dagger, half-concealed, against his chest. 'Begging your Royal pardon, Your Majesty,' he said, 'but I've been informed that the lad and his harlot are not supposed to be here, and I've come to remove them.'

'They're friends of mine,' Andra replied.

He noticed the assassin square up, as if he was prepared to defy Andra. 'I beg to think Your Highness is mistaken,' Sarcen said with mock politeness. 'The lad's just an apprentice I train. And the wench was sent here by Lord Ki to, shall we say, whet your Royal appetite for a bigger meal tonight. They've no reason to be here now.'

'I said they stay,' Andra replied.

Sarcen shifted uneasily and glanced out the door. Figures shuffled in the corridor. Andra glimpsed golden armour. 'Ah, I don't think Your Highness quite understands,' Sarcen said, in a conciliatory tone. 'Lord Ki has ordered I remove them at once.' He nodded to the doorway. Six Andrakian warriors shuffled in.

Andra shifted his weight. 'I don't think you understand, whoever you are,' he said, though he was masking his confusion at the apparent change in his status regards his relationship with the Chancellor. 'I am the King.'

Sarcen smiled graciously. 'Yes, Your Highness, you are. But Lord Ki has given an order and it will be carried out. Please excuse us, Your Majesty.' He motioned to the Golden Warriors, who headed for Milly and Aaron.

Enraged, Andra caused the sword to flare, and he struck the first warrior, cutting through his torso, sending him tumbling aside. Sarcen's eyes widened in shock at King Andrakis' unanticipated attack and bolted from the room. Andra felled two more Andrakian warriors, forcing the remaining three to withdraw and regroup.

'Andra!' Milly screamed. 'We can't stay here! Sarcen's gone to fetch the Chancellor. We've got to escape! We can't stay! Please!'

Andra heard the girl's cry. Edging backwards, keeping a watchful eye on the circling Andrakian warriors, he pointed to a stone panel in the wall behind Milly. 'Press the reddish rock that juts slightly. It opens a door into the King's Table chamber. Go through there.' Milly pressed the stone, as instructed, and dragged Aaron through. Andra followed and closed the door.

'What now?' Milly asked. Only one door led from the King's Table.

'We go out there and down,' Andra said indicating the door. 'Are the Maze ruins still accessible from the Deep Cave?'

'Yes,' Milly answered.

'Good. There's bound to be horses in the city. We'll take a couple and ride out. I need a couple of days to sort this out,' he said hastily. 'I fear you've got a lot to tell me, Milly, more than I'm going to like to hear. If what you say is true about the Chancellor, I need to be ready.' He hoisted Aaron onto his shoulder, opened the door, and led Milly into the corridor, heading deeper into the fortress for the old Maze ruins, and the safety of Kara's Guild.

Forty Two

Andra hunched over his horse and spurred it on, descending the shallow slope toward the rising darkness to the north, and the horse broke into a steady, tired canter as it reached the flat, feeling the young man's hands easing on the reins. The brittle pre-dawn air stung the rider's eyes, and he savoured its coolness in his dry mouth. With a gentle nudge of his knee, he steered his mount toward a gap between the rising peaks that darkened as the midnight blue sky faded through lighter and lighter shades. He wished he was riding Firebrand. He owed his life to the horse that carried him safely in battle, but there wasn't time for romantic notions in his escape from the fortress. He only had time to find Kara in the plateau's lower chambers and arrange a horse and provisions.

Milly's protests echoed in his mind when he told her he was riding alone. She pleaded to let her travel with him, begged him to say yes, but he knew taking her would be foolish. Riding alone, he could put a lot of distance between himself and A Ahmud Ki, before the Chancellor could muster riders to pursue him, and though he knew Milly was the better rider he didn't want to put her at risk in the open should A Ahmud Ki's people chase him. He wanted her safe. She broke the Chancellor's hold by severing his finger and shattering the spell. He owed her his life. The last thing he wanted was to let her step into the ring of fire he felt encircling A Ahmud Ki and him.

While Kara tended to his finger stump, he made the Guild Mistress promise she wouldn't let Milly follow, under any circumstances. Kara asked him where he was going, but he steadfastly refused to reveal his plan. To do so, he considered, would endanger his few remaining friends who had to remain in Andrakis under the Chancellor's eyes. His mind was still befuddled, hazy, chaotic. He needed time to think, to remember, to decide.

The weariness of riding ached through his bones. The sky east was turning cobalt blue. The highest tips of the Ureykyeu Mountains faded from grey to white, and as he let the horse slip into a slow walk the first morning rays made the snow peaks glow with golden light. How long since I've seen such beauty? he wondered. How long?

He coaxed his exhausted mount up a short, steep incline and dismounted at the summit beneath three twisted trees whose gnarled, skinny trunks intertwined, as if they were locked in an eternal fight for possession of the limited space on the hilltop. He studied the dark southwest landscape for movement, shook his head tiredly and smiled as he turned to rub his horse's ears. 'Keep watch, my friend,' he whispered, too tired to talk with effort. 'Whatever happens now, happens. I have to sleep a little.' He pulled a coarse woollen blanket that served as his temporary saddle from his horse's damp, warm back, and huddled between the trunks of the wrestling trees, wrapping himself tight to keep warm. Within a breath, he fell into a deep sleep.

Sweat beaded on Sarcen's brow as he faltered under the accusing glare of Master Ki who held a severed ring finger, daring him to look away and be damned. The trainer of the Royal assassins was riddled with guilt and fear that he, alone, was responsible for the King's escape in the Chancellor's absence.

A Ahmud Ki held Sarcen's attention without speaking or moving, as if wanting to drain every ounce of potential resistance from his victim before consigning him to his fate. Finally, he threw the finger into the burning hearth warming the chamber, and his face rippled with anger. 'A girl and a boy,' he snarled. 'Two children steal away the one thing that will make me Lord of all lands.' He wheeled toward Sarcen, making the assassin flinch. 'And you let it happen,' A Ahmud Ki snarled. 'You!'

Sarcen lowered his head, exposing the unprotected nape

of his neck.

A Ahmud Ki watched his act of submission and was seized with the desire to plunge a dagger deep into Sarcen's throat. No, he decided, too honourable for an assassin, too quick. For letting Andra break out of the spell, Sarcen had to suffer sufficient anguish and humiliation to warn others not to fail their master - ever again. 'Where have they gone?'

The question brought Sarcen's head up, but the assassin averted his eyes from A Ahmud Ki's gaze. Without looking, he knew what he would see. The Dragonlord Andrakis, who condemned him to a lifeless existence as a dracabeorn, had eyes that glowed red, full of fire and energy, and Master Ki had broken that Dragonlord's spell, returning Sarcen to his former human existence. To have such power meant Master Ki was a Dragonlord, a powerful Dragonlord. He sensed A Ahmud Ki's fiery gaze and tasted fear. 'The children are still in the city, or the plateau, Lord Ki,' he answered. 'But my men say they're under the protection of the King and the Guild. Lady Kara has hidden them from us.'

'Kara?' A Ahmud Ki queried. 'She meddles too much!' he cursed, recalling her ascension to Guild Mistress by killing Master Orrin, eliminating A Ahmud Ki's secret hold over the Thieves' Guild as the Shadow's Voice. 'She'll regret this petty act of defiance.'

Sarcen heard the cold threat in A Ahmud Ki's oath and felt claws of fear tearing at his stomach.

'And the King?' A Ahmud Ki asked.

'Word is the King took a horse, and rode out of the city, to the north,' Sarcen replied.

'Alone?'

Sarcen risked raising his eyes to sneak a glimpse of A Ahmud Ki's face, and stared into two blazing pools of liquid fire where he saw his cowering reflection.

I feed on your fear, a voice whispered in his mind. You should've feared me more when you had your chance. It's too late now.

He snapped out of his horrified trance and desperately tried to reassert his self-control. 'He rode out alone, Master

403

Ki.'

A Ahmud Ki turned from the assassin and walked toward the door, wrapped in thought. Why would the King ride away alone, he wondered? A heroic gesture to draw attention from the others? Possibly. His warrior code and training would undoubtedly lead him to such an act. Why north? Toward Mareg?

It dawned on him the fool was going to fulfil the prophecy alone. There were too many wild possibilities, too many unforeseen risks if Andra took that path. A Ahmud Ki could not afford to let him act alone. While he couldn't wield a sword to slay Mareg, Andra was his warrior extension to combat the Dragonlord enemy. If Andra succeeded alone, all A Ahmud Ki's planning to seize power would crumble. If Andra failed, how could A Ahmud Ki hope to defeat Mareg? He had to stop the wayward King and bring him to heel.

He turned angrily on Sarcen, and the assassin dropped to his knees to abase himself in the manner Lord Ki most approved of, hoping if he showed sufficient subservience Lord Ki would punish him, but not kill him. A Ahmud Ki stared at Sarcen's long golden ponytail, braided down his assassin's back, and sneered. It reminded him of the braiding the Aelendyell favoured. He hated the Aelendyell. He hated failure even more.

He turned to the door, opened it, beckoned two Andrakian warriors into the chamber, and pointed at Sarcen's back. 'Take this one to the dragon shaft and let my pets amuse themselves with him,' he ordered, and strode into the corridor, ignoring Sarcen's screams for mercy stifled under golden gauntlets.

Andra could hear voices in the mist, and he strained to catch words, but they were whisperings; gentle, distant whisperings. A horse galloped through. Firebrand. He called after his horse, but the swirling mist swallowed it. He felt the familiar corrugations of his sword and glanced down. It wasn't Abreotan's sword he held, but Cedwyn's, the sword his father passed to him: that Liam carried to his death in Cennednyss. Blood never stained the blade. But even as he remembered its magical feature, dark liquid oozed from the blade's gutter and dripped from its point. He shook the sword, but dark blood continued to spread across the shining surface, defiling it. Repulsed by the vision, he dropped the weapon, and heard it splash at his feet. He was standing in a murky swamp. Water rippled around his ankles, while ghostly voices encircled him, and closed in.

'They're your enemy,' a deep voice of authority warned.

He knew that voice. It was a familiar voice, a protective voice.

'Summon the sword against your enemy,' the voice coaxed.

Andra willed Abreotan's sword into his hand and felt a hilt materialise, but when he lifted the blade to gaze on the magical weapon, again he saw the crimson blade of Cedwyn's sword. Before he could recoil from it, a shadow emerged from the mist.

'Strike! Kill your enemy!' the voice urged.

Andra slashed at the figure, and it collapsed silently at his feet into the marsh. Another appeared. And another. Each time they loomed out of the mist, he cut them down. More shadows lurked beyond his reach, moving, and whispering to him. The oddest sound reaching his ears, out of the mist, was the wail of mourning women. It was crystal clear, ringing. Smaller shadows drifted through the mist. Children. One face appeared and sank back, but he recognised her short brown hair. Milly. She was mouthing something, but the vision was brief, too obscure. The mist swallowed her. A larger shadow charged from his left. He spun to meet the looming giant.

'Slay him!' the voice hissed. 'Cut him down!'

Andra lunged at the shadow, burying his sword deep into the enemy's belly, and heard a groan, and the shadow roared with laughter. As if swept aside by the sudden burst of merriment, the mist surrounding the shadow dissipated, until Andra found himself staring into the glittering eyes of

Claarn, the giant warrior's red mane flaming from his head. Claarn laughed, as if he had no sense of the sword blade buried deep in his midriff. Shocked, Andra released the hilt. He'd stabbed Claarn. He'd killed his friend.

His heel caught a body in the sludge underfoot and he fell, sprawling on his back in the freezing water. He rolled and caught hold of an arm. He turned the corpse over. It was Tim. He scrambled to a second body and rolled it over. Tim Gaelus' glassy eyes stared up again. Maddened, he lurched to his feet and stared at the other bodies in the swamp. Every corpse was Tim Gaelus. He'd used the sword, listened to A Ahmud Ki's commanding voice, and cut down Tim Gaelus as his enemy, not once but a dozen times. Claarn's laughter rose to an insane cackle and took on the frightening pitch of a dragon's screech. The giant erupted in flames and toppled into the marsh, the flames meeting the water with a sharp hiss of steam, and through the mist swept a dark shape on outstretched wings. It came toward him. He knew it was a dragon coming for him, but he couldn't run.

He willed Abreotan's sword into his hand and felt it ignite. The mist evaporated, running from the sword's bright amber flame, but the dragon shape expanded, until it became an enveloping darkness all round, and, from the darkness, new laughter bubbled, laughter he knew, laughter from A Ahmud Ki. His eyes glowed red. The darkness swept in, and he stood with Abreotan's sword, waiting to meet its full fury.

The frightened nickering of his horse woke Andra and he staggered to his feet, blazing sword in his hand. He squinted, to adjust to the mid-morning light, and searched the surrounding land but saw nothing. Then he heard the dragon's cry, and looked up to find the creature circling low, over the hilltop, a thousand paces to his right. It swept back and forth in a deliberate pattern, searching. Andra knew what it was looking for.

He let the sword return to its scabbard, caught hold of his

horse's reins, and patted the gelding's white nose to calm the frightened creature, but as the dragon's weaving path brought it nearer the horse became increasingly distressed, threatening to rear and hurt itself.

Andra realised he had little choice. He quickly checked the horse's hobbles were secure and headed down the steep slope to the small valley floor. On the open grassy ground, he would be easily visible to the dragon. Whoever rode the creature would soon see him.

He only just reached level ground before the dragon banked and flew directly overhead. The downdraft of its wing beats swirled around him, driving the cool air into frenzy, before the massive reptilian beast descended to land thirty paces away. He studied the creature's green-black hide, and one glittering golden eye slit opened to stare at him.

Two figures slid from a harness on the dragon's neck. Andra recognised A Ahmud Ki, in the Dragonlord's armour. The other was a shadowy dracabeorn, that prostrated itself on the grass as soon as A Ahmud Ki dismounted, and stayed there obediently as the Chancellor walked toward Andra. Andra saw arrogance in A Ahmud Ki's gait, the air of superiority the Chancellor adopted to impress everyone, and prepared to meet him.

'Irand shadu arat shehaal, Your Highness,' A Ahmud Ki said graciously. 'That's the formal Ranu greeting I've always preferred. It means very loosely 'May you live in light and peace'.' Andra reserved his greeting. A Ahmud Ki observed Andra's suspicion and shrugged in disappointment, asking, 'Why are you riding this way, Your Highness?'

The Chancellor's question made Andra consider for the first time, since leaving Andrakis and running from his confusion, where he was going. Understanding crystallised in his consciousness like first daylight on the mountain peaks. 'I'm returning home,' he answered.

A Ahmud Ki raised an eyebrow in curiosity. When the ring held the King's mind under its controlling spell, A Ahmud Ki penetrated the memories in Andra's mind and learned of

The Vale, and touched on the teachings of The Way, but he dismissed them as minor irrelevancies, common to an ignorant warrior, the trappings of a homesick youth who had not come to terms with the power thrust in his hands by a prophecy. He, personally, had no home, and no concept of the bonding strength of a family or community, because the Aelendyell village where he grew up filled him with loathing rather than longing. Love of home, he decided, was a weakness fools like Andra clung to, which only made them more vulnerable to manipulation. Andra was running in fear from him, trying to escape to the safety of his home, the idyllic womb from which he was dragged reluctantly by Thana's Haardrishii to serve in the war, and so he was vulnerable to A Ahmud Ki's whim. There was no point letting him run blindly away. Or had he missed some important detail about The Vale? Unlikely. 'Why return to The Vale?' the Chancellor asked.

Andra fixed A Ahmud Ki with a calm gaze, hearing the Chancellor's faint mocking tone, and countered with his own question. 'Why did you put the ring on my finger?'

A Ahmud Ki shrugged off Andra's question. 'If you run away now, your Kingdom will fall, and your friends will all perish,' he said, carefully beginning his attempt to convince Andra to return to Andrakis. 'The Dragonlord is ready.'

'Which Dragonlord?' Andra asked stolidly.

The faintest trace of a smile played across A Ahmud Ki's mouth as he accepted Andra's sharp observation. From the outset, the young warrior understood too much, and now, having broken the ring's hold, it seemed the King was going to be stubborn again. Perhaps he would acquiesce to persuasion from another source. He subtly attuned his senses to entering Andra's mind in the guise of Berak N'eth, the voice he utilised to convince the King he was the Ranu god's servant being Abreotan's successor. The instant he did, he received a surprise.

No, Lord Ki, Andra projected.

Stunned by the strength of Andra's defensive mental response, A Ahmud Ki withdrew, recognizing the pattern of resistance he encountered from Waeron Ardath. He blinked and saw the sword glowing white in the young King's hand.

'Why did you force me to kill my friends?' Andra asked in a low, determined voice.

'Because they interfered too much,' A Ahmud Ki replied. If Andra could resist his magical influence so determinedly, it didn't matter anymore if the King knew his reasons. Nothing could change events now. It was all too late. The die was cast and, if the words were as true to their ending as they'd proven to be so far from their beginning, the prophecy would be fulfilled, no matter what lies or truth he told Andra.

A Ahmud Ki's casual dismissal of Andra's friends' lives angered the young warrior, and in response to his emotion the sword's glow shifted hue from white to amber.

The Chancellor saw the change and increased his concentration as he continued, aware that he, not the King, was in the greatest danger in this confrontation. 'Open your mind to the reality of what's happening to you. The prophecy you must complete doesn't concern them,' he argued. 'It concerns you and Mareg. Everyone else's lives are dispensable.'

'Even yours?' Andra asked.

A Ahmud Ki heard the warrior's unveiled threat. 'You need me,' he replied, warily.

'Why?'

'Because I hold the key to Mareg's single weakness.'

Andra scrutinised A Ahmud Ki's handsome face, searching for the clue, the shift in his grey eyes, the line that would tell him the Chancellor was lying, but no such sign appeared. 'The prophecy says nothing about you,' he said. 'The final confrontation will be between the Dragonlord and me. I, alone, am fated to slay him. Even you know that is true.'

A Ahmud Ki chuckled, shrewdly gauging the effect of his laughter, trying to evoke enough curiosity to overcome, or at least temper, the warrior's anger for revenge.

'What amuses you?' Andra asked, disgusted with the

Chancellor's clear disrespect.

'You'll take an army to meet Mareg's army and the prophecy says nothing about them,' A Ahmud Ki argued. 'Who'll hold back Mareg's dragons while you fight Mareg? You can't keep his whole force at bay while you try to engage him.'

'And you can?' Andra cynically retorted.

'Whatever magic Mareg has, I can deny or duplicate,' A Ahmud Ki confidently replied. 'I hold the Fifth Ki. I am as much a Dragonlord as Mareg. I control my own four dragons. And the Andrakian warriors are my personal army.'

'You forget who controls the Golden Warriors,' Andra interrupted sharply. 'I'm their master,' he asserted. A Ahmud Ki smiled. It was then Andra realised the extent of A Ahmud Ki's ruse. 'You used me,' he blurted.

'Of course I did,' A Ahmud Ki admitted, regaining his confidence with Andra's show of astonished comprehension. 'I needed the sword's powers to enlarge my spells, so I could successfully re-animate the Golden Warriors. They belonged to Dragonlord Andrakis, they still do, except I possess his powers and he's dead. But it was Abreotan who sealed them permanently beneath Dragon Tooth, before he defeated Andrakis in his fortress. I needed your sword to release them. More than that, I needed your credibility to do it. Even if I had the power to release them, if I offered to animate them alone, who would've trusted me? Your precious friends? Even you? I don't think so. Yet, if I hadn't led you all to the catacombs under Dragon's Tooth, you'd never have unshackled Andrakis' warriors, and the Kingdom would've been lost. I used you for your own good. I used you to save the Kingdom from Mareg.'

'Then why place a spell ring on my finger?'

A Ahmud Ki glared at the King for returning to the ring question, realising his attempt to gain Andra's sympathy and trust, by explaining how he, as Chancellor, was the victim of mistrust, wasn't convincing the King as he hoped it would. He was running out of options, having no other choice than to use magic to return the King to Andrakis. 'To help you be a strong King,' A Ahmud Ki said simply.

'To help you be the King's mentor and rule through me,' Andra accused, understanding clearly what had been happening to him.

A Ahmud Ki's grey eyes flared, and Andra saw the colour dissolve into angry, red pupil-less balls of fire as the Chancellor challenged his accusation. 'What do you know about power and ruling others? Why should you be the sole King, the one ruler of the Kingdom? You might hold everyone's future in your sword arm because of promises prophets scribbled down hastily a thousand years ago, but you've no idea how to act or make decisions as King. To be a ruler, you must be trained to understand the nature of power, and how it must be used to ensure stability and security. That would take years of your lifetime. There aren't years to teach you in. The war against Mareg is now. The Kingdom needs a strong, experienced King now, not in five or ten years. Can't you see why the ring was needed? It turned you into the kind of King the Kingdom needs. It was a simple way to speed up the process of years, that's all. It gave you insight and authority -'

'It gave you control over me,' Andra cut in. 'It gave you the power, not me.'

So, thought A Ahmud Ki, the King learns too quickly and won't be led. He slipped off his gauntlets designed to protect his hands from the chill air encountered in dragon flight, and slowly, casually, started to weave a holding spell as he continued to embellish his explanation. 'Power's my birth right. I'm an inheritor, just like you. Of course, you realised that. It's why I can practise magic, destroy Andrakis Va'ristrin Nyavardenet, and subdue the dragons. It's why, inevitably, I will overcome Mareg. I am the Dragonlords' inheritor just as you are Abreotan's – except, for me, power and authority come naturally. What I hold, what I seek, what I am, is power. For you, it is a lifelong learning just to understand it and manipulate it in minor ways as a King.'

Andra listened intently to A Ahmud Ki's speech, fascinated by just how convinced the Chancellor was that he

411

was Mareg's successor, but as he listened he saw the subtle motions of the Chancellor's fingers and recognised the threat. 'You are the sword,' Ardath told him. He focussed, enough to remain attentive to A Ahmud Ki while conjuring the sword's magic to ward off the Chancellor's spell. He had no concept of A Ahmud Ki's intention, only an innate awareness a spell was being created, and so he willed the sword to protect him from danger. As A Ahmud Ki completed and cast his spell, the sword emitted a mauve radiance that enveloped Andra.

The Chancellor's eyes widened when he saw the magical aura repel his holding spell, or at least that's what appeared to happen, because when he tentatively tried to manipulate Andra's mind he perceived no weakening of the young King's resistance to his probing spell. The sword's magic protected its master. It negated A Ahmud Ki's power. Stalemate.

Their eyes met, locked like adversaries who've fought each other in battle, neither gaining ascendancy, neither accepting defeat, yet standing apart, caught between respect and loathing for the enemy's power, reluctant to let the issue end, yet knowing there could be no resolution on that particular battlefield.

Andra ended the silent confrontation. He turned, as if A Ahmud Ki no longer existed, and headed up the steep slope toward his tethered horse.

'You can't walk away from your destiny!' A Ahmud Ki shouted at Andra's back. 'If you refuse to go to Mareg, he'll come to you. And sooner than you think!'

Andra ignored the Chancellor's voice, walking with tired legs up the hill.

'A whole army waits for your order on the edge of Dragon Breath Plains!' A Ahmud Ki called, as Andra reached his horse and threw the makeshift cloth saddle over the horse's back. 'They wait for your order to march against Uz Erhaag and the Dragonlord. You can't ignore them and ride away.'

Andra hauled himself onto his mount and wheeled to face the entrance to the Valley of Rivers. He stared down at the gold-armoured Chancellor, standing only paces from his black-winged reptile, whose tail flicked, back and forth, across the yellowed grass. From Andra's vantage point, A Ahmud Ki looked too much like the Dragonlord he imagined in his nightmares. Did Mareg look like A Ahmud Ki, he wondered?

'You have to return with me!' A Ahmud Ki shouted. 'The Kingdom's fate is your fate! You can't ride away from that responsibility! You have no right to do that!'

'I am the King!' Andra called down to the Chancellor in a tired, firm voice. 'The army will march when I return! Remember that, Chancellor! Remember also that my word protects the lives of my friends in Andrakis! I hold you personally responsible for their safety in my absence! If any one of them comes to harm, I will come for you! That I promise! I am the King!'

His words trailed across the small valley, as he wheeled his horse and dropped from sight over the summit of the hill, leaving A Ahmud Ki clenching his fists in rage and frustration, staring at the three twisted trees caught in each other's wild embrace on the hilltop.

Forty Three

Light rain drizzled through the trees, as Andra started the slow climb, up the Outward road, into The Vale. He led his sore and weary horse, its fetlock bruised by a stumble three days earlier on a pebble creek-bed, one of hundreds crisscrossing the scarred road winding through the forest on the valley floor. Through the thinning tree canopy, he could see the low grey sky descending, bringing the first heavy falls of late autumn to begin the annual process of turning the Valley of Rivers into a vast floodway, that would isolate the scattered valley-dwelling communities from the rest of the Kingdom for two or three months. This year's rains are coming early, he observed. He was thankful to reach The Vale ahead of them.

The Outward road wound between two spurs forming the entrance to The Vale, and he carefully surveyed their summits, searching the granite clusters for movement. Traditionally, there would be two Guardians on either point, watching for travellers. He remembered the first time, as a Guardian, he spotted Thana's black-armoured Haardrishii riding into his home, led by Devi Senok. Their arrival changed his world, and his destiny. He saw no movement among the rocks, even though he knew exactly where the Guardians on watch would be stationed, but, he reminded himself, that is the purpose of their training - not to be seen. Even now, a Guardian would be running a hidden pathway to the village, to warn the Council an intruder was approaching.

Beyond the spurs, cradled between hills to the north and south, and nestling under the sharp faces of the Ureykyeu Mountains that rose like walls to the east, the valley opened. Though rises hid the village from Andra's view at this point on the meandering Outward Road, he could see the tree fringe encircling the valley, and the eastern ridge above the marshes where old pig master Flintok's sties were built.

414

He wanted to return home for more than two years; to come back to the sights and sounds and smells of The Vale, and be reunited with his parents and the faces of his youth. Now, as he followed the road, his old passions returned, stronger than ever, and he drank in the air's cool essence and the visions of The Vale. He was home. The world beyond this place faded like a terrible dream, a dream that held the constancy of reality for only so long as he held the dream. Here he was Andra, Guardian of The Vale, son of Malcolm and Anedra. King Andrakis did not exist. The Dragonlord was someone else's nightmare. Uplifted by The Vale's homely touch, he crested the last rise.

The village was gone. In place of the homes, the Hall of Council, the Guardian Hall, were blackened ash heaps, and every building, even the smallest enclosures to pen domestic animals, was burnt and scattered. The Outward road ran like a lost child between the darker patches in the grass.

Andra frantically searched the desolate scene for signs of life. The ruins were deserted. No cattle or sheep grazed near the stream that ran from behind the eastern ridge along the foot of the southern hills. Nothing. He stood for a long time, unaware of the saturating rain or rapidly fading light.

Not until a distant rumble of thunder rolled down the Ureykyeu cliffs did he shift his attention to the cold world surrounding him. He wiped the moisture from his haggard face, and started down the slope toward the ashen ruins, letting the horse trail behind.

In the rain and failing light, the blackened ground where his parents' hut had been was a dismal vision. He paused to reflect, before he crossed the sodden earth to the scorched patch where the Hall of Council had stood. In the ashen centre, he saw charcoal remnants of the log-seats the Councillors used for meetings. He recalled the ceremony the Guardian Master performed to make Erik, Alain and himself Guardians, and his right hand moved to touch the silver circlet holding his wet black hair in a ponytail, the Guardian's badge of office. Had fate made him the last Guardian of The Vale?

Another roll of thunder drew him from his mournful reverie. He squinted against the rain, whose intensity increased after the thunderclap, and considered where he could shelter from the encroaching storm. Finally, he decided to head for the trees in the foothills west of the village and build a temporary shelter from branches and the underbrush. He took the horse's reins and led it from the ruin.

The passing storm promised more violence than it delivered. When Andra woke the following morning, cold, hungry, and aching, he was thankful the rain hadn't washed away his humble shelter, but, despite his precautions, it had soaked into his rations bag and his flour was a wet doughy mess. He cursed his luck and grabbed a handful of dried seeds and fruit to appease his stomach. Pale sunlight struggled to break through the cloud ceiling, leaving him shivering with cold because his clothing hadn't dried. He rummaged through the bag of extras, Kara provided, and dragged out a dirty but dry beige tunic and a grey woollen cloak, which he gratefully put on. He only had the single pair of breeches and knew he'd have to suffer wearing them, damp as they were.

He had a far more serious problem than damp breeches. With the village gone, and the early rains surging into the Valley of Rivers, he faced a long, lonely winter, trapped in The Vale. I was stupid to come back, he thought. As much as he hated to admit it, A Ahmud Ki was right to talk him into returning to Andrakis, but not for the reasons motivating A Ahmud Ki's concern. There was nothing left for him in The Vale. Andra the Guardian was the distant dream: King Andrakis his reality. The past was consumed in the fires of war. He was a part of the present and the future, and he was foolish to try escaping it. Now he couldn't go back until the rainy season passed, trapped by his own folly.

He hung his wet garments and possessions on branches, to dry as best as they could under the circumstances, before he checked the horse's bruised fetlock. 'At least you'll be grateful for a long rest here,' he said, as he stroked the horse's cheek. 'I just hope the Chancellor takes my threat seriously and leaves Kara and Milly and the others alone. This was a mistake coming back.' He picked up his scabbard, buckled it on, and headed out of the grove toward the village ruins, in the forlorn hope of finding a clue in the ashes to the fates of his family and people.

When he crested the last hill, he spied dark figures moving through the ruins on horseback. Alarmed, he dropped to his belly beside a shrub, and studied the unexpected intruders. He estimated at least two hundred, a sizeable force, and they wore black armour. Mareg's Dammeraag warriors? Then he saw the armour was smooth, finely crafted, not at all like the vicious spiky suits the Dammeraag warriors wore, and knew the riders were Haardrishii. What were they doing here? Their leader attracted Andra's attention when she removed her helmet. Familiar black hair fell to her shoulders. 'Marella!' he yelled, leaping to his feet. 'Marella!' He broke into a wild run down the rise toward the wheeling horse riders. Marella spurred her mount forward to meet the running warrior. When she recognised Andra, she reined in her steed and dismounted to meet his embrace.

'By all the gods! What are you doing here?' she asked, as they parted.

'I've come home,' he explained, catching his breath. He gestured toward the remains of the village. 'At least that's what I'd hoped I was doing. But there's nothing left.'

'Not here there isn't,' she replied, shaking her head. 'The Haagii burned this place down a long time ago. The people fled into the mountains.' She lifted her hand and pointed to a cleft in the rock faces, high above the valley floor, and he realised she was pointing to the pillars his people called the Twin Guardians of the Dead. Beyond them was a maze of caves where The Vale's dead were interred.

'Are you sure they fled into the mountains?' he asked.

'Yes,' she said. 'We came here, on the way north to close the Valley of Rivers off to the Haagii, after last winter.

417

Remember?' He couldn't remember. Had he given the order? Or A Ahmud Ki? 'We found the ruins the Haagii had left the summer before, so we imagined the people had been slaughtered like all the others. Because it was late in the afternoon, we camped here for the night. It's as well we did, because after dark the people came down from the mountain to see who we were.'

'Was there a tall, red-headed woman among them?' he asked eagerly.

She grinned. 'Your mother, Anedra? Yes.' Andra's eyes lit up at Marella's news. 'She came down, with several others who said they were the Council of Law, and they had warriors with them who wore ponytails and silver circlets like yours, Andra. I knew they were your people, so I told them that you were King now. No one believed me. I'm not even sure they did by the time we rode out the following morning.'

He gazed up at the Twin Guardians wondering if Anedra, and his father, Malcolm, were watching him now. 'I'm going up there,' he said.

'You can if you like,' she said, 'but Creon informs me there's already a party coming down to meet with us.'

'No. I can't wait. I'll meet them halfway,' he said anxiously, and clasped Marella's arms. 'I praise Teka you're still alive.' He released his grip and headed toward the hidden pathway in the southeast corner of The Vale that led up to the Time-Old burial grounds. As he crossed the village site, Marella's Haardrishii watched in astonishment when they learned from their leader the ragged warrior, who appeared from the woods, was their King.

Andra studied the faces around the warm fire burning in the centre of the cavern. Artega, the Guardian Master, was there, steel blue eyes glittering in the flickering light, his face lined, looking older, and his dark hair pulled severely in the traditional ponytail. Beside him Bryon squatted, looking like Artega's younger brother, except his features were flatter, his nose broader. Other Guardians Andra remembered sat with them: Mark, Renwith, and Karl who had hair like Claarn. With them was Erik. Andra saw his blond hair and smiling face, and it hurt and pleased him to be reunited with his friend, because Erik reminded him of Alain and Stephen who died in the slaughter on The Rim Shield. They spoke, but the intervening time had carved a great chasm between the two friends. One was a hard-bitten guerrilla warrior who'd learned to survive and fight the Haagii in the mountains, the other an increasingly worldly-wise King caught in a prophetic web he could no longer escape. They hardly knew what to say to each other, and behind the joy of meeting their eyes registered an unspeakable sadness.

Anedra's red hair shone in the firelight. She wept with joy when Andra met their party at the foot of the pathway to the Twin Guardians, and she embraced her son as if she would never release him. She, also, was caught between laughter and sadness, and, while Andra related the core of his tale to the listeners at the fire, she searched her son's face for traces of the child she'd borne into the world in the man who had become her King. She studied the crescent scar on his cheek and shuddered. When he was carried from the marshes by his father, his cheek slashed open by a root, she worried he would carry the scar on a handsome face, and be marked apart from other Guardians because of it, but no one guessed just how important the accidental scarring would become. Her son, a king, destined to fight the Dragonlord, was marked apart forever.

Malcolm was glad to have his son return. Andra apologised for losing Cedwyn's sword, when they first met at the base of path to the Twin Guardians, but Malcolm waived aside concern. 'A weapon can be remade. A son cannot,' he said philosophically, and warmly clasped Andra's shoulders. 'But the question is,' he asked, stepping back and looking around at the others gathered there, 'do I hug my son, or kneel before my King?' Andra grinned as he held out both arms to renew the old bond with his father. Like his wife though, Malcolm studied his son's face and eyes at the evening hearth, reading the changes the intervening years had wrought in the young man. The stories Andra told belonged to the ancient tales and ballads of heroes, yet now they were his experiences, his life. Like his wife, Malcolm studied his son, but saw a stranger.

There were expected faces missing from the fireside – Master Renfrey, Mistress Orlin, and others – slain by the Haagii in attacks and skirmishes throughout the summer months after he left The Vale. Master Flintok was dead. Age caught up with the old Task Master in his sleep. The Haagii savagely butchered Master Neldrin only days after Andra left his home. He'd seen death on a massive scale, since the Dragonlord's hordes invaded the Kingdom, thousands slaughtered on vast bloodied battlefields, but he never envisioned the bloody hand of death reaching so deeply into the secluded world he grew up in. It had, and The Vale was changed.

There were strangers too, faces he didn't recognise, people from other valleys and places throughout the Valley of Rivers who fled the Haagii to seek refuge in The Vale.

One new face sat with the Council beside Artega, a burly man with a greying beard and equally grey hair pulled back in a Guardian's ponytail. He was called Dominic, and he had the charismatic appeal and latent physical strength Andra associated with his memories of Guardian Master Artega. He wondered why the man was in The Vale, or why he listened with increasing interest to Andra's story when he told how Thana had been assassinated, or described A Ahmud Ki's role in events. Only later, when Anedra informed him that Dominic had come from Great King Thana's court, did Andra put the jigsaw together. Dominic was head of Thana's Haardrishii before A Ahmud Ki arrived, before the war erupted. Long ago, when Andra and his companions were led unwillingly from The Vale to serve in Thana's army, Andra learned that, before he came to The Vale, Artega was a Haardrishii warrior, and ex-High Lord Dominic had been his master.

In turn, Andra, Marella and the Haardrishii listened to the

tales of Artega and The Vale people in the ensuing wintry nights; of hunting for Haagii in the mountains after Gavin's burial, of returning to learn how the Haardrishii had come for the Guardians, of the Council's bitter decision to let four Guardians be spirited away to keep the majority in The Vale. Artega described the burning of the village, the running battles throughout the summer with Haagii, and the encounters with those who'd seen the Dragonlord's vast armies massed across Dragon Breath Plains. Through it all, the people of The Vale survived, determined not to fall prey to the Haagii.

Andra said nothing about fighting dragons, but when he was out of earshot Marella and her Haardrishii told how he fought the dragon at Cennednyss and the dragons at Andrakis. Eventually Artega, Anedra and the others asked Andra to show them Abreotan's sword, and they studied the ancient arcane Elvenaar runes on its ragged blade, saw its cruel curves and keen edge, and knew the prophecy to which Marella referred was true. Andra was Abreotan's inheritor. He was the One True King.

The days when the winter rains eased, the Haardrishii and every able-bodied person busied himself or herself with rebuilding the village. The bursts of activity alleviated the boredom of being confined to The Vale and lifted everyone's spirits. The Dragonlord's hordes might come again, and they might destroy the new village, but what they couldn't kill was the heart of the people. Anedra and Artega reminded everyone of that truth. By rebuilding from the ashes, they showed defiance and resilience, qualities of The Way. No amount of hatred or killing could suppress those qualities.

The first reconstruction was the new Hall of Council. Tree trunks and beams were set upright and lashed together by teams, and the roof tiled with wooden shingles. Anedra oversaw its construction, as Renfrey's successor, and when the hall was finished everyone entered and swore the time-old oath Andra remembered hearing his mother speak the first time he was admitted to the old Hall of Council. The tradition remained unbroken. The Haagii could not break it.

Within weeks, the village re-appeared, sprouting from the ashes as if raised by the rain. Its growth, and the cooperation among the workers, sealed a lasting bond of friendship between everyone involved.

Andra worked beside the others throughout the weeks, laughing at the jests and oaths made about a King dirtying his hands and talking with common folk, and revelling in the freedom the hard work generated. Around the fires in the caves at night, surrounded by memories and the dust of the people's ancestors, he renewed his friendships, especially with Erik, enjoyed the company of his mother, and grew increasingly fond of the dark-haired, brown-skinned Marella.

Against the other women and the girls who lived in The Vale, Marella was a strong, beautiful woman with a sharp-witted mind. She lacked the demure shyness of the other women her age because she knew Andra through the war, had shared its adventures, and knew how he earned Abreotan's inheritance. She respected him and talked with him as an equal. She was also the one link he had to his memories of Claarn, Tim and Sasha. What he was afraid of doing was falling in love with her. Though he felt closer to her with every passing day, he made himself resist his deeper passions, believing it wouldn't be right to take their relationship beyond the level of friendship and warrior respect. And he couldn't explain why. Perhaps it was because she had loved Claarn, and he carried guilt for his giant friend's death.

The guilt always returned to him at night. When the others drifted to sleep, he forced himself to stay awake, for as long as he could, to avoid the dreams. When he did succumb to sleep, his dreams were always the same. He stood with Abreotan's sword blazing, in a sea of Haagii warriors, and every time he swept the sword through his seething enemy he heard familiar voices cry out, and when he looked down there were the corpses of everyone he knew or had known – Tim, Claarn, Kara, Milly, Stephen, Liam, Derik

422

O'Dale. Whenever he tried to throw the sword away, a dragon would stoop from the churning clouds overhead and retrieve it, and its faceless rider would hand the sword to Andra. Always the rider laughed malevolently. Always the rider bowed to A Ahmud Ki, who stood on a rise above the battlefield, laughing at Andra's dilemma and mouthing the words, 'I hold the key' while beneath his dark hood his red eyes burned. And the sequence would start again.

The night air was bitterly cold. Andra stooped to leave the cave mouth, wrapping the sheepskin around his shoulders to keep out the chill, and shuffled along the narrow ledge connecting one cave entrance to the next. He slipped into a smaller cave, and felt several paces along the wall until he kicked a bundle of kindling he collected earlier that day. He squatted to blindly arrange the kindling, and summoned the sword to his hand. Its blade glowed with amber light. Andra touched the sword point to the slivers of wood, willing them to ignite, and they burst into flame. He leaned the sword against the cold cave wall and rubbed his hands together over the small, warm fire, satisfied to be alone again, outside the sleeping circles in the larger caves, and away from his nightmares.

'Wouldn't it be simpler to use the sword's heat?'

Andra turned to face the intruder's voice and saw Dominic, Artega, and Marella entering. 'I like the fire,' he said, as the three settled around it, crowding Andra's tiny space.

'You've been coming in here, alone, every night, for the past week,' Artega noted.

'Why, Andra?' Marella asked. 'What's wrong?' He peered at her concerned face across the crackling flames, but said nothing, so she glanced at Artega and Dominic, and continued. 'You didn't kill Claarn, Andra. Or Tim. Or anyone else.'

Her unexpected disclosure of his innermost torment shocked him. His eyes widened. 'How - what do you mean?'

he stammered.

'Your dreams,' Artega replied. 'You talk in them.'

'Sometimes you scream,' Marella gently confided. 'We've heard them for weeks, ever since we arrived.'

'Then you know the truth,' Andra admitted. 'You know I killed all my friends. All of them.'

'This A Ahmud Ki killed your friends, Your Highness,' Dominic quietly told him. 'Not you.'

'I let him do it. Through me.'

'Not of your own free will,' Marella argued. 'He used you, fooled you somehow.' She glanced at the gap on his left hand where his ring finger had been. 'Through the ring. There was nothing you could do.'

'I was too weak. I couldn't fight him,' Andra gasped, emotion swelling in his chest. 'Can't you understand that? I couldn't resist him. I couldn't save my friends when it mattered most. All this so-called power I've inherited from Abreotan, and I couldn't even use it to save my friends!' An anguished sob escaped, and he buried his head in his hands.

Marella stroked his hair. 'There was nothing you could've done for Claarn, Andra,' she said gently. 'I knew him. He was always taking a risk, always looking for glory. You knew that too. How many times did you have to save his life? He would've chosen to go after A Ahmud Ki in his own determined way if he'd returned. There was nothing you could have done. Perhaps, perhaps one day we'll know the truth about his death, how and where he died, but I'm certain you could not have killed my Claarn, Andra. He would never have let you. It's the Chancellor, not you, who carries the guilt.'

Andra lifted his red-rimmed eyes to stare into the fire. 'But he doesn't carry it. He has no conscience, no guilt. I should kill him. For Claarn. And Tim. And everyone.'

'Vengeance is a poor and hateful road to travel,' Artega cut in. 'It is not The Way of a Guardian. This A Ahmud Ki will bring about his own end soon enough.'

'I'd kill him if I could. I'd be fulfilling justice,' Andra said coldly, 'but I can't even do that.'

'Why not?' Dominic asked. 'What protection does he have from Abreotan's inheritor when even a Dragonlord should fear you?'

Andra looked at Surdrok's predecessor, as Lord of the Haardrishii before A Ahmud Ki's arrival in Thana's court. Dominic trained Artega. Artega trained Andra. The world moved in circles. 'He says he has the only key to Mareg's weakness.'

'Another of his lies,' Marella sneered.

'No,' Andra replied. 'This time I know he's telling the truth. I saw the truth in his face. I know I'm powerless without him as he is without me. I need his knowledge when I meet Mareg.'

'He's planted doubt in your mind. You know that's how he works,' Marella insisted.

'Not this time,' Andra asserted. 'He can't get inside my head ever again. I can stop him with the sword's magic. It's not his doubt, it's mine. I can't explain how I know. I just know A Ahmud Ki has a key to Mareg and I have to use it.'

Artega shook his head and stared into the flames. 'When you leave one place, to travel to a place you've never been before, the path you follow is the only certainty you hold, beyond knowing you have come from one place and you are going to another. The mysteries of life unfold like turnings, and junctions, and other pathways leading off from the one you follow. If you are lucky, there will be signposts to guide you on the true path. You may even learn, one day, that there is a shorter way to your destination. Then again, it may not be signposted, and you might pass by it, never knowing the shorter way existed. In the end, the essence of your life is not in reaching your intended destination, but in the journey. It is The Way.'

Andra gazed at the Guardian Master's shadowed face, analysing his words. 'Are you saying A Ahmud Ki is a signpost to a shorter way?' he asked after a moment's reflection.

'I know only the words of the teachings, Andra,' Artega answered, casting a glance at Dominic. 'Perhaps he is. Perhaps he is not.'

'You travel a dark road toward a bright goal,' explained Dominic, adding to Artega's view. 'Your journey's end shines with the light of prophecy. But how you get to that end is as unclear to you as it was to the prophets who foresaw your road. The only certainty you have is to travel it.'

Andra touched the crescent-shaped scar on his cheek, and felt its raised edge, its roughness against his smooth skin. A memory stirred deep in the recesses of his mind. He repeated something he'd heard Tim Gaelus mutter once. 'He will bear a sword of flame that will cut friend and foe alike.' Andra's three companions stared at him.

'What did you say?' Artega asked.

Andra's attention returned to the tiny cave. 'The prophecy,' he said, taking a breath. 'Tim mentioned it several times to me. It had an Aelendyell version as well. The wielder of the sword would hurt friends as well as enemies. It's true, isn't it? Abreotan's sword cuts both ways. To defeat the Dragonlord, I have to go to war against him, and sacrifice my friends in doing so.' He focussed on the flames of the small fire and watched a flame leap from one sliver of wood to the next, consuming it with a steady passion. 'I walk a bloodied path, whether I fight Mareg or run from him.'

'It is The Way,' Artega concluded. 'You know a Guardian cannot escape from his path once he has set foot on it. Even one footprint on a trail will tell others who passed that point. What is done is done. Your inheritance from Abreotan is the future. It is always the future. When the Valley of Rivers begins to clear, you will return to the Kingdom, as you must, and we will go with you.' Their eyes met, and what Andra saw in the Guardian Master's blue orbs was trust and respect, understanding and acceptance. Dominic and Marella wore the same expression. 'You are the King, Andra,' Artega reminded him. 'The Kingdom's fate lies with you.'

Andra was astonished to hear A Ahmud Ki's words echoed by the Guardian Master. Dark the prophetic road might be, he thought, but the signposts are everywhere.

Forty Four

The dragon lowered its brutal black head, until its jaw rested in the cool white sand on the cavern floor, and a golden eye gazed lazily at A Ahmud Ki. The Chancellor placed his left hand on the soft grey scales around the reptile's snout. 'Bored, aren't you,' he said to the supine beast. 'Eaten too many cattle, and now you have nothing else to do. I sometimes wonder why the old Dragonlords persisted with your species. You're greedy and lazy.' The dragon's inner eyelid slid across the golden pupil and back again. 'Even so, you're still the most formidable creatures in the Kingdom,' he added, wondering how well the dragon understood Kingdom language.

A Ahmud Ki cast a cursory glance over his four pets, three of whom were snoring in deep sleep, curled around each other like dogs. He levitated from the cavern floor, up the long central shaft, to the surface outside the Upper Palace.

He paused to study the sharp curved sculpture of the stone buildings he designed. Stonemason slaves and Ranu freemen had worked beauty and power into the shining white buildings, and A Ahmud Ki was proud of what he brought into existence. It surpassed anything in any of the lands he visited in his lifetime, even in Yul Ithrandyr, the Ranu Holy City of Light. When the winter clouds parted to let the sun peer on the Upper Palace, the white marble surfaces shone. In summer, the Upper Palace was sure to dazzle all fortunate enough to gaze upon it. It was a palace befitting a Dragonlord.

He crossed the open space, reserved for the new gardens between the Upper Palace and his black tower, passed through the tower wall, and ascended the levels to his Study chamber, where he slid onto his stool and opened a colourfully illustrated text he discovered among the books Waeron Ardath possessed.

Entitled 'A Circumspectual History of Dragon Kind', he originally dismissed it as one of many ill-informed tomes in Ardath's library, fanciful works hastily concocted by pseudo-scholars of the succeeding rulers since Abreotan, but it turned out to be more informative than most. It was translated by a court scribe, Eran of Aken, who lived one hundred and fifty years after Abreotan's death, directly from an earlier Elvenaar text that must have inadvertently fallen into human hands. A Ahmud Ki knew the Elvenaar rarely committed much to writing, their oral tradition being strong, so he assumed Eran stumbled across a script from an Elvenaar or Aelendyell Lore Book.

He was astonished to learn dragons had been far more potent creatures than the beasts Mareg and he held under sway. The oldest legends described creatures, called draca, who could not only fly and breathe fire, but who were vastly intelligent, who could cast spells and speak, who held the greatest power in the land, and who were feared and respected by the Dwarven, Elvenaar and other peoples. Changes wrought by the Dragonlords, who discovered how to subjugate the draca to their wills, through magic and specialised breeding, reduced the omnipotent draca to beasts of lust and killing to suit their twisted ends. The dragons became pets, albeit awesome ones, but they were shadows of their former glory.

The text was speculative, that was certain, but its explanations fitted A Ahmud Ki's understanding of things. The Dragonlords usurped the power of the dragons and turned their former superiors into their slaves. He enjoyed learning that fact. It showed the extent to which the Dragonlords went to gain power.

The golden axe sparkled in the magical sphere's light, as A Ahmud Ki turned the weapon in his right hand, feinted left, and swung down viciously on the Haagii's unprotected shoulder. The Haagii screamed and collapsed, blood gushing from a severed artery at the base of his neck. A Ahmud Ki wrenched the axe from his victim and kicked the Haagii onto his side, leaving him to thrash around on the stone floor as he bled to death. 'Clean that up,' he instructed three Royal assassins, as he strode from the tiny arena inside the Upper Palace toward Devi Cullan, a former dracabeorn from Dragon's Tooth restored to human form.

Cullan was an impressive human warrior, in the days before Abreotan's arrival, but Andrakis condemned him to the status of dracabeorn for failing to complete a menial task. As A Ahmud Ki approached, his golden armour shining, his face hidden behind the golden helmet, Cullan bowed low, as was expected of all Lord Ki's servants, and patiently awaited his bidding. His task was to teach his new master, Lord Ki, how to wield his golden axe.

'Well?' A Ahmud Ki asked, pulling his helmet off to let his silver-grey hair drop to his shoulders.

'Good, Lord Ki, very good,' Cullan said, lifting his head carefully, so as not to offend his master. 'Your timing and defence are much improved this week. But,' he added, having already learned it was better to tell Lord Ki the truth, and take the abuse that came with it, than to hold back, only to have the Lord pry his true thoughts from his mind, and beat him for it, 'your footwork is terrible, my Lord. You're lucky your opponent is a clumsy Haagii with no better weapon than a rusted old sword. Think more of your balance.'

'Show me,' A Ahmud Ki ordered, and threw Cullan the battle-axe.

While he watched the consummate warrior display his deadly art, and listened to Cullan's instruction, he reflected on the passing weeks. The game had changed significantly. Andra, having been released from the holding spell in the ring by the meddlesome child who Kara kept hidden in the old thieves' quarters, called his bluff on the plains of Ky. Only one other had done that – Mareg. The three of them were locked together for a final struggle.

His plans had gone awry, to a degree, with Andra regaining his freedom, but he knew the outcome at the end of everything would be the same. Inevitably, Andra would have to face Mareg, after winter passed. The errant King couldn't forsake the destiny shaped for him. He would return. A Ahmud Ki kept the Kingdom's massed force facing onto Dragon Breath Plains, wintering at the toe of the Abreotan Ranges, in readiness to march into Uz Erhaag as soon as the King returned from his little sojourn home. The golden Andrakian warriors, reinforced with Ranu riders and soldiers and Kingdom warriors, and backed by A Ahmud Ki's dragons, would follow the King and the Chancellor into the heart of Mareg's land, and force the Dragonlord to meet them in combat.

Three in one struggle and only one victor would emerge. He hadn't lied to Andra when he said he had the key to Mareg's destruction. What he hadn't admitted was Andra was the key. He would use Mareg and Andra to destroy each other. Mareg gave him a clue to Andra's downfall when he lured A Ahmud Ki into Se'Treya, the Dragonlords' traditional fighting ground: the more potent the magical object through which the Dragonlords passed to meet, the more potent the impact of their meeting. What better key to Se'Treya than Abreotan's sword, the most potent magical object created?

In the final confrontation, A Ahmud Ki would lure Mareg into the sword, on the pretext he was ready to do battle, his golden axe against Mareg's black axe, to resolve once and for all who was destined to be the One Ruler. Then he would summon Andra to join them. Two against one: what chance would Mareg have then? Together, they would slay Mareg, and if he planned it right Andra would also die with Andrakis' golden battle-axe buried in his back. The sword's magic, like all magic in Se'Treya, would be nullified and unable to protect him. That was why A Ahmud Ki practised daily, under Cullan's instruction. He only needed to be proficient with the battle-axe to make one deadly stroke on a man whose back would be turned, but because he wanted no chances taken he forced Cullan to teach him everything possible to learn in the short winter months while Andra was absent. Only he, A Ahmud Ki, must return from the inner plane of the sword's magic to claim his inheritance as the One Ruler.

Cullan's voice disturbed his thoughts. 'Try it, my Lord,' the warrior said. The Chancellor grinned as he took his axe.

You persist, don't you?

A Ahmud Ki received Mareg's cutting transmission and grinned back through the crystal communication sphere at the Dragonlord. Goes with the territory, he replied.

Mareg laughed contemptuously, his eyes burning red. You're still ignorant enough to consider yourself a Dragonlord?

No ignorance involved, A Ahmud Ki retorted. I know I am a Dragonlord.

Prove it then! Mareg taunted. Meet me in Se'Treya again. Then he laughed with a mocking sneer. Or was last time too frightening for you?

The time is coming, A Ahmud Ki calmly replied. I have Andrakis' battle-axe for when we next meet. And a better way to get there too. Interested?

Mareg laughed again. Of course I'm interested, you weak-minded idiot. I look forward to spilling your guts in the dust and spiking your pathetic head on a pike above the gates to Azikhaag.

As you wish, A Ahmud Ki replied. And I give the same promise to you. I'm more than happy to put your head above Azikhaag's gates as the final act of my inheritance.

Inheritance! Mareg flashed through the crystal. As if you, an Aelendyell bastard, could ever inherit anything more than horses' dung for power.

Don't prize your own power so lowly, A Ahmud Ki replied derisively. Mareg followed his remark with a string of obscenities that made A Ahmud Ki laugh aloud, until he saw Mareg laughing as well, and stopped. What amuses you? he asked.

No compliment intended, Ki, or whatever pretentious title you call yourself, but it's been a thousand years since I last bested a foe with some potential. If you weren't such a pathetic being, I could almost enjoy renewing the old traditions.

Meaning? A Ahmud Ki inquired, his curiosity aroused by Mareg's remark.

You wouldn't understand, Mareg curtly answered.

Try me, A Ahmud Ki persisted.

Mareg paused in reflection, his handsome face shifting expression from annoyance to fond remembrance. Then his red eyes flared, and he grinned. It doesn't matter what you know. You're a dead Aelendyell already.

A Ahmud Ki flinched at Mareg's reference to his bastard inheritance, but he projected a calculated question. It's about the battle games, isn't it?

Mareg's eyes narrowed angrily. How do you know that?

I consumed Andrakis' memories, remember? What he remembered, I remember. That's why I know about Se'Treya. Now I understand what it meant to your Dragonlords.

Then you tell me, Mareg challenged.

This time A Ahmud Ki grinned triumphantly. Andrakis remembered that there were six of you, including him and you. There was Estridin, and Karega. Abreotan slew them, I think. And Jeraboam Ka'Effrem Vatnashanika was slain in Se'Treya by you as a warning to the others that you were their rightful leader. And Shamaron disappeared over the seas, fate unknown, when Abreotan entombed you.

And? Mareg asked.

You used to play wars to amuse yourselves. You created your own armies of magically sustained super warriors and chained the dragons to your service to wage constant, endless battles across the face of the earth against each other. No one ever won completely. You all had a tacit agreement not to annihilate your enemy of the time, and if one of you looked like trying to go too far in a conquest against another Dragonlord the others used to interfere in the game to ensure a fairer outcome, so that balance was maintained. Am I right?

Mareg maintained silence, staring out of the sparkling

crystal, his eyes a glowing mirror image of A Ahmud Ki's red pupils. A Ahmud Ki studied his sombre expression and thought he witnessed the slightest hint of humanity in the Dragonlord's character, but Mareg glared vehemently and projected onto the Sphere of Thought, You won't replace Andrakis, Ki. You are no Dragonlord. You never will be.

I have four of your dragons, Mareg. Never forget that.

Mareg frowned, his anger mounting. The challenge is Se'Treya, he declared. Only a true Dragonlord can triumph there.

And I will, Mareg, A Ahmud Ki boasted. I will triumph over you. Be prepared to meet me there a final time when our armies face each other in Uz Erhaag.

I will ensure it is a final time, Mareg warned. For you, you Aelendyell bastard!

The crystal flared into brilliant white light, threatening to blind A Ahmud Ki as Mareg broke communication on the Sphere of Thought, and faded into milky chaos, before returning to inert opacity. A Ahmud Ki sat back on his stool, shut his eyes, and smiled with grim contentment at his planning.

Kara made every possible effort to avoid confrontation with the Chancellor after Andra escaped. With Andra gone, she fully expected the Chancellor to use whatever means he had to punish Milly and Aaron for their daring rescue, so she organised the Guild network to send immediate warning to her if the Royal assassins, or the Chancellor, or any stranger associated with him, were spotted anywhere near the old Maze ruins or the thieves' quarters in the plateau. She hid Milly and Aaron under Patti's care in the old Maze, having them shift quarters every two to three days to newly excavated, or reclaimed, sections of the underground system in a plan to confuse anyone who tried locating them.

She was, therefore, surprised when A Ahmud Ki made no overt effort to find Milly or Aaron, which in turn made her suspicious because his lack of interest had to be a screen to hide his real intentions, but as days became weeks, and the winter season moved through its cycle, she was increasingly convinced the Chancellor had no desire to find the children, or intended to take issue with her over Andra's release. She put his unusual change of heart down to the possibility it resulted from a meeting with Andra the day the Chancellor flew out of Andrakis on his dragon. Informants in the Upper Palace told her the Chancellor returned in a foul mood and locked himself in his black tower for three days, and when he emerged he seemed more intent on spending time with his dragons and learning how to wield a golden battle-axe.

Kara knew the Chancellor's weapon skills were limited, but she never guessed he would adopt an interest in weapons. Yet he had, and he gave no sign to anyone all winter that Milly or Aaron mattered to him, despite the catastrophic interference they must have made in whatever megalomaniacal schemes the Chancellor was brewing.

In the King's absence, there were no meetings of the King's Table. High Lord Lori wintered with his army in the north, and High Priest Argwyllyn was disinterested in political matters, being more concerned with establishing a flourishing flock of believers for the Ranu god, Berak N'eth. Marella, as far as Kara knew, was in the north with her Haardrishii. She was expected to return before the onset of winter, but she hadn't, and it was generally assumed her force was isolated from the plains of Ky by the unusually early wintry weather. Kara, however, like many of her friends in the Guild, couldn't help wondering if the Chancellor had arranged an unfortunate accident for Marella as he did for Tim, Sasha and Claarn.

Without the King's Table functioning, and in the King's absence, responsibility for decisions fell to those overseeing specific duties. Winter rains, snow, and bleak weather closed the Kingdom, making encompassing decisions of state unnecessary. Beyond that, everyone knew the passing of winter would plunge them into a final confrontation with the Dragonlord's forces, especially since the unspoken plan was to go on the offensive and march into Uz Erhaag. All they awaited was the return of their King, Aian Abreotan's Inheritor, the bearer of the sword, to lead them into the final phase.

Forty Five

'The King! The King returns!' shouted a guard from the castle's eastern wall. Warriors and servants deserted their posts and ran to see if the long-awaited news was true. Kara's messengers carried the news to her, and within moments most of the resurrected city heard the cry.

Staring east, people on higher vantage points saw a column of Haardrishii riding toward the city of Andrakis, the same company that rode north the previous spring to hold Mareg's forces at bay in the Valley of Rivers.

At the column's head rode four people. Those with the sharpest eyes recognised Marella's long dark hair flowing above her black armour, and the warrior beside her held Abreotan's sword upright in his right hand, shining like a beacon of power proclaiming his return. The two in the vanguard were not so easily recognizable. Both were stocky warriors, and neither wore Haardrishii armour, yet they tied their hair back in a ponytail, like the King.

When the two hundred strong contingent reached the outskirts, where new buildings were beginning to stretch toward the old city's outer limits, a rumour spread that a rider in the leading group was Lord Dominic, the Haardrishii Lord who left the Great City before the war. The Haardrishii were returning to Andrakis in full glory to fight beside Abreotan's inheritor, and to the superstitious and unbelievers alike that was a mighty omen.

A Ahmud Ki left his black tower to observe Andra's entrance when he received the news. The King was back: not before time, he considered. Winter had settled into a mild spring season across the Kingdom, and the Valley of Rivers, he estimated, must've been open to travel for at least two weeks, but the snow hadn't yet melted from Central Gate, meaning the King had reasons to delay riding north to join his army. As soon as Central Gate became passable, the King had to commit to marching. A Ahmud Ki intended to put that very proposal to Andra at the King's Table. High Lord Lori was waiting patiently for the order to head across Dragon Breath Plains, but his bored troops, especially the Ranu and Kingdom soldiers, were restless for action after the long wait over winter.

As A Ahmud Ki entered the marble beauty of the Upper Palace, he issued orders to the servants to prepare for an assembly of the King's Table, before he headed toward the new palace gates to meet the King.

People flocked into the streets to greet Andra, cheering, and bowing respectfully as he rode by, pleased he had returned. He couldn't help but see their smiling and relieved faces as he rode to the junction on the King's Way, and as he turned to head up Castle road the city's joyous welcome filled his heart with happiness.

He glimpsed the green common, bordering Dragon River, where he dipped his crown in the water on his coronation and stood before the people, swearing his Royal oath to serve them and rid them of the Dragonlord's menace. At the time, he was caught up in the euphoria of the event, but the promise he made was from his heart. He took on Abreotan's legacy, as well as his inheritance, but only since retreating to The Vale did he come to terms with the depth of his responsibility as King; the significance of his promise to the people.

Under Guardian Master Artega's training, he learned how important it was for a warrior to serve as a Guardian, protecting The Vale from intruders who sought to destroy its people and its heritage. As King, he was even more a Guardian, but now his home valley was the entire Kingdom, and his responsibility was to protect it, without condition or compromise. Nothing had changed at the heart of his life, except the scale of things. He was a Guardian. It was The Way after all, just as Artega said it would be.

A Ahmud Ki studied the faces at the King's Table warily, assessing their moods and likely disposition. High Priest Argwyllyn and Ranu Ambassador Saleem could be relied on, because his former dracabeorn slaves served obediently, forever grateful for their release from the dracabeorn curse, and acutely aware that Lord Ki could easily return them to their former shadowy existence. Lori's absence was unavoidably necessary, being in charge of the army. Lady Jasmin, representing Targa, would support anything A Ahmud Ki proposed, so long as Targa could continue logging the small forests at the edges of the plains of Ky.

The others, though, were unaccountably Andra's friends. Lady Marella's return was no real threat because A Ahmud Ki was certain she, as a warrior, would be eager to march against the Haagii. Lady Kara would be content to support that move so long as her precious Thieves' Guild was safe. Her self-interest will be her undoing, once this conflict is resolved, he decided, and I owe her for hiding the children.

One thorn in A Ahmud Ki's side was the unexpected return of Lord Dominic, and Andra's insistence he sit at the King's Table. A Ahmud Ki remembered the burly ex-leader of Great King Thana's Haardrishii as a man with a short temper affixed to his intense pride in his elite warrior-knights. His confrontation with Thana over the role of the Haardrishii in the opening stages of the Kingdom's preparation for war against Mareg, three years ago, was the first evidence A Ahmud Ki observed of the serious instability and disharmony existing in Thana's court, and it showed him just how easily Thana could be manipulated. Nevertheless, he sensed a change in Dominic's personality, a hint that the man had mellowed and might no longer be drawn into arguments based on pride. Is that possible? he wondered.

The other new member at the King's Table was introduced as Artega. A Ahmud Ki's recollection of Andra's memories identified Artega as the Guardian Master, the source of Andra's fighting skills and philosophical beliefs. A Ahmud Ki was disappointed. He imagined the Guardian

Master to be mystical, a warrior with perhaps a little understanding of a Ki, one of the sources of magic, but the taciturn, steely-eyed man at the King's Table had nothing exceptionally charismatic about him, from A Ahmud Ki's point of view. He certainly had the muscular profile of an agile, strong warrior, and a determined glitter in his eyes, but nothing suggested greater talent than that. Of course, he had learned not to underestimate people. Perhaps Artega was artful about the impression he created, and therefore hid his true strengths from others. 'Never show your enemy, or your friends for that matter, the full extent of your power. That way you always hold power over them,' was one of A Ahmud Ki's core maxims. He wondered if Artega adhered to that principle.

'Andra!' Milly cried, sprinting along the corridor toward the King. He bent and embraced her, as she threw herself into his arms, and she kissed him eagerly, forgetting the others gathered around.

'I swear, Andra, you'd best be heading off to war at once,' Jen grinned as she appeared, leading Patti's rotund figure who waddled up the corridor behind Jen, puffing with the effort to move her bulk quickly. Milly flushed at Jen's comment, and pushed away from the King, much to the amusement of Kara, Marella, Dominic and Artega.

'I'm just pleased he's back and safe,' Milly said emphatically. 'I care about him.'

'There's no doubting the lass does that,' Patti huffed, as she gave Andra a welcoming hug. 'She cares more about you, my young lad, than many a lover cares about living.'

'Hush you - you -' Milly cried in exasperation, unable to finish her plea.

Andra smiled at Milly and reached out to take her hand. She looked at the others, and accepted his hand, triumphantly poking her tongue out at Jen. Andra grinned and introduced her to Artega and Dominic. 'I owe Milly my life,' he explained simply.

Then he saw Aaron's fair head at the edge of the gathering in the corridor and beckoned to the youth. Reluctantly, Aaron squeezed between Jen and Kara, and stood before Andra. 'And this is Aaron,' he said, 'who also helped. I owe both of them my life. Without their courage, who knows what would have happened?' Aaron shuffled his right foot and looked embarrassed, and he avoided Milly's gaze.

'And don't forget Artega,' Milly said.

Andra looked down and saw the dog's dark eyes and his black tail wagging.

'Artega?' the Guardian Master asked, an eyebrow cocked suspiciously.

Andra grinned, a flush of embarrassment glowing in his cheeks. 'It's a long story,' he said.

'Let's not stand in a corridor to hear it. There's food and drink where we've been hiding out,' Patti interrupted, 'fit for a King!' she added with an exaggerated wink at Andra.

'And you think it'll take seven days to reach the main force?' Artega asked, hefting his elbows onto the table.

'Yes,' Andra answered, nodding. 'A full week.'

'No shorter way?'

Dominic leaned toward Artega. 'Seven days hard riding is the shortest way to the edge of Dragon Breath Plains.'

'And first we have to wait for the snows to melt in Central Pass? That could take weeks,' Artega objected.

'Possibly,' Dominic agreed. 'But it might only be days. The weather will dictate that outcome.'

Andra remembered the Dwarven highways under the Andrakian Mountains that Bear revealed when he led Milly and Andra to safety. It seemed an eternity had passed since that time. After Milly released him from A Ahmud Ki's ring, his memories returned in flashes of understanding, often sparked by casual references to places and ideas. They didn't need to wait for the snow to melt in Central Gate. 'I have another plan,' he announced. 'We'll leave Andrakis when I say, not when A Ahmud Ki says.'

'So, when do you intend to lead us out?' Artega asked, as he handed the mead jug across the rough-hewn wooden table to Patti.

'In three days. That will give everyone time to organise gear. But we'll travel light and quickly on horseback. Basic provisions only.'

'Three days?' Dominic repeated, raising one grey eyebrow. 'What will we do? Sit at the bottom of Central Gate pass and watch the snows melt?'

'No. We'll go under Central Gate. We'll use the old Dwarven highways.'

Artega and Dominic exchanged astonished glances. 'When did you learn of this?' Artega asked.

'A friend led me through them, a long time ago.'

'Can you remember the way in and out?' Marella asked quietly.

'Yes.' he said, as he summoned Abreotan's sword to his hand, and his smile widened. 'The sword will lead us, if I lose my way.'

'Can you really use the sword like that?' Patti asked, wiping mead from her lips with the back of her pudgy hand.

'Since Milly cut the ring from me,' he began, and cast an appreciative smile at Milly beside him, 'I've remembered and learned more than I thought I knew. Waeron Ardath told me I had to focus on the sword and make it do as I bid, because the sword is me and I am the sword. In The Vale, I finally understood what he meant. The sword's limitations are only what I let them be. Its magic isn't the magic of spells, like A Ahmud Ki must use, or the Dragonlord. The Elvenaar wove the magic of imagination into it. What Waeron Ardath was trying to tell me is I don't have to learn the sword's powers, one by one, I make them as I please. They come from my needs and my desires. I am the sword, just as Abreotan was.'

He was aware of the stares of his companions in the chamber's dim lantern light, and felt very self-conscious, as if his explanation tore a chasm between himself and his friends, the magic he barely understood separating him from

441

them forever. 'I don't really understand it all,' he apologised, 'but somehow I know that's how it happens.' His friends nodded and smiled, but he could see they were in awe of his power, even Dominic and Artega, who he considered his mentors, not his underlings.

Kara stirred in her seat near the door, and asked, 'Why so urgent about riding north?'

Andra was unsure how much truth and speculation he should share with his friends after their reaction to his confession about the sword. He wasn't certain his reasoning for heading north urgently was sound. The memory that prompted his desire to reach the forest nestled between the Abreotan Ranges and the Andrakians was a fragment that leapt to his mind mid-winter in The Vale; a vague notion that answers to his most haunting questions were stored in the heart of Dragon Forest.

One reason he wasn't sure of his memory was that, when he associated it with Dragon Forest the first time he recalled it in The Vale, he called the forest a different name altogether: Ethelreddor. But there were no maps identifying it as Ethelreddor. There was no Ethelreddor Forest in the entire Kingdom. Yet he knew intuitively, from the clarity of the portion of memory he retained, it was the forest beneath the Abreotan Ranges. 'I have to talk with someone important before we march against the Haagii,' he said.

'Who?' Marella asked curiously.

Andra unconsciously rubbed his left wrist and thought he felt the faintest suggestion of hard ridging under the skin. Memories fluttered like moths in his mind. 'I'm not sure I know,' he answered vaguely.

A Ahmud Ki observed the King's contingent winding westward toward the distant Andrakian Mountains. He could see Andra's golden armour glistening in the morning sun at the head of the small army, and Royal golden pennants rippled in the light spring breeze atop long ceremonial lances carried by two hundred Haardrishii. The plan was in motion. Abreotan's inheritor rode to meet the Dragonlord, as the prophecy promised. Within a week, the King would join the vast Kingdom army at the edge of Dragon Breath Plains and lead it across the grey waste into Uz Erhaag. Within a fortnight, the war would be decided. Mareg and Andra would be dead, and he would ascend to supreme leadership over the lands.

Who would be left to dispute his right to be the One Ruler, the One Overlord? No one. He held the Five Ki. He was the single inheritor of the Dragonlords' powers, and the only true potential impediment to his final ascension, Abreotan's sword, would be powerless without a wielder, its master dead on the battlefield of Se'Treya where no one but Dragonlords could travel.

A Ahmud Ki smirked, as a bright ray of sunlight sparkled on Andra's shoulder. Like a god, in his own golden armour, A Ahmud Ki would fly astride a dragon to The Rim Shield, in ten days' time, to meet the Kingdom's army when it arrived. He glanced from the battlements at his tower. Inside its magical walls, three dracabeorn servants eagerly awaited their release to fly the dragons with their master. In formation, they would sweep in, and strike awe in the hearts of friend and foe on the battlefield. He would give them a spectacle of his true powers, show everyone what he had learned and mastered, through all his years of running, and wandering, suffering exile and humiliation, study and experimentation, defying limitations, striving to meld together what four cultures held apart since Abreotan's time. By the time of the final confrontation, no one could doubt his power, and no one could deny it. Everyone, even Mareg and Andra, would understand why they should bow low before Lord A Ahmud Ki.

Forty Six

Every day that Andra rode north, memories stirred and returned like waking dreams, until the evening his company approached Dragon Forest, crouching beneath the rugged Abreotan Ranges. He reined in Firebrand, beyond the vast encampment of the Kingdom army and the welcoming party riding to meet him, to gaze upon the dark forest verge sweeping east, and murmured the ancient Elvenaar name, Ethelreddor, to the soft perfumed breeze the forest exhaled.

Obsessed with his desire to plunge into the forest's depths, he begrudgingly endured the ceremonial greeting arranged by High Lord Lori. The High Lord insisted on feting the King on the first evening, and a Royal inspection of the troops was planned for the following morning, but, impatient to be alone, Andra ordered the inspection to begin at first light, and arranged to speak with Marella and Dominic at the end of Lori's formal feasting.

'I won't be inspecting the soldiers in the morning,' he informed Marella and Dominic, who joined him in the pavilion erected especially for the King. 'You'll carry out the inspection in my place.'

'What?' Marella gasped.

'I have a very important matter to attend to tonight,' Andra hastily explained. 'There's a chance I might not be back in time to do as I've promised. I need both of you to cover for me in my absence.'

'What are you doing?' Dominic asked. 'You're the King. You can't just go off somewhere on your whim.' He glanced to his left as the entrance rustled and the Haardrishii guards let the Guardian Master into the yellow lamplight.

'If I am the King,' Andra replied with a courteous smile, 'then I can come and go as I please.'

'But where?' Marella asked.

Andra retrieved a green cloak from a peg on the central

pole. 'I'm going into the forest.'

'Tonight?' Dominic asked in disbelief.

Andra slipped on the cloak and handed a second to Artega. He tightened his belt buckle and checked Abreotan's sword was secure. 'Yes,' he said.

'Why?' Dominic persisted.

'To find answers to questions I've been asking for a long time.'

'How?'

Andra shrugged and replied, 'I don't entirely know. All I remember is there's a place in the heart of Ethelreddor where I must go. And now the time is right to go.'

The sword's light threw distorted shadows across the gnarled trunks of the ancient elmoaks, holding the black unknown of the surrounding forest at bay. Before they plunged into Ethelreddor, Andra remembered the precautions Derik O'Dale and the Longbowmen took, and fashioned rough discs to fit over Artega's and his boots. Without the discs, the treacherously deep and soft leafy mulch underfoot in the forest would seriously hamper their progress.

'Can you feel it?' Artega whispered, as they moved forward in the sword's halo of light. 'The air. It moves. Like the forest is - is breathing.'

Andra felt the gentle air movement on his cheeks and remembered Alain's observation when they entered Ethelreddor the first time. Very little had changed. He noticed the devastation of the forest's margin from the Haagii invasions, but less than five hundred paces in the scorched and hewn patches abruptly ceased and the thick forest growth flourished as if it was impervious to Haagii fire and blade. He recalled Marvin's assertion the forest put out torches if anyone lit them. Perhaps Ethelreddor resisted the Haagii with its own magic.

'Do you know how far you have to go?' Artega asked, as they clambered over a gigantic tree root that rose from the forest floor like a serpent breaching river water.

'No,' Andra replied absently. He didn't see the Guardian Master's resigned expression, and pushed on, following the mulch-littered paths, dragging Artega in his wake, deeper into the ancient forest.

At a point where the surrounding tree trunks and interlocking branches, and foliage, formed a great natural hall, Andra paused and said, 'This is the place.'

Artega studied the vast forest hall, appreciating the majesty and beauty of the sanctuary hidden in the forest's heart because he'd never seen such a place in his travels, before becoming Guardian Master of The Vale. The girths of the trees were easily the span of thirty warriors' arms. The trees in the Valley of Rivers were children compared to the ancients forming this hall.

Andra stared at the vacant centre and a memory of his black pup asleep on the forest floor flashed into focus. There were answers hidden here. Something, no, someone else was left here. Marvin's serious face, framed by his blond hair, flitted through his thoughts. This was the place he was seeking. But what was here?

As he slipped out of his reverie, he was aware of the first sign of life, other than themselves and plants in the forest, when a huge moth, its wingspan twice the breadth of Andra's hands, fluttered aimlessly across the arc of the sword's light, its buff wings dappled with tan and green pigments. Motionless, it could blend against a trunk and be invisible to casual passers. How many such moths were pressed against the trunks they passed?

'Andra. To your left.'

He obeyed Artega's quiet warning and turned to a blue halo glowing on a trunk. In the blue haze, he saw a naked maiden, smiling and beckoning.

'Do you see her?' Artega whispered.

'Yes,' Andra replied. 'Close your eyes.'

Perplexed by the instruction, unaware of the danger inherent in the vision, Artega attempted to turn toward Andra, but to his horror he was unable to draw his gaze from the beautiful nymph in the blue glow. 'I can't,' he groaned. 'I can't, Andra.'

Andra saw the charm trap Artega. The Guardian Master's face relaxed and creased into a warm smile, and he walked toward the light, unable and unwilling to resist the nymph's attraction. Andra concentrated on Artega through Abreotan's sword. One step later, Artega was bathed in a lavender wash from the sword and he faltered, lifting his hands to rub his eyes, as if waking from a long and tiring sleep. Andra ceased the sword's spell and went to his old master.

Artega shook his head and looked up at Andra with a puzzled expression. 'What happened?'

'You were charmed by a Tree Keeper. She didn't mean you any harm, but if I hadn't broken her spell you'd have walked straight into her tree,' Andra explained. The vision wakened more of his memory. Now he understood what led him to this place.

Artega was more baffled by his explanation. 'Tree Keepers? What do you mean?'

'Stay here and wait for me,' Andra instructed the Guardian Master. 'I don't know how long I will be. Here,' he said, unhitching his small food bag and water skin, 'Keep these. I won't need them in Tree Home.' He ignored Artega's concerned and confused expression. 'Above all, while I'm gone, don't stare at any blue glows,' Andra added, though a faint smile drifted across his mouth. He headed for the pale blue aura glowing on the tree trunk and entered as if stepping through a door. The light vanished.

The forest hall sank into preternatural darkness that flowed in and threatened to drown the Guardian Master. He congratulated himself on hiding inside caves in the long fight against the Haagii in The Vale during the war, because the experience meant he could concentrate on relaxing in the pervading darkness without Andra's sword for light. Sounds magnified. He heard groans and creaking emanating from the trees, and the soft chatter of moths' wings as the insects shifted trunks in the darkness. His breathing seemed excessively loud in the silence.

What he marvelled at, as he adjusted to the gloom and isolation, was how much Andra, the raw Guardian he barely finished training in The Vale, had changed. Here he was, Guardian Master, barely three years later, waiting in the darkness like a lost apprentice for his master to return from a magical world he hadn't imagined to exist, and Andra strode into it as if entering magical worlds was a common practice. As much as The Way tried to reason the various paths of life, no one could ever predict where those paths led. It could only suggest a way of travelling. Now he was witnessing the truth of his teachings, and it filled him with awe.

'You expected me to return,' Andra realised, as he lowered the crystal goblet Hyacinth handed to him.

'You are the One King of All People, the One Who Bears the Mark of the Moon,' she replied with a smile. 'The prophecies are true. You were expected.'

'But A Ahmud Ki's spell ring nearly destroyed me,' he argued. 'Or was that part of the prophecy?'

Hyacinth shrugged, the sheer garment she wore shifting softly across her body, catching the sheen of the amber light permeating Tree Home. 'The Chancellor's ring failed.'

'Only because Milly cut off my ring finger,' Andra indicated, holding up his left hand for her inspection. His missing finger drew gasps from the six nymphs sitting in the chamber.

When he glanced at them, noticing their long, braided hair after the fashion of their Aelendyell cousins, more memories quickened. Hyacinth told him important details about the Kingdom's history the last time he visited – how the Elvenaar came, and humans, and the Dragonlord Wars, until Abreotan's bloody but triumphant victory over them all. He recalled the covenant Hyacinth and her sisters sealed between the dying trees and the last Elvenaar by sacrificing their lives to the task of tending the trees. He remembered his disbelief at being surrounded by a world of magic he never imagined could exist. So much had changed.

'The human girl did you a great favour,' agreed Hyacinth, 'but you wear Dyrenthanya's Bracelet to enable you to draw the sword from its protecting glyph. It also would've protected you from the Chancellor's magic.'

Andra stared at Hyacinth. 'I wear wha -?' he began to ask, but he stopped abruptly to examine his wrist. A spider web thin circle of silver-amber metal gleaming in the soft amber light jogged deeper memories. He remembered the nymph who slipped it onto his wrist. He remembered studying it, back in his human world, and then it disappeared, becoming nothing more than a hard impression under the top layer of his skin, a sensation, a barely perceptible presence he no longer understood or remembered. Now the links rose into focus. 'The mist,' he muttered, comprehending the possibilities. 'The bracelet you gave me was fighting the Chancellor's magic, preventing him from fully controlling me.'

She nodded. 'It is a gift we held in trust when our fathers offered us to become the Tree Keepers. The Alfyn knew the prophecy, and they interpreted it for the Elvenaar. They said that one day the chosen warrior would stumble into our world and when he did we would recognise him by the moon scar, and they told us we had to give him Dyrenthanya's Bracelet to protect him from the Dragonlords.'

'But why didn't you tell me all this then?' he asked, mystified by the revelation.

'Because you weren't ready,' she told him. 'You were a youth who blushed at the sight of our bodies. You weren't the One King. You were barely a warrior, and hardly a man.' Embarrassed by her frank comment, his cheeks flushed, but he didn't turn away. 'Now,' she continued, 'everything has changed. You are ready to face the Dragonlords as it was always intended you should.'

'Dragonlords?' he asked in astonishment. 'You talk as though there's more than one.'

'There are,' she confirmed. 'But you already know that.

The worst is the one who pretends to be your friend.'

A Ahmud Ki, thought Andra. Mareg and A Ahmud Ki. Two Dragonlords meeting on the battlefield to come, and I am destined their nemesis.

'It is time you were told the whole prophecy, the full vision that fate denied the generations following Abreotan's reign,' she said, and nodded to a companion nymph who rose and withdrew. 'Place the sword on the ground, point toward you,' Hyacinth instructed.

Andra summoned the sword and laid it along the chamber floor, where the rune-impregnated blade seemed stained with the amber magical light.

The nymph Hyacinth sent away re-entered, carrying a tiny silver flask, which she passed to Hyacinth before resuming her seat. Hyacinth uttered a string of words in a lilting, musical language Andra faintly recognised as Aelendyell from his time in Wynwuduholt, yet he sensed it was an older tongue because the words lacked meaning, despite their familiar structure. The Tree Keepers were the last Elvenaar, he reminded himself, immortalised in Tree Home by their people's magic for a thousand years.

As Hyacinth finished chanting, she removed the stopper in the neck of the silver flask and carefully poured a watery green liquid on the sword's blade. Where the liquid touched the blade, a sequence of light-enhanced fumes erupted, coiling and circling, until they wove into the fragile features of an old, silver-haired sorceress, her hair intricately braided in Aelendyell fashion, her almond-shaped eyes the deepest blue. The face hovered in the air between Hyacinth and Andra, gazing on the young King.

'Who -?' he tentatively began to ask.

'Ythysandranyll, High Sorceress of the Ethelreddor community,' Hyacinth answered, and added, 'my grandmother.'

'What is -'

'Shh!' the Tree Keeper ordered with a finger against her lips.

From the smoke-woven face, a quietly spoken woman

addressed him, a voice Andra decided came from a younger woman than the elder floating before him, and the woman's eyes glittered as she began her oration, though her face was grim and haggard. 'When the moon-faced warrior rides against the Dragonlords in the days to come, the sources of magic will be consumed and destroyed. The vengeful sword will sweep away the Dark Ones a final time and be consumed in consuming, it being the last relic of true Elvenaar power. As we've always known, that which sustains our life, the essence of magic, also feeds the dark lust of the Dark Ones. With the sword, we too will be destroyed. Without the sword, we will cease to exist. In it are the secrets of all magic. All that will remain, when it is nothing but a broken dream on an empty battlefield, will be the last fading rays of our setting sun, the last generations of the Elvenaar descendants, and in a short time, no more than two or three generations, they will lose the secrets of the old powers and become nothing more than memories in an alien world. The world to come, beyond the days of the Dragonlords, is a human world, a world without true magic, without true beauty or harmony. We have seen this to be true and know it will come to pass.' The aged face dissipated.

Tiny wisps of smoke drifted and vanished against the green glow of the ceiling, leaving Andra staring at Hyacinth. He thought he saw the sparkle of tears in the corners of the Tree Keeper's eyes, so he broke her steady gaze and studied the blade. The sword was a far greater burden than he imagined. 'I carry the key to the existence of all magic,' he murmured.

'To all Elvenaar magic,' Hyacinth gently corrected. 'There are other sources, weaker sources, other magics. And there were other keys, though I guess they are all gone by now.'

'Like the Orb of Radiance?' he asked. She didn't answer his question. He wondered if she knew how and when Mareg's Sharvan assassins destroyed it. He wasn't there. Tim told him the story. Like the pieces of a child's puzzle, he was drawing together the fragments of the world and magic he was trapped at the centre of.

What he kept to himself was his assumption, from Ythysandranyll's prophetic message, that he appeared destined to perish when he killed the Dragonlords, destroyed along with Abreotan's sword and all remnants of Elvenaar magic. Waeron Ardath told him he was the sword. If it was doomed, then logically so was he. The bond of magic united them. The inevitable could not be avoided. His destiny was marked for him and he had no choice but to seek it, resolved and ready.

He smiled at Hyacinth and her Tree Keeper companions. 'Then you've always known that I would come bearing the end to Tree Home and the covenant you hold.'

'We have always known,' Hyacinth replied softly. She cast an unusually shy glance at her companions. 'That is why we gave you what protection we could and what guidance we have to offer. These are things that will be because they must be. To all things, there are ends, even as there are beginnings.'

As it is, reflected Andra. As it is.

The Guardian Master leapt to his feet when he saw the soft blue glow form on the tree trunk and strode eagerly toward Andra as the young warrior King emerged, bearing Abreotan's sword like a shining lantern. The vision touched Artega's sense of duty, formed in his years as a Haardrishii warrior, and solidified in his later role as Guardian Master of The Vale. He dropped on one knee and bent his head. 'My Lord and my King,' he whispered harshly.

Andra set a hand on Artega's shoulder and drew his former master to his feet. 'Only those who need to beg my forgiveness, or fear my anger, will ever kneel to me, Guardian Master,' he explained with solemn reverence. 'And you, my friend, will never need do either.'

Artega cast an appreciative glance at the young man and smiled approval as he stood.

Andra saw Artega's expression, as he turned to lead him from the ancient forest hall of Tree Home, and inwardly warmed to his old master's acknowledgement. He was luckier than most, he decided, because his path was illuminated, its purpose and ending clear. Though he carried the double-edged sword of Abreotan, the death-blade that would sweep aside good and evil magic with the slaying of the Dragonlords, the weapon and key to the last Elvenaar magic and all it created, he was finally at peace, knowing through Ythysandranyll's prophetic vision that in the end it was The Way, as it always was meant to be for Andra. He strode out of Tree Home ready at last to embrace his destiny.

Forty Seven

Andra watched the dragon formation sweep across the summits of the brooding Fire Mountains. When the four black creatures banked and circled low across the sheer cliffs of The Rim Shield, he half-expected them to land, but they turned sharply toward the Kingdom army and glided gracefully down. They flapped their enormous wings, to slow momentum, and the downdraft pushed a curtain of grey, choking dust into the air.

The chaos caused by the dragons' arrival subsided as quickly as the dust itself, and the warriors nearest the beasts encircled them, ogling in dread and wonder, but remembering to keep a narrow space for safety. Shadowy forms clung to the necks of three dragons, while on the fourth sat a warrior in golden plate, resembling King Andrakis' in every detail except the armour had brutal spikes and razor-sharp edges adorning its joints and flat segments. A massive golden battle axe hung from the warrior's belt, its twin-bladed head gleaming in the morning sunlight.

The warrior unbuckled a black leather safety harness bridling the dragon's neck and slid casually from his mount. He paused to study the curious throng peering at him and lifted his golden helmet, letting his silver-grey braided locks tumble to his shoulders. A mixed gasp of relief and excitement rippled through the crowd, to become a cheer, as everyone recognised the Chancellor. The four dragons, curiosity aroused by the clamour, lifted their reptilian heads, and their movement quietened the outburst as the front row of people felt vulnerable so close to the fire-breathing, brutal jaws.

The circle parted to A Ahmud Ki's left, allowing High Lord Lori and a dozen Ranu Guards to enter. The High Lord prostrated himself in the dust before A Ahmud Ki, and his retinue followed his example, pressing their foreheads against the soft grey surface of Dragon Breath Plains. In the crowd, other Ranu warriors lowered themselves out of respect for the Chancellor, but the Kingdom warriors bowed, as much out of confusion from the reaction of their Ranu companions as from any genuine fear or respect for A Ahmud Ki.

Andra led Artega, Marella, and Dominic through, as warriors parted and bowed to the King, and entered the space before A Ahmud Ki.

A Ahmud Ki watched the King approach and bent his head very slightly to show the minimum respect. 'Greetings, Your Majesty,' he said, with a congenial smile. 'As promised, I've come to join you. But I expected we would meet on the escarpment, not here in the dust.'

'The Haagii were waiting for us,' Andra replied. 'The Rim Shield is the greatest defence Uz Erhaag and the Kingdom have against each other. Where else would the Haagii choose to meet us? Here, they hold the advantage.'

A Ahmud Ki looked over the heads of the warriors toward the cliff and the rugged pinnacles of the Fire Mountains rising above it. Mareg was cheating. The Dragonlord was going to use every wily manoeuvre at his disposal to wear down A Ahmud Ki's forces before there would be a final confrontation. He grinned at the idea. There was no point complaining. After all, if he was Mareg, he would do the same.

'What amuses you?' Andra asked.

A Ahmud Ki remained studying The Rim Shield as he answered the question. 'I was thinking how much I'm going to enjoy meeting Mareg on the battlefield. He must be very scared to know his doom is approaching, especially if he has to resort to petty tricks like this.'

Andra knew A Ahmud Ki's reference to Mareg's doom was to himself and the sword. Doom was approaching, not just for Mareg, but also for A Ahmud Ki. He studied the Chancellor's finely chiselled features, his hairless chin, high cheekbones and oval eyes, and his braided silver-grey hair. When he first saw A Ahmud Ki as Thana's Royal Advisor, three years ago, the Chancellor had a dark, neatly trimmed beard, and his Aelendyell features, though recognizably non-human, were muted compared to the faces of true Aelendyell, like Mirith and Terath. The changes, for there were significant changes, made the Chancellor's face finer, more handsome, identical to the features of the Elvenaar sorceress who Hyacinth conjured from the rune on Abreotan's sword in Tree Home. The sorceress confirmed the prophecy's wording that there was more than one Dragonlord, and confirmed for Andra that A Ahmud Ki was the second Dragonlord.

Not that Andra could doubt the evidence. Mounted on his dragon, wielding spells, wearing Andrakis' golden armour, A Ahmud Ki's metamorphosis into Elvenaar form all but complete, and the ever-present red energy glittering behind his grey Aelendyell eyes, Andra knew he was gazing at a reincarnation of a Dragonlord. A Ahmud Ki even revealed to him that he conquered the entombed Dragonlord Andrakis Va'ristrin Nyavardenet in the catacombs of Andrakis' fortress, but now Andra wondered who really had conquered who; who really controlled the outer husk of the being bearing the name A Ahmud Ki?

'Your Majesty?'

Andra blinked and realised A Ahmud Ki was staring directly at him with his cold, calculating eyes.

'You were thinking?' A Ahmud Ki asked, suspicion in his tone.

He knew A Ahmud Ki would no longer dare use mind spells on him to satisfy his curiosity, not so long as the Chancellor knew he could repel mental invasion at will with the aid of the sword. 'We have to plan an assault on The Rim Shield,' he replied, altering the topic of conversation. 'We arrived, yesterday afternoon, well-provisioned, but the sooner we get off this dusty graveyard the better. I suggest you order your servants to see to your dragons and meet with us in the pavilion immediately.' Andra looked down at High Lord Lori and his guards, whose foreheads were still pressed against the dust before A Ahmud Ki. 'I expect to see you there as well, High Lord Lori. Your opinion will be appreciated,' he said with a slight hint of irony, recognising who really served who in the chain of command. He gave A Ahmud Ki a direct look and turned toward the pavilion where the King's gold pennant drooped in the listless air.

'Andra?'

He turned to the dark shadow beside him, on horseback, where Marella ought to be. 'What?' he asked.

'Do you trust the Chancellor?' she whispered.

'No,' he replied. 'But we need him against Mareg, and he needs us.'

'What if he betrays us?' Her question hung in the dark silent pre-dawn air.

'He won't.'

'How can you be sure?'

'I'm not. I just don't think he will.' Andra felt Firebrand chafing at his bit and listened to the comforting sounds of horses snorting and moving restlessly in the cold, still morning air. To the east, on the flat, distant horizon, darkness was fading.

'He's a Dragonlord too.' Marella's words carried, despite her whisper.

Andra hadn't considered the possibility Marella's statement implied. Was that the Elvenaar sorcerer's warning? Was it possible the two Dragonlords might unite against Abreotan's heir, in a desperate bid to stave off their deaths? 'I know,' he said, but his attention was diverted, before he could explain why he knew, by a sound from his left. A horse approached. He heard its hooves crushing the soft invisible dust before he saw the shadow loom out of the darkness.

'They've left,' a voice informed him, as the horse and Haardrishii rider drew alongside.

'Then we're ready,' Andra said, but, within, he began to wonder when he would have to face and fight the first Dragonlord.

The light in the east quickened, filling that portion of the sky with vague patches of gold and purple and pale amber, heralding the swiftly approaching sun. Andra focussed on the dark line of The Rim Shield that was punctuated with small fires kept burning by the waiting Haagii. There was no sign of Mareg. But he remembered the last time the Great Armies of Thana gathered on Dragon Breath Plains no one even guessed at the resources Mareg had gathered to throw at them — innumerable warriors, darkness, and dragons. Death. What, Andra wondered, lies up there this time?

A ball of flame erupted on the western end of The Rim Shield, and a second, a stream of yellow fire, swept the earth where the Upward Road reached the top. Two more fireballs exploded at the base of The Rim Shield, deep in the ranks of the enemy camp.

Inspired by A Ahmud Ki's fiery signal, the front ranks of the Kingdom army, the Ranu riders and Andrakian knights, spurred across the dusty gap and plunged into the Haagii. A Ahmud Ki's dragons made a final pass across the base, lashing the terrified enemy with gouts of dragon fire, before turning their attention on the warriors and catapults assembled on the cliff top.

Andra summoned Abreotan's sword, and the blade burst into bright light as he held it aloft to lead the second wave. With a defiant roar, the warriors on foot charged into battle.

The Kingdom army seized the initiative. A Ahmud Ki's dragons broke the spirit of the Haagii defenders, and the Andrakian knights, their courage and ability to withstand pain enhanced by Dragonlord magic, overwhelmed the enemy at the cliff base. Pockets of Haagii resistance held out against the mortal Ranu soldiers, and the Kingdom warriors who joined the battle beside their King suffered losses, but the Haagii steadily succumbed as the press of numbers turned against them.

One dragon rider began scouring the Upward Road, swooping and burning Haagii foolhardy enough to attempt to descend to aid their fellows, and catching those unfortunate enough to flee the slaughter. The way up opened quickly. At the head of the Kingdom army, High Lord Lori organised the Andrakian knights to lead the advance to the top. Andra spurred Firebrand on and joined them, and Marella marshalled her Haardrishii to follow.

They met no resistance on the ascent. Charred and smouldering corpses clogged the road where the dragon struck. Throughout the steady climb, memories flashed through Andra's mind: memories of the fighting press, the struggle he was caught in the first time he was here. Thana's Great Armies fought for every bloodied space of ground, leaving the road awash with their blood as much as with the enemy's.

And he remembered the horrible silence that met them at the top, when Mareg's dark Haagii tide ran down from the valleys of the Fire Mountains with the dragons to sweep Great King Thana's warriors aside like flotsam. Were the Haagii waiting like that again? He remembered the startled face of A Ahmud Ki's Apprentice who saw him wielding Cedwyn's sword, and he remembered Claarn's anguish when Mareg's Dark Warriors refused to fight the handful of survivors who resolved to fight to the death. Claarn ought to be here, he thought. He should've been alive to witness our return to The Rim Shield.

The front ranks crested the lip, just as morning sunlight chased the last vestiges of night from the sky and replaced them with a pale blue wash that promised to deepen with the day. The rugged Fire Mountains reflected the sunlight in flashes of red and gold streaks along their ash-darkened volcanic faces, colours that contrasted sharply with the treeless, grassless broad valley the Andrakian and Ranu warriors rode onto.

A Ahmud Ki's dragons circled a thousand paces to the east, diving and climbing over a dark mass, and the ground between was littered with the burning wreckage of carts and siege machines, and hundreds of corpses. Haagii warriors gathered in tight defensive knots, preparing to fight the approaching Kingdom army, while smaller groups and individuals wandered aimlessly through the devastation, stunned by the ferocity of the dragon attack.

High Lord Lori reined in beside Andra and bowed low. 'With Your Highness' permission, I will take the Andrakian knights and pursue the enemy where Lord Ki is fighting.'

Andra agreed. 'Do that. I'll see the remaining enemy here are dealt with before I join with you further east.' The High Lord bowed from the waist and led the golden knights toward the main battle.

Andra returned Abreotan's sword to its scabbard and dismounted from Firebrand. He surveyed the reaches of the valley for hint of further attack, not yet willing to believe Mareg's army had been driven off so easily, but no smudges darkened the bare slopes and no dark clouds broiled menacingly in the sky. If he kept looking up, away from the carnage spread across The Rim Shield, he could easily believe it was a fresh, bright spring morning in the Kingdom, a long way from war.

Marella rode toward him. Beyond her, to the west, he heard shouting, and the ring of metal striking metal, as the warriors arriving at the top attacked isolated and desperate Haagii groups who still had fight left in them. 'Claarn should be here,' she said, leaning from her saddle, as she reined in.

He looked up and smiled. 'I was thinking that on the way up,' he admitted, 'but he would have been disappointed.'

Marella studied a spot on the valley floor where the fighting had become more serious, judging from the sound of the cries echoing there. A party of her Haardrishii rode toward the trouble. 'Too easy,' she said, without turning her attention from the skirmish.

'Exactly,' Andra agreed. 'Mareg did this to annoy us. He could've amassed a far more powerful force and made taking this barrier a long and bitter struggle. There were no Dark Warriors or dragons.'

'Then he's playing a calculated game,' she said, as she faced Andra.

Another voice broke across their conversation as two more horses cantered toward them. 'This Mareg is trying us out!' called Dominic, as he slowed his horse. 'Learning the potential of our army.'

'Good tactics,' said Artega, as the pair reined in beside Marella. Andra turned to peruse the distant battle where A Ahmud Ki's dragons circled. They'd ceased swooping. High Lord Lori and his knights were finishing off the few who hadn't retreated.

'He'll learn a lot from this encounter,' Marella remarked. 'He'll know he's not just facing Abreotan's Inheritor.'

'Somehow,' Andra said quietly, 'I think he already knows who he's facing. I think he's just finding out how strong his opponent is.'

'You? Or our army?' Dominic asked.

'Neither,' Andra replied and turned his eyes to the east. 'Him,' he said simply.

All four turned to watch a dragon gliding toward them out of the morning sun. The rider glowed gold.

Mareg's forces harried the Kingdom army throughout the six days it took to march east along The Rim Shield, and through the only pass north into Uz Erhaag. The Haagii attacked frequently and quickly, intent more on setting equipment alight and destroying goods than on causing injury, so Marella set the Haardrishii on constant watch. The specialist Kingdom warriors caught several Haagii raiding parties before they could attack the army's camps, but enough Haagii got through their defending net to wreak havoc during the nights. Mareg was intent on waging a war of attrition and nerves.

Each night, Andra called together High Lord Lori, Marella, Artega, Dominic, and A Ahmud Ki to assess their progress and review the plans. Andra noticed the Chancellor had very little to say at the meetings, except if mention was made of tasks or plans that directly concerned him or his dragons, at which point he intervened and determined the action that best suited him.

On the seventh morning, the Andrakian knights led the army onto a broad, rolling, treeless pasture, its sightline broken by unusual rock formations jutting between two to thirty arm spans out of the ground, especially on hillocks. Close inspection of one rock formation revealed it to be the ruins of a building corner, and the mound around it, when the grass and soft earth was scratched away, concealed rubble. The granite rock was hewn into long flat slabs to serve as building blocks, but the ruins were ancient because wind and rain had softened the slab blocks and blurred their outlines.

'What was this place?' Artega asked, as they rode past the remnants of a stone column defiantly standing above a rise like a weathered and calloused finger. 'It spreads in all directions. Was it a city?' His question went unanswered.

Andra surveyed the ruins, as they rode northwest, and wondered who built so vast a city on the plains of Uz Erhaag. Perhaps the Haagii knew. Whoever built it, and lived there, perished a very long time ago, perhaps even before the Dragonlords and Abreotan's time. It was a mystery, and a warning that time would conquer all things.

They passed hastily deserted villages, Haagii villages abandoned in advance of the Kingdom army. There were plenty of signs that a large Haagii army was retreating ahead of them in the discarded baggage and campfire ashes marking their path. Andra knew it was standard practice the Haagii utilised to draw their enemy into a trap. That was how Mareg sealed the fate of ten thousand warriors of Great King Thana's Armies at The Rim Shield three years before. He lured them across the treacherously dry Dragon Breath Plains and cornered them at the base of The Rim Shield, until their water ran out. Then he mercilessly slaughtered them. The signs were clear to Andra the major confrontation was coming.

At dusk, the army reached an unusual landmark that cut north-east to south-west across the vast plain; a two thousand paces wide river valley that bit deep into the earth to form a natural amphitheatre. A very shallow, tree-lined creek meandered through its centre. Beyond the valley, the plain melted into a low range, studded with trees and natural rocky outcrops that looked ominously like a waiting army in the fading light.

Andra ordered the Kingdom army to set up camp on the southeast ridge overlooking the valley and instructed Marella to send a party of Haardrishii across the valley to reconnoitre the neighbouring hills. Then he waited for A Ahmud Ki to settle his dragon flight and join the leaders in the King's pavilion.

They were six days from Azikhaag, the capital of Uz Erhaag, so if Mareg was determined to meet them in open battle he was certain to do it very soon. As far as the Royal mapmakers knew, beyond the ranges to the northwest, the country opened onto another flat plain and became a tapestry of hills and bush land all the way to Azikhaag. Uz Erhaag had no true forests, according to Haagii prisoners taken on The Rim Shield, and certainly none lay between the Kingdom army and the capital.

After the meeting, Andra withdrew to gather his thoughts in the cool night air, so he was surprised when A Ahmud Ki visited. 'You have nothing to fear from me,' A Ahmud Ki said quietly, and stopped a couple of steps short. 'I want Mareg as badly as you do. And we need each other to achieve that.'

'What do you want?' Andra asked defensively.

'Just to finalise a plan,' A Ahmud Ki said casually. 'An important plan. I want to explain it to you. Shall we keep walking?' As Andra complied, A Ahmud Ki continued. 'Have you heard of a place called Se'Treya?'

'No,' Andra replied. 'Is it in Uz Erhaag?'

'Not exactly. It's in your sword.'

Andra stopped to face the Chancellor though he couldn't see anything clearly in the darkness except a faint reddish glow where the Chancellor's eyes were.

'It's a place generated by magic,' A Ahmud Ki explained. 'The old Dragonlords used to meet there to settle differences of opinion.' He planted his seed prudently, deliberately trying to arouse Andra's interest. All he needed was the human's agreement to allow the sword to be used

463

to open the door to Se'Treya. Then his final plan would be ready to complete.

'What do you mean by settling differences of opinion?' asked Andra.

'Mareg, Andrakis and the other Dragonlords didn't always agree on things. Sometimes they had to resolve their differences, but naturally they didn't trust each other, especially since they each had so much magic at their fingertips and they all wanted to be the single dominating power, so they created a special place where they could meet, knowing their magic would be nullified so no single one of them could be a threat to the others whilst he was there.'

'You mean a magical place where magic was powerless?'

'You understand it well,' A Ahmud Ki declared with mock delight.

'That seems a paradox,' Andra argued. 'And wasn't there still a threat that one might kill another with a weapon? That wouldn't be magical.'

A Ahmud Ki appreciated the young King's shrewd thinking. 'They built in an additional assurance,' he explained. 'Two Dragonlords must agree before either can leave Se'Treya once they're there.'

Andra started walking again. 'So why do you tell me this?' he asked after a few steps.

'Because it's where you will slay the Dragonlord to fulfil the prophecy.'

A Ahmud Ki's statement made Andra pause again. 'How?'

'Se'Treya can be entered through Abreotan's sword. I'll lure Mareg in to meet with me, and then you follow us in. Two against one. Abreotan's sword will finish Mareg, and we can mutually agree to leave.'

'Enter the sword?' Andra murmured in disbelief.

'It's simple magic. You won't have to understand it. Just do what you always do with the sword. Make it take you to Se'Treya and you will be there.'

'If I do, how can I trust you?' Andra asked.

His accusation bit deep. The upstart King was challenging

him again. If he didn't desperately need him, he would slay the fool tonight and be done with the whole prophecy, but he couldn't do that. He didn't have the power to overcome Abreotan's sword in this world. In Se'Treya, though, Abreotan's sword was another matter. 'Without you, Your Highness, I can't leave Se'Treya. Two must agree, remember? I would be foolish to bring you to harm. Besides, you are the One King, and the Inheritor. I can't alter destiny.'

Andra held his tongue. He wanted to remind A Ahmud Ki he'd already tampered with destiny, especially Andra's destiny, but he knew saying it would be pointless, perhaps even dangerous. He suspected A Ahmud Ki had sinister motives in play, but he had little choice except to accept the plan. It had merit. Without the aid of magic, Mareg would be easy prey for a warrior and his sword. 'If I agree, how will I know when to enter this place?'

'Se'Treya,' A Ahmud Ki reminded Andra. 'You will know when it happens. Leave your mind open to my communication when the battle is joined between Mareg and me.'

Marella was uneasy throughout the night. The Haardrishii squad sent to check the distant hills failed to return, and no word of their whereabouts came from the watches. She sent word to the King, but her messenger returned saying he was asleep. She knew Andra wouldn't mind being woken by her messenger, but she didn't pursue the issue, deciding she was being over-cautious in hostile land, and Andra needed the little sleep the campaign could afford to give him.

When the early light of morning crept across the face of the northwest range, she stared across the broad river valley at the opposite ridge and saw what appeared to be a dark shadow spreading down the hills and valleys. As light increased with the rising sun peeping over the horizon, the expanding shadow took form; an army of warriors, some mounted, most on foot, and nine dark shapes rose and circled above the ranges, their wings catching the updrafts generated by the warming morning air. Dominic and other Kingdom warriors at the edge of the valley beside Marella gazed across the intervening space at Mareg's vast Dragon Army taking position, in all its varied glory, to face the Kingdom's invading force for a final conflict.

Forty Eight

The dragons wheeled in tight formation above the northern ridge, then peeled off from each other, two angling into the valley toward the battling armies. The third levelled half a thousand paces away and came on low at terrifying speed along the ridge toward Andra. Those it passed over, heard the wind whistling across its scaly hide, and flattened themselves against the earth, watching the black beast's passage through eyes wide with terror.

Andra slid from Firebrand's saddle as the dragon swept in, summoning Abreotan's sword while he stepped away from the horse, and when it seemed certain to the watchers the creature would snatch the warrior King from the ground a pulse of bright white energy surged from his sword and exploded in the dragon's gaping maw. Trying in vain to avoid what had already torn through its throat, the dragon baulked in its attack run, cartwheeled through the air over the startled troops nearest Andra, and crashed into the side of the valley two hundred paces away. The black beast thrashed its ebbing life out on the slope, before it shuddered twice and was still.

Spontaneous cheers of relief and victory erupted around Andra as the Kingdom warriors celebrated the dragon's death, but he sheathed Abreotan's sword and stared silently into the valley.

The river ran blood red in the late afternoon sunlight. The valley floor was littered with hundreds of corpses of mutilated warriors and horses, and thrashing in the bloodied river was a mass of fighting warriors, moving with no sense of direction or reason, bulging and shrinking, roving restlessly back and forth across the same breadth of ground and river like a grotesque, mindless beast of prey. Searching sunlight sparkled on golden armour where contingents of Andrakian warriors battled, and on fragments of silver mail not yet smeared with blood or mud. The terrified whinnying of horses and ten thousand battle cries locked together in the ebb and flow of a frenzied death dance echoed against the hills. The dragon pair that descended on the battle flashed above the milling chaos like fleeting shadows, shedding gouts of dragon fire indiscriminately on friend and foe, before they climbed steeply and banked west. As they started to stoop to another attack, three more winged shapes hurtled toward them from the southwest ridge as A Ahmud Ki's flight of dragons rose to drive away Mareg's pets.

With a weary sigh, Andra remounted Firebrand, and urged the horse from the knot of warriors around his pavilion, heading for a higher vantage point along the ridge from where he could more easily assess the battle's progress. He rode by hastily constructed tents where wounded and dying, brought from the valley, were desperately crying for attention from surgeons and healers. The walking wounded saluted the King, and Andra saw bed-ridden and horribly mutilated warriors feebly acknowledge him with nods or faint smiles as he passed. One warrior, his face and upper body utterly smeared with crusted blood, lifted one appealing hand toward him from his deathbed, and the vision so filled Andra with bitterness and guilt he spurred Firebrand away from the tents of the dying, and cantered through tired ranks of Ranu riders who were resting before a new assault into the valley where so many of their kin and comrades were dead.

At the base of a rocky outcrop, surrounded by a copse of low, stunted trees, he dismounted, patted Firebrand gently on the nose, and clambered up the jumbled rocks to the summit. For the past four days, he'd come to this spot because the trees partially concealed the position and the outcrop afforded the best vantage for viewing the valley's expanse. A Ahmud Ki's dragon flight, based less than fifty paces from the site, enhanced its comparative safety.

The battle at the river had altered little. There were bulges forming and disappearing along the central line of conflict as groups fought, won, and lost advantage, but neither army made significant ground. The thickest and bloodiest fighting erupted wherever Mareg's Dammeraag warriors met Andrakian knights. Fluctuations in the fortunes of the battle were brought about by the intervention of either of these groups against courageous, but less able opponents, although periodic arrow storms from the heights and headlong cavalry charges from either side occasionally swung the tide of battle in one army's favour, until reinforcements altered the balance again.

For four long, murderous days, the battle raged. The cost in lives reached staggering proportion, and Andra was sickened by the appalling carnage, all in the name of his prophecy. Thousands were dead, thousands dying, because he chose to lead them against Mareg: to gain what? Freedom? In that, the war was a disaster. He was sending them with futile hope into the valley and offering only death.

He lifted his eyes from the churning river of blood to scan the ranks of Mareg's army assembled along the opposing ridge and foothills to the northwest. A multitude of hide tents dotted the upper landscape and figures swarmed between them like ants. Coloured banners and tribal poles proclaimed the Haagii legions and other nations that flocked to serve Mareg. The Dragonlord's resources seemed limitless. Even after four days of relentless fighting, fresh troops still awaited their first blooding in the conflict. On the other hand, Andra's army was being destroyed by the protracted battle. Almost half the warriors under his command were dead or severely wounded. Two, perhaps three more days of this and the Kingdom would have no one left to defend it. There were thousands of Ranu waiting to join Andra's army, but they were still in their lands, and even if A Ahmud Ki could summon them through a gigantic portal would it matter if only the Ranu were left to return to the Kingdom?

Mareg hadn't come. Andra anticipated the Dragonlord's arrival from the first morning, but he hadn't appeared. In his place, he sent troops and dragons: nine dragons. Andra had slain three beasts, including the one he just killed, two on the first afternoon of battle when they made a bold attack on him.

Mareg's generals gambled on quickly routing the Kingdom force by killing Andra. Their gamble failed. Andra's slaughter of the black creatures bolstered his warriors' spirit and cowed the hearts of the Haagii sent into the valley. A Ahmud Ki had since tried to lure Mareg's dragons to him, as he successfully did the previous summer at the edge of Dragon Breath plains, but Mareg foresaw that initiative and the dragons that came with the Haagii army were immune to A Ahmud Ki's wooing. A Ahmud Ki's dragons met and frequently fought with Mareg's creatures in the skies above the battlefield, but the dragons were unable to effectively injure each other during their aerial sorties because of their tough scaly hides and manoeuvrability, though they gave and received countless minor bites and scorch marks. Instead, the dragons were used to terrorize the troops on either side of the valley, dropping out of the sky and lashing the warriors with their fiery breath, spreading panic and destruction wherever they swooped. Since the death of the first pair, Mareg's dragons remained wary of Andra's presence, and the recent attack heightened Andra's wariness since it was out of character with the dragons' established role in the conflict.

As he pondered the possibilities, he sensed a subtle change in the texture of the air. Recognising the presence of magic, he automatically turned, expecting to come face-to-face with A Ahmud Ki, but the flat space of rock on which he stood was empty. He moved cautiously to the edge and peered through the trees toward the Chancellor's pavilion. Three black dragons hunkered nearby, attended by shadowy dracabeorn, but A Ahmud Ki was nowhere to be seen. Andra wondered what game the Chancellor was playing?

He sensed another change, the light faltering, and rubbed his eyes, thinking tiredness was affecting his vision, but he saw the daylight was losing luminosity. A thrill of fear ran up his spine and he turned toward the valley. The sky drew his attention.

Out of the north, a dark cloudbank rolled toward the valley, moving low with unnatural speed, and ahead of the wall of darkness he spotted three dots he knew were dragons heralding the approaching cloud. The sunlight, free of the encroaching cloudbank, was tinged with an orange hue that tainted everything and everyone. He'd seen this vision three years before, on The Rim Shield, when Mareg's vast hordes swept down from the Fire mountains and slaughtered Great King Thana's unfortunate forces as a warning of the fate awaiting anyone who dared oppose Mareg's will.

He willed Abreotan's sword into his hand and felt its magic flow like adrenalin through his arm and across his chest. For the first time since marching out of the Kingdom in search of the Dragonlord, Andra felt fear's icy touch at the base of his spine, and he tightened his grip on the hilt. Mareg was coming. Destiny flew in the teeth of a violent sky to find him and was bringing whatever end their shared fates prophesied.

'Mareg comes,' said A Ahmud Ki.

The firm voice startled Andra, and he turned to find the Chancellor beside him. Ahmud Ki's grey eyes were fixed intently on the approaching dragons, and, as the clouds swept over, plunging the valley and the ridges into semi-darkness, Andra saw the grey replaced by a fiery red flash of energy. A moment later, a sharp wind rushed through, swinging the stunted trees into life, and it lifted A Ahmud Ki's silver-grey hair into a halo; an effect, which made the Chancellor seem possessed with madness. There are two Dragonlords, Andra reminded himself. The prophecy mentioned two. Hyacinth warned me there would be more than one to face.

'The dragons land. Mareg is riding the central one,' murmured A Ahmud Ki, out of the depths of his reverie, while his gaze remained riveted to the opposing ridge.

Andra stared across the dark space toward the distant ridge, but he could only see silhouettes in the dull light. He squinted into the mouth of the wind and called on the sword's power to assist his vision. As its magic coursed through him, he imagined a tunnel of light forming between him and where the dragons landed. At the tunnel's end, he saw a figure in shining black armour, adorned with brutal spikes, armour like that worn by the Dammeraag warriors, but the flat surfaces were etched with mystical runes identifying it as something more than mortal. The figure sat rigid, impatiently waiting for servants to unbuckle riding straps affixed to the dragon's neck. As Andra studied him, the dragon rider seemed to gaze straight back. His black gauntlets moved, as if to lift his visor, and paused, and for a prolonged time the figure remained motionless, staring from within the secrecy of his helmet. Andra sensed a disruption in the tunnel of light, a premonition of imminent danger, and relinquished his spell.

'He felt you prying,' said A Ahmud Ki, without emotion.

'You see him, can't you,' Andra said.

'We see each other,' A Ahmud Ki murmured. He shifted his hands gently, in small oscillating circles, and Andra felt the fabric of magic in the air shift again. The wind dropped and disappeared. Overhead, the boiling mass of clouds slowed, until it hung motionless, like a smothering blanket suspended over the world, and an eerie silence settled over the valley.

In the odd light, Andra saw warriors, paused in mid-battle, staring up at the far ridge and at the sky, some frighteningly curious, some enthralled by the prickling presence of awesome magic that brought the forces of nature to heel. They all knew the Dragonlord had arrived. 'What now?' he asked.

A Ahmud Ki maintained his silent, distant concentration. Along the base of the blanketing cloud, a red glow appeared and brightened, shedding its light into the valley's depths to bathe everything with its bloody hue. 'Open your mind to me,' A Ahmud Ki whispered steadily.

Andra studied the Chancellor's emotionless face and unblinking burning red eyes. As reluctant as he felt, having already once been made the Chancellor's pawn through his treachery, he knew he had to obey the command. Besides, he was ready for any trickery A Ahmud Ki might pull. He had the sword. Its magic would protect him.

'Open your mind,' the Chancellor rasped, as though the act of speaking was becoming increasingly painful.

Andra took hold of Abreotan's sword and let down his mental defence against A Ahmud Ki's magic.

Keep the sword ready. Mareg is here, A Ahmud Ki instructed.

At the edge of his consciousness, Andra sensed another mind pattern lurking, sinister and dark. A guttural, sneering voice intruded.

So, you've even taught your puppet how to come to the Sphere of Thought. How useful.

Mareg lacks manners, A Ahmud Ki projected.

Only equals deserve etiquette! Mareg scoffed. And there are no equals to me.

We shall see, A Ahmud Ki replied.

A ripple of mocking laughter spread through Andra's mind. He willed the sword to protect him and sensed a wave of disbelief break and vanish as quickly as it had come.

Learn something? A Ahmud Ki prompted.

Andra was about to reply when he realised the question wasn't directed at him, but at the Dragonlord.

Mareg's response was sharp and direct. There's nothing left for me to learn, Ki, and too much for you to learn before you die. I know the touch of that sword's power. The hatred I bear Abreotan has outlasted his death a thousand times. You waste your time on old prophecies. The imbecile with you is nothing more than a child carrying another's magic. If he was an Abreotan, I'd reconsider your proposal, but Abreotan is long, long dead. Only I, Mareg Dru'artha Sutnavanistra, am left. And no pathetic human who happens to carry another's sword will frighten me because others cried in the growing darkness for a light and called their cry a prophecy. I came to resolve our difference, once and for all, in Se'Treya, as you foolishly suggested, and when I've finished with you I'll crush this pathetic play King and his rag

473

of an army, and rule eternally, as has always been my destiny.

Andra heard the limitless authority and hatred of Mareg's words echo in his mind and felt the enormity of the Dragonlord's presence weighing him down. The Dragonlord's power was vaster than he imagined possible, on a scale that dwarfed his belief in Abreotan's sword. He doubted the validity of the prophecy that brought him to this moment. How could he destroy a being so immense, so determined, so ruthlessly powerful?

Get control of your fear, A Ahmud Ki cut in. Mareg's only trying to weaken your resolve.

There's nothing to weaken, Mareg interjected. This paltry excuse is already dead, and he knows it. Open Se'Treya, Ki. It's time you also learned the magnitude of your hopelessness. I am your master. Obey me.

Mareg's presence vanished. Lightning flashed across the face of the red cloud, chased by a peal of thunder, spreading from the centre to the far reaches, bringing Andra to his senses. Across the valley, the Dragonlord shone with a pale amber light against the dark hordes. Andra glimpsed shadowy masses moving awkwardly up both slopes of the valley: warriors withdrawing to their respective lines, overawed by the surrounding spectacle.

'Hold up the sword,' A Ahmud Ki ordered.

Andra wheeled to face him. 'Why?'

The Chancellor's red eyes glowed and the russet unnatural light lit his face with malevolence. 'Listen quickly, and do exactly as I say if you want the prophecy to be fulfilled. I told you I had the key to Mareg's destruction. Now it's time to use it. Your sword is the key. I've fooled Mareg into facing me on an ancient battlefield the old Dragonlords call Se'Treya. It can only be entered through a powerful magical item. Nothing is more powerful than your sword, so it's a perfect gateway. When you hold it above your head, Mareg and I will enter its fabric and thence enter Se'Treya. He thinks to fight me there and slay me. But after we've entered, you must come too, and then you can defeat him, as the prophecy promises.'

'But what about his magic?' Andra asked.

'It's useless in Se'Treya. That's the beauty of it. The Dragonlord's created his own trap.' A Ahmud Ki's face broke into a wide, hideous grin. 'A trap within a trap.' He laughed.

Lightning crackled across the sky. The amber light enveloping Mareg intensified.

'He grows impatient,' said A Ahmud Ki. 'Hold up the sword. Now.'

Andra slowly lifted Abreotan's blade above his head, until it pointed at the motionless sea of red clouds. By its own volition, the sword began to shine, a brilliant white light that radiated through the surrounding trees and chased the shadows from the rocks on which Andra stood. So brightly did it shine that Andra had to turn his eyes from it. Across the valley, Mareg's amber light flashed to red, and a red trace flashed across the valley and disappeared into the sword's whiteness. Andra sensed more than saw a second flash of red enter the sword from his left, but before he could turn to see what had happened to A Ahmud Ki he felt the handle's energy increase dramatically and magic pulsed through his arm. Mareg and A Ahmud Ki had projected themselves into the sword, to Se'Treya. He felt incredible stillness infect the air over the entire valley.

Bathed in amber light, the dark figures of both armies moved in a strange dream, moved in limbo, as if they'd lost direction and purpose. Andra saw horses galloping toward him, Marella, and Artega perhaps, but they were a long way along the ridge. They were coming to the light. The light from the sword was a beacon, drawing them to him, like moths to a lantern.

Come now, called the voice.

Andra knew A Ahmud Ki was ready. When he looked to his left, the body of A Ahmud Ki stood, enveloped in a vague amber glow, but Andra noticed the raging fire had dissolved from his eyes, and the Chancellor's dark sockets stared sightless at the shining blade of Abreotan's sword. A Ahmud Ki was gone, and he was waiting for Andra in Se'Treya, in the place of Dragonlords.

Andra shivered with fear. Or was it anticipation? Everything was happening too fast, too much out of his control. A Ahmud Ki had set the trap for Mareg. He had to go through the sword. Concentrate. Force his will inward. Wild magic rushed down his arms and flooded into his chest. His eyes erupted with the same brilliant light emanating from the sword's blade, and he felt himself flowing into the aura, being swept toward his destiny, out of control, and uncertain of its outcome.

Forty Nine

The first thing he noticed was the dust. He stood at the centre of a grey plain that swept to invisible horizons in every direction – flat, endless, dead – so dead he thought he was standing on the familiar surface of Dragon Breath plains, alone, except for two figures facing each other near him. One wore the familiar Andrakian golden armour: A Ahmud Ki. The Chancellor's head was bare, his braided silver hair looking fresh and alive beneath the harsh blue sky above the grey plain. The other wore shining black plate, from head to toe. A wicked double-bladed battle-axe dangled menacingly in his left hand.

The Dark Warrior turned his helmeted head toward Andra, chuckled sarcastically, and said, 'Welcome to Se'Treya. You're the first mortal to set foot in this place. Pity no one will ever know. They'd proclaim you a hero for it.'

Andra felt the impulse to summon his sword. It didn't come. He concentrated harder. No sword.

'You thought to trick me, did you Ki?' Mareg asked. 'Perhaps bring two to Se'Treya and overpower me?'

Andra willed the sword to come to him. His hand remained empty.

'You could've at least given your assistant a weapon to make this little contest a touch more challenging,' Mareg added reproachfully.

A Ahmud Ki's face broke into a confident smile. 'If you insist,' he said, grey eyes sparkling, and nodded to Andra. 'Call the sword.'

Andra concentrated harder. I am the sword, he reminded himself. Come to me. Come. He sensed an unusual ripple in the fabric of the air, and it seemed the place in which they stood blurred, but normalcy returned. He did not hold the sword. Instead, the plain echoed with mocking laughter.

'You fool! You amateur, Ki!' Mareg roared with delight.

'How can he summon the sword now? It's the key to Se'Treya. We entered through it. While we stay here, it functions to keep this place open. Let him call it. It won't come to him. It can't!' Mareg swung his keen blade and caught the shaft of the battle-axe in his other hand, turning the axe to admire its keenly honed edge. 'You set a trap to catch me and blundered into it yourself. And you claim to be a Dragonlord, Ki. You're a fool. I'm wasting my time here.' He advanced on A Ahmud Ki, whose face was set in shock at the realisation of his simple error when calculating the confrontation with Mareg. 'First, I'll crush you, as I should have done earlier, and then I'll dispose of your worthless apprentice,' Mareg scowled, with a malicious grin.

A Ahmud Ki back-pedaled, buying time while he desperately tried to re-order his thoughts. How could he have been so careless? Without the sword, how could Andra slay the Dragonlord? Mareg had the upper hand. They needed to escape Se'Treya. His plan to have Andra slay Mareg and then himself slay Andra was dust at his feet.

'At least pretend to make a fight of it, you gutless cur!' Mareg cursed as he spun his axe. 'You've got an axe.'

A Ahmud Ki stumbled toward Andra, frantically unhitching the golden battle-axe from his belt. The training in the winter months to use the weapon was all he could draw on to stall for more time. If necessary, he'd resort to the same form of escape he used previously: combining his thoughts and Andrakis' to work as the minds of two Dragonlords. Two Dragonlords had to agree to leave Se'Treya. That was the code. Mareg revealed that law to him in their last meeting. That's how he escaped before. It was his one insurance against a fatal blunder.

Mareg roared and lunged. A Ahmud Ki leapt aside, but not quick enough to avoid a glancing blow from Mareg's axe, and the blade rang as it crumpled the armour on A Ahmud Ki's thigh. 'First hit!' Mareg shouted triumphantly, and swept his axe back in a wide arc, narrowly missing Andra.

The warrior King dived to his right, to avoid the attack, and rolled through the dust to his feet again.

The Dragonlord cast a cursory glance at him. 'Impressive. You might be more fun to kill than I anticipated.'

While Mareg's guard was down, A Ahmud Ki saw an opportunity, and with a desperate swing he lunged at the Dragonlord's exposed side. Mareg was too quick. He met A Ahmud Ki's blow with the shaft of his battle-axe and turned the blade down and away.

'Pathetic! A real Dragonlord would've done much better,' Mareg remonstrated, and in the same breath he kicked out to send the Chancellor sprawling backwards into the dust. 'There's more to fighting than simply swinging an axe, Ki,' he scoffed, and closed on his quarry.

A Ahmud Ki reached deep into his past to revive his Aelendyell agility, rolled away from Mareg, and scrambled to his feet in a cloud of grey dust.

The Dragonlord laughed. 'Run, Ki. Run. But in Se'Treya there's nowhere to run. The dust will hold you down. Let's get this unfortunate charade over with. I have a world to rule.'

A Ahmud Ki switched his attention from Mareg, and focused inward, deep inside the chambers of his memory. He called on the psyche he drained from the crystal pyramid, the memories of the dead Dragonlord Andrakis, as he did the previous time Mareg tried to trap him on Se'Treya and directed his mind to escape. Nothing changed. When he blinked, he still stood on the grey plain. What was happening? Before he could shake off his shock, Mareg's axe blade bit into his breastplate; the force of impact winded him, and sharp pain shot through his chest and into his neck as he crumpled backwards into the dust. The world spun sickeningly inside his head, and when he opened his eyes Mareg was leaning over him, gloating. 'Had enough?'

A Ahmud Ki spat blood and dust as he coughed to clear his throat. Why couldn't he escape? What had Mareg done? Why was he still trapped in Se'Treya?

'You were never going to win Ki!' Mareg stated flatly. 'There can only ever be one Dragonlord to rule. That's why you came here, isn't it? That was your petty ambition, wasn't it? To rule? But now you can see how foolish you were to oppose me. You see, Ki, I promised myself, a thousand years ago, I'd rule as a Dragonlord should, even, if necessary, at the expense of my stupid brothers. But Abreotan ruined everything, just as I laid my plans to conquer. As it's turned out, he did me a favour by imprisoning and driving off my brothers. There's no competition anymore. I promised myself I'd rule. And I promised myself, if I couldn't, no one else would. But even that's unnecessary. I'll rule as I planned now, and no one can stop me. You saw to that just by coming here, Ki. You sealed your own fate. Now your destiny is complete.'

A Ahmud Ki watched Mareg lift his murderous battle-axe high, shining ebony against the bright blue sky. All for nothing, he cursed silently, trapped by his carelessness and his stupid belief in a prophecy. This much are prophecies worth, he judged, turning to glare at Mareg in one final act of defiance, as he felt the soft sand slip through his fingers. For a terrible instant, Mareg towered over him, the shadow of death, and then inexplicably toppled to A Ahmud Ki's left. When A Ahmud Ki rolled onto his elbow, he saw a cloud of dust enveloping a tangle of black and gold armour. The armour separated, and scrambled out of the dust in opposite directions, and the warrior in golden armour hastily snatched A Ahmud Ki's discarded battle-axe from the dust.

'You'll pay dearly for meddling,' Mareg scowled, as he strode arrogantly toward Andra.

Andra felt the weight of the battle-axe in his hand. Its balance was precise, a fine weapon. He timed the first sweep of Mareg's axe and turned it harmlessly away, dodged the predicted backswing and put a pace between himself and his opponent. Mareg spun with astonishing speed, and his axe glanced Andra's cheek. The warrior King flinched, feinted left, and drove the head of the golden axe hard against Mareg's right shoulder. Armour clashed against armour before Andra leapt aside.

Mareg stepped back to regain his balance. 'Sometimes a little luck can forestall the inevitable,' he said behind his visor, 'But not for long.' He twirled his axe as easily as a dagger, and made another sweep at Andra's unprotected head, but Andra met the blow with his axe and locked the axe heads together, pulling his enemy up against his chest. Mareg was taller, and broader, but lighter in weight than Andra expected. He could hear the Dragonlord's breath heaving inside his helmet. The warriors twisted and pulled against each other, trying to assert dominance with sheer strength and bend the other into the dust, but neither gave way. Mareg ended the struggle by deftly pushing against Andra's thigh with his foot, and they stumbled apart.

Dust drifted between them. Andra tasted it in his mouth, and considered again they could as easily be on Dragon Breath Plains, as he watched Mareg prepare his next attack. Everything was the same, except here there were no horizons, because, although the grey melted into blue in the furthest distance, nowhere was there a truly distinct line. Mareg had less arrogance in his approach. Instead he began to circle, stalking Andra, searching for a weakness to exploit.

'You've met your match, Mareg,' A Ahmud Ki announced from behind Andra. 'A human is going to best you, as the prophecy promises.'

A Ahmud Ki's jibe had brutal effect. With a frustrated roar, Mareg rushed at Andra, axe whirling in a blur of murderous motion, and he beat the warrior King back several steps, black blade slicing through the golden plate along Andra's left arm and slashing down the front of his leg in the flurry of action, and it took all of Andra's skill to turn it away from his head and shoulders. Carried further backwards by Mareg's momentum, Andra stooped and moved under Mareg's blows, catching his back against the Dragonlord's chest. He let Mareg's weight cross the fulcrum of his back and stood upright, swinging his left arm up, between the Dragonlord's legs to throw him over to land helplessly on his back in the dust.

Mareg let out a string of oaths, as he scrambled to his feet in front of A Ahmud Ki, and he ripped off his black helmet to shake out the all-pervading dust. For the first time,

Andra saw the Dragonlord's long silver braids in the clear light of Se'Treya. One vicious backswing of Mareg's axe caught A Ahmud Ki's left arm and the Chancellor howled in agony. 'Don't ever mock me again, Ki!' Mareg spat with satisfaction, and he turned toward Andra.

Andra had seen the tapestries and the pictures, and he knew the Dragonlord would look like A Ahmud Ki, would share the same handsome features and high cheekbones of their Aelendyell and Elvenaar ancestors, but now he could see the awesome truth in the flesh he understood how Mareg and A Ahmud Ki could have been brothers. He expected the Dragonlord's eyes to flare with the eerie fire he observed in A Ahmud Ki's eyes, but they were dark grey and in a mask of hatred that scarred the Dragonlord's face and made him all the more ugly because of the handsome features the hatred altered. He felt the enormity of a thousand years of expectation looming in the moment, bunching like the muscles in the Dragonlord's exposed neck. Mareg would make one more attack. One had to die this time. Like the awesome dragons Mareg commanded to do his will, Andra saw the prophecy flying out of the dust of time and descending on him, and Abreotan's sword was out of his reach. What twists of fate would prevail? 'Die!' Mareg screamed and charged.

Andra met blows with counterblows, parried, defended, and brought his axe up and through to thwart Mareg's rain of death-seeking sweeps. Armour crumpled, split, and the shafts of the axes rang in the still, dusty air as the two warriors met in desperate combat. In the panic of violence, Andra had a fleeting glimpse of a vision of his past – two figures moving in a fluid dance, point and counterpoint, in shafts of late afternoon sunlight streaming through the trees in the Valley of Rivers – Guardian Master Artega locked in mock combat with Devi Senok. The vision vanished as Mareg's axe clanged against his gauntlet. Andra's rhythmic Guardian training was useless in the wake of the Dragonlord's frenetic attack. Instead, he fought desperately for his life, blocking and swinging, feeling his blade cut deep

482

even as Mareg's bit into him.

Through the swirling, chaotic veil of dust, Mareg misjudged a step and faltered. It was a chance. With all his strength, Andra swept the golden axe across and up, catching the hapless Dragonlord under the ribs, splitting his black armour plate, piercing his chest. In the follow-through, Andra's axe caught Mareg's weapon and the ebony blade went spinning through the air, over Andra's head, to land in the grey dust.

Mareg grunted at the impact of the mortal blow and staggered back several paces, staring down in disbelief at his punctured chest. Then he lifted his grey eyes to Andra and fixed him with a steady gaze that didn't falter, even as he sank to his knees.

Andra felt numb, rooted to the earth, as if he couldn't break from the Dragonlord's staring eyes, and he let the golden axe drop, the handle slipping through his fingers. It was over. All the struggle was over. At last the prophecy was fulfilled.

If it wasn't for the register of astonishment in Mareg's eyes, he would never have expected the blow. As it was, the black axe blade smashed through his shoulder armour and cut deep into his back, but he instinctively rolled with the force and saved himself from a fatal wound. Dust filled his mouth, and dizziness overwhelmed him as he tried to struggle to his feet, only to collapse face first. He fought against the intense pain surging through his shoulder and flipped onto his back to find A Ahmud Ki standing over him with Mareg's axe in his remaining good right hand. 'Why?' Andra coughed, but even as he asked the question he understood the answer. Hyacinth warned him.

'One Dragonlord. One ruler,' A Ahmud Ki wheezed. Bright red blood ran from the gaping wound in his left arm and his battered chest. Mareg had sorely wounded the Chancellor. 'I'm that Dragonlord. You gave me that gift by defeating Mareg. I'd like to thank you, but I just have to tidy up the last loose end.' He smiled bitterly and swung down with all his weakened strength. The axe blade bit into grey dust. Andra had vanished. Stunned, A Ahmud Ki wheeled on the spot, searching for the warrior King.

'He's gone, Ki,' Mareg rasped from his kneeling position.

A Ahmud Ki fixed his eyes on the dying Dragonlord. 'How can he?' he blurted. 'It takes two.'

Mareg chuckled. Blood bubbled from his mouth, and he spat it into the dust. 'I lied,' he admitted, and grinned with bloodied teeth, 'and you took the bait.'

A Ahmud Ki's eyes widened. He lifted his axe and stumbled angrily toward Mareg. 'Explain it quickly before I finish what's already over,' he demanded.

Mareg gathered his ebbing strength, and reached forward to wrench the discarded golden axe from the earth as he staggered defiantly to his feet to confront A Ahmud Ki. 'You leave Se'Treya if you are the controller of the magic that opened it,' he revealed, clenching his teeth against the pain wracking his body. 'That's the only reason you escaped me last time, you fool. It was your crystal that opened the gate.'

A Ahmud Ki's eyes narrowed with skepticism. 'If I had the key with my crystal last time, then how did you get out?' he asked.

'I had a crystal too, remember?'

A Ahmud Ki understood the import of Mareg's statement. Andra had the key to Se'Treya in the sword. And Andra was gone. 'Then we're trapped here?'

Mareg forced a weak laugh through bloodied lips. 'How little you really know, even with the benefit of Andrakis' knowledge.' He lifted the golden axe menacingly. 'I've given myself a gateway, just in case you tried to outsmart me,' he snarled and cocked one eyebrow. 'You think I'd trust you with the only key?'

'What's it matter to you anymore? You're already dead,' A Ahmud Ki sneered. 'Even you won't survive that wound. I have the right to claim my inheritance as a Dragonlord.'

Mareg grimaced and drew in a deep, rattly breath. A cruel smile flickered across his lips, and dissolved into twisted hatred, as he bunched his rapidly failing strength into his left arm. 'If I can't be the one ruler, no one can! I swore that oath a thousand years past, Ki! You want to inherit that? Then here's your inheritance, Dragonlord!' he screamed, and hurled his axe with brutal accuracy.

The instant he felt the tingle of the sword in his grip, he screamed with pain and stumbled to his knees. At the furthest edge of his consciousness, he heard cries and gasps. 'By Holy Teka!' one yelled. 'Look at his back!'

'Andra!' a woman's voice cried. 'Oh, in all the eight hells, Andra, what's happening?'

Andra forced his eyes open, against the searing agony shooting through his upper chest and across his back, and he was overwhelmed by the sword's sharp light. Shadows moved at the light's edge. A Ahmud Ki's figure remained rooted to the stone platform, like a statue awaiting its first kiss of life. Someone reached for his arm. 'No!' he groaned in warning and pushed to his feet. 'Get back! Get away from me!' He held the sword directly before his face, staring into its pure white light, and turned in a circle. The light threatened to burn his eyes, but he gazed deeply through its blazing intensity, until he could see two figures facing each other on a flat plain. One was A Ahmud Ki; the other Mareg. Dragonlord faced Dragonlord. They stood in Se'Treya and Se'Treya was in the sword. The pieces were clear at last. A Ahmud Ki tried to kill him. At the last, the Chancellor tried to take it all and become the one Dragonlord. He tried to murder Andra to stop the ancient prophecy's fulfilment. But Andra was the sword. In the end, when it had not come to him, he returned to it. Waeron Ardath's advice won out. He was the sword.

He turned toward the circling crowd of warriors gazing in awe at him, and saw Artega, and Marella whose eyes were reaching for him from a great sadness. In the reflected light of their eyes, he saw other faces: Claarn, whose red bushy brows were knitted in a concerned frown; Tim grinning with irrepressible mischief; Derik O'Dale and Alain, Mirith, beautiful Mirith, and Terath, and the Tree Keepers in Tree

Home. In every face he read unmistakable trust, a belief in him, and at the head of the crowd Hyacinth smiled solemnly and nodded. The bracelet entrusted to him by the Tree Keepers, the last true Elvenaar, throbbed with magical power. The promised moment had come. At last he understood what needed to be done. Now and forever he had to seal the fate of magic, forge the lock that would forever separate the past from the future and destroy what was to ensure that what was promised would be. In his hands, he held the key to the prophecy's fulfilment.

He lifted Abreotan's sword high, drew in his breath as greater pain leapt across his back and up his shoulder, and screamed, 'Get back! Get away!' and roared, 'The Dragonlords are dead!' The circle of faces hesitated, unwilling to leave their King and Lord, so he focused in, until the sword's light drove them down from the rocky outcrop, and, with one determined cry, he swung the blade in a blazing arc of pure light against the edge of the rock and it shattered into a thousand spinning crystals that erupted like a shower of stars. He thought he was going to pitch over the edge with the effort, but he braced and straightened, as around him the still and eerie world began to change.

Lightning sparked across the blood red ceiling of clouds, and the stagnant air surged into a vicious wind that stirred the clouds into boiling fury. Wild sheets of lightning flashed as Mareg's amber hue dissolved, swallowed in the maelstrom and whistling hurricane that ripped across the valley and tore tents and possessions of both armies from the terrified grip of their owners. Shocked into self-survival, warriors clung to the earth, pressing their faces against the cold ground as if they were trying to burrow to escape the violence unleashed by the shattered sword.

The expanse of magical energy generated by the Dragonlords, and the ensuing cataclysm, swirled in ever-decreasing circles directly over the stone platform, where Andra swayed defiantly against the raging elements, and swept down into the broken sword handle, making it glow with such intense white heat Andra was forced to drop it and watch it clatter uselessly against the rock. His eyes rested on the upright form of A Ahmud Ki, whose silver hair flared in the tempest. The pretender to the title of Dragonlord seemed indestructible, even in the teeth of the magical storm lashing the valley, but there was still no light, no sparkle in the Chancellor's sightless eyes. They continued to stare outward from a great depth of emptiness. Then, as Andra felt the rising flood of his exhaustion reaching from within, he saw the Chancellor's body fold like a discarded rag doll. The golden armour of Dragonlord Andrakis crashed against the harsh stone and glinted briefly in a flash of lightning as it rolled over the edge and disappeared into the rocks below. Andra spun on his heel, away from the edge of the rock, felt a wave of darkness sweep over his mind, and collapsed into it, freed, at last, of the burden.

Fifty

From a rocky ledge in the heights of the Andrakian Mountains, above the rolling plains of Ky, the shadowy finger of Dragon's Tooth rising in the north like an ancient warning, Andra watched a white steed race across a low ridge, its rider leaning forward, urging the horse to greater speed, a black war dog racing in their wake. The rider was a girl, her brown hair flowing back in the wind of her passage, and she rode with passion, as if all eight hells had released their darkest horrors and were chasing her across the plains. 'She rides like the wind,' Marella observed, in her husky voice.

'She is the wind,' Artega said, and chuckled. 'Could anyone catch her?' He cast a sly glance toward Andra who was to Marella's left. 'Except perhaps the King?'

Marella smiled, but Andra ignored the former Guardian Master's comment, and continued to watch Milly. She wheeled her mount at the furthest end of the ridge, slowed to a canter, and headed down a shallow slope toward the foot of the mountains where the path led up to where Andra's party was gathered. 'You couldn't have given her a greater gift,' Marella said, touching Andra's shoulder gently.

'I promised her the horse a long time ago,' he said, remembering the promise made in the confusion of the prophecy and its fruition. 'She made me a King again.'

He turned from the vista to walk toward the warriors awaiting him on the narrow path. As he descended on Firebrand, he rubbed the stump of his knuckle where his ring finger had been severed to break A Ahmud Ki's arcane hold. Milly's intervention turned events out of the Chancellor's hands more than any other action. The intervening months, since the cataclysm unleashed by the breaking of the sword, had barely begun to heal the Kingdom, and it would be years before the Dragonlords' devastating impact would be erased sufficiently from the landscape to call the world normal again. And some, thought Andra, as he glanced at Marella, whose face, arms, legs, and body were scored with white welts, will carry the scars of the time for the rest of their lives.

He ran his fingers along the edge of the crescent scar on his left cheek, the prophetic mark that set him apart from the outset, then flexed his left shoulder and felt scar tissue across his shoulder and back pull against his movement. He could never forget either. Not that anyone would forget. Though a year had passed since the last bloody battle in Uz Erhaag, parents and children, husbands and wives, and friends still mourned the loss of loved ones. Wounds were still healing. Four long years of war consumed thousands upon thousands of lives, and reduced villages and towns to ashes. Yet out of the ashes, the agonies and victories of war, legends had risen, like mysterious phoenixes, new heroes were created, and minstrels were plying their trade from village to village, spreading ballads among the population to immortalise everyone, long after Andra and the people who lived through the time were dust.

'Is Your Majesty comfortable?'

Andra quietly acknowledged the Haardrishii escort mounted beside him, and replied, 'Thank you, Evan, I'm just thinking.'

'If Claarn was here, he'd say you're doing too much of that,' Marella teased and laughed. Andra turned to her, grinning at her hearty mood, but in her dark, sparkling eyes he glimpsed deeper memories stirring and looked away. Some memories of the past were still too close.

Jana leant on her elbow, resting her forehead in her hand, and pressed her left temple with her thumb. The taper on her desk was burning low, but there was enough time to write another page in the New History of Andrakis, before her task for the night was done. She reached for a fresh piece of vellum and steadily refilled her scribing reed with indigo ink.

For the first time, she noticed how stained her fingertips were becoming. Since King Andrakis sanctioned her appointment, at Lady Kara's suggestion, as Royal Drycraefter, she'd spent countless days learning her new craft. Not that she was a stranger to writing. The Thieves' Guild kept records: records of membership, of events, of certain transactions, of likely professional targets, and of every suspect who could prove to be a nuisance to the workings and members of the Guild.

The records were haphazard to say the least, probably a necessity for internal security as much as out of bad record keeping, Jana considered. She was one of three apprentices assigned by the Guild to Markham, a literate ex-thief in charge of the records, and Markham taught them rudimentary writing and reading skills, in the days before the rise of the Dragonlords, for which Jana was grateful, because she found, in herself, a hunger for writing. Whenever she could, she scribbled ideas, and snatches of ballads, and sketches of people on fragments of parchment that she pilfered from the records store in the Guild's maze, and she read avidly, though there was a distinct shortage of quality texts in the Guild's library.

Twice, Markham caught her writing creatively. The first time the older thief scoffed at her, telling her pretty words and ballads were for malingerers who couldn't earn a respectable living as a thief. The second time, Markham took what Jana had written, perused it with a frown that threatened punishment was following, and removed the fragment with a warning the piece of writing on stolen vellum would be shown to Guild Master Orrin.

Only after the siege of Andrakis, and Orrin's death, did Jana learn the writing had ultimately ended up in Lady Kara's hands. Markham died in the summer King Andrakis and the golden Andrakian knights drove the Haagii armies from the plains of Ky, and Lady Kara appointed one of Markham's apprentices, Tyrone, as his successor. Jana knew she was the most adept scribe of the three, and therefore the apprentice most deserving of her mentor's position, but she silently accepted the possibility she was passed over as punishment for her earlier transgression. In the chaotic months that followed, during the rebuilding of the city and the new palace under the Chancellor's manic direction, Jana buried herself in keeping records for the Guild, and training new apprentices in reading and writing skills for Tyrone, though she still wrote her stories in secret whenever opportunities arose.

When Kris, a Guild colleague, came to Jana, two months after the return of the army from Uz Erhaag, in the long period while the Kingdom waited for the King's health to be restored, with the news Lady Kara wanted a direct interview, she was surprised. Though Jana asked for clues as to the purpose of the interview, Kris frankly admitted she had no idea what it was about, so Jana went to see the highest-ranking person of the Guild with a degree of trepidation, wondering what she'd done wrong. The outcome was her appointment as Royal Drycraefter. The honour stunned her and left her speechless.

The immensity of the task initially daunted her. Waeron Ardath's death resulted in the old Drycraefter's library being locked away, in the Chancellor's magical black tower, and a thousand years and more of records, including the volumes of the Ancient Lore, the collective works of the successive Royal Drycraefters since the time of King Aian Abreotan, disappeared with the dissolution of A Ahmud Ki's magic. Nothing remained of the once-forbidding black tower, except an empty space in the palace gardens. The written history and knowledge of the Kingdom was gone. But Jana also knew her appointment opened a door to a vast world she longed to explore, and she finally accepted the challenge with quiet enthusiasm. Her task was to rebuild the Kingdom's written history, from the ashes of the surviving oral tradition, and the meagre written fragments stored in personal libraries beyond the city. She had to recreate the Ancient Lore as faithfully as possible, and continue the Drycraefter's role, blending into her writings a balance of truth, and a touch of genius, to inspire and warn future readers.

Jana lifted the last page she had written, its ink dry, and reminded herself where she had reached in the records. King Andrakis had collapsed on the summit of a rocky outcrop. The swirling red clouds had vanished, and bright daylight flooded the ridges and the valley. She bent to her vellum and began carefully forming the letters, avoiding a rush of ink that would smudge or blot her copy.

'The silence, following the dying wind, hung above the surviving warriors of both stunned armies, like a delicate question, and they stood motionless, rooted to the earth, awaiting a sign, a new marvel. In answer, dragons on both sides of the valley took flight, spiralling up to meet in the apex of the blue sky, where they rolled and cavorted, danced like wildly excited children, their black hides gleaming as they looped and spun around each other, and they peeled off, some paired, some single, flashing east, west, north, disappearing rapidly to the points of the compass, their keening echoing across the skies like exhilarating cries of freedom. The warriors watched in amazement, murmuring and pointing, wondering what new event might erupt with the breaking of the sword.

Then the air filled with a cacophony of agony, the wailing cries of thousands of spirits from the valley floor, and every warrior trembled, hearing the terrifying screams ascend and dissipate in the gentle breeze. One by one, the Golden Warriors of Andrakis, the tortured souls, not dead, not alive, toppled, as the Dragonlord magic binding their existence drained into the blood red waters of the dividing river. The last of the magic was gone, the last of the horror vanquished.

As if they, too, were released of a burden too heavy to carry further, the warriors of both sides turned their weary backs on the valley of death, where so many companions-in-arms lay, and began their long journeys homeward, freed at last from the blood and oaths of vengeance of those who brought them there.'

The taper flame flickered. Jana glanced up and saw she'd run out of time. She shifted the new entry of her volume away from the wax spillage and lifted the dying taper to light her way to her bedchamber in the Upper Palace. So much had yet to be written – so much more had yet to be rewritten.

Andra's gaze rested on Mirith's soft lips as she smiled. 'Please forgive my expression,' she said haltingly, her lilting Aelendyell dialect refusing to be subdued by foreign words. 'I am still learning your language.'

'Mirith,' was all the dark-haired King could reply, as he descended the throne steps in the Upper Palace and approached the Aelendyell delegation with outstretched arms, 'Mirith.' He embraced her fondly, while the accompanying Aelendyell Elders watched in fascination, and turned to embrace her brother Terath, taking a moment to read the deep respect in the young Aelendyell's eyes. 'I never expected you'd come,' Andra said, stepping back to gaze at his Aelendyell friends.

'Aelendyell always come when a hondgesella asks,' Terath answered quietly. 'We have not forgotten you, my friend,' he explained with his customary seriousness, 'but your messengers had a hard time reaching us in the ruins of Wynwuduholt. The news of the Ealdfeond's defeat came to our tun many weeks afterwards, and we had already heard stories from the Ieldran that the new King was under the thrall of a hateful enemy of the people, so Chanter Pyraneth and our Elders were loath to send a deputation. But when we learned the King was you, and that this A Ahmud Ki, like the Ealdfeond, was dead, we could not refuse.'

'I have done your people a great wrong, Terath,' Andra said sadly, and he glanced self-consciously at the six Elders. 'When they came with my friend, Tim Gaelus, to renew the bond of friendship and trust, I sent them away, empty-handed. To their deaths, Terath.'

'We have heard the story, my friend,' replied Terath with a gentle shake of his silver locks, 'but you were not yourself. You were held by the dark working of another. You cannot

493

be held responsible for what you had no control over. No one who knows the truth will blame you for the deceptions of the evil maegslaga who used you. And since then you have become a Maegencyning and completed a mighty deed, the Elvenaar ellen-weorc I sped you on, when you left Wudufaesten. Remember?' Terath's face broke into a warm smile, and in his features Andra imagined Tim Gaelus' grinning image.

'I remember,' Andra said. 'I never forgot it. But if I'd known how great the task was you wished me on, I don't think I would've ever left Wudufaesten.'

Terath broke into sparkling laughter at Andra's candid comment, and Mirith joined in. The Aelendyell Elders nodded approval.

Andra's spirit soared to the heights of the airy ceiling of the Upper Palace. When he sent Haardrishii envoys to Wudufaesten, to find and invite his friends to Andrakis, he was filled with grave doubt they would come. Why would they want to? The Aelendyell people had much to be bitter about. A Ahmud Ki's active vengeance took many shapes – deceit, theft, murder – all determined to obliterate the ties between the Aelendyell and human races, and although the long-term effects of breaking Abreotan's sword were yet to be felt Andra knew, from Hyacinth and the Tree Keepers, there would be repercussions on the existence of magic in future Aelendyell generations. If they didn't yet know the unpalatable consequences the prophecy's fulfilment held for them, as descendants of the Elvenaar whose magic shaped Abreotan's sword, Andra was obliged to tell them. Still, they came in renewed faith, and brought others. Mirith and Terath would be the first keys to unlock the prejudices A Ahmud Ki deliberately fostered, and they would help Andra restore diplomacy between the races. Some wounds could be healed.

'If he thinks keepin' the likes of me inside this place is goin' to turn me into a lady, he's got to think again!' Patti taunted, as she inspected the bedchamber set aside for her. 'Besides,' she added, running her fingers along the edge of a silken sheet, 'There's me girls to look to.'

Lady Kara smoothed her long silken black hair and sat casually on the edge of the eiderdown covering Patti's bed. 'The girls can look after themselves,' she said. 'Jen will fill your capacity admirably.'

Patti shot a sharp glare at her. 'What might you be implying?' she asked, the loose wattles under her chin shaking furiously.

Patti's mock anger brought a broad smile to Kara's face, and her dark eyes shone mischievously. 'Everyone gets too old for their trade,' she teased.

With her hands on her ample hips, Patti advanced on Kara to look her directly in the eyes. Even standing, she could only just match the sitting woman's height. 'I'll have you know, girl, that I've satisfied more men in a week than the likes of you have seen in a lifetime, and I can still do as much, if it pleases me to,' she asserted defiantly.

'That's a reputation I wouldn't want to argue with,' cut in a man's voice. Both women turned to see Andra entering the room.

'You cheeky whelp!' Patti scowled good-naturedly. 'King you might be, but I've still a mind to put you across my knee.'

'I wouldn't doubt you'd do it too,' said Andra, with a wink at Kara. 'But I haven't come to squabble. I have a favour to ask.'

'I knew there'd be a catch,' Patti muttered ruefully. 'Men always have more than kindness in their minds when they give gifts to a lady.'

Andra grinned, considering a ribald retort of the kind Tim would've made to Patti's remark, but he restrained himself, and said, 'There's a catch. It's called Milly, and the girls who will serve in the Upper Palace.' He sat beside Kara as he explained. 'I want you to make sure Milly is looked after, and taught to be a lady. She's learned a great deal in the Guild, and since, but if she wants to be a princess, she'll need to learn more than an assassin's skill. And I want you to make

495

sure the girls in the palace aren't too naive or silly.'

Patti's face mobilised into astonishment that made the old brothel madam appear a simpleton beneath her shock of red-orange hair, and at that moment Andra recognised the Shaddite heritage he always saw but never acknowledged in the woman. That he missed the obvious connection surprised him, because she reminded him of Bear and Hannah, the ferryman and his Shaddite wife who guided Milly and him through the old Dwarven ways in the Andrakian Mountains. 'You're asking me to teach someone how to be a lady?' she asked incredulously.

'I know no one more qualified,' Andra replied, with a generous smile.

'But -' blurted the woman, but she held her tongue when she saw Andra and Kara grinning, and broke into jovial laughter, and ended up sniggering, as she said, 'As my Lord so commands,' in a poor parody of an educated voice, while she swept into a low curtsey. She made a vain attempt to retrieve her decorum by adding, 'I think the King has made a wise choice,' for Kara's benefit. Kara cocked a quizzical eyebrow at her antics.

In the half-light outside Milly's bedchamber in the Upper Palace, Andra paused to pat Artega who sat on watch. He heard Milly giggling and Patti's cracked voice remonstrating her.

'You might've seen nearly sixteen summers, young lass, and lived through a great many events in the meantime, but I say you still need your beauty rest,' the older woman growled. 'Now snuggle down into that bed and be thinking of sleep.'

Andra smiled in the darkness by the window, pleased the old ex-madam had accepted her role in the new palace. Milly was close to his heart, and he wanted her to be pampered as the first princess of the new Kingdom, but not spoilt. She was growing prettier daily, becoming more a young woman and less a child. The turmoil of the past three years matured the girl quickly. The lost and whining child the Haagii tied up in a filthy bag to use for their cruel sport had changed into a confident, courageous girl who assumed responsibility during the darkest days of the siege and risked her life to cut A Ahmud Ki's ring from his finger.

'Patti?' Milly asked.

'What child?'

'Do you think Andra will marry Marella?' Andra smiled to overhear Milly's personal question.

'Andra will marry whom he chooses, young lady,' Patti replied.

'But will it be Marella?'

'Why? Such a question!' the old woman lamented.

'Well?' the girl persisted.

'Shh.'

'I only want to know what you think.'

'Well, it won't be Marella,' Patti replied.

'Why not? They're always together.'

'Because they're good friends, and it's her duty to serve him,' Patti explained. 'Besides, her heart is with Claarn, and he understands that. They both do.'

It is the truth, thought Andra. Even beyond death, the giant warrior of Tressel Deep lived in Marella's heart, and always would. That was a bond even the Dragonlord couldn't break.

'Will it be the Aelendyell girl then?'

'You mean the one that comes with her brother?'

'He never takes his eyes off her,' Milly muttered despondently.

'Nor do any of the men, if you'd notice,' Patti said. 'Perhaps he will. It would be a good match.'

'No it wouldn't!' Milly retorted.

'I hear a jealous child,' Patti frowned.

'Wouldn't you be?' Milly pleaded.

'If I was a pretty young princess like you, well then I'd be bitten by jealousy too. I admit that,' said Patti quietly. 'Some things aren't quite as we'd like them to be.'

'Do you think he might marry me?' Milly half-whispered.

Patti chuckled, as she answered, 'You saved his life. He saved yours. He'll always love you, little lass, and don't you never forget that. But he's the King, child, and the King marries whomever he wants to marry. Who knows? If you're really very unlucky, he might choose you.'

'Oh, you tease me too much!' Milly complained, and the interchange dissolved into giggles and laughter.

Knowing he'd spied too long on a conversation he shouldn't have heard, Andra moved from the window and descended the white marble stairs to ground level, passing three Haardrishii guards who bowed as he greeted them. From there, he crossed the shadowy courtyard, lit by a solitary lantern, and headed toward stone steps leading up to a portion of the old castle's western wall.

On the parapet, a single figure moved, a woman with whom Andra had prearranged a meeting, and she passed a dark leather sack to him, as they exchanged greetings. 'I kept it safe,' Marella said. 'No one could touch it after it was broken.'

Andra felt the familiar weight in the sack and opened the drawstring. A stream of amber light flooded out, nearly blinding him. He quickly pulled the sack closed.

'It was nearly lost at the base of the rocks, after you collapsed,' Marella explained. 'No one even thought of it, until several days after we left Uz Erhaag, and when we finally sent a party back to retrieve it they couldn't find it, because someone else happened on the site at night, and saw the light it casts shining like a beacon. It took fourteen weeks before we located it again, fortunately back here in the Kingdom, and another six months of bartering and negotiation before the mercenaries who found it after the battle would part with it.'

'Why did they part with it, if they knew what it was?' Andra asked.

'They realised it was no use to them, except to extract money from the Kingdom. None of them could touch it. Four of their group had terrible burns to their hands, and their leader was also partially blinded by its glare. The only way they could carry it with them was to keep it in a bag like this. In the end, they were glad to part company with it, in exchange for a tidy sum of gold, and horses.'

Andra edged his fingers down the outside of the sack to the bottom and felt a familiar sensation course through his hand and arm; familiar magic, and yet so more potent than ever before. He remembered the enormous power surge he suffered when the sword hilt absorbed the Dragonlords' energy, after he shattered the blade. 'Have you felt it?' he asked.

'It's heavy,' she replied, not fully understanding his meaning, 'but I haven't dared touch the thing. Not after what I've heard it's done to others.' She noticed an amber light shining in Andra's eyes and caught her breath. 'Can you still control it?' she asked tentatively, uncertain of what she was witnessing.

'I don't know,' he said, his voice quivering. 'There's more to it than there ever was before. The Tree Keepers told me the magic would be destroyed when I killed the Dragonlords, but it isn't gone at all. It's just concentrated here, in the handle.'

'What will you do with it?' she asked.

He shook his head and sighed, taking his hand from the hilt. 'I don't know yet. Perhaps there's a lot more to know about all this than we do know. Perhaps,' he hesitated, realising the implication of his wildest thought, 'perhaps it isn't over, just halted.'

Marella did not answer out of the darkness, leaving him to consider the ramifications of all the possibilities the still-powerful sword hilt presented, and they stood, each lost in their private thoughts for what seemed a very long time. Finally, she coughed, and told him she had to check the guard posts around the castle wall and Upper Palace before she was finished for the night. She vanished into the darkness.

Left alone on the wall, a luxury he rarely experienced since becoming King, Andra leaned against the cool stonework, and rested the sack containing the hilt of

Abreotan's sword on the parapet. The night sounds of the palace drifted to his ears, and voices rose and fell from the Haardrishii barracks. Near the southern gates, a stringed instrument broke into strains of a popular ballad about the slaying of a dragon on the arched bridge at Cennednyss, and a minstrel's voice wavered and faded through several verses. On the western plain, dots of yellow light randomly patterned the black carpet that night had spread, marking where people had returned to their homes and farms. The Kingdom was renewing. The Aelendyell agreed to sit at the reconvened King's Table, along with representatives from Targa and Ranu Ka Shehaala, and someone already suggested it would be politic to invite representation from Uz Erhaag. There were many issues to be broached. There were a lot of wounds to heal.

The distant minstrel broke into a new ballad, another popular piece Andra had heard many times in the months since the end of the war, about the red giant and the sly thief. It conjured memories of Claarn, the great giant of a warrior with red flaming hair and beard, and a bellowing roar everyone could hear in the heat of battle, and Tim Gaelus, the quick-thinking half-Aelendyell assassin who befriended Andra from the outset. How the pair would laugh if they could hear their exploits lauded in song, full of heroic embellishments that made them immortal. Each time Andra heard the tune, he smiled, imagining what they would say, the mocking jibes and not-so-feigned embarrassment, but deep within he suffered the heart pangs of loss for his two friends, and for all his friends who laid down their lives to return the Kingdom to peace. The Dragonlord, A Ahmud Ki, Abreotan's sword, and the prophecy wrought so much change in four years. The wounds might heal in time, but there would always be scars. Always.

The minstrel's ballad faded out of hearing, and the world around Andra slipped into grateful silence. He focused on the full moon, suspended in the clear night sky, its silvery light bathing the distant snow-capped peaks of the Andrakians, and reminisced about adventures and good times with friends, while his fingers, resting on the dark sack, continued to sense the restless energy trapped in the hilt.

He thought of home. The Vale was a very long way away. His parents, Anedra and Malcolm, journeyed to the new city to see their son, the King, proclaimed in the month-long celebrations following his return to health, after months of convalescence, and their quiet pride in his glory shone in their faces, but they graciously and patiently refused his invitations to live with him in the Upper Palace. Anedra was head of the Council of Law. She had time-old traditions to maintain. It was The Way. Hearing the familiar philosophical words that sat at the root of his understanding, Andra acquiesced. After all, before he was a King, he was a Guardian. The Vale was his parents' home, and before the winter rains settled into the Valley of Rivers they returned. On the morning they left, he vowed he would make a pilgrimage every spring to his birthplace to renew his spirit and his love for them, and they left knowing he would keep that vow.

A tiny shadow passed across the moon's milky face, a brief, insubstantial thing, except he saw it. Or, at least, he thought he did. It was so far away, and so obscure, it could've been anything, but the involuntary shiver that jumped along his spine told him the shadow was neither cloud nor bird. Somewhere out there, in the Kingdom, the dragons were loose, their own masters now, free to come and go as they pleased, and no doubt, in time, being predatory beasts, they would become a new nuisance in the world of Andrakis. The Dragonlords, like their potent magic, were gone, and the past was past – that was the prophecy's intended outcome – but the prophecy's ending left legacies for the young King to resolve, the roaming dragons one of them. Some wounds, he knew, were still open.

ABOUT THE AUTHOR

Australian writer, Tony Shillitoe, entered the fantasy field in 1992-3 when Pan Macmillan Australia published his popular and successful Andrakis trilogy. He followed the trilogy with a stand-alone coming-of-age fantasy novel, The Last Wizard, which was short-listed for the inaugural Aurealis Awards Best Fantasy Novel in 1995.

From 2002-2008, Tony published two more fantasy series – the Ashuak Chronicles trilogy and the Dreaming in Amber quatrology – with HarperCollins Voyager Australia, and Blood, from the Ashuak Chronicles, was shortlisted for the Aurealis Awards Best Fantasy Novel in 2002.

Tony branched into Adolescent/Young Adult novels in 1999, with the publication of Joy Ride by Wakefield Press. Tony's second teenage novel, Caught in the Headlights, a HarperCollins Angus and Robertson imprint, was listed as a notable read for Older Readers in the 2003 Children's Book Council Awards, and subsequently appeared on Premier's Reading Lists around the nation.

Tony has written and published short stories, scripts, poetry, professional writing course books and ghost-edited a variety of projects. More information about his work and life can be found at his web site The Phoenix Rises: http://www.tonyshillitoe.com.au

BOOKS BY THE SAME AUTHOR

FANTASY NOVELS
The Andrakis Trilogy
The Waking Dragon
Maker of Kings
Dragonlord War

The Ashuak Chronicles
Blood
Passion
Freedom

Dreaming in Amber
The Amber Legacy
A Solitary Journey
Prisoner of Fate
The Demon Horsemen

The Last Wizard

STORY ANTHOLOGIES
Tales of the Dragon
The Red Heart

TEENAGE NOVELS
Joy Ride
Caught in the Headlights
In My Father's Shadow
The Need